ACROSS THE
STAR-KISSED SEA

also by

ARLEM HAWKS

Georgana's Secret

Beyond the Lavender Fields

Along a Breton Shore

PROPER ROMANCE

ACROSS THE STAR-KISSED SEA

Arlem Hawks

SHADOW
MOUNTAIN
PUBLISHING

To everyone who has tripped up, messed up, or fallen short—

Keep going. There are brighter days ahead. I believe in you.

Library of Congress Cataloging-in-Publication Data

Names: Hawks, Arlem, author.
Title: Across the star-kissed sea / Arlem Hawks.
Other titles: Proper romance.
Description: [Salt Lake City] : Shadow Mountain Publishing, [2024] | Series: Proper romance | Summary: "May Byam seeks solace as a lady's maid aboard a naval ship, encountering Chaplain Elias Doswell, who soon comes to harbor secret affections. Amid shipboard tensions and the looming threat of war with the French, their burgeoning romance faces peril. As they navigate the challenges of their pasts, their love story unfolds within the storms of the sea"—Provided by publisher.
Identifiers: LCCN 2024012186 (print) | LCCN 2024012187 (ebook) | ISBN 9781639933211 (trade paperback) | ISBN 9781649333001 (ebook)
Subjects: LCSH: Great Britain. Royal Navy—Fiction. | Man-woman relationships—Fiction. | Clergy—Great Britain—Fiction. | Lady's maids—Great Britain—Fiction. | Seafaring life—Fiction. | Nineteenth century, setting. | Mediterranean Sea, setting. | BISAC: FICTION / Romance / Historical / Regency | FICTION / Romance / Clean & Wholesome | LCGFT: Historical fiction. | Novels. | Romance fiction.
Classification: LCC PS3608.A89348 A64 2024 (print) | LCC PS3608.A89348 (ebook) | DDC 813/.6—dc23/eng/20240412
LC record available at https://lccn.loc.gov/2024012186
LC ebook record available at https://lccn.loc.gov/2024012187

Printed in the United States of America
Publishers Printing

10 9 8 7 6 5 4 3 2 1

Chapter 1

17 September 1811
Portsmouth, England

MAY BYAM

Six years marked as the daughter of a convict had taught me one thing: I couldn't trust even the people closest to me. Watching Mama pack her trunk to leave only confirmed that. I buried my nose in Papa's old copy of Cowper's poetry to hide the unfathomable scene.

"Would you like this?" Mama asked, holding up a poke bonnet with a short brim trimmed in little white silk flowers. "I think my other will better suit my position."

She'd loved that bonnet when Papa had bought it for her. Before his arrest. She'd hardly worn it since.

A pang rippled through my heart as I peeked over my book. "If you do not wish to take it, I will not refuse. My bonnet is in tatters." We hadn't had funds to replace mine.

I turned a page, though I wasn't really reading. The one chair we had in our borrowed room dug into my back, but I couldn't give up my seat. In a moment, Mama would go to post her letter to my older sister, Agnes, in London, and then I'd make my escape. If I acted absorbed in my reading, there would be less opportunity for conversation, and she'd leave sooner. I just hoped I wouldn't keep my potential employer waiting. My previous employer had demanded punctuality. I swallowed back the little ache that tried to form in my chest at the thought of poor Mrs. Richardson.

"I'll put it on your trunk," Mama said.

My tiny book didn't hide the room well enough to block out her movements. As she returned to collecting her belongings, her eyes caught mine. I quickly looked away, but a moment later, her hand touched my knee.

Oh no. Not this again.

"May, I know you are angry with me for accepting this work." She sighed. "I felt I had no choice."

No choice but to leave her daughter to fend for herself. Ever since Papa's deportation, we'd had only each other. My brother, Lewis, had never sent funds home. Agnes and James had a house full of children and couldn't afford two more mouths to feed. Mama and I had scrounged for work despite the few options we had, given our connection to my father. The last six months, we hadn't had more than this ten-foot room to call our home. We'd survived. Together.

"I know." I didn't have much more to say than that. I'd already shouted my frustrations when she'd come in a few nights ago to announce Aunt Byam had found her a job as an abigail in a town several miles from Portsmouth. They were to work at the same estate for a mother and daughter.

"I understand the sorrow over Mrs. Richardson is still very fresh," Mama said, squeezing my knee in a way I'm sure she meant to be comforting. "But have you considered your aunt's suggestion of taking the scullery maid position? We'd be together."

I bit my lip to keep from shouting again and tried to breathe out the mounting rage. Mama cared enough to worry. It was more than anyone else in this world cared. "We *employed* a scullery maid once."

"That was a different life, May." Mama released me and straightened. "Mrs. Richardson took pity on you, even though she knew our story. Most of Portsmouth will not be that sympathetic. We have seen it over and over."

My eyes stung, and I willed myself not to cry. Mrs. Richardson, old and independent, thanks to her late husband's fortune accrued as an admiral, had not minded my connections. As long as I arrived to act as her companion precisely at eight in the morning and let her talk all day without reprieve, she did not care that my father had stolen a small fortune from the rope yard. Arriving on her doorstep yesterday morning to be informed by her unfeeling son that his mother had died in the night had not only deprived me of work but also of my legitimate excuse to reject my aunt's suggestion. "I will not wear my fingers to the bone for someone who could not care if I lived or died," I said.

Mama shook her head and turned her back on me. She closed the trunk with a sharp click. "I'm off to post this letter. Please consider it. We'd be together, and that is all I want." Her voice sounded tired, resigned. It was a tone I'd heard so many times the last few years.

I wanted to remind her that we would be together in theory, but she would inhabit a servants' circle far above mine. While she pinned up hair and mended hems, I'd scrub pans and empty chamber pots. If she wanted us to stay together so badly, she should have discussed it with me instead of surprising me with the information after signing a contract.

Mama donned her drab bonnet and made for the door. I pushed my nose closer to the pages of my book as I held my breath for her to leave.

"I love you, May," she said quietly.

A lump formed in my throat as the door closed. I didn't want to believe it. She'd chosen this with little thought for my situation. For five years, we'd made all our decisions—to leave our home, to live with my aunt and uncle, to find work well beneath our previous standing—together. But Aunt Byam had always been such a friend to Mama. And I could not convince myself that Mama hadn't chosen my aunt over me.

Mama's footsteps softened as she walked away, down the hall and down the steps of the tavern one of my uncle's former shipmates owned. I lifted the bonnet and fingered its little flowers, remembering Papa's pride-filled grin and Mama's pleasure at the gift.

A sweet memory turned bitter by the lies that would soon be revealed. The pang of sorrow I'd never been allowed to express pulsed within me. Byams didn't wilt under life's misfortunes. My aunt had enforced that the last six years, each time she'd scolded me for my tears.

I slipped to the window and watched Mama pick her way through the street until she vanished, then I drew in a fortifying breath and slid from my apron pocket the scrap of newsprint I'd torn out of an abandoned paper yesterday on my way home from Mrs. Richardson's. I set the worn apron on the chair and pulled on my spencer and the bonnet. It wouldn't do to look unpolished when interviewing to be a lady's maid.

I held up the piece of newspaper to check the ship's name again. HMS *Marianne*. I hoped I'd find it quickly. With how soon she'd set sail, the seamen milling about the dockyards should have directions for me. I raced down the stairs and into the street, my gaze automatically falling on the low wall where my cousin Charlie and I would sit and watch for his father's ship. I wanted to find the *Marianne* as quickly as possible, but surely I had a moment for Charlie.

The September sun shone brightly on our spot, warming me through my jacket as I leaned against the rough stone wall. The ocean breeze ruffled the scrap of paper in my hand. Jolly boats and longboats wove between sloops and frigates in the harbor, some carrying supplies and some transporting smartly dressed officers. Farther away sat the first-, second-, and third-rates, their hulking forms crawling with ant-sized seamen. My cousin Charlie used to tell me all about the different ships and how he'd wanted to work on one of the great ships of the line.

He hadn't made it higher than frigates.

"I'm doing it, Charlie," I whispered to the wind. "I'm going to sail, just like you. I only have to convince her to take me." My throat tightened, and my eyes smarted. I gritted my teeth. Now was not the time for grief to surface. I couldn't arrive with red eyes and a running nose.

Gulls called as they looked for perches among the forest of masts. Sails filled as ships crept out of the harbor. I breathed in the moment. If I convinced this captain's wife to take me on, this could be one of my last days in Old Pompey. I hadn't considered that.

Before the sense of loss could overwhelm me, I turned and hurried away. I could mourn the changes in my life later. In all my nineteen years, nothing had both thrilled and terrified me quite like today. Everything hinged on this captain's wife's seeing my worth.

I glanced once more at the scrap. HMS *Marianne*. And the captain's wife's name was Georgana Peyton. Most likely some middle-aged woman with grown children, so she could run off to heaven knew where with her husband. I'd have to charm her and hope for a bit of luck. Luck had never favored me, but I had to believe it would now, or it was the scullery for me.

ELIAS DOSWELL

I forced the best smile I could under my sister's probing stare. She stood inside the cramped cabin that would be my home for months, if not years, her arms folded. Her red hair, nearly the same shade as my own, had a brassy sheen in the light of the lantern that swung gently from its hook.

"I know you better than that, Elias. You cannot keep your feelings from me."

I gulped. "I am not keeping—"

"A man of the church lying to his own kin?" She clicked her tongue. "Papa will be mortified when I tell him."

My face heated. "Miriam, this is what I want. I promise you." I needed an escape. This voyage was the best way. "I will have a place here. A living. I won't get in the way of Isaac's family. Surely you can see that."

Her raised brow told me she saw straight through my words. Older sisters always did. "And you won't get your heart broken again."

I winced as scenes of vibrant gardens swirled across my mind. Lilacs and rosebushes and greenery laid out in welcoming perfection. A blue-sky day and warm breeze. And Eliza Somer walking toward me with the effortless grace for which she was admired by all. Her calm expression, solemn even for her, should have warned me.

Miriam walked toward my hanging cot and turned about. "I think that rug I gave you will do nicely in here. Though it's a pity you did not sign on with a seventy-four. A bigger ship would give you windows in the main room and gun ports for a little breeze."

"Such is frigate life." There would have been advantages to joining the crew of a larger ship. Miriam preferred the larger rates, as her husband, John, commanded one of them, but he already had a chaplain. So did our brother Isaac. I had to use my only other connection.

"She is a pretty little frigate though. Captain Peyton seems beside himself with joy." She laughed. "His new wife, less so. She is a very reserved young woman, is she not?"

After sailing with Mrs. Peyton a year ago, I did not blame her. We hadn't had the best of voyages.

Miriam completed her inspection of my cabin and took me by both arms. Though only three years older than my twenty-six, she'd mothered me as much as any of my four older sisters. The serious look in her eye belied an impending lecture. "You have tried navy life before. Twice. I am very seriously doubting your judgment, seeing you once again on board a warship."

I didn't have an answer to that. I doubted my judgment as much as she did.

"Father is too vocal in his praise of Isaac's career," she said. "You shouldn't let him make you feel like a coward or a simpleton because the life of an officer was not for you. He should have welcomed your desire to follow in his footsteps."

"I *am* a coward," I said softly, "but his criticism is not why I am here." At least not the biggest reason. I drew in a slow, steady breath, blocking out the old memories that were even more painful than Miss Somer's rejection. My first time at sea had changed me in irreversible ways. "I hope to make some small difference in the lives of these men." It wasn't untrue.

"Of course." She pursed her lips, eyes dropping to examine my attire. "Just remember that running from heartache does not solve your problems." She brushed something from my waistcoat, a fashionable green silk she and I had chosen the last time I'd returned from a voyage. Back when I'd vowed never to go to sea again. "You have to face your problems. Show life that it cannot beat you."

"We have already established that I am a coward," I said.

"You have a funny way of showing it, signing on for another voyage." She went up on her toes to kiss my cheek. The action nudged my spectacles slightly askew. "You have so much love to give, Elias. And a world of good to offer. Don't give up because one woman couldn't see that."

I adjusted my spectacles. "She hasn't been the only one." Three others had broken my heart before her. Clouds gathered, thick and heavy inside me. I needed air. "Shall we go above?"

"Ah, yes. I should be on my way." She retrieved her bonnet from the top of my trunk and put it on. "We are off to Southampton this afternoon, and then we will make for Brighton to see my mother-in-law." Her hands dropped to her sides. "I love the woman dearly, I truly do, but if she asks us one more time when we will have children, I think she shall get an explanation that will make her choke on her tea."

I laughed at her peeved expression, but as I had no experience with mothers-in-law, I didn't know what sort of sympathetic response to give.

"You do look nice today," she said as we left the gun room and made for the stairs. "It's a pity you aren't going to a picnic or for a drive in Hyde Park. Your taste in fashion will be lost on this crowd."

Along with many other things, such as the comfort of a delicate blend of herbs and spices infused into a hot cup of tea. I could use such a drink and a few moments alone just now. We passed the gun deck and emerged above to a brilliant sun and all the clamoring one could expect from a naval dockyard. The *Marianne*'s full crew had not yet been mustered, but the boatswain's and carpenter's mates, along with a few seamen, made inspections and moved lines about.

I removed my spectacles and shoved them into a pocket. In full light, I didn't need them unless I was reading. I could see far distances easily, but in close quarters, I struggled.

"Write as soon as you receive your orders," Miriam said, pulling on her gloves. "I am most anxious to know where you'll be. With war on practically every front, there is no telling where they'll send you."

"Of course." War. My stomach soured. Though I hadn't fought during my previous voyage, as a chaplain, I'd seen the aftermath. Broken bodies, bloodied forms. Scenes I'd fled as a ship's boy.

She embraced me, then hurried down the gangplank to her waiting carriage. I stepped to the rail to watch her go, a pocket of emptiness opening in my heart. We'd hardly seen each other more than a few times since I'd returned from my voyage on HMS *Deborah*, but she understood me better than anyone in my life and loved me for my oddities. Not many did.

"Is that the captain's wife?"

Not far up the deck, two young men stopped at the rail—the boatswain's mate and carpenter's mate, guessing by their jackets. They looked four or five years younger than I.

"Peyton's wife doesn't have blazing hair like that," the taller of the young men said. He must be speaking of Miriam, and the thought made me watch him warily. He wore a smirk that seemed permanently etched into his face. "Mrs. Peyton's a slight thing. Did you not see her up here this morning?" He lowered his voice to say something to his companion. The guffaw that followed attested to its vulgarity.

I clenched my jaw, hands balling into fists. This sort of talk was all too common in the service. Hearing such remarks on the subject of someone I knew and respected made it difficult to ignore.

The young man straightened. "Pity we're not gettin' this one. I wouldn't mind staring at that day after day." He raised a brow and, with a crooked grin, nodded toward the retreating coach. "I like 'em—"

"Show some respect," I snapped, surprising myself. My voice echoed across the deck, louder than I'd intended.

The young man turned. He looked me up and down, then snorted. "Lookin' is free, mate."

His companion hissed something at him, but all I heard was "chaplain."

The young man's mocking glance only deepened. He leaned back against the rail on one elbow, doffing his cap. "Saving me from my lecherous sins, Mr. Chaplain?"

"Your sins are your own business, but I will not tolerate such talk toward my kin." Least of all Miriam. He showed no remorse on the revelation that she was family. My confidence faltered. "Do you not have better things to attend to?"

The young man scratched his chin, a dull look in his eyes. "Better things? What better things? Sorry, Mr. Chaplain, but we simple seamen don't have the brains for knowin' which better things the likes of us should be thinkin' about. Perhaps you could enlighten us."

I swallowed. He was hardly a simple seaman. Officers couldn't tolerate insubordination like this taunting. Left unchecked, it had dangerous consequences. But I was only a chaplain and practically undeserving of inclusion among the ranks of officers. What right had I to reprimand his insolence, especially when I barely outranked him?

He turned back to the rail, making another comment to his friend that I couldn't hear. They seemed intent on enjoying a moment of gawking at and ridiculing the women who passed.

Elias, you idiot. What good did you think to achieve with men like them? I wasn't Captain Peyton, who commanded not just respect but also appreciation from all he met.

Well, most all.

"I like the looks of that one." The taller one gestured.

On the street below, a young woman in a muted maroon spencer and gray gown walked slowly up to the *Marianne*. She paused, the right distance to put her in perfect focus for my vision. She squinted in the glare of the sun through the rigging. With a hand holding the back of her simple bonnet, she swept the ship from prow to stern with her gaze. I straightened, cocking my head. Had I imagined the calculating look on her features?

"As though she'd look twice at your ugly muzzle, Frank."

"Think we can persuade her aboard?" Frank popped a coin from his pocket and flipped it before them.

I stiffened. When I'd boarded, Captain Peyton had requested I help the officers in preventing any extra women trying to stow away. On the other side of the idling mates, the boatswain's wife, Mrs. Hallyburton, with her stern glare, stood helping her husband on the forecastle. Not long after arriving, I'd seen her drag a girl off the ship in a terrible chorus of hollering and screeching. Heaven help the streetwalker unlucky enough to cross her path.

The shorter mate shook his head. "She'd charge double, that. Look at that face."

"Look at that figure." The pair snorted.

I ground my teeth. It would be a long journey with these cads. I could only hope they'd mellow their roguish talk with no women aboard. Or perhaps they'd worsen. Men like this often did.

People passed the woman below as she stared at our ship. She looked young, perhaps nineteen or twenty, common among those trying to sneak aboard to earn a few extra coins. I leaned forward. Though tidy, her clothing had a worn appearance. One of the women who solicited to officers rather than sailors? Most of the sea officers on the *Marianne* were married, though that didn't always prevent liaisons.

"Now's your chance," the shorter mate said. "Tell Hallyburton she's your wife."

He waved to get the young woman's attention. "I tried to say that last time. Didn't believe me. Thought the old hag would drag me off by the ear, too, so I made myself scarce."

Then he'd been the one to help the previous harlot sneak on board, and he clearly had no remorse for it. My opinion of this mate plummeted by the second.

Please let her move on. Checked and striped shirts dotted the upper deck, but no blue-and-white coats to signify the presence of a commissioned officer. I'd have to save this young woman from Mrs. Hallyburton since her gawkers clearly had no intention of protecting the girls they played with.

The young woman lifted her chin, then strode purposefully for the gangplank.

My stomach leaped to my throat, and I tightened my fingers on the rail. The mates hooted, elbowing each other. I didn't even know how much money she expected to earn, but perhaps I could pay her off. The same price for no . . . *effort* . . . would surely be more appealing. Whatever happened, I had to save her from the boatswain's wife.

I darted for the gangplank, dodging seamen. Mrs. Hallyburton's back was turned, but it wasn't a large ship. One wrong glance would draw her wrath. I had little time to avoid a scene. This young woman didn't deserve public humiliation, no matter her situation. So many of these girls and women were forced into terrible positions in which they had to sell themselves just for a roof over their heads and meager sustenance. They deserved empathy, not trouble.

She stepped onto the deck, clutching a paper in one hand, and made for the hatchway as though she knew the ship well. I jerked to a halt, throwing a hand out to stop her progression. She stared at it, then met my gaze.

"It would be better if you left, miss," I blurted. The brazen light of midafternoon caught the soft, honey-colored curls about her face. What was one supposed to say to a woman of her character? Especially one so nice to look at?

Imbecile. My pulse pounded, grateful she couldn't hear my thoughts.

Her brows lowered dangerously. "I beg your pardon." Her dark-blue eyes bored into me with a severity that fuddled my already scrambling mind.

"The captain has requested . . ." I licked my lips, which suddenly felt dry. "Women of certain repute are not to board."

Certain repute. Can you sound any more ridiculous? Or condescending?

The young woman's nose wrinkled, and she straightened her arms, her fists bunching at her sides in mustard-colored gloves. "Who exactly do you think I am, sir?"

My face burned hotter than before. It had to match my hair by now. Mrs. Hallyburton turned, making my skin prickle. "Please. I don't wish to make a scene." I stepped closer and lowered my voice. Murmurs from the mates drifted over. Chuckles at the chaplain trying to dissuade the harlot. "I'll pay you what you would have earned, but you should leave and save yourself the spectacle."

She stepped to the side, distancing herself from me but making no move to retreat. The livid fire in her gaze had cooled to steely disdain. "I am here for work." She spoke with a calmness that belied her agitated expression.

I let out a strained breath. "Yes, I know it. And I commend your efforts to find work, but surely there are better ways to earn a living." I tried to think of any connections I had in Portsmouth who might be in need of a scullery maid or washwoman. I didn't know many people in the city.

"I will make my own decision, though I appreciate your concern." Her cold voice suggested she did not appreciate it at all.

Mrs. Hallyburton had caught a whiff of disobedience. She stalked toward us, a tigress after her prey.

"Please, miss," I begged. Captain Peyton had given us clear instructions.

The young woman held up the paper in her hand. "If you would excuse me, I must find Mrs. Peyton. I am answering her advertisement."

I blinked. Why would Mrs. Peyton hire a . . . I inched back, taking in her spencer and gown, the latter of which had a more gathered skirt than this year's styles allowed, though it was only a couple of years out of fashion. From her gloves to the reticule hanging from her wrist to her pointed half boots, one thing was becoming humiliatingly clear—this young woman was no streetwalker.

Elias, you bumbling numbskull.

Chapter 2

MAY

I pursed my lips as the man paled. How dare this self-righteous fop, with his fine coat and expertly styled red hair, judge me before he knew a thing about me. His throat bobbed beneath his pristine cravat.

A young man appeared at my elbow, a crooked smile on his face. His simple linen waistcoat contrasted sharply with the other gentleman's patterned silk. He bowed grandly and offered his arm. "Frank Walcott, carpenter's mate, at your service, miss."

It was a ridiculous display, one I would have quickly dismissed if the accusing gentleman hadn't just tried to pay me off for work I would never aspire to. I turned my back on the insufferable dandy and curtsied briskly to the carpenter's mate. "Would you take me to Mrs. Peyton, please?"

"Certainly. We Mariannes live to serve," Mr. Walcott said with too much enthusiasm. I couldn't quite make out if he was taunting me or genuinely seeking to please. Perhaps a little of both.

I took his arm. "Thank you. It is comforting to know this ship has at least one courteous person aboard."

"Never you mind Mr. Chaplain." Mr. Walcott winked. "Not all of us think ourselves so high above our company." Though not handsome in the classical sense of the word, his enthusiastic expressions gave him an intriguing air. Unlike the tall and stylish chaplain, whose mouth opened as if he meant to speak but couldn't think of what to say.

"I am very sorry, miss," the chaplain finally said as Mr. Walcott steered me toward the hatchway. "I hadn't the faintest idea why you were here."

I halted, my arm yanking out of Mr. Walcott's grasp as I rounded on the penitent chaplain. No doubt he was one of those fashionable vicars who thought so highly of himself despite making very little money. He probably didn't earn much more than this carpenter's mate. Attending university and living under the patronage of the Royal Navy hadn't taught him to respect his fellow man. Or woman. "I know very well what you thought I was." Someone despicable in his eyes. "Keep your apologies for someone who will accept them."

Mr. Walcott snickered quietly as I took his arm once again. I would have joined him if my stomach didn't feel like it was stuffed with rocks. What an excellent start to what I'd hoped would be the solution to my difficulties. I'd clung to that hope, that boarding this ship would make things different, erase the censure of Papa's shame that had haunted me these six years. Clearly, it didn't matter, even if no one here knew about the crime. How stupid of me to think a change of scene would bring a change of respect. No matter what I did, no matter how hard I worked, I'd always come up short.

My spirits sank with each step down the ladder. The deck below, with its short headspace and ominous rows of cannons, only darkened the emptiness mounting inside me.

"The great cabin is just there," Mr. Walcott said, pointing toward the stern. "She was inside not long ago."

"Thank you very much." I twisted the scrap of newsprint. Voices filtered from the cabin, but I couldn't make out words. My new employers, if everything turned out.

"If things go poorly in there, you're always welcome on the mess deck."

I grimaced in an attempt to smile at him, then walked quickly toward the doors, my mind not functioning enough to decipher if he meant something improper. One of the doors was ajar, light spilling through.

"I finally convinced them to give me a pair of long nines," a male voice said. "We can't very well give chase without guns at the bow."

"We'd be the laughingstock of the service," a wry female voice said.

I put my eye up to the opening. A dark-haired woman sat with her back to me, facing a tall man standing by the windows. His fine wool coat with gold buttons and his windswept hair made him the image of a noble captain.

"Are you mocking me?" he asked through a grin.

She shook her head coyly. "Your passion commends you, Captain."

"You would—"

I knocked quickly on the door. Eavesdropping on them before I'd even secured the job. I pulled off my gloves, suddenly too warm, then removed my bonnet.

"Enter," the captain said.

Poise. Serenity. Confidence. I pushed the door open and stepped inside. "Begging your pardon." I curtsied. "I've come to answer Mrs. Peyton's advertisement."

The woman had turned to regard me. My eyes widened. The girl looked no older than I was. *She* was the captain's wife? Skinny as a hairpin, she chewed the corner of her lip like a girl unsure how to act at her first assembly. This was to be my employer?

"Advertisement? I thought you didn't want to bring a lady's maid," Captain Peyton said.

She must not have had any others answer yet. The captain would have found this out earlier. I held tightly to my gloves. That bolstered my chances. As did her age. I might have better luck convincing a younger woman.

Mrs. Peyton rose swiftly and leveled her chin. "Your mother convinced me otherwise. She insisted a woman needed a companion with all these men."

"You know I support it. I'm simply surprised you changed your mind." He watched her carefully. "I shall leave you to your interview, then. I wanted to track down Doswell."

I almost envied this Doswell as I watched the attractive captain squeeze his wife's hand before quitting the cabin. What a shame he was already married. But then, I wouldn't be here if he weren't, and it wasn't as though I were in a position to catch his eye.

"What is your name?" Mrs. Peyton asked.

"Margaret Byam, ma'am." I curtsied again. An abundance of propriety would help my cause.

"Won't you sit, Miss Byam?" She gestured to a chair across the table from her.

I hurried to the indicated seat. The table took up the center of the room. Behind me, a large cot hung from beams, its curtains drawn. Only one cot, large enough for two. That was odd for members of the gentry.

I sat primly, settling my bonnet and gloves in my lap. I felt the curls surrounding my face to make certain nothing had fallen out of place or been smashed by my hat. She needed to see that I could make someone look presentable.

"Do you have family in the navy?" She spoke softly, with a calculating gaze.

"Yes, one brother." Lazy, negligent Lewis.

Her brows pulled together, and my stomach dropped. What if she knew of him? I didn't know how he acted at sea, but if it were at all similar to how he acted on land, he could not have a good reputation. I should not have claimed him.

"My uncle was boatswain of HMS *Deborah*, and my cousin was his mate. Both died at sea last year." The words came out so calmly, untouched by the vortex of grief lurking in the recesses of my heart. The fact that I could say it with so little emotion both surprised and hurt.

Mrs. Peyton's expression softened. "I see." She looked away. "Have you been a lady's maid before?"

I cleared my throat. "No, ma'am. But I was a companion to Admiral Richardson's widow for several years and helped when she didn't have an abigail for a time."

"I was sorry to hear she recently died."

"Yes, ma'am." Death had been my constant companion the last year.

She rose and paced toward a small desk that sat below the windows. She picked up a paper, then set it down and lifted another. Her simple cotton dress fluttered in a breeze off the harbor. She didn't dress as elegantly as other captains' wives I'd seen, even for the daytime.

I surveyed the room while she collected her thoughts. The cabin wasn't grand, by any means, much smaller than many of the great cabins of ships my uncle had worked on, but it was tidy and homey. I could see myself working here, even if it had fewer books and comforts than Mrs. Richardson's parlor.

"Have you had much experience with children?" She set down the papers.

I blinked. What did children have to do with this? She hadn't mentioned any children in her advertisement.

"We have several children aboard." She wrung her hands. "I was hoping for someone who might help with them."

She meant ship's boys. Older children. They couldn't be more difficult than the little ones I'd tended to. "Yes, I helped my sister frequently with her children before my employment." Until Agnes and her family had moved to London.

Mrs. Peyton's rigid posture relaxed. "How old were your nieces and nephews?"

Visions of little feet sprinting down the hall to a chorus of laughter pricked at my sentiments. It had been two years since I'd seen them last. They all must have grown so much. "At the time, the oldest was five years old. Then four and two, and the twins had just been born." And my sister had just written to announce yet another little one on the way.

"Good heavens," she whispered.

I laughed. "They are clearly a happy couple."

At that, Mrs. Peyton's face reddened. I winced. She must be a young bride, uncomfortable talking about such things. What was I thinking, bringing that up to someone I hoped would hire me?

She cleared her throat. "We will be gone quite some time, I understand." Changing the subject. I wanted to kick myself. Causing her discomfort would do me no favors. "Your service would be required for many months, and it could be difficult to find you return passage to England. Our orders are not certain."

"I understand." We never knew where Charlie, my uncle, or Lewis would end up when they left. I'd assumed the same for this voyage.

"Navy life is not for the faint of heart," she said.

I knew that better than this delicate bride did. Even if she were a captain's daughter, she couldn't understand the hardships of most seamen and officers. She must have sat in a comfortable home on land all her life, with servants to do her bidding and pin money to fund her fancies. Most officers' families did. I doubted she knew the horrors of being buried at sea and never seeing your loved ones again. This voyage would open her eyes more than mine.

I only nodded. Despite it all, I wanted to experience this life that Charlie and Uncle Byam had shared. To feel closer to them than I had in more than a year. And to take control of my own future, not waiting on parents or kin to disappoint me.

"Very well." She chewed the corner of her lip. Then she clasped her hands behind her. "I will expect you aboard the morning of the twentieth with all your things. We sail with the early tide the following day. Shall we go over the contract?" She plucked a sheet from the desk and brought it to the table.

I stared. "I have the job?"

She extended the page, then hesitated. "Unless you need time to think it over."

I fingered the flowers on Mama's bonnet. It had been too easy. My mind spun. Ever since I'd found the advertisement, I'd counted on getting this job, and I had planned the next steps of my life based on securing it as I'd watched Mama prepare to leave. However, I hadn't expected so short an interview to get me what I sought.

"You have no other candidates?" I'd prepared answers to questions about my skills and refutations to inquiries about my inexperience. She hadn't even asked for references, not that I could give them with my former employer dead. Would she snatch the sheet away and laugh, the way Lewis had liked to tease me with sweets when we were children?

She shrugged. "I've made my choice." She sat and pushed the paper toward me.

I leaned forward. My insides leaped in dizzying flips as I took the contract with shaking hands. At last. I was going to sea like Charlie. No thoughtless family members or judging chaplains would deter me. My eyes smarted, and for a moment, it felt like Charlie was there with me, his smile chasing away the frustrations and worries. I was taking the reins of my destiny, and life couldn't stop me now.

ELIAS

I stood on the quarterdeck, leaning against the rail and trying not to lose the tea and biscuits Miriam and I had shared before boarding. Of all the humiliating situations to get myself into—accusing someone without knowing the facts of the matter.

"Doswell!" Captain Peyton bounded up the steps to the quarterdeck. He carried himself with such agility and self-assurance as to make any man hate him if it weren't for his contagious friendliness toward equal and inferior alike. Though if he'd heard the carpenter's crewmen discussing his wife, the friendliness would have vanished in an instant.

"I confess I was surprised to receive your letter, Doswell." He joined me at the rail, folding his hands atop it. "The navy life didn't agree with you when last we met."

"Yes, I . . ." How did I tell him I'd come all this way because of a broken heart? A lovesick puppy slinking away with his tail between his legs. "My situation, it . . ." *Think, Elias. Sound intelligent for once.* "I needed a change. This seemed the best fit."

"We're glad to have you, of course. This will be a smaller party than we're used to." He put his back to the rail and observed the upper deck. "We've a few from the *Deborah* coming with us. You might have seen Étienne below."

I nodded. The French surgeon had greeted me in the gun room when Miriam and I had arrived.

"A few of the crew as well. Walter Fitz. Do you remember the lad?"

He'd had a way of drawing attention, first through beating others and then by getting beaten himself within an inch of his life. "But no Mr. Jarvis," I said.

Peyton's expression darkened. "Thank heaven for that."

"I saw our friend in Town a few months ago," I said. The backstabbing former lieutenant had pretended not to know me, crossing to the other side of the busy London street and losing himself in the crush.

A mirthless smile crept onto Peyton's face. Jarvis should have hung for his insubordination on the *Deborah*. The navy didn't usually let even their officers get away with serious crimes. Politics had rewarded Jarvis a slap on the wrist with an ejection from the navy. He likely didn't see it as a light punishment, however.

"Oh, to have friends in high places," the captain finally said.

Indeed. Some men were born with all the good fortune.

"I am glad you came, even if I don't understand it," he said. "It's good to have friends aboard."

"I can imagine, on your first voyage as captain." My brother served as captain of HMS *Lumière* my single year as a ship's boy, and he was the only reason I'd managed to pull myself away from my mother and sisters to board that first day. It hadn't been enough to make me stay, however.

"It's daunting," he said quietly.

I nodded. That I could understand. What aspect of life didn't daunt me? But then, I made a fool of myself in every situation, regardless of how much I tried to do things the correct way. Like with the young woman a moment ago. Her voice still drifted through the open stern windows. Though I wished her no ill, I hoped she would find a situation better suited for her. Elsewhere. I'd never be capable of looking her in the eye again and prayed I'd never be forced to.

"You'll earn their respect in no time," I said. "I have no doubt." Unlike me, Peyton had charm and charisma. He didn't spout nonsense when he didn't know what to say or quake in his shoes when faced with awkward situations.

"Thank you, Doswell." He looked as though he wished to say something else but then thought better of it. He straightened his coat. "Well, I'm off to the victualing office on a tiresome matter. If you have need of anything, seek out Mr. Howard in the galley or my steward."

"Yes, sir."

He glanced back when he'd cleared the quarterdeck. "Dine with me and Georgana tonight, won't you?"

I nodded, and he disappeared down the hatchway. I'd have at least one friend aboard. It eased the tension inside me. Though we'd hardly been more than acquaintances on the *Deborah*, if the Peytons were glad of my presence, perhaps I could find some sense of belonging. More so than I'd found at my brother's house in Kent.

The sun's brightness reflected on the murky harbor. I rubbed a hand over my face. *If you do not wear your hat, you shall be red and even more freckled. Never forget your hat.* Miriam's words oft repeated through our younger years played through my mind, as they did every time I ventured outside without a topper. If nothing else, I'd regret it when my skin stung from too much sunlight.

I turned to follow Peyton. When I passed the helm, I brushed the wheel's handles with my fingers. As a ship's boy, I'd learned to steer at the elbow of the oldest seaman on the *Lumière*. I'd loved feeling the strength of the ocean as it had passed the rudder, tugging at the wheel, and the power I'd felt guiding the ship against the waves. Despite its strict laws, the life at sea had been freedom itself. Until our first battle had turned it into a prison.

Perhaps I could rekindle that spark. This life would never again hold the magic it had those first weeks as a twelve-year-old boy. I'd experienced too much of its terror since. If I could set my sights on the beauties and simplicities, maybe this new chapter would not be purgatory. Perhaps I could enjoy myself at sea again.

Something slammed into my head, sending me staggering backward. Ratty fibers swept across my eyes as the thing dropped to the deck. I blinked rapidly and pressed the heels of my hands against my burning eyes.

"Sorry about that, Mr. Chaplain." Walcott's voice drifted from somewhere up the mast. "Didn't see you there."

Highly unlikely. I forced my eyes open and tried to make them focus. A piece of chafing gear, little more than a mat made from old rope to protect the sails and lines from wear, lay at my feet. Just in front of the sun, a figure stood on the platform at the top of the first length of the mizzenmast.

"Perhaps you'll think before harassing harmless women next time," he muttered.

Most certainly not an accident. I ducked my head, grateful for the excuse of injured eyes to not look at him for long. Praise the heavens I hadn't been wearing my spectacles. They'd have shattered.

"Walcott!"

The blast of a screeching voice farther up the deck made me flinch. I straightened, even though the woman's shout hadn't been directed at me.

"Captain won't tolerate the least insubordination, you slobbering mutt." The boatswain's wife, though tall and thin, stormed aft like a winter squall, her apron flapping.

"My dear Mrs. Hallyburton, you are looking lovely this afternoon," the carpenter's mate crooned.

She hardly glanced at me as she snatched up the chafing gear and shook it at Walcott. "How dare you insult your superior, the church, and the crown itself with your blasted tomfoolery."

I felt the crew's attention settling on us. *Not again.* If only I could melt through the deck.

"A simple mistake, madam." He oozed politeness.

"Mistakes by idiots get good men killed. Mr. Hallyburton has a cat begging to meet your lazy skin, and I'm not keeping it stowed a moment longer than I have to."

A cat o' nine tails, the whip boatswains used for flogging, inspired fear in the most hardened of seamen.

The young man snapped to attention with a salute, never mind the woman wasn't an officer. I couldn't tell if he did it to mock her or out of fear. I certainly wouldn't cross this woman.

"I've had enough from you, Walcott, you pickthank son of an eighteen-pounder," she said, throwing the chafing gear back down. "Now, get back to work, or I'll see to it Mr. Jackson needs a new mate before you've had time to fish a splinter from your pretty little palm."

She finally rounded on me. "There, Mr. Doswell. You aren't hurt, are you?" The vicious she-wolf had turned to a docile mother ewe with terrifying swiftness. "These boys hardly know what's best for them. Mr. Hallyburton and Mr. Jackson will whip some respect into them."

I laughed uneasily. "Thank you, but I'm certain it isn't—"

"Shall I fetch something for you, sir? A chair? A pint of grog? You look positively red in the face."

A mixture of exposure to the sun and blinking fibers from my eyes. "That is very kind of you, but I believe I will—"

She went on as though she hadn't heard me. "Perhaps some tea? Mr. Howard put the kettle on for Mrs. Peyton not long ago."

After the events of the last hour, I couldn't say no to that. I sighed. "If you would bring a little water to my cabin for tea, that would be just the thing."

The boatswain's wife beamed. "With pleasure, sir. And you will inform me if there is anything else." She didn't wait for an answer but grabbed the sleeve of my coat and proceeded to the hatchway.

Walcott's snickering sounded above us. I let her lead me. Whatever got me to the safety of my cabin the fastest.

This day had lasted long enough.

Chapter 3

MAY

My throat tightened as we ambled through the streets of Old Pompey. The wagon Mama, Aunt Byam, and I rode in clattered against the cobblestones. In the front of the wagon, the old man who'd taken pity on three women trying to haul trunks down the street whistled through the din of voices, carts, and gulls. It wasn't the peace of a country town, but it was home.

Mama's arm stayed around my shoulders, which didn't help me keep back the tears. When I'd told her about signing on with Mrs. Peyton, she'd, of course, tried to dissuade me. It hadn't lasted long, however. We could both hear the same arguments I'd used when she'd taken the job with Aunt Byam. We were going our separate ways, and while a few days ago I'd welcomed it, now the regret mounted inside so powerfully I thought I'd choke.

"You'll have quite the adventure," Aunt Byam said. "I never got to go to sea." She wore a plain blue dress and a draconian knot in her hair. I'd blame it on her servitude, but she'd started this when we'd found out about Charlie's death and was only reinforced when we got the news of Uncle. It was as though because her life had changed forever, she did not want at all to resemble the even-tempered and unaffected person she'd been before.

I nodded, not trusting my voice. Uncle had requested permission to bring his wife along on the voyage, as many boatswains did to help with their work, but the unreasonable Captain Woodall had refused. No one had known it would be Uncle Byam's and Charlie's last. Aunt should have been there with them. Would that have changed Woodall's mind? She doubted it. There had been whispers in Portsmouth of his obscure orders, ambiguous reasoning, and secretiveness. Very few of his former crew members respected him and had no qualms voicing it. He didn't care whether he had their respect or not, from the sound of it.

We passed the Church of St. Thomas, vibrant morning light catching its tan stone and red roof. Papa had taken me there on summer evenings to catch the sunset through its windows. Tomorrow I'd be far from this place that held so many memories of him. Memories tainted by the revelation that our comfortable life had been a sham. Through it all, I wished in the deep recesses of my heart that I could tell him about my position and see the pride in his eyes. He was always so proud of any accomplishment.

"You said the ship was the *Marianne*?" Aunt Byam asked.

"Yes," I said, sweeping away thoughts of Papa. "She's a new frigate." Uncle Byam would not have known her.

"Who knows how far you'll be from us?" Mama said, voice wavering.

"May was born for the sea," Aunt Byam said, turning her face toward the harbor. A distant look touched her eyes. "No need to worry for her. She'll come home with acquaintances from every quarter of the earth, songs from every land, and tales from every city. She won't be our little May anymore."

The corners of my lips pulled upward. At least my aunt supported my choice. She'd watched her life crumble when the men in it had been taken, but she'd determined to pull herself up hand over hand. And she meant to drag Mama up with her. With Aunt Byam around, Mama hardly needed me anymore. My smile dissolved again.

A pair of sailors stumbled by with a raggedly dressed woman between them, nearly knocking into the side of the wagon. They laughed and continued on toward the public house we'd just passed. The snooty chaplain had thought me someone like that. My stomach

soured, and I groaned inside. I'd have to see that ginger-haired mor-
alist every day. It was fortunate officers didn't mingle with servants
and seamen. I'd have to console myself with that and find ways to
avoid him at all costs.

"Who is the *Marianne*'s captain?" my aunt asked.

"Peyton is his name."

"You cannot be serious," Aunt Byam hissed as though I'd said I
was to work for Bonaparte himself.

I sat up ramrod straight under her fiery glare. "What is it?"

She clutched the side of the wagon. "Dominic Peyton?"

I lifted my shoulders. "I didn't hear his Christian name." A chill
swept over me. Why did it feel as though I'd committed a heinous
act?

"What was the wife's name?" Aunt demanded.

"Georgana." I looked to Mama's worried face. Understanding
seemed to dawn, and her mouth fell open.

Mercy. What had I done?

The blaze in my aunt's eyes flared. "Of course you would plow
headfirst into something like this without thinking. You always act
before you consider."

"Margaret," Mama said, pulling her arm from around me and
reaching toward my aunt. In that moment, I wished I hadn't been
named for this woman who looked at me with such fury. She'd trans-
formed from a supportive aunt to a raging harpy. "She couldn't have
remembered. I did not even recall the connection."

Aunt Byam sat back, clapping a hand to her face. The driver
glanced at us over his shoulder.

"What did I not remember?" I asked, shrinking.

"Captain Peyton was the lieutenant who brought word when the
Deborah docked," my aunt said darkly.

The one who had told her about Uncle's death. I gulped. Neither
Mama nor I had been home for the terrible visit. I would have remembered a man such as Captain Peyton. She couldn't fault me for
not recalling the name of a man I'd never met. "But you said he was
all compassion and gentility."

"He married Captain Woodall's daughter. He is in league with that villain."

My stomach sank like an anchor plunging into the deep. I covered my mouth, bile rising.

"The captain hid her on the *Deborah* that voyage, despite his own orders of no women aboard."

Orders he'd cited when he'd told Uncle my aunt couldn't join them. I tried to breathe. That little slip of a girl had not only been to sea before, which I struggled to reconcile after what I'd seen of her in our meeting, but had also been the reason my aunt hadn't been there with Charlie or Uncle in their final moments. Now she was my employer.

"What will you do?" Mama asked, face pale.

"What can I do?" I said through my fingers. My aunt had cursed the Woodalls so many times in the last year, her cries echoed in my head in moments of stillness. "I've given her my word." If I didn't show up, what would Mrs. Peyton do? She wouldn't have time to find someone else. That would be cruel of me after the kindness she'd shown.

"You can break a contract," Aunt Byam said. "Let that cosseted darling wash her own gowns."

Break the contract. Stay here. Find work as a maid and hope for something better than cracked, bleeding hands and endless days of scrubbing pots. I wrapped my arms around my middle. That thought made me as sick as the thought of working for one of Captain Woodall's kin. Would she be just as reserved, just as incomprehensible as they said her father was? I should have known a situation so perfect would come at so steep a price.

All my excitement fled, leaving a hollowness in its wake. I couldn't stay in Portsmouth. We'd quit the rented room. Mama and Aunt Byam were off to Fareham and their employer's estate as soon as they deposited me at the *Marianne*. I had nowhere else to go.

"I'm sorry," I whispered. How could I go back on my agreement with Mrs. Peyton? Contract or not, I'd made a promise. I knew too well the effects of broken word and broken trust. My life had been shattered by them. The dockyard blurred, buildings turning into mountains too steep to climb and masts becoming forests I could not cross.

"You said HMS *Marianne*, yes?" the wagon driver asked. "I believe she's just ahead."

"If you would let us out here," Aunt Byam said.

My limbs shook as we descended. Mama thanked the man and gave him a penny for his service. I stood stupidly as my aunt and mother dragged my trunk and hers from the wagon bed.

Aunt Byam hugged me goodbye, her whole body stiff and her farewell clipped. She stayed with Mama's trunk and let us carry mine on together. My grip on the handle kept slipping from the sweat on my palms.

"You still have time to reconsider, love." Mama's voice seemed to come from far away, my brain whirled so swiftly. Like the hands of Papa's clock at his desk in the rope yard when he'd wound it each morning. Too many things pulled me in all directions—wanting to go to sea, wanting to support my aunt, wanting freedom from the weight of the past, wanting to stay far away from anything connected to the dreadful Woodall family. In nineteen years, I'd learned life didn't give you perfect situations wrapped in pretty bows, like a new hat from the milliner, but it didn't stop me from wishing it did.

Why did this feel as though I had to choose between my family and myself?

"Come with us," Mama said when we reached the gangplank.

I panted from the exertion, eyeing the incline we'd have to brave. The ship's black and yellow paint gleamed fresh and new. She beckoned me to climb aboard, to see what excitements and dangers awaited on the ocean.

"Might I help you with your trunk?" The rich voice curled around the words in an accent I hadn't often heard in Portsmouth. Not when we were at war with the country the accent belonged to. An olive-skinned man with wild, dark curls bobbed his head in a bow. He seemed to be about forty but moved with the carefree nature of someone half his age. "Trunks can be rather troublesome things."

Mama said nothing but looked to me. I swallowed slowly. The Frenchman waited patiently for my answer.

"Yes, thank you," I said.

"*Très bien.*" The man turned to hail someone near the gangplank. "Doswell, will you help me with this?"

The tall man hurried over, the tails of his fine green coat undulating with each step. He wore a straw top hat nestled over red hair.

Lud. The chaplain! I hadn't even made it onto the ship before having to face him. I nearly took back my approval of the assistance.

"You are Miss Byam, Mrs. Peyton's lady's maid?" the Frenchman asked.

I nodded, scrambling to find a way to refuse his assistance before the chaplain arrived.

The Frenchman smiled kindly. "Gilles Étienne. I am the ship's surgeon."

I opened my mouth to tell him my mother and I could manage my belongings, but the chaplain stopped before us.

"Who is . . . ?" He paled as he met my gaze. I expected him to pivot and flounce away, irritably waving his handkerchief in our direction at the thought of helping me.

"Miss Byam, this is Mr. Doswell, our chaplain," Dr. Étienne said, hands on his hips. He dressed rather sloppily compared to the chaplain. "And a rather good one, I must say, though I am not much for religion." He leaned toward me and said in a hushed tone, "The clergyman from my last ship, HMS *Propriety*, he was a buffoon."

"Shall we?" Mr. Doswell tore his gaze away and gestured toward the gangplank.

"Yes, yes, yes." Étienne waved a hand. "We will put it in your cabin, miss."

I mumbled my thanks as the two men lifted the trunk with greater ease than Mama and I. The stocky Frenchman had to take two strides for every one of the chaplain's rapid steps. The man practically sprinted up the gangplank and onto the deck.

"*He* is handsome," Mama said.

"*He* is an imbecile." I turned to her, my hovering tears suddenly gone. The chaplain's presence would not cow me. I was ready for this challenge. I'd made my choice, just like Mama had and Papa had and Agnes had and Lewis had. Though my heart ached as she drew me in for one last embrace, the rightness of the decision permeated every part of me. Come storm or battle or critical clergyman, I would remember this moment. When I returned, I would be a different May, a better May. They would all see. I could break free of the chains of Papa's guilt on my own.

ELIAS

"This is Miss Byam's cabin?" I asked, balking at the entrance. It was the empty cabin sharing a wall with mine. "You're certain?"

Étienne nodded. "This is what that hawk woman told me."

He meant Mrs. Hallyburton. Only Captain Peyton knew this ship better than she. "She's . . . she's sleeping in the gun room?" The gun room—with its nicer cabins divided by wood partitions—was usually reserved for lieutenants, the sailing master, the surgeon, the purser, and the chaplain. Even the standing officers like Mr. Hallyburton were relegated to canvas-enclosed cabins outside the gun room's bulwark. While I cared little about breaking such customs, the oddness of having a servant housed among officers struck me. As did the impending regularity with which I would be forced to relive my blunder because I would surely cross paths with her often. A man couldn't avoid his neighbor very easily. Not on a ship. So much for my hastily concocted plans to stay away from her during the voyage.

The surgeon shrugged. "Mrs. Peyton requested it. Because the captain did not bring a clerk, there was an empty cabin."

"I see." We shuffled through the narrow door and deposited the trunk against one of the partitions.

"It will be odd having a few women aboard, will it not?" Étienne said as we exited.

"Quite." I wouldn't have minded until I'd humiliated myself in front of one a few days ago. "It should be a very different voyage." This was the longest conversation I'd ever had with the Frenchman.

During our voyage on the *Deborah*, he'd kept to himself unless summoned to meet the needs of the crew.

He pulled a folded square of paper from his pocket and held it up. "If you'll excuse me." A letter from home, perhaps?

"Of course," I said. No doubt he received those infrequently.

He made for his cabin and closed the door behind him. I glanced through the doors separating the gun room from the rest of the mess deck. The young woman, Miss Byam, had not descended the ladder. Perhaps she had continued her goodbyes with her mother, or maybe she had stopped at the captain's quarters to inform Mrs. Peyton of her arrival.

I slipped into my cabin and lit the lantern. Then I pulled out my little chest of herbs and spices. I sat cross-legged on the sage-green rug Miriam had given me and carefully opened the lid. Whiffs of cinnamon, cardamom, and nutmeg hit my nose, followed by the earthy tones of sage and thyme. Dried lemon, candied ginger, and delicate jasmine buds. My shoulders loosened, and my stomach muscles relaxed. What concoction today? Something with jasmine, to be sure.

I glanced toward the wall and sighed. In the next months, I had a feeling I would be brewing quite a few infusions, given whom my neighbor had turned out to be.

Elias, you truly have the most rotten luck.

MAY

I stood near the wall—or perhaps more appropriately, the bulwark—of the great cabin with hands folded as Captain Woodall's daughter tapped her chin. I had seen her tall, light-haired father only once, when I'd drifted to the dockyard in a grief-fueled stupor after my aunt had told us the news. This short, dark-haired girl looked almost nothing like him, and on our first meeting, she had seemed so inexperienced with this life. But even so, she had earned a touch of my respect in that visit—how could I not, at the very least, appreciate her when she'd accepted me so quickly?

But now it made much more sense. She'd recognized my name and pitied me. I took a breath to calm myself. It wouldn't do to let her know the realization of her parentage smarted within me.

"I suppose bringing me breakfast would be your first responsibility in the morning," she said. "Dominic . . . Captain Peyton usually rises before me. The steward will attend to him."

"What time do you expect your breakfast?" I asked evenly. Did she support her father's decision regarding my aunt? Did she even know of it? Each thought made my heart turn a little colder.

She hesitated, searching my face as though she could sense something was amiss. "At the beginning of forenoon watch. Whenever it is convenient."

Convenient? I nearly scoffed. Aunt had told me how demanding the Woodalls were, based on what she inferred from Uncle's stories. My uncle was too loyal to speak ill of his captain. Was Mrs. Peyton attempting to appear a fair employer only to chide me later when I brought things too late for her taste? I translated the time in my head. Forenoon watch began at half past eight o'clock. That was more than reasonable. It was later than Mrs. Richardson had expected me at her house, and I'd had farther to walk to get to that job.

"Is that too early?" Mrs. Peyton asked.

"No, ma'am. What else?" She would have worse demands, no doubt.

"I will dress before eating. Though I can do much of that myself."

Did she doubt my abilities to dress someone? I straightened my gown. "I am perfectly capable of dressing you, ma'am." That was what a lady's maid was for, after all.

She opened her mouth as though to protest but paused. Then she gave a little sigh. "Very well."

How terribly inexperienced she seemed. No wonder the sailors we'd heard speak of HMS *Deborah*'s last voyage had snorted and guffawed at the very mention of her. If my aunt had been aboard, she might have been a friend to Mrs. Peyton and helped her understand the way of things. What a terrible mistake the Woodalls had made.

A little voice in my head protested that I was being both irrational and unkind. The blurring memory of Charlie's face filled my mind. He would have scolded me for this. He was one of the few boys I had ever met who I could genuinely say had a heart of gold. Very well. I would be kind for Charlie, even if I would also not forgive Captain Woodall's actions. As much as I wanted to be like Charlie, I had too much of my aunt in me.

"Mrs. Hallyburton said she can show you how we do laundry aboard. I can help as well. Everyone must see to their own clothes on a voyage."

I frowned. Did she even need me here? She seemed so intent on not inconveniencing me. I had to make sure she saw the value in keeping me here. We were still in port. There was plenty of time to change her mind. A flash of worry shot through my limbs. She wouldn't reconsider, would she? I couldn't crawl back to Mama and Aunt now. "I will, of course, oversee all the laundry for you and the captain," I said firmly. "I am more than capable."

She nodded. "Of course. I did not mean to imply that you were not." Her cheeks pinked. "Once you have settled into your cabin, I will show you where our things are stowed. If you would like."

It was all I could do not to cross my arms in irritation. Had she been without servants all her life? She spoke as though she were a servant-turned-lady, but I knew that could not be true. All accounts said that the Woodalls owned a comfortable estate outside London. Comfortable estates meant an army of servants. "Will that be all?"

"Yes. Please see to your own cabin, which is the first cabin in the gun room on the larboard side."

The gun room? That was where the sea officers stayed. Uncle hadn't even been allowed a cabin there. I'd be living among men far above my station, enjoying the most privacy one could find on a ship, except for the captain's great cabin. "Are you certain? There aren't things to organize here? Schedules to learn?"

Mrs. Peyton fingered the short curls at the back of her neck. "My husband and I have much to discuss on the subject of schedule. And there will be plenty of time to set things to rights in the great cabin. Settle your things first." A glimmer of concern crossed her eyes. She motioned toward the door in an awkward dismissal.

I curtsied stiffly, torn between not wanting to be too civil with a Woodall and wanting to appear a competent servant. "I will be brief."

"Take all the time you need," she said. "Though we sail with the navy, we do not always have to adhere to their customs." Such as housing servants with officers. Odd as it was, I couldn't complain.

"Yes, ma'am," I said, walking toward the door.

"Byam?"

How odd it felt to be called that. But it was what women of rank usually called their lady's maids. I turned.

"I'm glad you are here," she said.

Glad? I swallowed. I couldn't say the same about being her servant, not when her family had caused ours so much pain. The genuine gratitude in her expression made me squirm inside. I curtsied once more and rushed from the cabin, not wanting my disgust at the situation I'd found myself in to come tumbling out. I would need to repeatedly remind myself that anything was better than the scullery.

MAY

The crew had already begun their supper when I descended the ladder with my rough-hewn tray. They'd pulled down the tables usually secured against the hull and gathered their sea chests and barrels around for seats. The comfortable rumble of conversation washed over me, and I paused when my shoes met the deck.

Dozens of accents hailing from many lands across the seas mingled in the dank air. Men from the North Sea sat beside crew from the Mediterranean and Caribbean seas, talking and drinking and eating.

Mr. Walcott and the other mates sat at the nearest table, their laughter louder than the rest. He raised a hand when he spotted me and motioned me over.

"Join us," he said. "I insist."

I didn't need much urging. He slid to one side of his trunk, allowing me a narrow seat. It kept us in rather tight quarters, with my arm and leg pressed against him. I scooted to the edge of the chest, as far over as I could be without falling off, but we still touched.

"What was your name?" he asked. "I don't think you mentioned it the other day. Rather impolite, as I so graciously gave you mine."

I laughed, uncertain how to respond. "My name is May Byam."

He nodded. "This here is John Catterick, boatswain's mate, and George Shelby, gunner's mate." He indicated a large young man on the other side of the table and then one whose eyebrows seemed locked in a scowl.

"I'm pleased to meet you." I took a spoonful of the lobscouse. The salty, hearty, thick mound of fish, onion, and potato warmed my mouth.

"Enjoy that bread." Walcott pointed to the slice on my plate. "Won't be long before we have ship's biscuit forced on us."

I wrinkled my nose. Charlie always complained about the rockhard, tasteless disks the navy used for bread.

"First voyage?" Shelby asked.

I nodded, trying not to look too enthusiastic. Lack of experience, especially overly optimistic inexperience, always drew out terrible tales from experts. I already knew the horrors of life at sea. "But I have many family members in the service, and I've lived in Portsmouth all my life."

"You hail from Old Pompey as well?" Walcott drew out his Portsmouth accent, brash and wonderful to my suddenly homesick ears.

"I do." Mama and Aunt Byam would have made it to Fareham hours ago. I mechanically shoveled in my next bite. Did she like her employer and the girl she'd be fussing over? The daughter couldn't be older than I was. How would it feel to have someone so young ordering her about?

"Look here, Miss May," Walcott said with a sly grin, elbowing me in the ribs hard enough to hurt. "It's your Mr. Chaplain."

The clergyman took one look at the mess deck and hurried toward the gun room with an air of displeasure. Good heavens. And

I'd have to pass him each day coming out of my cabin. I could only hope his cabin was in the opposite corner from mine.

I nearly refuted his suggestion of my interest in Mr. Doswell, but Walcott wanted me to respond so he could tease. I refused to give him the pleasure, especially if the teasing was over a pompous dandy like the chaplain. Instead, I rubbed my side, grateful that the boning in my stays had softened the blow of Walcott's elbowing. Good natured as he had meant to be, I wished he'd learn a little more gentility.

Walcott got a twinkle in his eye, so like Lewis and Papa used to when teasing me. "Think he'll ask you for—"

"What time do you think we shall depart in the morning?" I asked. I did not care to hear the end of his question. On my brother and father, that expression meant distasteful words were about to spew from their mouths.

"Tide will be early," Mr. Catterick said, scraping his spoon across the wooden plate. "If you want to catch the last sight of the city, you'll have to be up before sunrise. The Isle of Wight blocks our view fairly quick heading south."

"Miss May doesn't need a final look." Walcott nudged me again. Why did he call me that? I hadn't been Miss May in years. Not since Agnes had married. "Her eyes are on the horizon. She sails for death and glory."

I swallowed, the taste of lobscouse souring in my mouth. That was hardly what I wanted in this journey. Charlie. Uncle Byam. Where was the glory in their deaths? I stood, the deck suddenly tilting and not from the waves. I grabbed onto the bulky rope that supported the table.

"Miss Byam." The sharp voice made us all turn. Mrs. Hallyburton loomed near the standing officers' cabins outside the gun room, arms folded. "A word."

I excused myself, grateful for a reason to get away, even if it meant conversing with the shrewish boatswain's wife. She wore a checked apron over a dull crimson gown. Her steely expression sent gooseflesh over my arms, and for a moment, I thought to scurry into my cabin and barricade the door.

"You're not to fraternize with the crew," the woman said.

"Pardon?" She couldn't be serious. These were the only people I could converse with for the next months. She couldn't expect me to remain silent for all of it.

"You'll stay away from the crew, mates and officers included." Mrs. Hallyburton looked me up and down. "Our crew have no need of your wiles."

I curled my hands into fists, heat flying to my cheeks. First the chaplain's insulting episode a few days ago and now the boatswain's wife suggesting the same thing. "I will associate with whom I wish, thank you, ma'am." The honorific left a nasty taste in my mouth I couldn't attribute to the lobscouse.

"My word is law," the angular woman growled. Take away the dangerous scowl and she would be a rather handsome woman north of forty. With the scowl, she was a veritable sea witch. "You won't like the consequences if you cross it."

I pressed my lips together. I knew navy life better than that. She didn't earn one ha'penny on this ship. Only her husband did, and they had to share his cabin, share his rations, and share his hammock, unless they could pay for additional supplies with their own funds. My aunt and uncle had discussed it for long hours last year when trying to get her aboard. Why Mrs. Hallyburton thought she had any right to set rules was beyond me.

"You think you've found friends your first day aboard," she said. "I hate to be the bearer of bad news." In truth, she seemed gleeful to be the messenger. "These men—none of them—have your best interest at heart, girl. The unmarried women usually aboard these ships don't have anything left to lose."

"I will decide who I interact with for myself." I retreated a step, keeping my chin high. A few tables of seamen had stopped their chatter to watch us. Mrs. Hallyburton recoiled, but I rode over her before she could open her mouth to complain. "You have no authority," I said, digging my fingernails into my palms. "Not from the Admiralty nor from Captain Peyton."

"I am the—"

"Woman who lodges with the boatswain, yes. Meant to help him with his duties rather than harass those you deem yourself above." I'd seen her scolding a trio of young boys earlier while I'd been setting Mrs. Peyton's things aright. The whole crew seemed to tread carefully around her.

"How dare you," she hissed.

"You have no authority where I am concerned. I answer to the Peytons. And the Peytons only." Much as it pained me to say it.

I turned on my heel and stormed to my cabin, slamming the door with a satisfying crack. Sailcloth had been tacked over the window, blocking out the gun room's lanterns. No doubt Mrs. Hallyburton's attempt to save the innocent officers from my "wiles."

Now plunged into darkness, the reality of what I'd said hit me like a first-rate's broadside. I'd just made an enemy of the least agreeable person on this ship. I reached out, feeling for my trunk. The faint rocking of the ship I'd hardly noticed before now unsteadied my steps without the comfort of light. I stumbled into my belongings and fell to my knees. Rather than using the chest to push myself back to my feet, I folded my arms over the lid and buried my face in the sleeves of my spencer. The trunk creaked as I sank against it.

My aunt's words, my mother's pleadings, and Mrs. Hallyburton's commands roared in my ears. But somehow, the face I saw was that of Mr. Doswell, his eyes wide in bewilderment at my presence.

No one wished me here. So many had tried to dissuade me. If the Peytons knew I shared in my family's hatred of Captain Woodall, they wouldn't want me here either. I lifted my head, setting my jaw. But I would not let them deter me from making this voyage. Tomorrow, we would get underway, and I would be at the bow. No looking back, only ahead. And I'd spit in the face of anyone who tried to stop me.

Chapter 4

ELIAS

The Isle of Wight receded to the north and with it, the piercing ache of Miss Somer's rejection. I couldn't hope it would abate completely, not for some time, but my heart lifted nonetheless. Wind filled the columns of sails above me, carrying us farther into the English Channel.

Whispers of the balmy Mediterranean drifted through the crew. Leaving in September, we'd get there too late in the year to enjoy the warm waters, but if Napoleon kept up his attacks on countries throughout the region, we'd likely remain long enough to partake of the sea's pleasures next year. Between battles.

I tapped my fingers against the stern rail as England shrank along the horizon. The other officers had long since left the quarterdeck to return to their duties, but as chaplain, I had few responsibilities beyond morning prayer and Sunday service. School for the younger ones would start soon, but I'd already recorded in great detail my teaching plans for the next few months.

"The trick, Mr. McDaniel, is not to overcorrect."

I turned at the voice. Captain Peyton stood at the helm, a young midshipman beside him grasping the handles. The poor lad's rigid shoulders had risen practically to his ears.

"She'll follow your lead. Just give her a moment."

The scene brought back memories of learning the helm. How I missed Mr. Riddley's deep voice telling stories as he let me steer.

"Mind your weather helm." Peyton stepped back. "Ah, Doswell. Having second thoughts?"

I laughed, trying not to consider his question. "Good morning, Captain."

Peyton breathed deeply. "It's a fine day to set out, isn't it?"

He'd have said that whether the sun shone or rain poured. However, it was a lovely morning of placid skies mottled all shades of rose and violet.

"Your wife didn't come above for a last sight of England?" I asked.

He shrugged. "She said she was tired. My mother has gone to stay with friends, and her father is in London, so there was no one to see at the dock. But her maid is just there"—he gestured with his head—"so I would guess she has risen by now."

I followed his indication. Miss Byam stood near the aft hatch, smoothing her skirts. My stomach clenched against the wave of humiliation that always followed a glimpse of that young woman. The brim of her bonnet rippled in the breeze, blocking my view of her face as she wandered toward the starboard rail.

I needed to apologize to her. Bile rose in my throat. I'd made her feel unwelcome and looked down on. That hadn't been my intention, but I was a fool. Could I apologize without making a greater fool of myself?

Based on history, the answer is certainly not.

Now she was alone, and the sailors above were engaged with setting sails. As good a chance as any, with a smaller audience to witness another potential blunder. I needed to take my chance. "If you'll excuse me for a moment, sir." I touched the brim of my straw topper and stepped down from the quarterdeck.

Before I could reach Miss Byam, Mr. Walcott appeared at her elbow, stopping me in my tracks.

"A lovely morning to you, Miss May!" The carpenter's mate was the last man I wanted to observe my apology. He took her arm, leaning closer to whisper in her ear, as though old friends.

My apology could wait. I fiddled with the buttons of my coat. Yes, of course. I had plenty of time. We had months left on this mission. Perhaps years. No need to rush. I might as well think out what I would say and do it properly. I retreated back to the quarterdeck, breathing slowly and trying not to blush.

If only preparation could guarantee my success.

MAY

"Allow me to introduce you to His Majesty's Ship *Marianne*," Mr. Walcott said as though orchestrating a meeting with a duchess. I couldn't help a laugh, silly as he sounded. Why he'd taken such an interest in me, I couldn't say, but I allowed him to pull me toward the mainmast.

"These are her masts," he said, thumping the wood between the many lines surrounding it. "Foremast, mainmast, mizzenmast." He pointed to the mast closest to the bow, then the one above us, then the one closest the stern. "The forward deck is the forecastle, and where we're standing is the waist. Then we've the quarterdeck, where the likes of Mr. Chaplain mingle, sipping their tea." He pretended to drink from an invisible cup, fluttering his eyelashes.

The chaplain was on the quarterdeck, and he looked away quickly when our eyes met and turned his back. Was he truly so prideful that he couldn't stand the sight of me?

"I regret to interrupt your discourse," I said, prying my eyes away from the chaplain's finely fit jacket. "My knowledge of ships is a little more advanced than this lesson." Uncle Byam had drilled Charlie and me on different parts of ships as children.

He leaned his shoulder into the mainmast. "Ah. An expert, have we?"

"Hardly. But my uncle was a boatswain and my cousin his mate. I spent many hours aboard various vessels."

"If Hallyburton ever tosses Catterick overboard, I'll give him your name."

Mrs. Hallyburton wouldn't approve of that. Not after our encounter last night. Her fiery glare still blazed in my mind. "Is Mr. Catterick in danger?"

He pushed off the mast. "Not if he'd remember his duties once in a while." He offered me his arm with a flourish, like he had when we'd first met a few days before. I couldn't keep back a smile as I took it. Blatant flattery or not, he knew how to make a girl feel appreciated. "I'll only point out the pieces of great interest on this tour, seeing as I am in the company of so knowledgeable a lady."

Was he mocking me? Everything seemed like such a joke to this young man. We worked our way toward the bow, not a long walk on so small a ship. "*Marianne* boasts twenty-eight guns, besides her long guns and a swivel," he said. "All twelve-pounders, which, if you ask me, are superior. Longer range, and all." A sly glint crossed his brown eyes. "Would you like to see the figurehead?"

I hesitated. "I suppose." Was it terribly bawdy? Many figureheads portrayed questionably dressed women. I couldn't think of another reason for his mischievousness.

"She's a vision, to be certain." He guided me to the rail. "If you'll look just—"

"Miss Byam, may I speak with you?" The anxious question sounded behind me, and I turned at the unexpected entreaty. Mr. Doswell sped toward us, face aflame.

Would this man never leave me alone? He'd caused enough embarrassment. I released Mr. Walcott's arm, searching for something to say to make the chaplain keep his distance.

"Is . . . ?" Mr. Doswell cleared his throat, glancing toward the bowsprit and back to me. "Is Mrs. Peyton well?"

I folded my arms. "You were just with her husband. Why did you not ask him?" His hands wrung before him. He wanted to talk of something else, it would seem, but couldn't spit out the words.

"You saw her more recently than he has." Again, he glanced behind me.

"You've interrupted our tour of the *Marianne*," Mr. Walcott said, mouth twisting oddly. "It's rude to disrupt." The two men stared at each other, the carpenter's mate with a smirk and the chaplain with a disapproving frown. They both knew something I'd missed. Mr. Walcott put a hand on my shoulder as though to block me from Mr. Doswell and tried to turn me toward the prow.

I resisted. Mr. Doswell was clearly frustrated by something Mr. Walcott was doing. A little feeling told me not to let Mr. Walcott drag me about until I knew.

A form rose up over the starboard side. I startled, shuffling back as the seaman hauled himself across the rail and onto the deck. He glanced between the three of us, one eyebrow raised, then brushed his hands together and strode off.

Oh . . . I ground my teeth, face heating. So much for boasting about my knowledge of ships. I'd forgotten one important feature that Mr. Walcott had sneakily tried to draw my attention to—the head. The only place a sailor could go for a few moments of privacy on this ship. The carpenter's mate burst out laughing as I recoiled from his touch. Vulgar brute.

"Ruder still," the chaplain said softly, "is purposely throwing someone into an awkward situation. You saw him go down there."

Mr. Walcott snorted and sat on the rail. "Quite the killjoy, aren't you, Mr. Chaplain?"

"No need to make others uncomfortable for your own amusement." An edge of something—embarrassment? timidity?—colored Mr. Doswell's voice.

Mr. Walcott leaned forward. "Where was this white knight when she needed him the other day?"

"If you'll excuse me," I said and rushed aft toward the farther hatch. The way they carried on as though I were some delicate lady in need of protecting made me want to take Walcott by his patterned neckcloth and Doswell by his pristine cravat and give them both the Hallyburton treatment with a toss over the side.

No wonder the boatswain's wife had hardened into such a woman. These men wouldn't respect a female if she didn't.

⁓

MAY

I closed the door of my cabin and put my back against it, block-ing out the sounds of the ship's crew hanging their hammocks in preparation to sleep. One day at sea behind me. I'd easily managed the work itself, but the company . . .

I trudged into the darkness. Mama and I hadn't had the funds for a lantern of my own. I'd assumed I would be in a space that better took advantage of the common-area lamps and lanterns. The luxury of an officer's cabin had its drawbacks if one did not bring in an officer's salary.

As I knelt beside my trunk, faintly outlined in what light came through the canvas, something crinkled against my knee. I pulled a little packet out from under my skirt. I hadn't put that there.

I opened it and pulled out a bumpy strip of . . . fruit? I held it to my nose and breathed in.

The cozy brightness of peach enfolded me in memories of sunlit walks along the harbor. Dried peach? I sank my teeth into it, relish-ing the sweet tang. For a moment, I was a little girl clutching tightly to Papa's hand as we walked home from the rope yard sharing dried-and-sugared peach slices. His favorite and mine. I could almost see his wide smile and hear his booming laugh.

Had Mama slipped these into my trunk? My heart swelled for a moment at the thought of her doing something so kind after all that had happened. The feeling quickly dissipated. This packet was sitting outside my trunk. I'd already done a thorough perusal of everything inside. If she'd put the fruit in before leaving, I'd have found it yester-day.

I sat back, chewing slowly. Who would have set these here, then? Practically no one knew me. Most of the crew hardly glanced at me. The Peytons, while kind, were caught up in their own little world just as Agnes and John had been right after their wedding. Mrs. Hal-lyburton . . . I snorted, unable to even consider the thought, then clapped a hand over my mouth. Their canvas cabin leaned against the wooden partition of my cabin. I didn't want the nosy woman investigating my laughter.

That left only Walcott and Doswell. I scrunched up my face. After this morning's altercation, I didn't want it to have come from either of them. Perhaps it was some sort of peace offering. I put the half-eaten piece back in the packet and knelt, opening the lid of my trunk to bury it under my things.

The happy flavor still danced along my tongue. I paused. It would be a shame to let the slices go to waste to satisfy my pride. I sat back on my heels, slowly closing the lid. Eating these didn't mean I had to forgive the giver. And if they hadn't left a name, how was I supposed to know who to forgive? They wouldn't know if I'd eaten the gift or not, so it wasn't as though I were depriving them of the satisfaction of my enjoyment. I fingered the treat, tongue begging for more.

Unless they'd written a name on the packet. I turned the packet over but couldn't make out any writing in the dim light. All the better.

I crawled over to the bulwark—the opposite wall from the one I shared with the Hallyburtons—and sat against it. I popped the other half of the first peach slice into my mouth and couldn't help a grin. Irritating as it had started, the day was resolving itself quite nicely.

I pulled another slice from the packet, and my eyes fell on a yellow splotch across the deck. I took a bite, then reached toward the shape. The shadow of my hand made it disappear. Light from the cabin beside mine.

I scanned the panels and located a crack about waist high in the wall. A knot in the wood must have separated and fallen out when seamen had previously taken down the cabins. I went up on my knees to investigate, tracing the hole with a finger.

The opening gave me a glimpse of the cabin beside me, lit with a bright lantern against the nearest wall. I froze, finger still on the rough wood. In the center of the room, a man stood with his back to me in shirt and breeches. The light caught his hair, turning it orange as autumn leaves, and passed through the fine linen of his shirt, defining his shoulder blades and trim torso. His bare feet paced the width of a sage-green rug. He murmured faintly to himself, a steady thrum that tickled my ear.

Lieutenant Roddam? I'd seen him on a few occasions in the last two days but hadn't had a good look at the *Marianne*'s only lieutenant. I clearly needed to amend that, if only he'd turn so I could see his face. If it was the lieutenant, this brassy light gave his blond hair a reddish sheen. It was too difficult not to stare. His shirt hung in just the right way to give him that undone attraction, and his breeches were expertly tailored. Heavens, why did the rank of lieutenant make a man so attractive? He halted again, and my eyes strayed to the lean muscles of his calves. Mercy. This was as treacherous as it was thrilling to have such a neighbor. And a crevice between our cabins. Mrs. Hallyburton would flay me alive if she knew what I was doing just now.

The man turned, and my heart skipped in anticipation. For a moment, the spectacles he wore delayed my discernment. His brows sat low as he stared at a little book in his hand. The other hand tapped a pencil against his firm jaw.

"If you instead start with verse six," he muttered, "then you could lead with an entreaty to faith."

I blinked as recognition smacked into me like round shot dropped from the mainmast. The chaplain. I gasped much louder than I'd intended. He raised his head with a look of concern, glancing toward the partition, though not in the direction of the hole.

The packet crackled as it fell from my hands. I scrambled back and dove for my hammock, but the cursed bed evaded me. My hand swept down the canvas side as it swung out of my way, and the force of my efforts to jump in quickly dumped me to the deck, my cheek grating across the coarse fabric of my hammock on my way down. My elbow thudded against the floor. Tingling pain shot up and down my arm.

"Miss Byam? Are you well?" His soft voice carried clear through the hole in the panel.

I held my breath as I grasped the side of the hammock, wanting to rip it to shreds. I carefully lifted myself into bed and lay still. My arm throbbed. My face stung. Neither hurt so much as my pride.

"Miss Byam?"

I wouldn't respond. It appeared fate had more cards to play besides the Woodall connection. Whatever higher power I'd angered in my life surely must have been cackling at the chaos He'd orchestrated. Next door to the chaplain. Of all the cruel tricks.

Chapter 5

MAY

Mrs. Peyton steadied herself with a hand against the hull as I laced her stays the next morning. I cinched the laces snug until the edges of the stays nearly touched.

Ten months ago, I would have turned up my nose at lacing Captain Woodall's daughter into her stays. How my life had changed.

"Is that comfortable?" I asked. Whatever my feelings about her father, I would do my job the right way. I would be the best lady's maid she'd ever had and prove to myself and my family that I could do this.

"Yes, thank you."

I tied off the laces and bent to lift the plain yellow gown I'd laid out across her chest of clothes. She had a very simple taste in fashion. Some of my own gowns had more frills. The simplicity made my job easier, certainly, but it all seemed too modest for a captain's wife.

Mrs. Peyton turned slowly, holding her forehead in her hand. I paused in gathering up the dress to put over her. Her face had gone pale as a dinner plate.

"Are you ill, ma'am?" I asked.

She shook her head slowly without looking at me.

"Let's get you dressed and open the windows." She looked as though she could use some fresh air and perhaps a proper meal. She hadn't eaten much of what the steward had me deliver that morning, as evidenced by the tray of practically untouched food on the desk.

The young woman nodded once, then swallowed slowly, breathing deeply.

I tilted my head. "Are you certain—"

She groaned and whipped around, knocking into the dressing screen as she dashed for the starboard privy. The door clattered shut behind her, and I winced at the sound of her retching. Aunt Byam would say to hope she didn't get it on her stays for me to clean. I frowned, banishing the horrible thought.

I deposited the gown on the cot and retrieved a handkerchief from her trunk. I dipped a corner in the bowl of water I'd brought for her to wash her face. She'd be right as rain in a day or two, once she got used to the rocking of the ship. I praised the skies that seasickness hadn't hit me.

When she finally slipped out of the privy, her cheeks had taken a green tint. Her eyes shone as though she were about to cry.

I extended the handkerchief toward her. "Would you like me to get the captain?"

She took the damp square of linen and murmured her thanks. "Oh, no. I don't wish to bother him over this." She wiped at her mouth, then started to breathe heavily again.

"Do you need something to drink?" I volunteered. "The steward brought tea."

"No," she said tightly, eyes closed. "Thank you."

I retrieved her dressing gown. "I don't think you're well enough to go to services this morning." I certainly wouldn't want to sit and listen to Mr. Doswell's self-righteous preaching while ill. "You might feel better with a little more rest."

Mrs. Peyton stared at the dressing gown. Finally, she put her arm out for me to fit into the sleeve. She didn't say anything as I wrapped it around her. I could feel her trembling through the fabric. For someone who had supposedly gone to sea before, she didn't act the part.

After I'd helped her back to bed, I headed for the gun room. I might as well inform Captain Peyton of his wife's illness. As I came down the ladder, Mr. Doswell exited his cabin in a solemn black coat, waistcoat, and breeches. I grudgingly admitted the ensemble suited him so well as to make up for the dreary colors, and his copper hair added a vivacity that made him almost . . .

No. I'd given enough sympathy to people I'd sworn to hate this morning. That high-and-mighty man would get none of my good will, attractive or not. I jumped out of his way, keeping my eyes down and ignoring his greeting.

Captain Peyton stood in his dress uniform beside the sailing master, Mr. Merkley, who pointed to a spot on a large map laid out across the dining table.

I stepped inside the gun room. "I beg your pardon, sir," I said with a curtsy, "but Mrs. Peyton won't be attending services today. She's fallen ill."

His attention snapped quickly to me. "She's ill? How is she ill?"

The same way several of the crew were at this point in the journey. "Seasickness, I would expect, sir."

He gave me a look of confusion. "That's unusual."

I shrugged. He must have overestimated the fortitude of his wife's stomach. "She returned to bed."

"I'll look in on her. Thank you, Miss Byam."

I backed out of the gun room and wandered toward the ladder. The crew would be called to worship soon. Could I find a corner near the great cabin to hide from view of two men in particular?

"Miss May."

I inwardly groaned. Frank Walcott. Some girls might leap at the chance to sail, what with all the unmarried young men of varying heights and complexions and intelligences. My experience, however, had proved humiliating. I mounted the ladder without acknowledging Mr. Walcott.

"Oh, come now," he said. "You're not still sore about yesterday?" The ladder shifted beneath me as he followed close on my heels.

It wasn't the joke but the fact that he respected no one. Why should I have expected him to show me any regard? When he'd rescued me from the chaplain's embarrassing accusation, I'd given him more credit for gallantry than he'd deserved. His ridiculous trick concerning the head had proven that.

Something caught my ankle as I reached the top of the ladder. I fell forward, nearly smashing my face against the gun deck. My palms smarted as they slapped the planks. I kicked, but what I figured out was a hand held tight to my foot.

"I'm warning you, Mr. Walcott," I hissed, regaining my balance with one foot on the ladder and frantically gathering my skirts to keep them from flying up, "if you do not leave me be, I will . . ." I aimed my boot at his chest, but he twisted away, still holding on.

"No need for threats, Miss May," he said through his laughter. "Only, you can't be too angry with me. It was nothing more than a bit of fun." He finally released my ankle, and I scurried onto the gun deck.

The Royal Navy might raise sailors, but it did not raise gentlemen. I shot toward the great cabin. I'd stupidly assumed officers and mates would be like Uncle and Charlie—kind, dutiful, and chivalrous. One more way ignorance had made my life miserable.

"You can't run from anyone on this floating washbasin." He snatched my hand, and the force whipped me around. "I'm sorry about yesterday. It won't happen again." A twinkle in his eyes made that hard to believe. I tugged against his grip. "Promise," he said quickly. "Forgive an old friend."

"Ha! We are nothing near to old friends," I said. His apology felt as sincere as Mr. Doswell's.

Walcott dropped my hand. "We can fix that." Then he threw me a smile that could have melted ice. "You've no one to sit with during services. Come sit with me and the mates. At least you'll have someone to share in your boredom during Mr. Chaplain's blathering."

"I take it you aren't very religious." I folded my arms, trying to keep my stern visage.

Mr. Walcott wagged a finger heavenward. "We've an understanding."

The sentiment sounded too familiar. Papa might have been standing before me. I could practically hear his voice in Mr. Walcott's words. I unclenched my teeth. The little girl deep inside wouldn't let me refuse him.

"There now." He could see it, my softening. "Sit with us. A girl needs friends in a mangy crew like this." He took my arm and pulled me toward one of the guns before I could make an excuse to check on Mrs. Peyton.

Friends. I hadn't had many of those since Papa's conviction. I didn't need them. I'd survived six years without. And yet the word resounded in my soul. I may not need friends . . . but was it so terrible if a small part of me wanted them?

ELIAS

My first sermon of the voyage. I sat at the little table set out on the gun deck for me and arranged my notes and Bible. Stoic faces stared back. As usual.

Why do you do this if they don't want your preaching?

I gave a silent sigh. Why, indeed. In a country parish, most worshippers came by choice. In the navy, though not required, it was expected.

A trio of tawny-haired boys sat together near the front of the gathering. The smallest stared up at me with wide, glazed eyes. The other two stared at the deck, shoulders slumped. New ship's boys. Poor lads. They must be exhausted.

Captain Peyton arrived without his wife and nodded at me to begin. I took a deep breath. I was here to share hope. Even if it touched only one soul, my work was worth it. Miss Somer's father had told me that a few months ago, back when it had seemed certain I would soon become both his curate and his son-in-law.

Visions of Miss Somer threatened. I cleared my throat. I did not need her face before me just now. With a deep breath, I lifted my gaze and caught a pair of deep-blue eyes boring into me with the force of a whaler's harpoon.

Miss Byam. She of all people would not wish to listen to me. I hadn't found a time to apologize in the twenty-four hours we'd been at sea.

Liar. You haven't found the courage.

Yes, that as well. She had spent a good deal of time with Mr. Walcott, and after the uncomfortable situation yesterday morning, I didn't relish the idea of trying to have a conversation with her in his presence. I cleared my throat again. My sermon. "'And the Lord said, if he had faith as a grain of mustard seed, ye might say unto this sycamine tree, Be thou plucked up by the roots, and be thou planted in the sea; and it should obey you.'"

Oh, to have that sort of courage.

Miss Byam sat with the mates, who all spoke quietly among themselves without an attempt to look as though they listened.

"How often have we sat at the bottom of an abyss with no way out?" I said. It didn't matter if they listened. My message wasn't for them. It was for the weary boys in the front. "When towering waves crash down around us, and we have little hope that the sun will rise again on our seemingly insignificant existence?"

Her look softened as I continued, and her head tilted to one side as she studied me. I'd written these words as much for myself as anyone, and suddenly, I felt terribly exposed. It was as though she saw straight through the sermon into my soul. The words stopped. I sought my place in my notes, mind suddenly muddled.

Quiet chuckles from the mates' corner made my face heat. They laughed at their own jokes, but it felt as though they laughed at my stumble. She still watched me.

"And he . . ." *No, you already said that line.* I ran my thumb over the numbered paragraphs I'd written. Had I made it to part six? Or was it seven? I swallowed. "As we put our faith in the Holy One, the impossible becomes possible. He will lead us over the mountains and through the ravines life throws in our path."

What I wouldn't give to emerge from this ravine and throw off the weight of my former love's refusals. A few weeks at sea in the company of people with no connection to her would make it fade, would it not? I had to keep believing it would. Perhaps avoiding Miss Byam could prove the distraction I needed.

No, I couldn't avoid her. At the very least, I had to set things right. She might still hate me and shoot those unnerving, soul-searching looks in my direction, but I had to try.

The mates' talking crescendoed until seamen's heads turned to watch them. Mrs. Hallyburton, sitting near the officers, eyed them darkly, and I almost expected her to pull a cat o' nine tails from under the stool she sat on.

I was losing my audience. Time to skip to the end and finish the service before I lost control completely. I couldn't compete with the rowdy mates, and I did not wish to try. Those who wanted to listen to me would hear. "'For the time would fail me to tell of . . . the prophets: Who through faith—'"

One of the mates snorted loudly, drawing everyone's attention. I groaned internally. What was the use?

"Hush!" Miss Byam glared at Mr. Walcott, then at anyone nearby who dared to laugh at whatever joke the mates had told. The gun deck quieted. She waved toward me to continue.

Miss Byam had been listening. And had either enjoyed it or taken pity on me. Whichever it was, that meant she had some sliver of kind feelings toward the man who had utterly embarrassed her. The corners of my mouth pulled upward, a renewed desire to finish rising in my chest. "'Who through faith subdued kingdoms, wrought righteousness, obtained promises, stopped the mouths of lions.'"

When I ended with a thrown-together conclusion, the men dispersed quickly, to my relief and theirs. I was out of practice, not having given sermons since my time on the *Deborah*. The next would be easier.

I gathered my things as the captain came over. "Thank you, Doswell." Captain Peyton slapped my arm. "Join us for dinner tonight."

I glanced around the other officers. Dining in the captain's cabin was an honor, especially if the officers hadn't also been invited. "Will Mrs. Peyton be well enough for that?" She hadn't missed Sunday services on our last voyage.

He laughed. "I'm certain she'll recover by then. She hasn't been seasick in years."

It hit the most hardened of sailors sometimes. "I look forward to it, then," I said.

Peyton turned and disappeared into his quarters just as Miss Byam stood. The carpenter's, boatswain's, and gunner's mates had left.

I gripped my books. Now was as good a time as any. I crossed the deck before she could run off. "Miss Byam." I bowed.

She folded her arms. "Mr. Doswell."

A cold reception. *Keep going.* "Thank you for . . . for helping restore order." Did that sound as awkward as it felt coming from my mouth?

She lifted a shoulder. "They were telling terrible jokes. Your sermon was better than listening to that." She wrinkled her nose.

I laughed uneasily, unsure if I could take that as a compliment. I didn't know what to make of her brashness.

She straightened her back and dropped her arms to her sides. "Though I thought perhaps you should have based your sermon on Matthew 7, given the circumstances."

Chapter seven? She walked hastily away from me to go below before I could form a response. So, she hadn't forgiven me. I drummed my thumbs against the covers of my books. I knew chapter seven, with its entreaties not to judge, very well. It would appear she knew her Bible.

Once a few minutes had passed and I could safely assume she'd made it to her cabin, I tucked my books under my arm, adjusted my spectacles, and made my way down the ladder. After so awkward a sermon, I should have withered under the humiliation as I relived each stumble in my head. Even now her unyielding stare distracted me from my usual self-critique.

She'd meant the jab about Matthew 7 to discourage me from speaking to her, perhaps even to anger me. It had done just the opposite, though I didn't know how. The quickness of her response brought a grin to my face.

First you insult her, and now you smile at her anger.

I sobered instantly. I hadn't accomplished my task of making things right. If only brewing this apology were as simple as mixing a flavorful blend of herbs for a tea. I'd have mastered it by now.

But a good concoction took careful thought, and a proper steeping took time. There might be hope of success yet. I needed to think some more. Over a cup of tea.

MAY

By evening, the *Marianne* had hit rough water, and my stomach would not tolerate it. A light-haired boy delivered dinner, though I hadn't left my cabin in hours and hadn't asked anyone to fetch it for me. I sat in the dark, picking at the salty pie, but I quickly gave up and stumbled to my hammock.

Mrs. Peyton had stayed in bed the whole day, much to my relief. The gun deck, being higher on the ship, rocked more than the mess deck, and the mess deck was bad enough. With one hand on my aching head and one on my protesting belly, I closed my eyes and tried to imagine I lay on solid ground. The hammock helped minimize the feel of movement, especially if I couldn't see the cabin turning about me. This was not quite the adventure I'd anticipated when scheming with Charlie. He'd failed to mention the horrors of seasickness.

For the briefest moment, I wished I were a child once again, curled up in Papa's arms near the sitting room hearth. He had always taken it upon himself to watch over me when I was ill, making sure I felt safe and cared for. Now he was on the other side of the world, and I was alone.

A soft tap sounded on my door. Mrs. Peyton must need me. I sat up, my body objecting to the movement. I thought I'd had the better luck, finding an unusual position at sea. Clearly, Mama had been the luckier one. She didn't have to do her work while her insides fought to come out, and she had Aunt to keep her company in her work. I had a ship full of men, few of whom I wished to know better and fewer still who cared about my health.

The moment my feet hit the floor, the dark cabin began to spin. I stumbled, smashing into the wall before falling to the floor. It took all my power not to relinquish my dinner all over the deck. The smell would not help me, of that I was certain.

The door opened quickly. "Miss Byam?" The gun room's lanterns caught my visitor's red hair. Mr. Doswell. My stubbornness wanted to moan, but all I felt was relief. My predicament might repulse him, but at least he wouldn't poke fun. He was not the fun sort.

I pushed myself to sitting and leaned my head back against the wall. "I hate ships."

"I've thought the same thing before." He pushed the door open wide, letting in more light, then knelt beside me. He extended a teacup. "I noticed you've been in here quite a while and wondered if you were sick like the rest. I thought this might help."

I took it with trembling hands and brought it to my face. The ginger-laden steam wafted against my clammy face. I touched the surface of the herbal infusion with my upper lip. It was hot but not burning. The spicy liquid washed down my throat, brightened by a touch of lemon and cooled at the end with a brush of mint. I took a breath, and this time, my stomach didn't lurch as badly. "Thank you," I managed.

"We'll be past the Bay of Biscay in a couple of days. The weather should settle by then."

A couple of days! I took another sip, wanting to cry. I couldn't take this for a couple more days.

"We should get you above after you've finished that," he said, flipping out the tails of his coat and sitting back. Golden lantern light painted one side of his face, igniting the green in his eyes. His black attire, which should have given him a severe look, warmed in the mellow glow. Like when I'd seen the old Dutch paintings Papa had taken me to as a child, I couldn't look away from how the light played across his face, nor from the way the shadows of my cabin outlined the angles of his brow and jaw.

"Are you trying to redeem yourself from our first encounter?" I asked, breaking my stupor to study the diamond pattern across the teacup he'd brought.

He dropped his chin and drew a circle with a finger on the knee of his breeches. "I never wanted to embarrass you. Quite the opposite."

He sounded so sincere, I almost believed him. "You assumed you knew who and what I was."

He blushed. "When you've heard young women dragged off by Mrs. Hallyburton for violating the captain's rules, it makes you wary for the others."

I could imagine the tumult.

"Many of them are just trying to earn enough to eat," he added quietly.

I lowered the cup. That wasn't a sentiment one heard from a clergyman very often. No condemnation. Not even self-righteous pity. Sincere sorrow for their state. I'd taken such offense to his offering to pay me off, but it seemed he'd done it because he'd wanted me to have the funds to eat.

"I am truly sorry for my mistake," he said again, scratching the back of his head. "I feel terrible that that was your welcome to the *Marianne*. It isn't an easy situation to enter, surrounded by so many blundering buffoons."

I laughed and took another sip. My head's spinning had slowed. "You mean boarding a ship full of men who only give you strange looks? Why would that be so difficult?"

"This life isn't for the faint hearted." His expression grew serious, and he returned to tracing shapes on the leg of his breeches. He'd said that to himself as much as he'd said it to me. In a better composed state, I might have inquired further. Only that morning, I'd harbored a rather poor attitude toward this man. Either he'd added something strange to this infusion to muddle my mind, or we'd both misunderstood each other.

I slowly finished the tea while I watched him. Two vastly contrasting apologies from two dissimilar men in one day. I hadn't expected that. Something loosened in my chest, allowing room for comfort to drift in and take up a small corner.

He motioned to the teacup, and I returned it to him. With surprising agility, he got to his feet without jostling the cup in its saucer, then he reached down to me.

I set my hand into his, and his fingers wrapped around it as gently as if he were holding a little bird fallen from a nest. Warmth spread from my fingers up my arm. Gentlemen didn't wear gloves very often on ships. It made sense for the seamen and even the standing officers, who constantly had to work rope and sail and wood, but the rest of the officers followed suit. Feeling his skin against mine made me hesitate. Part of me still did not wish to feel comfort from this clergyman.

"Slowly," he said, allowing me to pull on his firm arm instead of yanking me up himself. He steadied me as the ship rose rapidly. When it righted, he kept hold of my hand. "Shall I help you above?"

I quickly shook my head, releasing his hand and cutting off the odd sensation his touch had given me. Was *odd* the right word? It hadn't been unpleasant. "I can manage," I said, trying to sound certain.

He did not look convinced. "Might I recommend the forecastle? Setting your sights on the horizon will help."

"So long as I don't set my sights on the head." What an idiotic thing to say. The illness had turned my brain to mush. It sounded like one of Mr. Walcott's jokes.

He chuckled. "I would avoid that." He hesitated and then bowed. "If you are certain you don't need help, I'll leave you to it."

As he turned to go, I remembered my manners. I followed him through the door. "Thank you, Mr. Doswell." And I truly meant it. Someone had remembered me. I hadn't expected it to be the very man I'd determined to hate on my first day. "You are too kind."

"I can bring you more if this keeps up. Do not hesitate to ask." He pointed toward his door. "I'm only right . . . ." His voice trailed off to end the obvious statement.

"Yes, of course." Did he know about the hole in the partition between our cabins? I expected not, and I would not be the one to tell him. One benefit of not having a lantern was that he would not be able to see into my cabin as well when he did discover it.

When he discovered it. Good heavens. I'd have to take care in here. My one place of privacy on this ship was not so private with that crack in the partition.

He bowed again, stiffly this time, and shot into his cabin. I would have stood there staring at his closed door for a moment longer, laughing at his awkwardness or pondering this new perspective of the *Marianne*'s chaplain, but my stomach started to turn again, and I raced for the ladder.

Chapter 6

ELIAS

I placed my *veilleuse-théière* on the gun room table and lit its tiny candle. Supper had finished some time ago, and sleeping hour for the mess deck had nearly arrived. Officers either readied for bed in their cabins or stood watch above, leaving the gun room quiet and still. I set the veilleuse-théière's small teapot over its chimney-like stand. The cylinder concentrated the candle's heat to bring the water in the teapot, which was just enough for two cups of tea, back to a simmer.

The flame swayed inside the chimney, sometimes following the movement of the *Marianne* and sometimes snapping its own direction. Unpredictable. Mesmerizing. Soothing. The tension of the day loosened and dissolved from my shoulders as I watched, and I steadied the veilleuse-théière against its base to keep it from plunging off the table.

A week at sea, and things had begun to settle into a familiar routine. I instructed the young gentlemen in mathematics and the classics in the morning, then taught the regular ship's boys to read in the afternoon. I dined with the officers in the evening or sometimes Captain Peyton when his wife had a brief respite from her lingering seasickness.

And all day, I passed Miss Byam, wondering which version of her I would meet. Some moments, she wouldn't glance at me, even if we brushed shoulders. Other times, she gave me a stiffly polite greeting, as though the apology hadn't quite made up for my offense. Like the candle before me, I couldn't guess which direction she would lean—toward or away from me.

I arranged the jars of jasmine buds, mint, and dried peaches with one hand. My stock of peaches had nearly vanished. I didn't know if they'd have them in Malta, but I could hope.

A feminine laugh skipped through the partition between the gun room and the rest of the mess deck. Miss Byam seemed to enjoy spending her evenings with the mates. It made sense, as Lieutenant Roddam hadn't invited her to dine with the officers, and who wouldn't want to pass her time with the charismatic and flirtatious Mr. Walcott?

"Are you well, Mr. Doswell?"

I straightened in my chair. Étienne stood on the opposite side of the table. I hadn't noticed his entrance. "Yes! Yes, of course."

"You looked as though you had eaten something foul."

I blinked. "Oh, no. I'm right as rain. To be sure." Blast it. I'd never mastered keeping a tight rein on my emotions, but to have someone sneak up on me when my guard was down did not help. I hadn't realized I harbored such disgruntlement over Miss Byam's friendship with Mr. Walcott, something I had nothing to do with and no reason to care about one way or another.

He only nodded and continued toward his cabin, as he did every night, to sit alone until morning came. Just as I did.

"Would you care for tea?" I asked as he opened his cabin door, surprising myself as much as him.

"I think I . . ." He gave me a thoughtful look. "Yes, thank you."

The Frenchman and I had exchanged pleasantries, and I wondered if he'd found comfort in the sight of a familiar face among a largely unknown crew, as I had in our conversations. Perhaps he preferred to not get more familiar than passing acquaintances, surrounded as he was by his country's enemies after being pressed into service, but every man needed a friend. Few on this ship wished to befriend me—clearly, Miss Byam had found her friendships in a rowdier crowd—but I could be a friend to those no one else wished to talk to. If Étienne was willing, I might even have an opportunity to practice my French. Or would that be too awkward a favor to ask of him?

"Have you ever been to the Mediterranean?" I asked. This wouldn't be the relaxing evening I'd anticipated, not with the task of thinking of what to say, but there was always tomorrow night.

He sat in the chair opposite mine and draped his arm across its back. "A few times."

Did I ask where he was from, or was that too personal?

Miss Byam laughed again, further jumbling my thoughts. What was she laughing at? One of Mr. Walcott's questionable jokes?

"I have not seen many of these outside of France," Étienne said, motioning to the veilleuse-théière.

"Nor have I. I brought it back from Paris while traveling with my father. During the peace time." England and France had fought all but a few years of my lifetime. If only the journey with my father could have been as peaceful.

"I have never been to Paris." Étienne's accent was pronounced, though he had a solid grasp on the English language. "I have heard it is stunning."

Overwhelming was more accurate, especially with my father directing us to and fro from sunup to sundown. "It was quite an experience." I carefully pulled the lid off the teapot, whose water had begun to bubble. I tipped a little of the jasmine and mint into the pot, followed by the last of the peach slices. My father had questioned my desire to bring home one of these sets. Even then, I'd been too obsessed with my herbal concoctions and infusions for his taste. He didn't know, and I reckoned he didn't care, that these nightly rituals had saved me.

I returned the lids to the jars and teapot, then blew out the candle below to let everything steep in the hot water.

"Perhaps it is not my business, but you seem rather more"— Étienne waved his hand as though searching for a word—"*burdened* this voyage."

It was all I could do not to duck my head. Had it been so obvious? "I suppose things did not go as I had hoped during my time on land."

The Frenchman twirled the gold ring on his little finger. "Life has a way of throwing such things in our path, does she not?"

A few more minutes and the herbs would be properly infused. "Sometimes I wish, for once, life could go as planned." I'd take even a single day.

I excused myself to fetch another teacup and couldn't help a glance out one of the gun room doors. Miss Byam sat at the end of the table in close quarters with Mr. Walcott.

Why does it bother you so much? You wanted to avoid her the rest of the voyage.

I didn't have an answer to that. Walcott and Catterick's discussion of Miriam, Mrs. Peyton, and Miss Byam did nothing to help. That first exchange with Walcott and my defense of the women they'd ogled repeated in my head nearly as much as the following encounter with Miss Byam. Would I ever learn how to prevent myself from sounding like a dunce? Someday, it would be nice not to relive every conversation in painful detail for years to come.

The teacup lay toward the bottom of my trunk, wrapped carefully to prevent breakage. I pulled it out and unwound the cloth. I fingered the diamond pattern along the porcelain. Another gift from Miriam from before I'd left on the *Deborah*.

Hearing the things they said about Miriam had made me suspicious of Walcott's and Catterick's intentions. Miss Byam could decide for herself who she wanted as friends, but I couldn't help feeling that Mr. Walcott had concealed some of his true nature in his attempt to win her attention. Not all of it, however, as evidenced by the joke he'd tried to play on her.

I rose and shut the trunk. The tea would be done. I deliberately kept my eyes on the gun room table as I returned. It wasn't as though I could tell her what a cad Mr. Walcott was. Any ground I'd made up in our brief conversation Sunday evening would be lost threefold. It wasn't as though I'd find the courage to do it either. She didn't need any more reasons to hate me.

"It isn't a true tea," I said as I retook my seat. I lifted the teapot from the base and poured the steaming and fragrant liquid into the cups. The delicate jasmine hit my nose, but it did not send the comforting warmth through my body as it usually did. Discomfort and worry remained.

"It smells wonderful." Étienne took the cup from me.

We sipped our drinks in silence, and I tried to banish my misgivings. I had no place judging whom Miss Byam chose to spend time with. It should not affect me in the slightest. And yet I could not lose myself in the details of my tea or distract myself in conversation with my fellow idler. My ears strained for any snippet of her conversation, any note of her laugh.

It was almost as though my weary brain and aching heart wanted nothing more than to set off once again down a path that ended at another impassable cliff, just like it had with Miss Somer and the other women I'd fallen for. I had to close the gate before that path even became a possibility. My soul could not take it one more time.

MAY

I tried to laugh at Mr. Shelby's jokes, but as the night wore on, it became more of a struggle. I did not find him amusing in the slightest. At least Walcott was funny, even if his teasing rankled me.

"I'm afraid we aren't your high society, Miss Byam," Shelby said, taking a swig from his cup. The thick, spicy aroma of grog mixed with the heavy air of the mess deck. A couple of days ago, it would have soured my churning stomach. At least I hadn't had seasickness as terribly as Mrs. Peyton. She still could hardly look at a drink without gagging.

"I haven't any worry about high society." I wasn't high society either, though Papa had put us in position to slide between social classes with ease. If my father hadn't been caught swindling, would I feel right sitting here among these young men, or would I prefer the stilted company of Mr. Doswell and the officers?

I glanced toward the ladder. Mrs. Hallyburton would not take pleasure in seeing me here. That fact made me more determined to stay, despite the dismal humor.

The plinking on the table brought me out of my reflection. Catterick dealt out the cards to start another round of their game, and the others threw in chips. It didn't serve to dwell on things that could never return, like the life Papa had tried to make for us. I would focus on the camaraderie before me. Reality meant more than wishes.

"Do you want to play now, Miss May?" Walcott asked.

I shook my head. The fatigue I felt did not lend itself well to cards.

"Care to sell your jack of diamonds?" he asked. Catterick stroked his square chin, staring at his faceup card. As he considered, Walcott leaned closer to me. "And how have you found your first week aboard? You've found your sea legs, it would seem."

How had I found the first week? Lonely in my dark cabin. Dull with so little to do. Strange, being in such close quarters with so many men after years of living only with Mama and Aunt Byam. "Not as I expected." The boredom had surprised me. I'd thought I'd have more work under Mrs. Peyton's employ.

"Sea life isn't as exciting as you think it will be," Shelby said wryly. "Don't you worry, miss. The French will give us enough excitement to last you a lifetime." He thought me weak, like all the others new to sea life. I bristled. Of course, Charlie had told me only the thrilling parts, but I wasn't naive enough to count on a blissful voyage.

"On the contrary, I've found the last few days fascinating." It wasn't a complete lie. Seeing a glimpse into the lives Charlie and Uncle had lived while away from us had given me a new appreciation for those two wonderful men I missed so much. My throat swelled. I rubbed the cloth of my skirt between my fingers, focusing on the woven texture sliding across my skin. I'd let the past creep into my head too much. If I didn't push back the memories, they'd keep me awake late into the night.

"Wait until you've eaten nothing but salt pork and ship's biscuit for four weeks," Catterick grumbled. Then he waved Walcott off. "No sale. I'm keeping the jack."

"I've found a bit of dried fruit helps with that," I said. The peach slice's brightness still lingered on my tongue from dinner. I'd saved the packet, rationing it so I could have a little dessert. As long as I had that to look forward to each evening, I might survive the tedious meals.

"Indulgent, aren't we?" Shelby said. "Did you bring along tea, sugar, and cream for after your supper as well?" He'd changed his accent to sound like a fine matron of London Society.

I pursed my lips. "No." Shelby would get my boot to his shins if I stayed here much longer. "Someone left it for me."

What the devil did I admit that for? I wanted to clap a hand to my face, but that would only make it worse. Of all the idiotic things to admit. Why had I brought up the fruit?

Walcott pressed his shoulder against mine. "Sweetmeats from an unknown giver. Miss May, have you already secured an admirer on this voyage?" His brows lifted knowingly.

My face grew hot. "What a ridiculous notion." Especially since he had probably been the one to leave them. The comical face he made and the too-enthusiastic tone he used gave him away.

"Who could it be?" Walcott thrummed his fingers on the table. "Mr. Howard would have the easiest time of it, what with having access to all the food stores, but he's got a wife and child, does he not?"

"As if that matters. Are you playing cards or matchmaking?" Catterick asked.

Heaven forbid Mr. Walcott take to matchmaking. There wasn't a man I wished to wed on this ship. The only ones worth looking at were already married. Well, except Mr. Doswell, but I'd rather die an old maid than marry a dull clergyman. Even a kind one who brought tea to a sick neighbor. Clergymen had to care for the sick, of course. It was expected of them.

Walcott nodded toward the other side of the table. "It's Shelby's play." He flicked the corner of the topmost card on his stack, looking about the mess deck. "An officer, perhaps? They'd have the means for little luxuries. Who have you been cozying up to in the gun room?"

Shelby flipped over his card, a ten of spades that wouldn't best Catterick's jack.

"It's your turn, Mr. Walcott," I said through gritted teeth. He'd gone too far with his teasing, just like my brother, Lewis, did. Perhaps I didn't enjoy the similarities after all.

"We don't stand on ceremony here." He plucked up the card and held it close to his chest. "You're practically one of us. Mrs. Peyton's mate, if you will." He tilted his head so it nearly rested on mine. I wanted to pull the brim of his knitted cap down over those mocking eyes. "You might as well call me Frank."

He'd left the packet of fruit. My eyes narrowed. The teasing, the flirting, the theatrics, the familiarity—it all made sense. He'd taken some sort of liking to me. Because I was the only unmarried female on board? The only one unprotected by connections? Had Mrs. Hallyburton been correct?

I swallowed. No, I would not believe that. It wasn't fair of me to instantly assume the worst. Mr. Walcott had offered friendship when I'd had nothing. He could have sneaked the peaches into my cabin as a kind gesture to a lonely shipmate. Why did I assume it had come from romantic feelings? From what I knew of this young man, he'd use anything as an excuse to tease. He could simply be trying to put me off his trail.

"If I call you Frank, will you take your turn?" I asked.

He laughed and tossed the card onto the table. The ace of diamonds. He'd won the round with the highest trump, and his companions voiced their displeasure as they gathered the cards.

Frank planted his elbow on the table, turning toward me. "We will find your sly beau." He tapped his fist against his mouth. "I have a few possibilities."

His calculating expression, so exaggerated, made me all the more certain. Did he not want his friends to know? If it wasn't romantic, why would he want to hide? I scraped the bottom corner of the trunk with my heel, the nails of its iron-capped corner pushing against my boot. I could easily picture Frank winning over young women who appreciated his flavor of humor, his crooked grin, and his magnetism. I didn't see myself among that crowd, though I couldn't deny how flattering it felt that I might have caught his eye. I twisted my hands together in my lap.

"You should ask Peyton's wife," Shelby said as he raised his mug. "I hear she's the master of secrets." It earned him a few guffaws.

"What do you mean by that?" I asked. Secrets?

"She fooled the *Deborah*'s crew for three years," Frank said in a loud whisper. "Made them think she was a ship's boy. Trousers and all."

She wasn't just on the *Deborah* . . . She was part of the crew? I opened my mouth to speak, but no words came. I'd grown up with stories of women like Hannah Snell and Mary Lacy, who'd run off to sea disguised as boys, but how could a delicate little thing like Mrs. Peyton, who couldn't overcome her sickness after days at sea, have kept up such an act for so long?

No wonder Captain Woodall hadn't allowed my aunt on board. She would have seen through the act in an instant. My insides coiled as the implications set in with even more certainty than before. Mrs. Peyton was the sole reason my aunt had been denied her last moments with her husband and son.

"I . . . I hadn't heard that," I finally said with great effort.

"Miss Byam is about to faint from the shock." Shelby's delight grated on my nerves. He imagined me distressed. I was far from that. My jaw ached from clenching it.

"We are sorry to turn your opinion of your employer," Frank said, giving my knee a reassuring pat. Could he feel that it was as rigid as one of the beams above us?

"That's very interesting, to be sure." What did this new story change? Nothing and everything at the same time. Not only had Woodall barred my aunt, but he'd done so to cover an even fiercer lie than I'd imagined. My disgust over serving one of his relatives had eased since the start of our voyage, but now it surged back into my chest.

Catterick shoved the cards at Frank to deal, and the game continued, but I didn't try to follow it. I bid them all goodnight, not pausing to hear Frank's parting joke. I'd think over what to do about his gift and the potential feelings surrounding it tomorrow.

In my cabin, I dressed halfway between the door, with its canvas window covering I didn't completely trust to keep out unwanted views, and the crack in the wall I shared with Mr. Doswell, which I didn't trust at all. My buzzing mind made it difficult to go through the motions. I felt around in the dark, wishing for the hundredth time already that I'd had the money to bring a lantern.

Mrs. Peyton had gallivanted as a ship's boy? I clutched my gown with both fists. My cousin died without his mother because that girl wanted a little adventure?

Trembling, I placed my clothes back in my sea chest. My fingers brushed Papa's little book of Cowper. I needed Cowper tonight to calm my reeling thoughts. More than Cowper, I needed my papa's calming voice to help me make sense of all this. I pulled the book out and held it to my chest. So often in the last years, I'd beaten down any thought of missing him. Since Mama announced that she'd be leaving, I hadn't had the strength to push the feelings down. I needed to douse my whirling brain in the poetry my father had loved. But how would I read? I didn't dare go out to the gun room in my dressing gown. Could I borrow a little of Mr. Doswell's light?

I crept to the gleaming ray coming through the partition. The hum of Mr. Doswell's gentle muttering seeped through the opening like steam from a teacup. I could almost smell the ginger and lemon from the drink he'd brought me the other night.

I sat with my back to the wall, careful not to lean into it and make the wood creak. For now, he seemed oblivious to the encroachment of privacy, and I wanted it to stay that way. I did not turn to take even a peek through the crack. He'd been in such a state of undress the last time I'd foolishly looked. I ducked my head and forced myself not to relive the moment or the sight. Whatever happened, I could not reveal that I'd stared at him, even if it meant lying to a clergyman. There had to be a special place in purgatory for people who lied to clergymen, but the price was worth it to avoid this humiliation.

I held up the book so it caught the light of Mr. Doswell's lantern and trained my eyes on the print. The glow revealed a vertical sliver of words on one side of the page. As I read, I slowly rotated the book, illuminating the text word by word. Papa's voice, painful and soothing all at once, read the words in my head.

> *Come, peace of mind, delightful guest!*
> *Return and make thy downy nest*
> *Once more in this sad heart.*

Peace of mind. What I wouldn't give for a few hours of that. The tension in my body loosened.

"What if I included another story here?" The voice sounded directly behind me, as though the bulwark had been removed. It took all my power not to turn around. Who was he speaking to? I hadn't heard anyone enter his room. "People like stories. They help show ideas better than lecturing."

He was talking to himself. And not in the unthinking way most people muttered to themselves but truly conversing. A smile slipped across my lips. He'd reassured himself of the new idea with all the enthusiasm of a supportive friend.

"Of course I don't wish to bog down the sermon with too many stories." Mr. Doswell's voice quieted a little as he moved away from the wall we shared. "You have to take care. The men easily lose interest if you speak too long."

I held my fingers to my mouth to keep back a laugh. I shouldn't laugh. Who didn't act in embarrassing ways when they thought they were completely alone? Such as crouching in the dark, trying to read with light from a crack in the wall.

That snapped my attention back to the page. I must look pitiful at the least, huddled here like a frightened mouse.

> *Nor riches I, nor pow'r pursue,*
> *Nor hold forbidden joys in view,*
> *We therefore need not part.*

Cowper's thoughts entwined with Mr. Doswell's conversation. My neighbor seemed to have such peace of mind, memorizing his sermons and walking the deck at all hours in quiet bliss. He'd chosen his path rather than being forced into taking whatever work could be found. Some men had all the luck.

Perhaps that was what kept drawing me back to Frank Walcott, besides how much he made me remember my father and brother before life had turned upside down. Unlike Mr. Doswell or the Peytons, Frank came from much simpler means and had to prove his strength and smarts to get to his current position. If only I could do the same.

Chapter 7

MAY

The weight of the day's anniversary made my movements slow that morning. It should have been just another day. After two weeks at sea, I knew my duties and routine. But even so, dressing had proven harder than I'd expected.

I slid a hairpin into place, then pulled my cap on over the messy knot. Mrs. Peyton wouldn't care if I looked a sight. I tied the ribbon, not worrying if the bow felt straight. Thank the skies I didn't have a light to check my reflection in the mirror. I didn't want to know. Not today.

My arms felt weak as I pulled myself up the ladder to the gun deck and trudged to the galley. The steward handed me the Peytons' breakfast tray. The steam rolling off the food turned my empty stomach. No doubt Mr. Howard had cooked it well, but I was in no state to appreciate the smell.

I took the food to the captain's cabin while the steward waited for water to boil in the galley for their tea. Why did the tray feel so much heavier this time? It wobbled as I balanced it on one arm to free my other hand.

I knocked, the hard wood thudding dully against my knuckles, then opened the door. Nothing moved in the cabin except the Peytons' cot, which swayed faintly with the roll of the *Marianne*. No papers or maps sat on the table or desks as they usually did by the time I arrived each morning.

"Dom, she's here," came a nearly imperceptible whisper. It was followed by a masculine sigh. Two forms nestled in the cot rather than just the slight form of Mrs. Peyton.

My cheeks heated. The captain hadn't started his day yet.

"Breakfast," I announced loudly.

Good heavens, he was usually ready by now.

I set the tray in the middle of the table, the plates and utensils clinking. For a moment, I didn't let go. Should I run? Stay and wait? A servant shouldn't mind whatever state she found her employer, but I clearly hadn't been a servant long enough. "I'll return in a moment." Where I would go in the meantime, I didn't know. I hadn't anticipated the perils of serving a newly married couple.

A shout sounded from the hatchway as I hurried out of the great cabin and pulled the door shut behind me. A boy bolted up the ladder toward the upper deck.

"You can't hide from me." Mrs. Hallyburton appeared a moment later, a stick clutched in her fist. She shot up the ladder in pursuit of the lad.

My heart jumped to my throat at her wild expression, and without thinking, I dashed for the hatchway after them.

ELIAS

The screech of a banshee shattered the early morning stillness I'd sought on the quarterdeck. I flinched, glancing at First Lieutenant Roddam, who had taken position not far away as officer of the watch. He closed his eyes and drew in a breath. A couple of weeks at sea hadn't given anyone time to familiarize themselves with Mrs. Hallyburton's outbursts.

A small form flew through the hatchway with the boatswain's wife on his heels, swinging a foot-long handspike from one of the capstans.

"You little rat!" She paused at the top of the ladder, breathing heavily. The boy had vanished, but soft sobbing filtered across the deck in the silence that had overtaken all seamen and officers.

That same leaping in my gut I'd experienced when Miss Byam had boarded overcame me. Whatever the lad had done, surely it didn't warrant this rage. I scanned the deck. Someone needed to step in.

Roddam tugged at his black neckcloth. As the highest-ranking officer above deck, it fell on him to intervene.

"It makes one wish to follow the Admiralty's ban of women with exactness," Roddam muttered.

Mrs. Hallyburton cried out as she advanced toward one of the boats. "You'll do as you're told, or you'll never see land again." Her handspike hit the boat, letting off a deep thud. The boy she chased let out a yelp and scrambled out from under it on the opposite side.

What was she thinking? She could badly injure him. I hurried toward the quarterdeck steps. I had little say in what happened on this ship, but I wouldn't sit back and watch her beat that boy senseless. Grown seamen could take her walloping and cursing. The young ones shouldn't.

Lieutenant Roddam brushed past me, slowing me with a hand on my arm. I let him take the lead, following closely behind. The boy scrambled toward us, face red and eyes wide. The boatswain's wife spied him and charged.

I sucked in a breath. Before I could run to them, someone flew through the hatchway and planted herself in front of Mrs. Hallyburton. A skewed cap covered Miss Byam's head, and the ends of her hair awkwardly splayed out from under the white linen. The older woman plowed into Miss Byam with a grunt, nearly bowling her over.

Mrs. Hallyburton snarled. "How dare you—"

"Let him alone." Miss Byam held out her arms to block the boatswain's wife.

The boy stumbled to a halt before Lieutenant Roddam. The officer took him by the shoulder, firmly but without roughness. He walked the ship's boy back toward the women.

Mrs. Hallyburton raised the handspike as though to strike Miss Byam. My chest tightened, and I rushed past the staring crewmen. The young woman stood unflinching, her Saxon blue gown catching the morning breeze.

"It is my duty to keep these vermin in line." Mrs. Hallyburton caught sight of the lieutenant advancing on them and lowered her weapon. Her gaze did not soften.

Miss Byam folded her arms. With her back to me, I could not see her face, but I could imagine the indignation in her eyes. "Does it say so in your contract?"

"What contract?"

The lieutenant pulled the boy up behind them, blocking me from getting closer to the women without tricky maneuvering through lines and seamen. Not that Miss Byam would appreciate my intervention should Mrs. Hallyburton raise her handspike again. Miss Byam fought her own battles, I was beginning to discover.

"The contract or orders that gave you the right to beat the ship's boys," Miss Byam said.

Mrs. Hallyburton snorted. "Of course I haven't a contract. I don't need orders. My husband has 'em. And you parade around calling yourself a boatswain's niece as though you know the job."

Miss Byam shifted her weight to one side and tilted her head. "I mention it only because to my understanding, you have no right to enact discipline, deserved or otherwise, on this ship."

"I told you to watch yourself, lass." The older woman's mouth twisted. She straightened, turning her attention to Lieutenant Roddam as though to dismiss her.

Miss Byam hadn't finished. "Everyone else on this ship acts under orders, but you seem to think you've been given a free hand to act as you wish, ordering and disciplining without authority." She advanced, and the boatswain's wife took a step back. "Everyone else is paid to perform their contracted duties. You, Mrs. Hallyburton, do not even earn a wage. You terrorize us all out of the goodness of your heart."

I winced at her forthrightness but not because I didn't agree. Most on board, even Captain Peyton, had wanted to say these very words. Though perhaps without such force.

Lieutenant Roddam cleared his throat. "Miss Byam."

Miss Byam turned, meeting the officer's gaze with calm determination. "Lieutenant." She gave a short curtsy. She didn't wear a coat over her short sleeves. Not even gloves to protect her bare arms from the morning chill.

"You'll forgive my interruption," Lieutenant Roddam said. "What is the meaning of this outburst?"

"He has his duties, sir." Mrs. Hallyburton glared at Miss Byam. "From my husband. And he's not fulfilling 'em."

The boy's chin trembled. Heavens, he looked young. Too young to be at sea. "I dinnae know how." The little Scottish brogue tugged at my heart.

"You'll speak when you're spoken to," the woman snapped, pointing her handspike at the lad.

"Pipe down, Hallyburton." Miss Byam swatted the stick aside. "You're no officer."

Mrs. Hallyburton pursed her lips, hand tightening on the wooden handle. Miss Byam stood her ground, a sleek frigate staring down a battle-worn ship of the line. Outgunned and outmanned, Miss Byam wasn't about to be outmaneuvered. Little ships had taken down great ones before.

Something burst to life in my core, filling my body with a warmth I hadn't experienced in weeks as I watched this young woman, seemingly alone in a new world, not only rise to the challenges of her circumstances but also stand for those who couldn't.

How I wished to remove myself from that list of her adversaries. Would she ever forgive me?

"Here now," Lieutenant Roddam said, holding up a hand, "let's be civil."

"Coddling the boy will only turn him soft as this lubber." The boatswain's wife nodded at Miss Byam.

The young woman opened her mouth to retort, but I blurted out, "It hasn't even been two weeks." Their eyes all turned to me, and I swallowed. "Surely . . . surely there is place for mercy for a lad with so little experience."

Mrs. Hallyburton's jaw worked, but she remained silent. She had too much respect for my office to say anything, though she clearly wished to.

Beside her, Miss Byam's indignant features softened. She tended to look at me with such wariness, but this morning, with the pale light painting her cheeks, the tension usually reserved for me had vanished. Her gaze sent a strange little thrill down my arms.

"What is your name, lad?" I asked, quickly turning away from Miss Byam before the sensation overcame me.

"Harvey Carden, sir." He sniffed. Carden. Two older boys with the same surname had come to my reading lessons, but he'd never shown. Had the Hallyburtons been keeping him too occupied? His tawny hair stood up at odd angles, and stains spattered his rumpled shirt.

Lieutenant Roddam sighed. "Leave him here, Mrs. Hallyburton. Thank you for bringing this to my attention."

"Yes, sir." She threw a scathing glare at Miss Byam before stalking toward the hatchway.

Harvey's shoulders slumped as she disappeared below, and for a moment, I thought he'd faint.

"How old are you, Mr. Carden?" I asked.

He glanced warily at the lieutenant, who seemed deep in thought. "Not yet ten, sir."

Yes, far too young to be at sea. I'd been twelve, and that was too young. What had Peyton been thinking, signing him and his brothers on? Their family must have been in dire straits.

"I will discuss this situation with Captain Peyton and Mr. Hallyburton," Lieutenant Roddam said. "For now, go find your brothers."

The boy grabbed for the brim of his cap in salute, despite not having one on his head. He looked to Miss Byam, then threw a grateful glance at me before dashing away.

"How can you leave him in such a situation?" Miss Byam muttered.

"Miss Byam, in the future you will stay out of disciplinary matters on this ship," Lieutenant Roddam said. While his voice held no rudeness, he was firm. "You also have no authority, and Captain Peyton will agree with me."

Her hands clenched at her sides. "Captain Peyton hardly seems the type of man to beat little boys for ridiculous reasons."

"What you deem ridiculous reasons could be life or death for the entire crew." Irritation flickered in the usually stoic lieutenant's eyes.

Hostility blazed in hers. "No one deserves—"

"I suggest you keep to your duties, miss. The order in our way of life stems from the danger we face. Please, try to understand."

I could practically see steam rising from her flushed face, a stray spark from a cannon that could send the whole interaction up in flames. "There must be another position for the boy," I said, wringing my hands. "The boatswain has quite a bit of help with his wife aboard. What of Étienne? He hasn't a loblolly boy or a mate." I hadn't realized he'd never secured a mate until our conversation four nights ago. No one wished to serve under a Frenchman, it seemed. "He might use young Mr. Carden's assistance."

Lieutenant Roddam nodded. "I will discuss it with the captain. Now, if you would excuse me." The lieutenant nodded in my direction. "Miss Byam," was the only farewell he gave her. He strode toward the fore of the ship.

I let out a slow breath. Miss Byam watched him go, lips pressed together. It didn't take much imagining to guess what sort of praise for Lieutenant Roddam circled through her head. I stood between them, seeing both Roddam's insistence on order and Miss Byam's demand for mercy. Their desires didn't contradict necessarily. Only their means of achieving those desires.

"Miss Byam, would you join me in a turn about the quarter-deck?" I asked.

She'd refuse me, but if she went below, she'd have to pass the Hallyburtons' cabin to get to hers. She and the boatswain's wife looked ready to keelhaul the other. Another altercation could lead to worse explosions than we'd just seen. If I could keep her above decks until feelings cooled, would it prevent the worst of it?

I offered her my arm, and she hesitated just as she had when I'd offered to help her stand Sunday evening. This wouldn't work. Perhaps I could entreat her to check in on Mrs. Peyton. I hadn't seen the captain or his wife yet this morning. Or Miss Byam couldn't have eaten yet, so a visit to Mr. Howard in the galley would stall.

Her hand slipped through the crook of my elbow, and she turned her face up toward mine. Wisps of honey-colored hair framed her forehead, curling softly about her temples. Her blue eyes ran over me, drawing heat to my skin.

A jolt rocked through me as I studied her. She shared too many similarities to Miss Somer, in her light-brown locks and well-defined cheekbones. No wonder she'd held my attention more than she should have. My heart faltered for a moment as I imagined the last time a young lady not of my family had taken my arm. It had been that afternoon in the garden when my perfect world had fizzled into oblivion.

"Only for a moment," she said.

Her quiet acceptance should have calmed me—a reprieve from the battle that certainly hadn't resolved—but as I led her aft, it took all my strength to keep the pain at bay.

MAY

He only wished to pacify me, to keep me from running straight down the hatchway to grapple Mrs. Hallyburton's stick from her and beat her over the head with it. Mr. Doswell liked peace above all.

What an exceptional clerical specimen.

Despite it, I allowed him to lead me up the steps to the quarterdeck. A cherry sunrise peeked over the horizon. Few men walked this upmost deck reserved for officers and helmsmen. When Uncle had first received his assignment to HMS *Deborah*, Charlie and I had sneaked up to the quarterdeck and pretended to steer when she was docked. That was just before Charlie had gone to sea and left me behind.

"It's a lovely sunrise," Mr. Doswell offered, guiding me toward the stern's bulwark.

"It is." My hand warmed, wrapped around the wool sleeve of his greatcoat. I needed only to exchange pleasantries for a moment, then make my excuses of needing to see to Mrs. Peyton.

I released his arm and steadied myself against the bulwark. The wind filling the sails swept past my uncovered arms, sending bumps along my skin. Had Mrs. Hallyburton snatched up little Harvey belowdecks? She'd looked ready to eat him with gruel for breakfast and wash him down with a dish of grog.

"Something is troubling you," he observed.

A strip of hair fell out of my hasty pinwork and slipped through the ruffles of my cap to hang limp against my neck. Wonderful. Loose hair, bare arms, no coat. Some streetwalker I was turning out to be. "Why would you think so?"

"You wrinkle your nose when you are displeased."

Did I? My hand flew to my nose before I could stop myself. How humiliating! I must have done it often if someone I knew so little had noticed. No one had told me I did that before. Had I recently picked up the habit? I pinched the bridge of my nose as if that would erase the tendency.

"But something is distressing you, isn't it?"

Too many things, none of which I wished to discuss with him. But the gentle tone he used made it difficult to resist.

"You needn't tell me, if you don't wish to," he said. "I do apologize. It isn't my place to pry." He fidgeted with the cuffs of his sleeves. An indigo jacket, a more brilliant blue than any other coat I'd seen aboard, poked out here and there from under his tan greatcoat. His neckcloth was sprigged with lighter blue diamonds. Everything about him seemed in perfect harmony, from his polished shoes to the way his red hair swooped stylishly off his brow. And yet he lowered his eyes and shuffled about as though uncomfortable in his own skin.

"If, however, you do wish to talk about it . . ." He straightened his fingers and pulled them from his cuff. "That is, if you haven't anyone else to talk to about it . . . What I mean to say is that I listen very well." His words quickened the longer he spoke.

I couldn't help a laugh. Poor man. Though I wanted so badly to hold on to my anger at the humiliation he'd put me through, my conviction had steadily slipped since he'd brought me the tea. The sincerity of his jumbled volunteering had broken down the last of the ramparts protecting my belief of his being a judging and pomp-ous peacock.

"I'm sure you wish to be alone in your thoughts," he said, step-ping back from the rail. "I'm sorry to have intruded. I should—"

"It is the twenty-fourth of September."

Rather than giving me a confused scowl or congratulating me on keeping track of the date, he waited.

I sighed. I did wish to talk to someone. Mama and Aunt Byam, specifically. But they were a distant dream now. Somehow, I knew Frank would brush this off, and I could hardly tell Mrs. Peyton my woes. Ladies told maids their troubles, not the other way around.

"My cousin died on this day last year." Saying that aloud felt strange. Had it only been a year? It might have been a lifetime.

Mr. Doswell returned his hands to the rail. "Yes, I remember. Charlie Byam."

The familiarity in his voice struck something inside me. "You knew him?"

He nodded. "I was on the *Deborah*."

I pressed a hand to my stomach. If only I—or more importantly, my aunt—could have sailed with them. To sit with him in his final moments. I scrunched my eyes shut as the hatred for Captain Wood-all swirled in fiery torrents through my whole being. Letting these emotions rage would only make my situation harder to bear.

But, oh, how I loathed holding it back.

A hand rested on my elbow, and I looked up into Mr. Doswell's full, green eyes. The steady pressure of his fingers around my arm anchored me in the storm. I couldn't say why I did it, but I curled my fingers over his. The warmth of his skin against mine seeped into me, banishing the morning chill.

"I oversaw his burial," he said hesitantly. "And I was with him his final day."

The thought of kindhearted Mr. Doswell sitting in when my aunt couldn't eased the tearing in my heart. "Were you?"

"The captain had us secure a little piece of land outside the port town, where it was quieter and more peaceful."

To relieve his own conscience, no doubt. "Tell me about it. Please."

He tilted his head, eyes focusing on something far in the distance. "It was near the beach, encircled by waving palm trees. The water was clearer in that area, and there were more birds about." He gave my arm the barest of squeezes. "It was a beautiful place."

"I wish I could see it." His touch felt so different from Frank's. Whenever Frank took my arm, he seized it and dragged me where he wanted. Mr. Doswell, on the other hand, offered and let me come to him. Well, he had until this hesitant gesture, but even this was gentle, not demanding.

"Perhaps Mrs. Peyton could draw it for you."

"She was there?" She could hardly make it out of bed these days, let alone draw. Although this morning might be different.

"Both she and her father. She was . . . not her usual self." He gave a nervous laugh. She'd been a boy then, of course. "Captain Peyton wished to come, but he took command in Captain Woodall's absence. He would have been there if duty had allowed."

"I believe it." I shivered, half from the cold and half from the memory of the next terrible information we received not long after news of Charlie's death. "Captain Peyton was the one to bring my aunt word about Uncle Byam."

"Ah, yes."

"But Captain Woodall was at Charlie's burial?" I couldn't help the incredulity that crept into my voice. Why would an unfeeling captain, unconcerned for anyone except his own, attend the burial of a boatswain's mate?

"Yes."

"I find that shocking when he paid no mind to my family before."

Mr. Doswell's fingers drifted from my arm, exposing it once more to the cold. "He was the one who instructed us to make a marker, as no one had brought one. Your uncle was understandably distraught."

I couldn't fault Mr. Doswell for loyalty to a captain, much as I wanted to. My uncle had similarly spoken well of Captain Woodall, even after he'd refused to let my aunt on board.

"What did the marker say?" I asked. Of course I didn't expect him to remember. Mr. Doswell must have officiated in several burials during his time as chaplain. More if he'd been a curate or vicar before his time at sea, though he seemed too young to have been ordained more than two or three years.

"I think I still have the plans of it, if you'd like to see."

I lifted my brows. "Do you copy all the grave markers?"

"His was the only burial I've officiated on land. Most of them die at sea and are buried there."

Like Uncle Byam. I bit my lip to distract myself from that line of thought. Burial at sea seemed the harshest end to a brutal way of life.

"I only have it because I helped the carpenter design it," Mr. Doswell said with a shrug.

"I'm certain you did lovely work." I smiled at him, not certain why. With how carefully he dressed and spoke, I could easily imagine his attentiveness to planning Charlie's marker. The cool air seemed distant, as though we stood in a pocket of sunlight. Sometime in our conversation, I'd leaned toward him. Too close. I shuffled back. "I apologize. I didn't intend to fill your morning with my grief."

Thoughts swirled behind his eyes, as clear to see as the *Marianne*'s wake below us, but I couldn't decipher them. "You needn't apologize for grief."

The lapping of waves against the hull filled my ears as Mr. Doswell withdrew to his thoughts. No one had said that to me before, that my mourning was not a burden to them. Aunt Byam and Mama dealt with their own sorrow. Mrs. Richardson was the only other person I had talked with regularly, and I never would have confided in her. The grief I knew in my life—for Papa as well as my uncle and cousin—had always been hidden. My family expected me to hide it. Only anger was allowed.

"From our conversation, it would seem you do not like . . ." He bit his lip.

"Captain Woodall?" I asked.

Mr. Doswell paled and pointed to the deck. No, not to the deck. Just below it, where Captain Woodall's daughter and son-in-law slept.

I covered my mouth with a hand. I'd said that too loudly. Bless him for remembering when I had not. What if they had opened a window? I shivered.

"I'm so sorry. You must be freezing." He rapidly unbuttoned his coat and pulled it off. He held it out to drape around my shoulders.

"Oh." I sidestepped. This was unnecessary. "No, thank you. I'll just return below. You are very kind, sir."

"Are you certain?" His face fell, and he lowered the coat.

"Yes, quite." My mind had ceased to function, except to cycle through memories of the evening Agnes had come home simpering and giggling about a young man giving her his coat when she'd been cold at an assembly. Then she'd gone and married him. "I do appreciate the offer. Truly." I backed toward the stairs, mind grasping for excuses. "I should see to Mrs. Peyton. She's about to wake, you know. She'll need her tea. And to dress."

"Of course. I won't keep you." He gave a small bow but made no move to put the coat back on.

I scurried down the steps, my hair falling more quickly from its pins. I grabbed the sides of my cap to hold it on and keep my hair contained. What a simpleton! Men offered coats to women they didn't have feelings toward. It was a considerate gesture, and Mr. Doswell was a considerate man to his core. Even when he'd incorrectly identified me on our first meeting, he'd done so out of worry for me.

Worry for me? I hadn't thought of that before. I stopped at the hatch to let a few seamen pass. Gentlemen did not always do such considerate things for women below their status, however. Society did not expect it of them.

Mr. Doswell stood where I'd left him, greatcoat now draped over the rail and his back toward me. He *had* been worried about me that first day, hadn't he? Not judging, not self-righteous. Simply concerned, both for my feelings and for heeding his captain. When was the last time someone had truly considered my feelings? Had anyone since Charlie?

Chapter 8

MAY

Dice bounced down the length of the table and plunged off the edge as the ship tipped. The movement drove me into Frank's side.

"Rather flirtatious tonight, aren't we, Miss May?"

I groaned and readjusted my position, futile as it was. The *Marianne* could throw me back into Frank's lap in a few moments. I hadn't been the flirtatious one. His renditions of "Adieu, Sweet Lovely Nancy" and "Spanish Ladies" had put him in an odd mood, or so I thought. I'd hoped Shelby's pulling out the dice for a game of Hazard would have distracted him, but clearly, his flirtatious mood hadn't been from the singing. Was there any water in the mug of grog before Frank, or was it straight rum?

"I like a girl who can reel you in and toss you back out the next breath." Frank stretched, then dropped his arm around my shoulders.

I stiffened and pulled back, but his arm stayed in place.

Mr. Shelby gave no notice to Frank's actions. "Think we'll make it to Malta this week like Merkley told us?"

"If this fog doesn't clear out, it will add to our journey," Mr. Catterick said, dumping the dice back on the table.

Fog had rolled in off the coast of Portugal that afternoon. Now, nearly time for the hammocks to come down, the conditions had held, much to the crew's disgruntlement. With little wind to blow it away, the *Marianne* hadn't made good progress.

"Merkley doesn't know what he's talking about half the time," Frank said, drumming his fingers on my arm. "But that's most of the *Marianne*'s officers, isn't it?"

Shelby and Catterick glanced about nervously but didn't contradict him.

In their silence, I couldn't help myself. "Captain Peyton is a good captain. And Lieutenant Roddam is . . ." I recalled his sternness after I'd butted heads with Mrs. Hallyburton. "Worthy of his position." Even if he'd made me want to spit on his boots that day.

"Is he, now?" Frank's suggestive tone made me grimace. What had he consumed tonight? He spoke too openly, even for him. "Well, I do hope their *worthiness* does not slow our voyage. I'd much rather have experience than nobility." The other mates snorted.

A pair of shoes stepped carefully down the ladder, followed by tan breeches and a green coat. Mr. Doswell. I squirmed, but Frank did not have the consideration to let go of me.

"At least there's good company to keep us warm," Frank said. I couldn't tell if he meant the company of friends or me specifically, but the way he squeezed my shoulder suggested he didn't refer to Catterick and Shelby.

Mr. Doswell halted by the gun room partition. Lantern light reflecting off his spectacles made it difficult to tell where he looked, but I sensed his gaze. Suddenly, this sea chest was unbearably small and its other occupant stifling.

"Shove off, Frank." I jumped to my feet, freeing myself from under his arm.

"Pity's sake. What's the matter with you?" Frank asked. I didn't like the grin he gave me. "Off to reassure your chaplain?"

Words spoken from jealousy, clear as morning. I crossed my arms. "I am not—"

A thundering boom rent the air. I clutched the thick cluster of rope that held up the table. Frank jumped to his feet. The crew looked around, tensed and waiting. My stomach tied itself in knots. That sound had become too familiar after two weeks of gun drills.

The screech of a boatswain's call followed and then drums. A deluge of vulgarity erupted as the seamen cursed everything from Boney to the ocean and rushed for the ladders.

"What is it?" I asked, knowing full well the answer.

"We just found ourselves a little company." Frank dug the heels of his hands into his eyes. "You'd best get your mistress and hurry below." For once, no teasing tainted his voice.

Mr. Doswell stood frozen in the doorway as sailors began breaking down the bulwark. His jaw was taut, his posture stiff.

I hurried over to him, trying to stay out of the way of the men working. "Are you well?"

He gave a nod. "I'll see you below." He turned on his heel, more abrupt than he'd ever been with me, and for a moment, I frowned after him. That didn't seem like Mr. Doswell at all, to be so curt.

How could I blame him though? This wasn't a gun drill. A chill ran down my spine. When the ladders had cleared, I raced up to the great cabin. They'd already cleared the partitions, leaving the captain's quarters open to the gun deck. I slipped past marines and made for Mrs. Peyton. She stood by her husband and the lieutenant as Captain Peyton shrugged into his coat.

"Did she even post her true colors before the shot?" Captain Peyton grumbled.

"We didn't see her in time to know," Lieutenant Roddam said.

I leaned toward Mrs. Peyton. "Are you going below, ma'am?" I asked quietly so as not to disrupt the officers.

Captain Peyton paused and glanced at his wife. She returned his gaze for several moments, as though silently discussing.

"We'll help Étienne," she finally said, and the captain's shoulders relaxed. She motioned toward the hatchway, now in full view with the walls removed. The lowest deck was as safe a place as one could find on a fighting ship, but it would not save us from seeing the carnage.

I reached up and felt my wrinkled nose. Blast. Mr. Doswell was right.

Mrs. Peyton walked briskly toward the ladders without another word, but the captain grabbed her about the waist. He whipped her around and kissed her fiercely. I expected a brief display, a parting affection, but after a few moments, Lieutenant Roddam and I shared a confused look. Had he lost his senses? Such tenderness against a backdrop of preparations for battle felt out of place. Never mind they were in plain sight of half the crew readying the guns.

Mrs. Peyton pushed the captain away with a huff. "I expect a full report." Then she turned on her heel and marched away unaffected.

I hurried to catch up. As we rapidly descended, I nearly tripped when my skirts tangled with my legs. The image of my employers' intimate exchange moments before stayed at the forefront of my mind. The disgust I wanted to feel didn't come. What would it be like to have someone to kiss as the world turned against you? Someone to draw courage from when faced with the unthinkable.

The blast of another cannon didn't let me consider it long.

ELIAS

I rubbed my hands together, pacing from one end of the cockpit to the other. Battle. Again. It never grew easier. Even from the belly of the ship, far removed from the scenes of battle.

"Ah. Welcome, ladies." Étienne's greeting made me halt. Miss Byam and Mrs. Peyton entered. The latter had a hand over her nose and mouth. Mrs. Peyton had experienced the foul bilge stench countless times before, but now her shoulders raised and fell in shallow breaths.

"Are you certain this is where you wish to be, madame?" Étienne raised a brow, throwing Mrs. Peyton a knowing look.

She nodded slowly.

"I cannot help but notice you are looking rather green." He moved a few tools to one side of the table we'd dragged into the center of the cockpit.

"I'll be right in a moment." She looked ready to keel over.

Miss Byam retrieved the bucket near the door.

"We'll bring in a barrel for her to sit on," the surgeon said, throwing me a wry grin. "I leave that bucket there on purpose. In case someone's stomach disagrees with them."

He was referencing our last battle together on the *Deborah*, when I hadn't been able to handle the aftermath of cannon fire. My neck heated. I'd sat in the corner, images from the past and the present crashing into each other until I couldn't breathe, much less help Étienne and his mate.

Too cowardly to even tend to the wounded. Typical for you.

I wouldn't allow myself that weakness tonight. I'd asked, practically begged, Peyton to bring me on. I knew what duties came with it.

"Harvey, help Miss Byam find a barrel. Mr. Doswell, if you'd help me fix these hammocks."

We shook out the canvas and secured the ends to beams. Three hammocks wouldn't be enough for a vicious battle, but we couldn't know the need now.

Deep blasts. Distant shouting. My mouth went dry. Everyone in the cockpit stilled. Above us, our shipmates stood in range of those cannons. Friends, acquaintances, kin. Étienne stared toward the upper decks. We were fighting his countrymen, possibly his friends or family. How many on both sides wouldn't see tomorrow?

I fumbled with the next hammock as scenes from a different battle, a different time, filled my waking eye. The helmsman, Mr. Riddley's, final words rang in my ears—*Hold steady. It'll pass.*

Battle always did, but it never passed without leaving scars.

We'd just finished with the hammocks when a pair of seamen limped into the cockpit. In the orange light, I recognized the smaller one, a young midshipman named McDaniel.

"Mr. Sanchez was hit in the head," the youth said. "He's bleeding terrible."

"Head wounds always do," Étienne said. "Harvey, help us get him on the table."

I moved forward to assist, keeping my eyes away from the wide and growing stain across Sanchez's collar, but Mr. McDaniel stopped me. "Captain Peyton asked that I fetch you. Lieutenant Roddam's manning the helm with Sanchez down. We've got all the other helmsmen captaining gun crews. Captain said you could do it."

I opened my mouth but couldn't get words out. I hadn't touched a ship's wheel in nearly fourteen years. Peyton knew that.

"She's turning to engage us," the youth said. "We must hurry, sir."

I nodded, glancing at Miss Byam. She clasped her hands before her, face pinched. Worry for Mr. Walcott, no doubt. With my luck, I couldn't hope it would be for me.

The midshipman rushed from the cockpit, and I followed, feet heavy as lead. Suddenly, I was twelve again, stumbling up the ladder with canisters of gunpowder. Each step shaky. Each rung hard to grip. Steeling myself against the explosions and fumes and blood that would soon encompass me.

ELIAS

I held to the wheel, awaiting Peyton's instruction. Wearing the ship with such little wind and even fainter visibility was something Mr. Riddley had never let me do all those years ago.

"Up mainsail and spanker! Brace in the afteryards! Up helm!"

I turned the wheel left, toward the wind. Smoke from firing the long nines at the bow drifted across the deck, mingling with the mist, its acrid scent burning my nostrils.

"How many guns?" Peyton called near my side. His question repeated up the length of the ship.

The *Marianne* tilted lazily into her turn as we tried to pull her parallel to our foe. The *Fatalité*. I adjusted my grasp on the handles, my palms sweating despite the chill evening. We were fortunate *Fatalité*'s raking broadside had only incapacitated Mr. Sanchez, but we would still be in a perilous position until we brought her around.

An answer passed back toward the quarterdeck. "Forty-eight guns, sir."

The hair on my neck stood on end. Forty-eight? Nigh on twice *Marianne*'s armament. And we'd sailed within a hundred yards before even catching sight of her?

Captain Peyton swore under his breath. A little frigate like ours could hold her own against bigger ships in favorable conditions with a bit of luck. The lingering fog and weak wind didn't give us much to work with. Then there was the starless sky. Firing in pitch black meant lanterns near cannon and gunpowder, not to mention greater chance for mistake.

"Ready the port battery," the captain called.

"Will you try to face her?" I asked.

"I'd prefer to outrun her," Peyton said. "I don't like the conditions."

I couldn't agree more.

Peyton adjusted his hat, eyes trained on the aggressor. "Blasted fool. Couldn't even wait until morning."

"She must be afraid of losing us in the fog," I said.

"Or she hasn't realized how much smaller we are yet and doesn't think she can outrun us."

Lieutenant Roddam made his way quickly from the bow, weaving between gun crews and seamen handling the yards and hopping lightly onto the quarterdeck. "What are your orders, sir?" He was close to my age. If I'd lasted in the navy, we might have had our lieutenant's examinations together. "She'd make a fine prize."

Only if we could find a way to overpower her.

"I don't fancy a court-martial to end my first command," Peyton said. A captain who lost his ship, regardless of the cause, stood trial to ensure he hadn't done anything stupid. This engagement was a high risk. He glanced toward the sails. "Get her around boys," he growled. "Don't let her rake us again."

Before we could bring the *Marianne* parallel to the enemy, guns up and down the *Fatalité* erupted. Shot barreled past overhead, whirring shadows crossing at an angle all down the deck. Lines snapped. One of the yards cracked, raining splinters down on the crew. Something sliced the side of my hand. My grip faltered at the sting that erupted across my skin.

Splashes sounded behind us. A little lower and half the crew might have been hit.

"Doswell?" Roddam steadied the wheel so I could look at my hand.

In the faint light from the binnacle lanterns, a line of blood trickled toward my sleeve. I dabbed at it with the opposite shirt cuff, turning to catch more of the light housed in the cabinet-like case set directly in front of the helm.

"It isn't deep." I flexed my hand, wincing. It might bleed all over, but I could still manage my task. I straightened, glancing behind us.

A light winked through the fog, past the stern rail. I narrowed my eyes, adjusting my spectacles. Were the *Marianne*'s lights reflecting off something to the north? Or perhaps it was *Fatalité*'s reflection? Tendrils of mist rolled lazily past us, unconcerned about the impending battle.

Peyton strode to the edge of the quarterdeck. "Lay the headyards square! Shift over the headsheets!"

"Lieutenant," I said, pointing with my bloodied hand. It wasn't just one light to the north. And it was the opposite direction of the shore.

"What is it?" Of course Roddam couldn't turn when at the helm.

"Lights off the stern to starboard," I said.

Without a word, he handed me his telescope. "Investigate."

My legs shook as I hurried to the stern rail, bringing the telescope to my eye. It slipped against the lens of my spectacles as I trained it on the pinpricks in the darkness. The impression of rigging crisscrossed the clouds. My breath caught. A ship, if I read the angles right, and she was turning toward us.

"Another ship," I called. I homed in on what I thought to be a stern lantern. Would she have her colors posted? If she was sailing toward the sound of battle, it could only mean she wanted a piece of the action. But was she ours or theirs?

Peyton appeared beside me. "What do you see?"

Very little in the dark. The new ship's stern lantern rose in a swell, catching the ripple of a tricolor flag. Ice shot through my veins. "French."

Peyton slapped the rail with a curse. "Frigate?"

"That would be my guess with the height of the lantern." It didn't really matter how big she was. We were already outmatched with the *Fatalité*.

Captain Peyton turned on his heel. "Haul aboard! Haul out!" Wearing, firing, leading. I did not know how he kept all the orders straight. I hurried back to the helm, exchanging the telescope for the wheel with Lieutenant Roddam. Surrounded. Were there more Frenchmen out there? Had we sailed into the middle of a squadron? My fingers trembled against the wood. For fourteen years, I'd fought down memories of that dogfight with French ships of the line that had ended in Mr. Riddley's death. I'd kept them at bay, closed up in the chest of memories I rarely opened. But at sea, that lid opened as easily as Pandora's box.

Peyton strode forward but halted near the helm. He regarded our first opponent, scanned the deck of the *Marianne*, then looked over his shoulder toward the newcomer.

I took steady breaths, trying to drown the images of my first battle in the darkness around us.

"Guns are ready, Captain," the lieutenant said.

I watched him out of the corner of my eye. This decision could define his captaincy. Marked in logbooks, recounted for Admiralty reports, and spoken of among officers' circles.

His jaw went taut. "Set the topgallants and royals. We'll give her a broadside and make our escape."

Escape? How could we escape with two large frigates herding us in?

"When the new ship gets into position, we douse all lights. Every one. Pass the word. No light, no noise, as much as we can help it. On my signal."

I snapped my head around. "No lights?" How was I to steer in the complete blackness? How were the men to tend the sails? Clean the guns?

"Not one."

Mr. Hallyburton relayed orders, and seamen glanced toward the quarterdeck in confusion. The *Fatalité's* gun ports glowed a dim yellow a hundred yards southwest of us, no doubt waiting for the new ship to get into position before dealing us a devastating blow.

The *Marianne* crested a wave, and as she descended, Peyton cried, "Fire!"

The broadside rattled my whole being. Smoke billowed, filling the night air with its choking stench.

"The other is coming straight at us," one of the midshipmen called. More lights flickered to life as the new ship approached.

"Thank you, Mr. Kingdon," Peyton said. "Just as we want."

I pulled my brows together. What could he mean by that?

Peyton motioned to me. "Steady as she goes, Doswell. Roddam, ready the starboard guns."

For the first time under his command, I hoped he knew what he was doing.

MAY

Étienne and I helped Mr. Sanchez into one of the hammocks, his head wrapped. Mrs. Peyton sat with eyes closed and one hand still over her nose and mouth. I had nothing to help her, and yet a part of me wished I could sneak into Mr. Doswell's chests to find some ginger to help settle her stomach. If only I knew where they'd stowed everyone's things.

Fretting over Captain Woodall's daughter. I pulled my gaze away, huffing inside. I was accomplishing my duties. That did not include upsetting myself over her seasickness. Aunt Byam would ridicule me.

The wounded man reached for his head, but I grabbed his hand and settled it at his side. He mumbled something in Spanish, his eyes unfocused.

"It is the blow to the head I am most worried about, not the wound." Creases appeared around Étienne's eyes. "What is your name, sailor?"

Worried. About an enemy. I didn't understand it.

When the man didn't respond to the question, Étienne said something in halting Spanish and watched the man's face.

"Raimundo Sanchez Olibar," the seaman said, his words slurred.

Little Harvey peeked over the side of the hammock, a bowl of water and a cloth in hand. "Will he be a madman the rest of his life?" he asked, looking pale despite the orange lantern light.

Étienne chuckled as he wiped off his hands. Then he tousled the boy's hair. "I don't think so. Give him a few days, and he will be on the mend."

Sanchez said something else in Spanish, which Étienne responded to. I watched them converse, not comprehending a word. The surgeon spoke with care and compassion, never mind all his shipmates were firing on his countrymen above.

He said something in what sounded like French and looked at me. Had he asked me something? Étienne blinked and shook his head. Switching between multiple languages must have made him forget which I spoke. "Apologies. Will you wash his face while we wait?"

I nodded. *While we wait.* Because there would certainly be more. I took the cloth from Harvey and dipped it into the bowl. Sanchez continued to mutter in Spanish, breathing strained. A few years ago, the helmsman would have been England's enemy, back when Spain had sided with France. Now he was a friend.

A shot rumbled through the hull, vibrating my boots. I glanced toward the upper decks. Frank was up there. And Shelby and Catterick. Mr. Doswell. I swallowed. I hated the thought of him up above most of all. Gentle Mr. Doswell, in the midst of such chaos. Like Mr. Sanchez, he had once seemed an enemy. But now . . .

I dipped the cloth into the water to rinse it and then squeezed it out. I hadn't managed to get all the blood off Mr. Sanchez's face, but it was better than before. His shirt had started to dry stiff and would need a good scrubbing. I'd offer to clean it for him when he could think more clearly.

Across the cockpit, Mrs. Peyton had lowered her hand, but she still looked pale. I sighed. Here was another enemy of sorts. When had I let my life fill with them? I chewed the inside of my cheek. Or rather than allow enemies into my life, had I instead *chosen* to see them all as enemies? Perhaps I did not have as many as it appeared. Mrs. Peyton certainly didn't look like much of an enemy right now.

I crossed the room to my employer. "Are you well, ma'am?"

She rubbed her brow, a look of disgust on her face. "I'm sorry. What a great help I am."

"You cannot help feeling ill."

She planted her elbows on her knees and dropped her head to her hands. "I shouldn't have come."

"To the cockpit?" I knelt beside her.

"On this voyage," she said so softly it was nearly a whisper.

If she hadn't come, I wouldn't be here. I wouldn't have met Frank or Mr. Doswell. I'd be the lowest of servants working my fingers to the bone for a few guineas a year. "Why do you feel that way?" I asked.

She fixed me with a long look, chewing the corner of her mouth as though she had something to say but wasn't sure she wished to say it. Her whole body tensed as she contemplated, and I tensed with her. Dread began to spill into my chest the longer she paused.

"Byam, it would be best if you knew—"

Agitated voices came from the hatchway, punctuated with blasts from a distant broadside. We both turned toward the sound of labored footsteps.

"Here comes another," I said, scrambling to my feet. There was no time to press her now.

Two men stepped into the light, dragging another between them. The wounded seaman looked younger than I was by a few years. Fair hair fell into the lad's eyes. His clothes were torn and bloody down one side of his body.

"Fitz." Mrs. Peyton flew off the barrel.

Étienne motioned to the table. "Bring him here. Lay him down."

"Harvey, move the bowl," Mrs. Peyton instructed as though she hadn't been about to vomit a few moments earlier.

I backed out of the way as the men brought Fitz around. The red hair and finely tailored coat of the nearest one made my heart skip a beat.

"There's another coming," Mr. Doswell said, breathing heavily as they lowered Fitz to the table. The young seaman groaned.

"Badly wounded?" Étienne asked.

"About the same." The chaplain didn't look at me, just turned on his heel and made for the door.

The surgeon nodded as he pulled out a tool. "We'll have to work fast. Harvey, the lantern."

"Mr. Doswell?" I said softly. Something was wrong with him. He walked too stiffly. Like another person had donned his clothes and taken his place. When he didn't turn, I grabbed for his hand.

He turned his head sharply, his features graver than I'd ever seen them. His hand felt slick against mine. He winced. Red stains appeared on my palm.

"You're injured."

Mr. Doswell drew his hand back, shaking his head in a leaden motion. "I need to return." His glazed eyes trained on something past my shoulder.

"Let me wrap it for you," I said, snatching his sleeve. The wound didn't worry me as much as his actions.

Fitz cried out, and Mrs. Peyton murmured something.

"We're making a run for it," he said. "My duties are above."

I didn't let go. He hadn't come aboard to fight.

"Miss Byam, fetch the laudanum," Étienne said behind me.

"You're needed," Mr. Doswell said, trying gently to pull his sleeve from my hands.

"You're not well." Why did it worry me so? The hollowness in his voice shook me to my core. "You shouldn't be above." Étienne had said Mr. Doswell didn't have the stomach for blood, and now the chaplain was in the middle of it.

"It's not as terrible in the dark." The phrase held back so many thoughts. I could sense them, almost hear them in the shadows that swayed across the room.

"Miss Byam," Étienne barked.

I released Mr. Doswell and let him slip away. I retrieved the laudanum, then helped Mrs. Peyton administer it to a trembling Fitz.

"We need to strap him down while I dig out these splinters," Étienne said, almost to himself. He widened the tear the wood had made in Fitz's trousers. "Harvey, the rope."

"I forgot to duck, Taylor," the injured boy said, giving a wry grin.

Taylor? What did he mean by calling Mrs. Peyton that?

"How clever of you." The seasick captain's wife had vanished. Perhaps I'd too quickly given her my pity. She'd come alive to help this ordinary sailor.

More men entered, and I went to help the next patient as the others tended to Fitz. I kept watching the door, anticipating Mr. Doswell's walking through again. Why did I so badly want him here instead of up there? If he did return, it could be seriously injured. I should prefer him to remain above. I rushed about, woodenly heeding Étienne's orders. Wounded men needed caring for, yet my mind had wandered. More than anything, I wanted to attend to Mr. Doswell's unseen hurts. Deep down, this bloodshed pained him more than most, and for some reason, I needed to know why.

Another burst stopped me short as I retrieved a bandage. The *Marianne* shuddered, sending a chill down my spine. Men around me glanced above. I tried to quiet my spinning head. Would I get the chance to ask him, or would that conversation never be?

Chapter 9

ELIAS

My jaw ached from clenching my teeth, and my eyes felt as though they'd been dredged with sand as I stared ahead into the now-familiar lines of the *Marianne*'s masts and rigging.

"Topgallants are set, sir," Hallyburton said.

To my left, Captain Peyton regarded the *Fatalité* and then the newcomer to starboard. "Man the lights. Load the guns. We'll give them a parting shot and make a run for it."

A broadside from the starboard opponent snapped through the rigging. I'd stopped flinching at the deafening roars. They wanted to make a prize of us, leveling out our masts without damaging the bulk of the ship. But they didn't care how many of the crew they took out with the masts and rigging.

A ship's boy, one of the Carden brothers, appeared near the binnacle before me, ready to extinguish the lantern.

"Guns ready," Roddam said.

"Fire as they bear."

A breath, shouts, and then eruptions from prow to stern. The *Marianne* seemed to tense beneath me as guns on all sides flared in the darkness. Sparks pulsed in my vision.

"Douse the lights!" Peyton cried, the shots still echoing.

In moments, everything went black. I clung to the handles, locking my arms to keep the wheel in place. The nothingness around us pressed into my soul, driving out emotion and thought until I hardly remembered my own name.

The lights on either side of us steadily receded as the breeze caught our topgallants. Though all in this battle were frigates, *Marianne* had the speed advantage at nearly half the tons in burthen as the Frenchmen.

Bursts flickered out of the corner of my eye. More shots.

"Steady," Peyton muttered.

Geysers burst up from the water around the stern, but nothing hit home. A trickle of sweat wound down the side of my face, leaving a trail on my skin for the wind to catch and chill. Distant shouts echoed across the water. Though I'd studied French for years, the fog muffled the words enough that I couldn't make out their meaning.

We stood still as mountains in the dark as the *Marianne* pulled away. It seemed an age before the lights at *Fatalité*'s bow fell behind us. I knew better than to allow myself relief. If they had swivel guns at the stern to engage us early on, they'd certainly have swivels at the prow when they tried to chase us down.

A broadside to starboard shook the night, and I tensed, holding my breath. No crashes or cries. They'd missed again.

"They're still firing," one of the midshipmen whispered.

I heard rather than saw Peyton's answering grin. "But not at us."

Praise the heavens.

"They're firing at each other, and they don't even know it," another midshipman said, a laugh in his voice before Lieutenant Roddam quieted him.

We sailed on in eerie silence, at every moment expecting a volley from the French chasers. Each time the wind played with the sails, my heart faltered at the resulting snap. But the enemy ships didn't seem to notice we'd slipped out from between them. Broadsides continued, quieting as we went. They were fighting friends, the smoke and mist all around hampering their views.

"Roddam, man the helm," Peyton whispered. "Stay the course. We need to get away before they realize what's happened and can still track us down."

It should have calmed me, knowing I was being relieved of my duty, but my body remained rigid, my limbs tight as pulled bowstrings. Roddam's shoulder bumped mine, and I relinquished the wheel, stepping back to give him space.

I dropped my arms to my sides. They hung tired, weak, thrumming from how tightly I'd grasped the handles and how long I'd held them up. Turning, I took in the ships behind us. They were little more than orange blurs in the blackness, slowly fading. We'd made it for now.

"Thank you, Doswell," came the captain's whisper again.

I couldn't answer, my voice having fled. I'd faced equally terrifying situations on our last voyage that should have desensitized me like it did every other man on this ship. And woman, for that matter. I'd seen Mrs. Peyton stare down danger without blinking. Mrs. Hallyburton ate danger smeared on her ship's biscuits, a feat in itself, as one could break a tooth on the barely edible disks. And Miss Byam hadn't let the sight of terrible wounds affect her in the slightest.

You're just a coward, Elias Doswell. No wonder so many women have turned their backs on you.

My skin tingled where Miss Byam had grabbed my hand. She'd seen that cowardice. She'd perhaps pitied me for it. Pity would do me no favors in her eyes.

"Hallyburton, light the binnacle lantern," Peyton said. "Merkley, let's check our course. Block the light as best we can."

Rustling preceded a faint glow, outlining the boatswain's and sailing master's forms. The light caught Captain Peyton's cocked hat as he skirted them and knelt to check the compass.

"Still due south. Very good." He instructed Roddam to bring the ship slightly more west, then he called for a sounding to be taken and the crew to clew up the topgallants. Traveling too fast in this fog was perilous now that we were out of the Frenchmen's grasp. Officers lit a few lanterns down the length of the deck.

The crew didn't snap into action as usual but crept along and spoke in low voices. I went to the stern rail, a slice of which had been blown off by one of the French shots.

"You didn't think we'd make it, did you?" the captain asked, joining me.

I laughed sheepishly. "I did not doubt your abilities, if that is what you mean. Only our odds." He could hardly blame me, caught between two much larger French frigates.

"Never say die, Mr. Doswell." He extended a telescope and lifted it to his eye.

"Do you think they will give chase?" The shattered wood's splinters dug into my palms as I steadied myself against a wave, praying we wouldn't repeat this engagement tomorrow. Too many factors at sea could negate our speed advantage. The mists closed over the Frenchmen's lights, leaving us completely alone in the blackness.

"It would depend on their mission. Working together, a twenty-eight-gun frigate would be an easy prize. In better conditions, of course."

A spark burst into view, and a boom echoed across the water, louder and deeper than cannon fire. Peyton leaned forward with the telescope. The flickering light remained, haloed in the thick air.

"One of them is on fire," Peyton whispered.

A chill moved over my arms. Had a cannon exploded, or had the ship caught fire and blown up the magazine? "Do we return?" I asked. The idea of men floating on debris, trying to stay afloat, filled my mind's eye. Fire was a ship's worst enemy, and as such was highly regulated on board. But you couldn't escape that in battle.

Lines strained above us. Sails murmured as seamen hauled them in. Tackles tapped against the masts.

Peyton sighed and shook his head slowly. "She'll have to rely on her comrade. I cannot risk my men or my ship." He closed the telescope. "There are too many unknowns. If we return and the fire was quickly controlled, we'd be a sitting duck. We have to protect ourselves."

"Of course."

He left the rail to give orders, but I stayed until the light dissolved, praying the souls aboard hadn't met a watery grave.

MAY

When Captain Peyton entered the cockpit, the tight coils inside me released. The room had filled with several more seamen needing attention for less serious injuries. They had brought word that we were most likely out of danger, but the captain's presence gave the confirmation I needed.

The coherent men grabbed the brims of their caps. He waved them off from standing to properly salute. "A report, Étienne."

"No casualties, sir." Relief flooded the Frenchman's voice. The captain clapped him on the shoulder. So friendly a gesture for an enemy.

I finished wrapping a seaman's arm in linen and tied it off. He nodded his thanks, and I took the leftover cloth and salve I'd used back to Étienne's medicine chest. Across the cockpit, Fitz muttered something in his laudanum-induced stupor. He'd have scars worthy of boasting about when he healed. I didn't envy him that.

Captain Peyton pulled his wife into a corner and said something I couldn't hear. I paused as I tucked the salve into its place. Mrs. Peyton didn't show much emotion most days, but tonight, pride shone in her eyes as she listened to her husband. She took his hand, earning her a grin and a kiss on the forehead.

To have someone caring for you like that must be a wonderful thing. I closed the chest's lid and rose. I'd envied Agnes her comfort in finding a husband and not having to fear for her future, but I hadn't thought on the comfort of having someone to confide in, someone to share in your hopes and sorrows. How much easier to recover from a night of fear and anxiety like tonight knowing you had someone not far away. In body and in mind.

The captain moved to the wounded men in hammocks. "Fitz, I see you've managed to earn yourself another spot in the sick bay."

"You know she's closer to my age than yours," the boy growled, barely intelligible.

Peyton chuckled. "Étienne, I think you were heavy-handed on the laudanum."

Étienne looked up from the seaman he was bandaging with one of his sly smiles. "Miss Byam gave it to him."

I frowned. On his orders.

The Frenchman's eyes twinkled. "She has been as helpful as any surgeon's mate. She did her work well."

I furrowed my brows further. I didn't hear praise often. Mrs. Richardson hadn't given it frequently under her employ, nor had my mother or aunt at home. Now this foreigner, practically a stranger, gave it to someone who'd tied a few bandages and had supposedly given a wounded seaman too much laudanum.

"We are grateful for your service, Miss Byam," the captain said.

I curtsied briskly. I didn't do this work for praise, but hearing the gratitude softened the tension that had taken up residence within me that night.

"We're finished here," Étienne said. "I'll have the crew help me transfer these men to the sick bay, if the ladies would like to retire."

The fatigue hit like a squall, my eyes suddenly dry and eyelids heavy. What was the hour? The bells hadn't resumed yet. "If you are certain," I said.

I followed the Peytons to the ladder and up to the mess deck, clenching my jaw against the yawns that came in quick succession. I didn't want to draw in deep breaths of this bilge-tainted air.

Captain Peyton offered me his hand and helped me up through the hatchway in the same manner he had his wife, with care and courtesy.

"Doswell seems a little dazed," he said before releasing my hand. "Would you talk to him? He always perks up after speaking with you."

Me? I wished to talk to him more than anyone, but what good could I do? His vacant stare when he'd helped Fitz to the cockpit had stayed with me through my work, the fear of not having the chance to speak with him again a constant throbbing in my heart. I hoped Frank was also well, of course. I couldn't rest easy until I knew they were both unharmed. I nodded to the captain. I'd do my best.

The carpenter's crew hadn't come below yet, so when the Peytons ascended to their cabin, I hurried into the gun room. They'd set it to rights quickly, a feat I'd doubted after seeing the crew's first attempt during the first week of gun drills. Mr. Doswell's door was closed, but his lantern glowed within. I tapped on the door, then shifted so I couldn't be tempted to peek through the bars.

He opened the door, eyes bloodshot, as though he'd just rubbed them.

"Mr. Doswell, I . . ."

He'd removed his coat and cravat. His unbuttoned waistcoat hung loosely from his shoulders. The undone collar, which left his shirt open halfway down his torso, made me swallow slowly. I'd seen him in such a situation two weeks ago, though with how far we'd come, it seemed forever since I'd discovered that crack in the bulwark. Mr. Doswell so carefully presented himself that seeing him in this state felt strange. I forced my eyes to lift and lock on his face.

He hastily fastened his collar. "Miss Byam. How may I be of service?"

I couldn't remember. I'd had an assignment. Mouth open like a caught fish, I stood there racking my brain. The captain had put me up to this. He'd said Mr. Doswell perked up after speaking with me. A sudden urge to pivot and hide in my cabin welled within. What had Captain Peyton meant by that?

"Are you well?" Mr. Doswell asked.

I needed to say something. "Your coat," I blurted. "I came for your coat."

"My coat?" He still had that distant look. Tonight had muddled his mind—it had all of ours, as evidenced by my odd disposition—but this battle's effect on him seemed deeper. The usual thoughtfulness in his pale-green eyes had given way to this despondency.

"I know it must have been dirtied tonight." I'd seen stains from Fitz's blood. And Étienne had mentioned his queasiness. "I can clean it for you."

"Oh, you needn't bother yourself." He withdrew a step.

"I will clean the captain's coat tomorrow, and I might as well do yours too." I put my hand on the door lest he try to give a quick goodbye and close it between us.

"That is very kind of you." His desire to refuse still tainted his words.

"I can fetch it." I made to squeeze through the door. He needed a little nudging.

"Oh, no. I'll get it."

I paused in the doorway as he took the coat from the lid of his trunk. He moved stiffly, haltingly, as though he'd just set foot on the frigate and needed to learn the motion of the waves.

"You shouldn't have been above," I said softly so the rest of the gun room didn't hear.

His hands jerked in and out of pockets, removing his spectacles, a little book, and a pencil. "We all have our duties. Peyton needed me there."

And it had taken all the strength of his mind to obey those orders. "That was very brave of you," I said.

He dropped his gaze. Then he held up the coat. "Really, you do not need to exert yourself for my sake."

I gathered the fine green wool into my arms. He hadn't appreciated my offer of comfort. It made me want to give it all the more. "How is your hand?"

He drew it back, pulling the cuff of his sleeve down to hide the wound. "Much better." Another attempt at enthusiasm. "Nothing to worry about. Thank you very much, Miss Byam. If you'll excuse me."

I backed up until he could close the door, scrambling to find something more to say. I couldn't think of anything as his door clicked shut.

Hugging his coat tightly, I slipped into my cabin. I wasn't usually so at a loss for words. A night of battling the French had muddled my thoughts. I held up the coat to the faint light coming through the canvas nailed across my window, trying to find the bloodstains, but I couldn't see well enough. I would try again tomorrow.

A light whiff of cologne tickled my senses. I held the coat to my nose and drew in the scent of jasmine, both deliciously sweet and deeply musky. A little like him.

Mr. Doswell's downcast face tore at me. Why, if he found this life so difficult, had he agreed to it? Surely a little country vicarage with a thatched roof, encircled in hedgerows suited him better. Someplace he could lead a quiet life doing good to his fellow man.

I draped the coat over my trunk and crouched by the crack between our cabins. He stood near the wall, so close I could only see his untucked shirt and breeches. A moment later, the cabin went dark as he blew out the lantern. Faint light from the gun room lit his back as he trudged to his cot and fell into it. He sighed, long and wearily.

And for some inexplicable reason, my heart sighed with him.

Chapter 10

MAY

Fierce winds tore at my gown and bonnet as I stood near the stern rail watching Frank at his work. The *Marianne* had sustained less damage than I would have guessed, from what I'd heard below. Superficial, as Frank had called it, but the splintered planks and yards made me shiver. Étienne had pulled similar-looking pieces of wood out of Fitz and the others two nights ago.

"Is the captain's wife going to stay in her cabin the whole voyage?" Frank asked, lining up a new length of wood to replace the mangled section.

I shrugged. "She seemed rather ill again this morning, except when the captain was around. But the moment he went above, she was back to the cot."

"What a luxury to spend the day in bed whenever one wishes." Frank fished a nail from a pouch at his waist. "As you have nothing else to do, would you hold this here?"

"You could ask without the niggling," I said, moving to hold the piece of wood.

"Nothing against you, Miss May."

I pressed my lips together. Though she didn't empty her stomach every morning, I had no doubt of Mrs. Peyton's genuine illness. What if it were something grave? I'd brought it up when I'd passed Étienne yesterday in the gun room. He'd seemed unconcerned, though that had done little to comfort me. He must have been distracted by his work with the wounded.

I'd thought perhaps Mrs. Peyton's fatigue had been a sign of the week all women loathed, but I hadn't found any napkins in my laundering. No additional articles to clean. We'd been at sea nearly three weeks, so it had to be coming soon, but her fatigue had lingered relatively unchanged since she'd first taken seasick. Having just ended myself, it was on my mind. How uncomfortable dealing with feminine struggles on a ship full of men.

The soft tapping of Frank's hammer joined the whistle of the wind in my ears, which Mama's bonnet didn't completely shelter. I turned so the brim blocked the afternoon sun, pointing my face directly at Frank, who grinned.

I instantly dropped my gaze to the rail. Frank's treatment of me hadn't changed since I'd boarded, but I couldn't help worrying about feelings forming on his part. The attention he gave me, the way I caught him shamelessly staring at me, the nudging and bumping, the teasing—either he was Portsmouth's most audacious flirt, or he'd formed an unreciprocated attachment.

"Your Mr. Chaplain seemed ill during the service yesterday," Frank said. It was as though he sensed whenever I was wondering about his feelings toward me and tried to throw me off his trail with jokes about Mr. Doswell.

Mr. Doswell hadn't seemed ill to me. Just withdrawn, as though he were sheltering himself behind a wall to recover. He'd hardly spoken to me yesterday or today, despite my attempts to engage him. When I returned his coat this evening, I would corner him. I gripped the wood tightly. Make him tell me what the matter was, the way I had to force my family members to if I wanted to know anything going on in their heads.

I frowned, imagining him backed against the bulwark, his eyes untrusting. Perhaps cornering was not the best approach with him. If he were trying to recover, as it seemed, a gentle approach might be best.

How exactly did one do that? Gentle approaches were not my specialty.

"You're deep in thought this afternoon," Frank said.

"Am I?" I flinched as the ribbons of the bonnet swept across my face. Drat. The bow had come untied. Thank goodness for the pin that held it on my head.

"You didn't respond to my comment about our estimable chaplain." Frank waved me off. "You can let go."

I stepped back. "I was only wondering . . ." What to say in order to not give him fodder for teasing. "Why he chose the topic of charity for his message." That was ridiculous. Why would I be wondering that? Besides the fact that his words had lingered with me the past few days. It would have made a very good sermon if he'd applied himself. That dullness in his voice, though, had dampened everything.

Frank snorted. "Perhaps he was trying to call Mrs. Hallyburton to repentance."

"Perhaps."

"Poor man," Frank said without a hint of sympathy in his voice. "Couldn't handle Saturday's battle."

I bristled, putting more distance between us. "Mr. Doswell wasn't brought on for fighting. Of course a person unused to such danger would find it difficult to bear."

Frank chuckled, running a hand along the seams between the new section of rail and the old. "No need to get defensive, Miss May. I won't hold it against the coward too much."

"You shouldn't hold it against him at all." I folded my arms, trying to keep back the rising heat inside me. "I know you dislike him, though I don't understand why. He is a good man. A caring man. And I will not hear you ridicule him any longer."

"This is a different tune from the one you sang when first you boarded." His words had an edge to them.

He was correct. I'd simply grown tired of Frank's criticism of anyone and everyone aboard. I rubbed at my nose, realizing I'd crinkled it again. When had that habit started? "I simply realized we'd had a misunderstanding, and it was little use holding on to my offense."

"Then, I hope you can offer me the same courtesy." A wicked gleam touched his eye. In one swift movement, he caught hold of the pin holding my bonnet and pulled it from my head. The knot of hair at the back of my head loosened, and my bonnet skewed.

"Frank, give that back." I held out my hand. "We are not children." Though sometimes I wondered when it came to him, despite his being two years older than I.

He tapped the dull end of the pin against his cheek. "Are we not, Miss May? Adults are not really as different from children as we purport to be."

"That much is clear." I swiped for the hat pin, but he moved out of reach.

"What will you give me for it?" He ticked it in front of his face, from one side to the other, like the hand of a clock. Mocking me. "Perhaps a few dried peaches?" He waggled his brows at me, which did him no favors.

I scowled. "I already finished them." And craved them now, but I wouldn't admit that to him and boost his ego.

"A kiss, then."

"Never." It was a hat pin. Let him have it if he was going to make preposterous demands. And may he stab his hand with it for suggesting that. I clenched my fists at my sides, teeth grinding. This was exactly the sort of teasing he'd doled out our entire voyage. Why this afternoon's prodding finally irked me past my limits, I couldn't say. I pivoted. Time to check on Mrs. Peyton anyway.

As I turned, the wind caught the brim of my bonnet and tore it from my head. It sailed toward the port rail, ribbons whipping behind it. I lunged, but Mama's bonnet hit the rail, bright sun catching the little white flowers, and tumbled over the side.

Frank cursed and ran to port. We arrived just as the bonnet got pulled under the *Marianne* in the churn of her wake.

"It'll resurface," Frank said. "We'll fish it out." He called to one of the carpenter's crew to bring him a line.

I stood at the rail, staring into the ocean. It was a hat, which I would have worn to pieces and replaced without thought in a few years. Why did this numbness open up inside me as I scanned the waves?

I trudged back toward the stern, eyes smarting. It was a stupid bonnet. One Papa had given Mama before practically abandoning us. And then Mama had given to me before abandoning me. I shouldn't have any feelings about it besides appreciating it as my only hat.

"You're never going to see that again," Catterick said, leaning over the rail. When had he come over?

The churning waters below us showed no sign of the bonnet. Even if we could find it, the straw would be terribly misshapen, the silk flowers ruined. I tried to swallow, but my throat felt thick and dry.

Frank glanced at me, panic in his eyes, and continued to swear under his breath.

Without another word, I left the quarterdeck and strode toward the forecastle, my insides roiling. The child May, who still lived somewhere deep down in the recesses of my heart, wanted to weep over the loss, not just of the bonnet but also of my entire family now spread to the far corners of the earth.

Another part of me wanted to scream at Frank. His unfeeling teasing had caused this. When would I draw the line with him? But the part of me that spoke the loudest simply wanted, against my better judgment, to go below and seek out—

"Miss Byam?"

The gentle voice washed over me like a sip of warm ginger tea. Mr. Doswell stepped to my side, brow knit. "Has something happened? Where . . . where is your bonnet?"

Of course stylish Mr. Doswell would notice something like that. I couldn't help the corners of my mouth ticking upward. He'd spoken to me. He hadn't done that unprompted since before the battle.

"Lost at sea, unfortunately," I said, attempting indifference.

"How did that happen?" The concern in his eyes lifted my spirits, though I couldn't say why.

"A mishap with my hat pin."

He swept his straw top hat off his head and extended it toward me. "Here. Use this until we can get you another."

Another? I didn't have the money for that. I didn't even have funds for a lantern, and I needed that more than a bonnet. I wouldn't be paid for another month. "Oh, I couldn't. I'd look ridiculous." He always wore that hat above decks. It was how I could spot him through the crowds. The crew's straw hats tended to be flat with much wider brims, and the sea officers wore felt cocked hats.

"Plenty of fashionable women sport toppers when they ride," he insisted.

I shook my head. "I am not a fashionable woman." By any stretch of the word. And even if I were, Frank's taunting about wearing it would be unbearable to add to my frustration with him. I couldn't manage both.

"It's terribly easy to get burned at sea."

"Yes, I know." I held up my hands, half expecting him to put it on my head without my consent. But no. That was what Frank would do. Mr. Doswell wouldn't dream of it. "Truly, I will manage. Thank you for your concern."

"Of course." The disquiet didn't leave his face.

My cheeks suddenly warmed under his attention. Why should he worry over me? I smoothed back my hair, finding the knot at the back of my head sagging and strands of hair loose, flailing in the wind. Gracious. I must look a sight. How many times would he catch me like this? A disheveled hackney horse toe-to-toe with a thoroughbred stallion.

"If . . . if you'll excuse me." I hurried for the hatchway like a ninny, not waiting to hear his response. Losing the bonnet, with all its strange emotions, had left me unprepared to speak with Mr. Doswell. I seized the ladder's rungs and descended as fast as I could. Yes, that was it. How else could I explain how utterly tongue-tied I'd become conversing with a simple chaplain, of all things?

A well-dressed, soft-spoken, far-too-caring chaplain.

ELIAS

I sat against the wall of my cabin, turning my straw hat over. I should have been writing my sermon for Sunday or going over my notes for tomorrow's trigonometry lesson with the midshipmen. Important things I hadn't been able to focus on while trying to still my mind after the battle two days ago. But filling my head was Miss Byam's brave face as she'd attempted to mask the sorrow at losing her bonnet that morning, and I clung to the change of focus.

Worrying over her lack of head covering was silly of me. We'd make it to Malta in a few days if the weather held, and she could find another bonnet there. If she could afford it. *I* could buy her another, though Walcott deserved to pay for the damages. I clenched my teeth. Michael Carden, the oldest of the three brothers, had recounted Walcott's thoughtlessness that had resulted in the loss. The cad.

I selected a piece of charcoal from my writing box, which sat in a heap of shoe ribbons and sewing supplies. Without some sort of hat, she'd have to take care not to go above in the heat of the day. As much as I enjoyed walking the deck under a sky full of stars, I knew she liked to take in fresh air in the warmth of the day. A few days below would drive anyone mad.

On the underside of my hat, I drew a line slanting across the brim on either side, then a semicircle to connect them across the crown. I held the hat next to my head, trying to visualize my scheme. The brim stood at a right angle to the crown—not ideal for a bonnet—but with some steam and coaxing, I might be able to get it into a better shape. I rubbed at the semicircle and redrew a better hollow to fit about her neck. If I went more conservative on the first cut, I'd have more room to adjust later.

I took up my shears and brought them to the brim. She might laugh at this attempt. I swallowed. Why was I doing this? Ruining my favorite hat to turn it into a makeshift bonnet for someone who didn't like to accept my help. She was a woman who preferred to do everything on her own, to not bother anyone. But every person needed someone to care for them, and I could make do with my felt hat. With one last look at the straw topper, I took a breath and began to cut. The lines of plaited straw crackled, trying to resist as the blades sliced through.

It wouldn't be a terribly fetching bonnet, with its black band across the crown and edged in black shoe ribbon I'd brought just in case, but it would do the job well enough.

A tapping at the door made me pause with the shears. Too soft to be any of the officers. "Who is it?" My heart started a strange pattering at the thought of who might be standing on the other side of the door.

"Mr. Doswell?" I knew that voice too well, though it carried a greater tone of uncertainty than I tended to hear from her. "Might I ask you something?" She stood to one side, her face not visible through the window. Just one shoulder of that Saxon blue gown. Confound it. I jumped to my feet and threw the hat, its cut piece flapping, into my trunk.

I felt for my cravat, making sure it was there. The last time she'd arrived at my cabin, I'd already removed it. I did not want multiple instances of her catching me in such a state of undress. "Yes. Yes, of course." I opened the door, revealing her upturned face. Had she seen what I was doing? "How can I be of service?"

"You don't always need to be of help to me." She tilted her head as she regarded me, one of her gentle curls falling across her brow.

I glanced around the empty gun room. "But I . . ." I *liked* to, but I couldn't say that. "I simply thought . . . That is to say, I do not mind helping. Not if it's you." *Stop talking, for all love.*

The corners of her lips curled upward, but in a split second, the smile vanished. "In truth, I wished to inquire after you."

"Me?"

"Might I come in?"

Come in? I glanced over my shoulder at the pile of shears and shoe ribbon surrounding my sewing kit and writing box. Even without the mess, I couldn't very well invite an unmarried young lady into my cabin. How did I express my concern without resurrecting the same humiliation I'd brought upon myself at our first meeting? She'd think I was suggesting her forwardness to be improper.

"Only for a moment," she said, moving my arm from the doorframe and brushing past me. She paused just inside. "Are you repairing something?"

I hurried over, nudging the disarray closer to the bulwark. "Yes. Repairing."

"Would you like me to mend it for you?"

"No, no. I am quite proficient at mending." *Humble, Elias.*

"I suppose I shouldn't be surprised." She finally looked up from the pile on the deck.

I cleared my throat. "You wished to ask me something?" The door creaked shut as the *Marianne* tilted to starboard. A little thrill raced up my spine. She stood so close, studying my face in a way that turned my brain to mush.

"I simply wished to know how you fared. After the battle."

The battle. Our engagements on the *Deborah* hadn't shaken me nearly so much. It was strange how memories I thought long buried had resurfaced, not just in my head but in my entire body, as though it remembered the paralyzing terror I'd experienced as a boy of twelve. My shoulders tensed, and the tautness traveled through my limbs.

Surely she meant the scratches I'd sustained, not the mental strain it had thrown me. I held up my hand with a forced laugh. "Healing well." It hadn't bled for long, and I wouldn't need a bandage by tomorrow. This mounting tension from simply mentioning the battle suggested I had a ways to go to return to the place of healing I'd found in the aftermath of my time as ship's boy.

"That isn't what I referred to." She pulled her lips to one side and seemed to consider. Then she sighed. "It seemed to affect you. In ways it didn't affect the others."

My stomach twisted. It certainly had. I tugged at my collar, holding my breath and steeling myself for the flood of memories. I didn't have the strength to be here, and I failed to even pretend I did. "I'm a blasted coward, Miss Byam." The words shot from my mouth, harsh and cold, before I could consider the consequences.

She flinched, expression hardening. "I apologize for asking. It wasn't my place. If you'll excuse me." She yanked open the door.

Dolt. "Wait, I did not mean to imply you were—"

The door clattered shut behind her before I could find the right explanation. I clapped a hand to my forehead. Why had I let that slip out? Raw emotion never led to good ends. I'd learned that long ago. I couldn't think through the emotions like Miss Byam could, saying the right thing at the right moment and not regretting it.

I leaned back against the bulwark that separated our two cabins, my project all but forgotten. She'd seen the cloud that had filled my soul the last two days and had made an effort to approach me about it. Few but my sisters had made any such attempts. I'd unintentionally rejected the outstretched hand by hurrying her out.

I groaned. And here I was accusing Mr. Walcott of being a cad.

MAY

I slogged toward the galley, my sour mood from the previous day clinging to me like a barnacle. Stupid Frank and his callous idiocy. I buttoned my spencer against the chill of the gun deck, with its open ports. Though only the first day of the month of October, it had hit us with a distinct chill I hoped would ease as the day progressed. Not that I could go above and enjoy it for long without getting burned and miserable. Unless the captain had ordered the awning, which he'd rarely done this voyage.

Perhaps I should have swallowed my pride and accepted Mr. Doswell's top hat. Was my refusal his reason for the short response when I'd tried to bring up his reaction to the battle? No, he'd seemed more cordial, if not a bit flustered, before that. I wrapped my arms around myself. I'd need my threadbare coat before too long.

Mr. Howard stood at the galley stove filling the Peytons' silver teapot with steaming water. At his side stood . . . Mr. Doswell? He retreated a step, shoulders hunching, with a sheepish look on his face. Or was that embarrassment? He gripped his hat behind his back, the straw brim just visible around the wool of his jacket.

I trained my gaze on the tray and cleared my throat. "Good morning, sirs. If you'll excuse me." I seized the tray from the cook. If the chaplain felt awkward every time I came near, I'd simply have to avoid him. Quite the feat with our cabins sharing a wall. I moaned inwardly as I hurried toward the great cabin. The teacups rattled in their saucers with each step across the rolling deck. No, avoiding him was impossible. I'd have to pretend nothing was wrong. If only I knew what *was* wrong.

The marine on duty nodded to me as I stopped before the cabin door. I took a deep breath and steadied the tray on one arm to knock. I'd learned my lesson not to barge in in the morning. Before I could knock, the door swung open to the jovial smile of Captain Peyton.

Praise the skies. He was already dressed and about his work.

"Miss Byam, you've arrived at the perfect time." He held the door open for me to enter.

"Thank you, sir," I mumbled, waiting until he'd quit the room before setting the tray on the table. "Have you an appetite today, ma'am?" I certainly didn't after seeing Mr. Doswell in the galley. His rosy complexion—from the heat of the galley or the morning light, I couldn't tell—made him almost seem normal. He was still coltish as ever. I fought against my lips, which wanted to grin for reasons I couldn't determine. Mr. Doswell was a conundrum, and I didn't know if I had the capacity to decipher him.

Mrs. Peyton pushed herself up, making the hanging cot sway. "A little."

"Cook just poured the water for your tea," I said. "Would you like to dress as it steeps?"

She nodded and stretched, then slipped out of bed with more energy than I'd seen since the beginning of our voyage. I went to fetch her stockings and stays from the trunk, keeping a careful eye on her. So she was finally getting used to the motion of the ship. Good. She rubbed her stomach for a moment as I rummaged through the trunk. Not fully adjusted, clearly. I mustn't get my hopes up too high.

"How is Mr. Doswell this morning?" She sat in a chair and pulled on her stockings without help.

I lifted a shoulder, untangling the lacing on the stays. "I don't know." The Peytons were unusually concerned about the chaplain. But then, so was I.

Mrs. Peyton stood and lifted her arms so I could wrap the boned material around her. "The captain says he talks to you more than anyone." She held the stays in place as I began threading the lacing through the eyelets.

"He speaks to you and the captain far more than he speaks to me." Especially the last few days. I missed a hole, and the stays' lace slipped through my fingers. For some reason, the thought of him talking with the Peytons irked me. It shouldn't. He'd known them far longer than he'd known me. Did he confide in them when he dined in the great cabin? I laced with vigor, spiraling the cord and tugging like a crew of able seamen jumping the halyard.

What could I do about Mr. Doswell? Nothing, really. Attempts to force him into conversation would make him retreat further. Perhaps I could pretend an illness or discomfort and ask for help. I paused at the bottom of the stays. That wasn't a half-bad idea. Mr. Doswell couldn't resist being helpful. If I played the distressed damsel, would he have a choice but to speak with me?

I returned to the top of the stays to cinch them snug. Yes. Appeal to his charity. His empathetic heart wouldn't allow him to keep away. If he saw vulnerability, he'd feel better inclined to vulnerability himself. I pulled sharply at the lacing about Mrs. Peyton's lower back. But what injury or misfortune could I believably invent?

Mrs. Peyton grunted, hands flying to her stomach. "A little too tight."

"Apologies, ma'am." I glanced down. How was the lacing too tight? The bottom edges of the stays weren't even close to touching. I'd laced the top normally. It wasn't as if she'd eaten enough the last few weeks to fatten up. I'd noticed the ill-fitting stays but hadn't thought much of them.

I froze. Then blinked. Seasickness that lasted longer than anyone else's despite years of experience at sea. Fatigue to the point of sleeping great stretches of the day. Stays that seemed increasingly too small. I bit my lip. Was Mrs. Peyton with child?

"Is that better?" I asked, mind whirling. No wonder she'd asked about my experience with children. No wonder she'd changed her mind about bringing a lady's maid.

"Yes, thank you."

I tied off the cord. What had possessed Captain Peyton to bring his wife on a voyage like this in such a state? Of course many women delivered children on navy ships, but they didn't usually set out in that condition. Surely Mrs. Peyton would have been better off staying in the comforts of her home surrounded by family than wasting away on a soggy old ship.

Unless . . . Did Captain Peyton know? I let my arms fall slowly to my sides. Would he be so chipper if he did?

Mrs. Peyton glanced at me over her shoulder, an eyebrow raised. I instantly looked away, certain my shock was written plainly across my face. She clearly did not desire anyone to know her secret. How long did she think she'd get away with it? Was that what she'd started to tell me when we'd been helping Étienne?

"Ma'am, during the battle you had something you wished me to know," I said. "Then we were interrupted. Was it important?"

She turned around, feeling the back of her stays with one hand. Was she checking how noticeable the gap was? "Oh. No, it wasn't. Never mind that."

She didn't want to tell me. "Tea?" I hurried to the table. What was I to do now? Pretend as though I didn't know? Ask directly?

"I think I'd prefer a gown first," she said, still standing in the middle of the cabin in her shift and stays.

Good heavens. I was a failure at pretending. "Yes, of course." I rushed to the trunk and retrieved the first day gown on top, not bothering to ask which she'd prefer. She rarely had a preference. I lifted the gown over her head and helped her fit her arms into the sleeves. I couldn't assume Captain Peyton was ignorant of the situation. If I figured it out, he certainly could. But then, he was a man. They didn't always notice these things.

I smoothed down the gown's skirts. The only man I could think of who might notice was Mr. Doswell. He noticed everything. I tied the gown closed. He even noticed destitute lady's maids who were the daughters of convicts and hardly had any friends in the whole world.

I poured the tea, the spicy ginger steam hitting my nose instantly. The underlying notes of jasmine flooded my head with visions of him.

Mrs. Peyton slid her feet into slippers and sat at the table. I placed the teacup in front of her, which she lifted and drank from eagerly. Her color had returned compared to the last few weeks. Had she passed the worst of her illness? She couldn't be very soon confined, but heaven only knew where we'd be when the time came. I swallowed. Thank goodness for Étienne, or I'd have to take charge with the sparse knowledge gained from assisting in one of my sister's children's births. I only hoped Étienne was familiar with delivering babies.

My thoughts still spun in a dizzying torrent when I made my way to the gun room to retrieve my sewing kit. The revelation answered many questions but also presented many more. I paused just inside the door of my cabin, kneading my forehead against an impending headache. Mrs. Richardson hadn't been nearly this confusing of an employer.

As I crouched by my trunk, my eyes fell on something peeking out over the edge of my hammock. The crown of a straw hat. I pursed my lips, which tried to smile against my will. For all his timidity, Mr. Doswell was persistent. I sighed. Perhaps the hat wouldn't look as silly on me as I imagined.

When I lifted it from my bedding, long black ribbons fell out behind it. I held it up to the lantern light from the gun room. This wasn't a top hat. The crown had a similar look to his, and the ribbon around it looked the same, but its shape was that of a bonnet. I fingered the ribbon trimming the brim, with its practically invisible stitches placed with great care. Little bows graced each side in the same stately black as the rest of the trim.

A lump welled in my throat as I placed the bonnet on my head. I couldn't say why my fingers trembled as I tied the ribbons loosely under my chin. This was the hat Mr. Doswell always wore, and he'd cut it and shaped it just for me. Any other man on this ship would have brushed aside the inconvenience, but given Mr. Doswell's appreciation of style and the great attention he paid to dressing himself, this could not have been an easy sacrifice to make.

This was what he'd been hiding in the galley earlier. I brushed my palms over the stiff straw. He must have been shaping it with Cook's steaming kettle. And last night when I'd gone to his cabin to try to talk, he had been working on this. No wonder he'd been flustered. My vision blurred. It seemed like so long since someone had done something this thoughtful for me. I wanted to march into the next cabin and scold him. I could have managed without a bonnet. But he was too tenderhearted to watch someone suffer, even over a small matter.

I removed the bonnet and set it gently back into my hammock, then tucked the ribbons beside it. Mr. Doswell was a mystery. A gracious, kind mystery. Perhaps I didn't have the capacity to decipher him, but I certainly wished to try.

Chapter 11

ELIAS

I pushed my book closer to the gun room table's lantern to better make out the lines forming Europe on its pages, then I glanced at my drawing on the two pasted-together sheets. I'd made Norway a little too close to Denmark. It wasn't as though the boys would notice, but I rubbed at the pencil line anyway, smearing it. Going over it with ink in the final version would mostly mask the mistake.

Nudging my spectacles back into place, I leaned forward to try forming the outline of Norway once more. Around me, the quiet of the ship drifting to sleep formed a bubble of calm. The *Marianne* rocked peacefully in the shelter of the Maltese harbor's waters, and seamen slept soundly, knowing they wouldn't be attacked by storm or foe tonight.

I turned the pencil to use the sharper point on the other side of the lead. Employing my hands had proven helpful in my attempts to banish the sinking despair that had holed up inside me since the battle. I thought that making land in Malta would have restored my mind to its previous state—more controlled, less spontaneous in the memories it chose to bring before me—but the fear and guilt still lodged in my heart. Constant companions I'd dealt with all my life but had learned to ignore in most situations.

A cabin door creaked open, and a head popped out. My heart flipped.

"What are you doing so late?" Miss Byam asked, slipping out and closing the door. She wore a cap over her hair and held a coat wrapped around her like a sultana.

"I thought I heard you go to bed," I said, setting down the pencil.

Excellent. Now she knows you listen to her getting ready each night. How awful that sounded. It wasn't as if anyone in this gun room could help but hear his neighbors in adjacent cabins. I opened my mouth to explain, then snapped it shut. Speaking would only make it worse.

Miss Byam shuffled to the table and sat in a chair across from me. "You have been nearly impossible to find the last week. One would think we resided on opposite ends of the ship."

I'd done it on purpose. I didn't want to witness her anger at me for trying to help when she'd already refused. "Coming into port is a busy time for everyone."

She planted her elbows on the table. "Not for the chaplain."

I rubbed the back of my neck, not meeting her gaze. "I still have duties to attend to. Of a clerical sort." I worked my pencil along Norway's coast, heading northeast.

Miss Byam placed her hand on the map, stopping my pencil's progression. "I wanted to thank you. For the bonnet. You didn't have to do that."

And yet catching glimpses of her wearing it the last three days had given me greater pleasure than wearing the hat myself. She could walk about freely without waiting for the awning or running from shadow to shadow. She did not seem the type to take well to being caged, and I did not want to see her caged.

"It was nothing," I said with a shrug. I wanted to lose myself in the safety of drawing again, but she hadn't moved her hand.

"It meant the world to me."

I couldn't help the grin that sprang to my face, though I instantly attempted to reel it back in. Her smile in return made that difficult to do. My body warmed despite the coolness of the lower deck.

"What is keeping you awake so late?" she asked, pulling her hand back and nodding to the sheets of paper on the gun room table.

"Part of my lessons with the midshipmen." I moved my arm to show her the half-finished map.

She came partway out of her chair to examine it. "What are these numbered circles?"

I traced my finger along the map. "You spin a teetotum to advance to important cities around the world, and the first to arrive back in London wins. I played an old version of this game with my grandfather as a boy, and I thought the mids would appreciate the change of routine."

She put her finger on the map and followed mine in the trek across Europe. "It sounds more exciting than just reading the names of places in books."

"I can't say I mind the reading, but I have a feeling the young gentlemen would agree with you."

She paused, then set her finger on Portsmouth. Slowly, she moved through the English Channel, along the Bay of Biscay, around Spain and Portugal, and past the Strait of Gibraltar, following the path of our voyage. "Where is Malta?"

I moved my finger to the little island off the coast of Sicily. "We are here."

She brought her finger through the Mediterranean Sea to tap against mine. "We've come a long way, haven't we?"

I nodded. In so many ways. The *Marianne* had taken us around Europe, but she had also taken Miss Byam and me from misunderstanding strangers to trusting neighbors. Trusting? I studied her face as she contemplated the map and our position. Did I trust her? In some ways. I trusted that she respected me, but I wasn't so desperate that I'd open the door to someone and give them free rein to examine every corner of my heart.

"Where will we go from here, do you think?" She kept her finger pressed against mine.

"Northeast to the Adriatic, Southeast to the Nile, North to Provence. There are many places they could send us."

"It's a bit exciting, isn't it? Not knowing what adventures await us."

I pulled my finger away. "Storms and battle await us." I'd finish the map tomorrow night. Fatigue was getting the better of me. I had only so much strength to keep the fear and worthlessness at bay. I pocketed the pencil and let the book I copied from fall closed.

"You can tell me," she said softly.

"Why would I do that?" I murmured, not looking at her. Hearing the explanation as to why the battle so much affected me would not strengthen my standing in her eyes. I laid my ruler atop the book.

"Because we've hardly spoken the last week, and I've missed our conversations."

She had? I halted before I could sweep the map out from under her hand. I had missed our chatting too. It was difficult to want to talk to someone when thoughts and memories overwhelmed me. Not to mention the embarrassment.

"I've been worried about you," she said. Lantern light caressed the side of her face, catching in tiny stars on the tips of her eyelashes.

I cleared my throat. Confound this stirring inside me. My lungs refused to expand as her pleading tone rang in my ears. Hadn't I learned from Miss Durant and Miss Starle and Miss Page and Miss Somer? I'd tried to let them in, and each instance had ended in heartache. None of them had asked though. Even Miss Somer, kind as she was, had never looked at me with so much concern. Pity, perhaps, but not genuine worry. "Why would you worry about me?" I finally said.

"How could I not worry about a friend?"

The corners of my mouth turned upward. A friend. My heart, still stubbornly clinging to naïveté despite its experience, thudded rapidly.

Miss Byam stood, and for a moment, I feared she'd retire to her cabin. She rounded the table and pushed a chair closer until it tapped mine. Then she sat. "Tell me. Please?" she said in a near whisper.

I glanced around the gun room. Most of the officers' cabins were dark.

"Why was it so difficult?" She clasped her hands together on her knees, eyes trained on me.

I wanted to push away. It would be easier than the pain women caused that was certain to follow. Why could I not resist? Like the first hint of jasmine drifting from a cup of tea, she'd captured me with her guileless care.

Don't do it, Elias. Don't give in. Though my head screamed I'd regret this, my heart would not be swayed. "I went to sea at twelve aboard the same ship my brother served in, HMS *Lumière*. Ship's boy, first class."

She inclined her head. "You meant to be an officer?"

"My father meant for me to be an officer." I blew out long and slow. "I hardly made it past the first battle."

"Did you want to be an officer?"

"I wanted nothing more than for him to esteem me as much as he did my older brother, who'd already made a name for himself in the navy." Why was I admitting this to her? I ran a hand through my hair. "I did love the sea. And ships. I thought I wanted this life." It had proven too harsh for a boy sheltered by four older sisters, who barely knew his brother at sea.

She nodded as though it made sense, but I couldn't understand why she thought so. "Even when we are born into the same family, that does not make us the same," she said.

Truer words had never been spoken. More than one of my sisters would have fared better at sea than I had. I could easily see Ruth or Anna getting promoted to post-captain faster than Isaac.

"My sister takes more after my mother and my brother after my father," she said with a little laugh, a twinge of something melancholy in her tone. Regret? "I thought I took after my father as well until a few years ago."

"What made you change your mind?"

She ducked her chin. "He did something so dishonorable I nearly wished there were a way to sever all ties with him." Even in the orange light, I could see her face reddening.

I leaned forward, stomach sinking as a dozen scenarios passed through my mind. I wanted to ask but did not wish to pry.

She smiled as though reading my thoughts. "He was a clerk at the rope yards and swindled money for years."

I closed my eyes, imagining the repercussions such actions would have on a family.

"We lived rather grandly for our station, not knowing it was all a lie." She brushed at the skirt of her coat. "Now he is in New Holland paying for his crimes." She sighed. "While we pay for his crimes in England."

I nodded. A guilty person tainted his family, however innocent the rest of them were. The authorities would have taken everything from her. My chest ached. She must have endured so much. How many friends had turned their backs on the Byams? And then to lose her uncle and cousin in a matter of months . . . No wonder she faced the world with such fierceness. She'd been forced to in order to survive.

"But you are not in England anymore," I said, nodding to the map. A warship might not have been the best choice as a sanctuary, but it would get her far away from the troubles of home. I'd come for the same escape.

She regarded the papers thoughtfully. Then she nudged my knee with hers. "You distracted me."

I raised my shoulders. "Not intentionally." Talking about her past was much safer waters than talking about mine.

She tipped her head toward me, playing with the ends of her plaited hair, which fell over her shoulder from under her soft linen cap. "If you do not wish to tell me, I will not hold it against you. I only thought . . ." She bit her lip. "That perhaps I could help the next time if I knew why it affected you so." Her voice diminished before she ended her thought, and she looked away. Then she stood swiftly. "Good night, Mr. Doswell."

Without thinking, I grabbed her hand as she started away. Her skin was cool and smooth against mine. "Wait."

She halted, tense.

How did I put into words the warmth that rushed through my veins at her care and concern? Dared I tell her how she had reignited the spark of life I'd thought lost? I softly tugged on her hand, and after a moment, she sat.

"I'll tell you," was the best I came up with.

She didn't release my hand as she waited for me to speak. The low-burning candle flickered, sending wispy shadows undulating across her face. Her dark blue eyes, nearly black in the dimness of the gun room, regarded me without judgment.

I took a breath. For some reason, I wanted to tell her. "In my first battle, I witnessed a friend—a mentor, really—blown to pieces by grapeshot. Just steps from where I stood." Visions of the gruesome scene flashed through my head with such sharpness, such clarity that I couldn't speak for a moment. I glanced down, half expecting to see my stockings splattered with Mr. Riddley's blood as they'd been that day.

Miss Byam's hand tightened around mine, and I clutched it, my lifeline in the torrent of memory.

"So many fell." Each one remained branded into my mind, from the coxswain to the sailing master to the ship's boys. I'd mourned, for the lives cut short and for the families shattered. The inability to perform my duties had led to punishment, humiliating to both me and my first-lieutenant brother. "I couldn't put my head to rights. The dreams. The terrors. Every gun drill was paralyzing purgatory. When we made port for repairs, my brother set me in a coach bound for my father's vicarage. We both knew I wasn't fit for the navy. Much to my father's regret."

How pathetic. I straightened, blinking against the deprecating voice in my head. "And now you can see what a coward I am." I tried to laugh.

Her thumb rubbed back and forth across my fingers, cutting off the laugh. Almost cutting off my breath. "I told you before—I think you are very brave," she said. "You kept going, even with the world against you. I dare someone to discredit that."

I stared at her lips forming the words that slowly swelled in my heart. She didn't care that I lacked Captain Peyton's charisma or Frank Walcott's incorrigible pluck. The weakness that had immobilized me throughout my life, she'd turned into a commendable strength.

"I think we could use a few more people who care as you do, Mr. Doswell," she said.

What she didn't see was that she was the one who did a better job at caring than I did. She stood her ground in people's defense, even when the odds were not in her favor. Sometime while she spoke, I'd leaned closer. Or had she?

"I'm not sure how many would agree," I said.

"What does that matter?" Her grip on my hand tightened. "I believe it. And so should you. If we believe, who else is needed?" Her voice slowed as she spoke.

We. My head buzzed, not making sense of her words but loving the sound of them all the same. She talked as though something connected us, and sitting here with her in the darkness of night— *Marianne's* lulling creak the only sound besides the pounding of my pulse—I desperately wanted that.

Her eyes flitted to my mouth, then slowly back up. Was I imagining her rapid breathing?

This is ludicrous. Burned time and again and you still go back for more.

This was different. I pulled her hand closer to me, and she didn't resist. Her face neared mine.

You always think that.

A crash rattled the partition between the gun room and the rest of the deck. I startled, and Miss Byam jerked away from me, jumping to her feet. Wailing like that of a wounded animal pierced the quiet we'd enjoyed.

"Gracious," she hissed, leaning to one side to see through the doorway.

I seized the lantern and held it toward the commotion. The wailing turned to whimpering as something shuffled around the floor. Lantern light caught a blond head.

"Harvey?" I asked, moving around Miss Byam. The lad moved fitfully on hands and knees. I knelt beside him and placed a hand on his shaking shoulder. "Harvey, what are you doing?"

I received only mumbles in answer.

"I don't think he's awake," she said. She helped me get the boy to his feet, and he immediately collapsed against my side. I wrapped my free arm around him before he fell. Poor boy. He blinked against the light, but no comprehension cleared his eyes.

Miss Byam glanced around as stirring rippled through some of the gun room cabins. A sharp voice muttered beyond the partition.

"I should get him back to his hammock before Mrs. Hallyburton comes," I whispered, trying not to let disappointment taint my voice. Whatever spell our time alone had cast was broken.

She nodded quickly, wrapping her coat more tightly around her and avoiding my gaze. "I should return to mine as well." She slipped away, pausing at the door of her cabin. "Good night."

I bobbed my head toward her. My shoulders sagged as her door clicked shut. That wasn't a very nice trick fate had decided to play.

"Come, Harvey." I hung the lantern on a hook on the wall, not wanting to wander through rows of sleeping men with a light, and guided him toward the occupied hammocks. I had to hold his shoulders with both hands to keep him from swaying like he'd downed too much grog.

That was fortunate.

Hardly. My lips twitched, eager for the kiss they hadn't received. *Have you no sense of self-preservation, Elias?*

I sighed, correcting Harvey's course again and attempting to banish the image of Miss Byam's candlelit face. Clearly, I did not.

MAY

I ascended the ladder to the gun deck with more vigor than I had the whole of our journey. Perhaps it was Mrs. Peyton's renewed health or that I'd finally grown used to sleeping in a hammock after more than a month at sea. I brushed down my skirts as I came off the ladder. It could also be the fresh rations or the fact that we were once again underway toward our next destination, Malta being only a brief stop to deliver correspondence.

I knocked on the great cabin door and entered at Mrs. Peyton's answer. She sat near the window, sketchbook open, which she had started doing more frequently the last several days.

"I finished mending the hem on this yellow gown, ma'am." I laid the gown I was carrying on the hanging cot.

"That is the white gown," she said, head cocked.

I glanced down. So it was. This gown needed a stain on the hem treated, and I hadn't seen to that yet. I'd snatched the wrong one on my way above. Gracious.

"Byam?"

I blinked. "Yes? Forgive me."

"I asked if you wished for me to treat the stain. I am not busy at the moment and do not mind the work, if you have other things to attend to."

"Oh." Did I have other things? Memories of the shadowy gun room and Elias's lulling voice had cleared all thought of duties from my mind.

"Are you well?" my employer asked. "Perhaps you should rest this afternoon."

"I am quite well, I assure you." More than well. It was just that my mind had been a muddle of wonderings all morning. Perhaps speaking with Mr. Doswell for a moment would clear my head. "I do have a question for Mr. Doswell. Might I be excused to find him?"

Brows knit, she nodded and motioned for me to go. I left the gown on the cot and hurried from the captain's quarters toward the opposite end of the ship, in the direction of the place I knew the chaplain liked to hold his classes.

The gun deck glowed with midmorning light coming through the larboard gunports, illuminating the scene of boys encircling Mr. Doswell near the galley. I'd passed this sight innumerable times since we'd set sail from Portsmouth, but today, it made my heart skip. How strange that one evening conversation surrounded by sleeping shipmates could cause such a reaction inside me.

I slowed myself and took on a pretense of mindless wandering as I approached the lesson. A boy asked a question, and Mr. Doswell removed his spectacles, twirling them back and forth between his fingers as he listened intently. When he answered, he spoke slowly, without any air of haughty authority. At a following question from the ship's boy, he dipped his head as though trying to hide a smile, but he failed miserably. A dimple creased his cheek as he fought a laugh.

Mercy. My heart melted like lacy frost at the touch of a spring sun. That dimple would be the undoing of me. The corners of my lips turned upward like his, but I was no better at hiding my grin than he.

The boys turned back to their slates, and Mr. Doswell raised his eyes to me. A glimmer of warmth touched them, the same one that had filled his eyes last night as he'd pulled me ever closer. I'd never wanted to give in to someone so badly, not that I had ever been the object of a man's affections before.

Affections? I gulped. The word rang strangely in my head. Was I seeing things I wanted to see, not what they really were?

He rose from his chair, tucking a reading primer under his arm and keeping his head ducked against the shortness of the gun deck. "Good morning, Miss Byam."

"I had a question for you, sir." Blast, what was it?

"I cannot promise a satisfactory response, but I will do my best to answer," he said.

I stood there stupidly gazing at him without saying a word. I couldn't remember the last time something or someone had made me so inarticulate. At least not something good.

A few of the carpenter's crew tromped down the fore ladder not far from us, loud and brash, as always. I looked away quickly, not wanting to catch Frank's eye if he was among them. I had no desire to run into him this morning.

"We fixed that orlop leak last week, but Captain wants us to check it again," one of the young men grumbled as they went.

The captain! I blinked, remembering. "Yes, I had a question about the captain." I lowered my voice. "One of a more delicate nature."

He took my elbow, sending a little thrill through my arm to my fingers, and guided me a few paces away from the gathering of boys between two of the big guns.

"What is it?"

I folded my hands. Surely, as Mrs. Peyton's lady's maid, I had a right to know her condition. Would the captain have confided in him? I couldn't be certain, but the only other man I could think of near Captain Peyton's level in Society was Lieutenant Roddam. I couldn't very well ask the lieutenant something like this.

"Does the captain ever speak to you of his wife's condition?" I asked, wringing my hands. Suddenly, this didn't seem like as good an idea as it had in my cabin.

"He mentions frequently how sorry he is that she is ill." He tilted his head questioningly.

"Does he mention, or perhaps hint at, another reason for her illness? Beyond seasickness, I mean?"

He frowned, shaking his head slowly. "Do you think it is more serious than seasickness?"

I took a deep breath. "In a way." Should I tell him? Mr. Doswell seemed the type who could keep a secret.

The worry on his face made me want to reach out and smooth his troubled brow. Perhaps sweep back the lock of ginger hair that had fallen across it.

"I think she is . . ." I paused, scanning the deck. What was I thinking? No place on this ship was truly private. Mrs. Peyton would have my neck if one of the crew heard me. The whole ship would know before the afternoon watch.

I grasped the little book peeking out between his side and coat sleeve, and he loosened his hold on it as I slid it out. The Child's New Spelling Primer. Mama had taught me to read from a copy of this. I flipped it open to the page filled with large capital letters and pointed to the B. He nodded. Then I tapped on the A, waiting for his nod. B again, and last Y.

He didn't move for a moment, and I feared he'd somehow missed it. I repeated the sequence, but he was focused on me. His brows shot up. "You think that is it?" he asked.

I nodded gravely.

"He hasn't mentioned a word of it to me."

"I think . . ." I balked. What if I was completely wrong? But how could I be? I'd observed the captain for nearly a week. He seemed the sort who would show an increase of tenderness if he knew his wife was carrying a child. While he was as loving a new husband as I'd met, I hadn't seen the sort of softness in speech and action I would expect. I closed the book and hugged it to me. "I do not think the captain knows."

Mr. Doswell's eyes narrowed in thought. "That's a serious thing to keep from her husband."

I stepped closer to him, as much to hide our conversation as to get a whiff of his cologne. "Would he have brought her on this voyage if he knew?"

He brushed his freshly shaved jaw with his knuckles. "I would think not." He dropped his hand to his side. I waited for him to ask me why I shared this with him. I didn't have a good answer, only that I couldn't stand not having someone to discuss it with. "I cannot say I am an expert on this subject," he said, "but having four sisters, three of whom have been in this situation several times, I must believe your guess has merit."

"And there are other things." What was I saying? I couldn't talk to him about not fitting into her stays or the lack of more soiled clothing than usual. It had been a month, after all. Most women would have had their time by now. I cleared my throat. "More personal things."

He nodded in understanding, not seeming embarrassed by my implication. Strange. Men usually hated talking about female issues. I supposed that having four sisters made him more comfortable with the subject.

"You cannot mention this to the captain," I said quickly. "If Mrs. Peyton caught wind that I knew and informed on her, she would probably have me flogged."

He chuckled. "She isn't a very vengeful person."

"But if she—"

A voice echoed across the gun deck. "Is Mr. Doswell neglecting his duties?"

I ground my teeth at the voice. Once, it had sounded so much like home. Now it only meant frustration.

Frank stood near the gathering of boys, arms folded. "A bit beneath a clergyman, wouldn't you think? How are these boys supposed to learn their letters when their teacher is off flirting with the laundry maid?"

Mr. Doswell flushed. I balled my hands into fists, fingernails digging into my palms. How dare he shout that where dozens of crew members could hear him.

"Mr. Doswell teaches us just fine," Michael Carden growled.

Frank crouched beside him, and I hurried over. This would lead nowhere good.

"If Mr. Doswell has taught you your letters so well, write the word *boatswain* for me."

Frank smirked as the boy formed shaky letters on the gray surface.

"Frank, that's hardly fair," I said. Sailing terms weren't spelled the same way seamen pronounced them.

He ignored me. "No, you're very wrong. It isn't *B-O-Z-U-N*. It's *B-O-A-T-S-W-A-I-N*."

The boy scowled at his slate. "But that's how it sounds."

"You see?" Frank rapped the boy on the shoulder. "Mr. Doswell did not even have the decency to teach you to spell useful words. Try *forecastle*."

Michael wiped the incorrect letters away with his sleeve and painstakingly attempted the next word.

"You don't have to do that, Michael," I said. "He isn't your teacher." The boy valiantly forged ahead, as though intent on proving Mr. Doswell was a good instructor.

Frank snickered. "*F-O-K-S-U-L*? What sort of spelling is that?"

Michael reddened, quickly smearing the letters with his hand.

"I have another," Frank said. "Spell *topgallant*."

I snatched Frank by the neckcloth and yanked. He staggered to his feet, chuckling. "Those aren't the sort of words you teach to a beginner, Walcott," I snapped. "Leave him alone."

"So, it's Walcott now, is it, Miss May?" His eyes took on a steely glint.

"These boys don't need your harassment," I said, releasing him and moving between him and Michael. "Their teacher doesn't either."

Frank rubbed his neck under the cloth. "You'd make a terrific wife of a *B-O-Z-U-N*."

I pressed my lips together, not deigning to give the jibe a response. I didn't care if he thought I was acting like Mrs. Hallyburton. I only wanted him to leave.

"But perhaps it's a *C-H-A-P-L-A-I-N* you have your sights on." Frank's voice turned frigid, accusatory.

"That isn't true!" Even I could hear the panic in my denial. And deep down, I knew he was more correct than I.

Frank leaned in, glaring. The wood dust on his shirt made my nose itch. "Enjoy your little country cottage, Mrs. Chaplain," he spat. He turned on his heel and shot down the ladder after the rest of the carpenter's crew.

I squeezed the book against my stomach, hands shaking. I glanced back at Mr. Doswell, whose look of praise should have filled me with sunbeams. It only brought gusts of confusion. I shouldn't regret losing Frank's friendship. There had been little respect on his side from the beginning. But a dark cloud inside me swallowed the energy I'd had to start the day.

I handed the primer back to Mr. Doswell. "I'll leave you to your work," I mumbled, not waiting to hear his response. A little night magic had made me think deep down in the hopeful pieces of my heart that Mr. Doswell could be a new adventure I hadn't expected. What had I been thinking? The way Frank had relegated me to a little country cottage made my skin crawl as though he'd spoken of the dungeons of Dover Castle. Did I want to be trapped in the country the rest of my life, shackled to the duties of a parson's wife? Finding my own work and taking to the seas had given me a taste of freedom I could not find in the country.

Frank's words were a warning against the coziness of dreaming about Mr. Doswell. I had to decide whether I would heed them or suffer the consequences.

Chapter 12

MAY

As though the sea had sensed my turmoil, not two days after my confrontation with Frank, a full-blown gale unleashed its wrath on the *Marianne*, and with it came the return of Mrs. Peyton's illness in force. By afternoon, the waves tossed us with such violence, I expected them to tear our hull to shreds.

Mrs. Peyton lay in her cot, hands covering her face. I attempted to comfort her, but the motion of the ship made it difficult to do much more than cling to the cot's ropes as the deck bucked and lunged.

"Can I fetch something for you, ma'am?" I called over the roar of the sea. In the dimness, I could barely see her shake her head. The deadlights covering the windows rattled in a gust of wind. The *Marianne* pitched, bow rising sharply. I tightened my grip on the ropes, yelping as my feet skidded out from under me. My stomach leaped to my throat.

The deck rolled back, allowing me a second to regain my footing and brace myself against the bulwark before the stern shot skyward. When we gained a moment of levelness, Mrs. Peyton groaned and threw her legs over the side of the cot. I helped her out, and she dashed for the privy. I sighed, rubbing my damp brow. If only there were some way I could help. She shouldn't have anything left in her belly by now, and still, she retched.

Shouts and the pounding of feet announced another half hour had passed. Cold air swept in under the door as seamen opened the hatches for the watch change. Water washed across the deck to a chorus of squelching from sodden shoes. I closed my eyes and leaned my forehead against the cot's ropes. A little cottage in the country sounded just fine to me right now. Adventure had a steep price. My limbs ached from all the bracing I'd done that day.

Mrs. Peyton opened the privy door just as we hit another swell. I reached out to help her back to her cot. Perhaps I should try to take her down to the orlop. She wouldn't appreciate the smell, but there was less motion below.

The *Marianne* slammed to the side, knocking me down. I hit the deck hard, elbows first, and pain flashed through my bones. I couldn't breathe. Seawater soaked my face and hair. My eyes smarted. After a moment, the pain subsided to a dull ache. When I could finally get air, I lifted my head. The great cabin had been cleared of anything not easily nailed or tied down, but something lay on the floor unmoving.

Mrs. Peyton.

I pushed myself up, the ache suddenly gone. "Ma'am!" I crawled toward her, hands slipping on the slick deck. "Ma'am, are you hurt?" I scrambled around to see her face, praying she hadn't been. Anyone else on this ship, but not her.

Her eyes were wide, the faintest light reflecting in them. She had her arms cradled around her abdomen. Even in the darkness, I could see the ashen hue to her skin.

Please, no. I grasped her arm. "Tell me. Is it the baby?"

She turned her face toward me and stared. Her brows pinched together. "I don't know." Her voice was nearly lost in the storm.

"Let's get you back to the cot." It was safer there than rolling about the deck. She clung to me, trembling, but before I could get us both to our feet, the ship rocked. We huddled together, bracing ourselves, until the deck leveled again.

Mrs. Peyton gasped for breath as we stood.

"Everything will be all right," I said as much to myself as to her. I tried not to think of the dangers of such a hard fall to a woman in her condition. "Let's get you safe, and I'll go for the captain."

"No!" She halted. "He can't know."

I wanted to ask her why she insisted on keeping it a secret from him, but I let it pass. "Étienne, then. We need *someone*."

She shook her head. "I just need to lie down. I'll be well in a moment."

I helped her back into the cot. She moaned with every movement. She needed a doctor, if for nothing else, to calm her fears. And mine.

"Does Étienne know?" I asked, returning to gripping the cot's ropes.

She stiffly rested her head on the pillow. "I haven't spoken of it with anyone. Except you now."

I'd spoken of it with Mr. Doswell, but I didn't mention that. I wiped my face with my sleeve, grit scraping my skin. What a burden to bear. I couldn't help her with these matters. Though he was a ship's surgeon and likely more familiar with grapeshot wounds than babies, I had to hope the Frenchman knew more than I.

"Promise me you won't tell him. If he knew, he'd leave me behind."

I wiped damp hair out of my eyes with the crook of my elbow. "You should tell him, ma'am. It isn't—" We hit another wave, and I fought for balance.

Mrs. Peyton gripped the side of her cot. "Promise me."

"I promise," I said reluctantly. I couldn't fault her not wanting to be left. I knew the feeling far too well.

The storm raged on, and I stood watch over Mrs. Peyton, who'd gone still as stone, holding her stomach. Once in a while, she would rub at her hip where she'd landed, but she always returned to the same position. Amid trying to keep upright, I mulled what to do. I didn't dare try to take her below now. She was hurt—I hoped with no more than bumps and bruises—and we only risked worse injury on the ladders. Her sickness seemed to have calmed, perhaps from the distraction brought on by pain.

I licked my lips, salt and grime filling my mouth. Here I'd thought my employer a delicate flower, not suited for the harshness of the sea. That wasn't right at all. She was stubborn as the ship's goat, unwilling to be left behind or to trouble anyone else. Even her hired maid. Perhaps it wasn't so difficult to imagine her playing the part of a ship's boy.

Her breaths came rapidly, and after a particularly violent pitch, she covered her face.

"Does it hurt?" I asked. Given the intensity of my own soreness, I could only imagine hers. She shook her head, but I didn't believe her. Her breathing didn't slow. "You'll worry yourself sick. I'm getting Étienne."

I launched myself toward the door, not waiting for an answer and not hearing one. I practically slid down the ladder, it was so wet. Curse the slippers I'd decided to wear that day. They found no grip on the rungs. My knees would be as bruised as my elbows from banging into the wood with each slip down the ladder.

At the bottom, I bolted for the gun room. "Étienne!" Someone sat slumped against one of the cabin doors in an oilskin cloak, not raising his head at my shout. Too tall to be the Frenchman. The table had been stowed below, so I dashed uninhibited toward Étienne's cabin. "Étienne!"

I grabbed hold of the bars across his cabin window, peering into the darkness. Something swayed. His cot, but it looked empty. Devil take it. Where was he? He must have gone to the orlop. Without light, it would be near impossible to maneuver. I pounded my head against the bars. What did I do now?

"Miss Byam?"

I turned. Mr. Doswell stood at the door of his cabin. When the deck steadied, I ran across the room to him. "I need to find the doctor."

He seized my arm. "Are you hurt?"

"It's Mrs. Peyton. She had a fall."

His grip tightened. "Étienne is above."

"Above? What is an idler doing above?" I put my hand over his, needing the strength of his touch.

"He has as much sailing experience as many of the men. He's helping the captain."

But he needed to be below. I pulled away, heading back toward the ladder.

"Where are you going?" Mr. Doswell cried.

Midshipmen shouted. Men stumbled up to the gun deck. Nearly time for another watch change.

"I need to find him," I said, darting into the mass of seamen.

"Miss Byam, wait!"

I made it up the ladder, and moments later, the hatchway opened, releasing a deluge of seawater on me and the crew. Wind howled across the opening. Weary bodies jostled. No one stopped me as we mounted the ladder.

When I emerged onto the upper deck, the rush of the storm took my breath away. I stumbled toward one of the masts, momentarily forgetting which direction was fore and which was aft. I caught the nearest line for balance and wiped at my eyes. Though brighter up here, the rain drilled into my face, making it even harder to see. Waves raced across the deck. White spray erupted on all sides.

How was I to find the surgeon in all this? I could barely make out individual forms, let alone faces. I shielded my eyes. The bow broke through a waterfall of ocean several yards away. That meant I stood at the mizzenmast toward the stern. I inched around the mast, stepping over lines and cables while trying to keep hold on something that would prevent me getting washed out to sea. Officers in oilskins stood around the helm. Was Étienne among them?

My coat went from damp to drenched in a matter of moments. Water dripped from my hair down the back of my neck. I clenched my teeth against a gust of wind.

I spotted the tallest of the officers. Captain Peyton, for sure. He lowered his head to listen to a shorter man beside him. Long, dark hair poked out from under his brimmed hat. My heart leaped. Étienne! The captain nodded, turning to the helmsman and shouting something in his ear. I doubted I would be able to get Étienne without drawing the attention of Captain Peyton, but I didn't care. I had to get him below as fast as I could.

"Hold fast!" someone bellowed behind me.

I glanced around. A wall of water bowled into me, breaking my grip on the line, stinging my eyes, cutting off my air. The world spun, frigid and gray. I couldn't find the deck.

A hand snatched my wrist as the water tore at my body—both above and below me—sucking me toward its icy depths. Wood cracked, deep and sickening, in the distance. I couldn't tell where it came from in the enveloping wave. The hand keeping me from being washed away pulled me down until I rested on the deck. The water still covered me, and my lungs began to burn.

Something clamped around my ankle, nearly breaking the grasp of my rescuer. I clawed at his arm as I kicked against the thing shackling my foot and threatening to lose me in the ocean. A rope? A sail? It stayed firmly around my ankle. I wasn't going to make it. This thing would drag me down. I whimpered, bubbles flying out around my face. The thing readjusted its grip. A hand. A person had grabbed hold of me. I instantly stopped kicking. I was his one hope as much as the other man was mine.

My face cleared the surface, and I gasped. The water in my eyes didn't let me see my rescuer well, but I clung to him with both hands and all of my might. I tried to clear my eyes by wiping them on the shoulder of my coat. Mr. Doswell filled my blurry vision, hair dark and plastered to his face. Of course it was him. I sobbed as I turned to see who had caught my ankle.

"Another!" Mr. Doswell shouted. The man holding on to my foot lifted his head. It was Frank. I barely caught my breath before the next wave enclosed us. The force twisted me around, wrenching at my grip on Mr. Doswell. Frank's hands cinched around my leg, so tight I thought he would rip it off. We skimmed across the deck. My face scraped against the wood. The pain in my leg intensified until it took over all my mind.

Please. Let it stop. I dug my fingers into Mr. Doswell's sleeve, screaming silently. *Please!*

Suddenly, the pressure released. Cold wind and rain whipped at my face as the sea raced by, receding. My body shook. I couldn't feel Mr. Doswell's hand anymore, but my arms were still fixed above my head. Masts and yards rose above me, their rigging leaping to and fro in a strange dance.

A voice, seeming far away in the din, shouted, "Man overboard!"

I sat up. Frank. Where was Frank? I stared dumbly at my feet. One of my shoes was gone.

Arms encircled me as I lunged toward the rail, broken and jagged with a chunk missing. I struggled, trying to get free. In moments, men blocked my view, searching the brutal waves.

"It's Frank," I choked, my efforts to get to him weakening by the moment. "Frank!"

"You can't help him," Mr. Doswell said into my ear. "Let them try. They know what they're about."

"Frank," I whispered, covering my mouth. It couldn't have been him.

A tall figure strode to the seamen gathered at the rail. "Ready lines. Do you see him?" He pulled a man out of the way to get a better view.

"Not yet, Captain."

Mr. Doswell eased me back as the men scurried about despite the tossing deck. Another man came over to us and grabbed the chaplain's shoulder.

"Miss Byam—why is she here?" It was Étienne.

"Something is wrong with Mrs. Peyton," Mr. Doswell answered for me as I continued to stare toward the rail where Frank had disappeared. They'd find him. They had to. Captain Peyton wouldn't let one of his men drown. "She came to find you."

"Let's get her below."

I gripped Mr. Doswell's coat. "No. Frank."

"You have no experience, mademoiselle," Étienne said firmly. "You will only endanger yourself up here."

I let them lead me toward the hatchway, but I kept my head craned toward the group of men at the port rail. My mind numbed. The water couldn't have taken him far. Perhaps he'd managed to hold on to the boat. They'd pull him over the side, he'd cough and sputter and make an idiotic joke. Then he'd flash me a smirk. The sea couldn't conquer Frank Walcott. *Did you worry about me, Miss May?*

I can see it on your face. You did. Never fear. I can take care of myself better than your Mr. Chaplain.

His words in my head quieted as we descended below. Softer and softer until they snuffed out like a candle on a midnight breeze.

ELIAS

I swallowed, glancing around at the still gathering before me. Seamen stared at the deck, officers stood at attention, all hats were solemnly in hand. Sails snapped above in the lingering remnants of yesterday's wind. Lines sat limp and sodden on the deck amid splinters from cracked wood. And the hole in the port side rail gaped, its spiny fingers emphasizing the emptiness.

I dropped my gaze back to my worn copy of The Book of Common Prayer and continued with a wooden voice, "'We therefore commit his body to the deep . . .'" Fear snaked around my heart, and the images of yesterday made it difficult to read the text. The wave overpowering us. Miss Byam getting swept from her feet and lost in the foam. My wild grab. The miracle of catching her.

"'To be turned into corruption, looking for the resurrection of the body—when the sea shall give up her dead—and the life of the world to come.'" I'd come so close to being forced to state Margaret Byam alongside the name of Frederick Walcott in this morning's service. I couldn't think on that possibility too much without the notion paralyzing me.

I tried to avoid looking at her, but my eyes kept returning to her corner of the deck as I finished the reading. She stood with fists pressed to her face as though trying to hold in a torrent as fierce as what we faced yesterday. Mrs. Peyton put an arm around her. Both women looked pale and haggard, their gowns dirty and rumpled. None of the crew had changed since before the storm.

No one moved when I finished, except one of the carpenter's crew, who brought forward a scrap of wood in which they'd carved "Frank." He paused beside the hole in the bulwark, then solemnly tipped the wood into the sea.

Walcott had been liked by many and avoided by many, but every eye was touched with red this morning, and every face was taut with sorrow. Even Mrs. Hallyburton lowered her head. Harvey kept wiping at his nose with his sleeve.

"Let this be a reminder to us all," Captain Peyton said, stepping up beside me, "that each day is a gift. We mustn't waste it."

I nodded my agreement. Miss Byam covered her face with her hands, and Mrs. Peyton hugged her tightly. How close I'd come to losing opportunities for nighttime conversations with Miss Byam. My stomach twisted at the thought of never again seeing the fiery flash in her eye when she was indignant or the soft smile when she felt safe enough to let down her walls.

So, what will you do with it? All this pent-up fear over things that didn't happen.

What *would* I do with it? How would I make the most of the time I had, as the captain had implored us? The only thing I wished to do just now was enfold her in my arms and banish this sick terror of nearly losing her to the deep.

So, you finally admit it. You fool.

Captain Peyton dismissed the men to begin wash and repairs, then turned to me. "Thank you, Doswell. That was respectfully done."

I shrugged, closing my book. "I simply read what I was supposed to." My pulse had taken up a rapid gait as realization dawned in my heart. I'd done it again. I'd let myself stumble down a path I'd sworn never to follow. So many times I'd offered my heart only to have it thrown back at me in tatters by ladies of good breeding and style. It had been done with pity, with disregard, with regret for a plethora of reasons. I still hadn't learned.

Captain Peyton replaced his cocked hat, surveying his men at their work. "But you do it with an air of sincerity that I've rarely observed in a clergyman."

Why do something if I couldn't do it sincerely? In my duties or my friendships. Or love. I licked my lips. "Thank you, Captain." I couldn't keep wandering this frigate, ignoring the truth before me and pretending these feelings hadn't taken root. I couldn't keep lying to myself that I didn't want to try again. With her.

Just as my hope soared, I dampened it quickly. She was grieving. I would need to give her time. Though her opinion of Mr. Walcott seemed complex, especially given how harshly she'd told him off when he'd teased my students a few days ago, she clearly esteemed him. Was it evil of me to wish she esteemed him only as an unaffected friend?

"How is your wife, sir?" I asked, snapping myself out of my pondering. Had he seen the maelstrom of emotions swirling across my face?

"Well enough, thank you." A hint of concern colored his voice. "She is a little stiff from yesterday's fall but, otherwise, fit as usual." He stroked his chin. "Though I am, of course, grateful for Miss Byam's dedication to Georgana, I cannot understand why she would risk her life over a few bruises. Georgana is not a fragile woman."

I tried my hardest not to wince. He most definitely did not know about her condition. The fact that I knew and he didn't made my skin crawl. Surely she couldn't keep it a secret from him much longer. "It is easy to act brashly in the anxiety of a storm."

"That it is." He clapped me on the shoulder, face still solemn. "You seem to be coming around since the battle. I'm glad of it."

My face heated. It was all because of her. Having someone to listen, to comfort, to care for made the storms of life easier to bear. She was the anchor I'd desperately needed without knowing it. As I watched her fight to stand in the shadow of her mountain of anguish, I knew I wanted to be that anchor for her as well. I only needed to figure out how.

"I apologize that it took me so long to sort out," I said.

But the captain shook his head. "Never apologize for that, my friend. We've all been there at some moment or other."

He patted my shoulder again and left to see to his duties. Silence hung heavy about the deck, all commands muted and conversation gone. Miss Byam stood alone at the port rail, clasping it beside its broken edge as Mrs. Peyton made her way to her husband with ginger movements. I whispered another prayer that her injuries weren't serious. Then I took a deep breath and walked to Miss Byam's side.

She'd locked herself in her cabin yesterday when word had spread that Mr. Walcott couldn't be recovered. I hadn't seen her until she'd come above for the service. She hadn't made a sound the whole night. I'd lain awake most of it listening.

"Miss Byam?" I asked. Though I kept my voice quiet, it seemed to ring across the deck.

She stood rigid, staring out into the gray-blue expanse as if perhaps she might succeed in finding him where the crew had not. Her knuckles were white, her face flushed, her eyes glossy. No cap or bonnet held back her hair, and it freely whipped across her face in the breeze, long and uncurled.

"I would rather be alone just now," she said with a raw voice. She didn't look at me.

My throat tightened, but I nodded. I could not force her to accept my sympathy. Nor did I know just what was going through her mind, despite my myriad guesses: guilt, sorrow, regret, so many more. Conflicting feelings all at once. Perhaps with time, she would let me in. Patience was the only path.

I reached out and took her arm, my hand barely touching her. A wave of longing to hold her burst through me, but I kept it at bay. It wasn't the time. I had to forebear, and I would as long as she needed me to.

I released her and retreated, my selfish heart hoping she wouldn't need me to keep my distance for too long.

Chapter 13

MAY

My brain hadn't stilled in days. I could feel it—the crazed energy twitching through every limb. Wanting to collapse but not having the ability. Words didn't make sense, whether I spoke them or someone else did. My lungs couldn't draw in enough air, even standing stationary as I was in the middle of my cabin. It was like the emptiness inside me the day they'd dragged Papa away without warning. The darkness of the lower deck, punctuated only by dim light coming through the canvas over my window, seemed to swallow me whole. The crashing of vicious waves roared in my ears despite the calm. Everywhere I looked, I saw Frank's pale face just moments before the sea had taken him.

I held my brush limply in my fingers, but my hair had become such a rat's nest after the storm that I'd quickly given up trying to get the pins out. If not for Mr. Doswell's grip, I might not have had to worry about my stupid hair. The thought should have chilled me, but my heart had reached its limit.

The *Marianne* tilted, and the brush flew from my hand and clattered to the deck. My legs wobbled as though uncertain if they wanted to give way or hold me up against the motion. I stared at the brush's outline. My mother would suggest tending to my hair, for it would only get worse the longer I waited. I usually followed the advice. Looking presentable was part of my job, after all. How unimportant it seemed now. Why did it matter what I looked like when Frank was lying at the bottom of the ocean, never to see the docks of Portsmouth again?

My vision blurred. I'd never hear that familiar Pompey accent teasing me again. Frank had sounded like home. The distance seemed impossibly far now. Why had I agreed to this journey? I should have stayed safely in England, even if it had meant a position as a scullery maid.

A knock on my door filtered through the haze of my mind. I didn't move.

"Are you well?" Though it wasn't a Portsmouth voice, somehow, its softness yanked the tears from my eyes. I covered my face, trying to hold them back, but a sob managed to escape.

The door opened, and footsteps crossed the room. Arms encircled me and with them, the scent of jasmine and tea and ginger. I buried my face in the delicate linen of his cravat as my body shook. Mr. Doswell held me tightly, as securely as when he'd grabbed hold of me against the force of the waves. He wouldn't let go, and I didn't want him to. I sank into his warmth, willing it to take away the ice inside me.

"He was there," I said as I wept. "And then he was gone." My words wavered almost to incoherence. My leg throbbed as though being torn away from Frank's grasp all over again.

Mr. Doswell rested his head protectively against mine. "I know."

"I should've . . ." What more could I have done? Something. Tears seared my face before getting lost in his cravat. I gasped for air, the emptiness of Frank's loss pressing so heavily against my chest.

Mr. Doswell pulled me closer, and I slumped against him, knees buckling. I gripped his waistcoat as the sea of grief threatened to drag me under. He alone anchored me through the deluge.

"He's gone," I whimpered. Ripped away in the blink of an eye, just like Charlie and Uncle Byam. Never to be seen or heard again by those who cared.

Mr. Doswell didn't speak as I blathered, the anguish flowing out in words even I couldn't understand. He stroked my matted hair and didn't hush me. Nor did he tell me it was God's will that Frank should die. We swayed in the darkness, either from the ship's motion or from him rocking me, I could not tell.

My sobbing finally quieted to uncontrollable sniffling as he held me. My head ached, and my eyes burned. I burrowed my face against his neck, my mind too drained to think better of it. The ground had been swept out from under me, and I wanted only the safety that seeped into me from the strength of his arms. How could I feel such despair and yet such solace all at once? If only I could stay here in his embrace instead of facing the morning and the realities it would bring. The duties I'd have to drag myself through in the midst of missing Frank. I'd have to face them, whether I wished to or not.

I pulled my head back and released his waistcoat. His arms held for a moment, then reluctantly let me go.

"I'm sorry," I said, wiping at my eyes.

"You needn't be." Sadness nearly as sharp as my own creased his face. His eyes glimmered with unshed tears in the faint light. Why was he sorrowing over Frank's death? Frank had mistreated him— practically to the point of insubordination—the entire voyage.

Mr. Doswell cleared his throat as though he could read the questions on my face and reached down to retrieve my brush from the floor. He gently set it in my hands.

I gave a mirthless laugh. "I don't think I have the fortitude to untangle this shambles tonight." I tugged on my knotted hair with a sigh. "I'll have to see to it in the morning." At which point, I would curse myself for not taking care of it before bed. What a sight I must look with my eyes red, clothes rumpled, and hair a disaster. I smoothed my apron, for what good it would do. Mr. Doswell, of course, looked as polished as ever.

He swallowed, then tentatively held out his hand. "May I?"

I froze, gripping the brush. He would do that for me? My heart launched into a funny pattering. No one had helped me with my hair since Agnes left. We hadn't had money for hairdressers since Papa's conviction, and I'd been too young before that to ask for my parents to pay one of the well-dressed men to cut and style my hair. I couldn't let Mr. Doswell handle this knot.

I handed him the brush, uncertain why I did, and turned my back to him. It wasn't odd for a man to fix a woman's hair. It happened in every city across Britain. But they weren't usually handsome young gentlemen with hearts of gold doing it in private cabins in the dark.

He softly pulled at a pin, wiggling it back and forth until it slid free. "I'm sorry about Mr. Walcott," he said. "Losing a friend leaves a hole in your heart that is impossible to fill."

I nearly didn't hear him, I was so focused on the feel of his hands working through my hair. "Thank you," I managed.

He slid out another pin and then another without tearing or catching my hair. Clearly, he had done this before. His feather-light touch sent tingles across my skin.

My hair fell down my back with an ungraceful plop. He offered me the pins, and I snatched them. Perhaps I should take over from here. That was the sensible and proper thing to do. But I kept my lips shut as he gathered my hair in his hand and began brushing the ends. He moved slowly up the length of my hair, never forcing his way through a snarl, taking more care than I ever did. My eyelids drooped as his strokes with the brush lengthened. The sleepiness came from the exhaustion of crying, not his soothing touch, I was certain.

"If you decided to retire from the clergy, you could make a good living as a hairdresser," I said. The brush reached my scalp, gliding across as gentle as a morning breeze.

He chuckled. "With four older sisters and a brother at sea since before I was born, I had a healthy dose of lessons in arranging hair."

That made sense. I let my eyes fall closed, a part of me wishing he'd never stop. My arms hung limp at my sides. I could have fallen asleep on my feet. The harsh world around us, with its death and pain, dissolved into this moment. I clung to it, this dark peace full of quiet and comfort. Full of him.

His fingers traced up the nape of my neck. A spark flashed through my veins, and my eyes flew open. He methodically divided my hair into sections to plait as though he hadn't just caused my whole body to wake.

"I suppose you could get any sailor aboard to do this just as well," he said. "The men with long hair help each other plait their queues."

I didn't want any other man on this ship doing this to my hair. I bit my lips, which suddenly felt dry. I was enjoying this far too much, and I didn't like what the appreciation implied. Was it so terrible to take a liking to a clergyman more humble than most of his station? Frank's taunting voice echoed in my head that there was.

The thought of Frank reopened the wound inside me. I'd forgotten it for a few blissful minutes.

"Do you have a ribbon?" Mr. Doswell asked. Why was his voice a balm to my soul?

"Yes." I took the end of my hair from him and hurried to my trunk. I fumbled around for anything that could tie it off. My fingers finally found a ribbon in the corner, and I hastily knotted it around my hair. "Thank you, sir. That was very kind of you." Never mind that he'd cast some sort of spell over me in the act.

He retreated a step. Did he sense my distress? "Is there any other way I can be of service?"

I shook my head, unsure if he could see it in the dark. Always thinking of others. Someone like me did not deserve someone like him. Kind, gentle, respectful of everyone, no matter their station. I was brash and stubborn and so far beneath him. The spark that had burst to life under his touch fizzled. "No. You've done so much already."

He hesitated at the door. "If you need someone to talk to about him, I am here. Grief is a hard road to walk alone."

I knew that. Even with my mother and aunt beside me, I'd had to find my way along that path by myself. Mama had had to help Aunt Byam through her grief and hadn't had the capacity to support me as well. I didn't resent it. Aunt Byam had needed more care than I had, with it being the deaths of her own husband and son. But it hadn't been easy. Mr. Doswell knew what it was like as well as I did.

"I will try to find your cabin if the need arises," I said.

His lips curled. "It is a little difficult to locate."

With mounting dread, I realized how much I did not want him to leave. Even if we would be separated by only a flimsy wooden partition.

"Promise you will tell me if you need me?" he asked.

"Promise."

He nodded once and bid me good night, leaving me alone for the chill to creep back in. I removed my boots, my shoes now unusable after losing one in the storm. Frank had most likely ripped it off when the wave had taken him. My throat swelled as I climbed into my hammock and pulled the blanket over my head. Life was cruel, taking away young men as lively and engaging as Frank and putting others on a pedestal too high to reach, such as Mr. Doswell.

Tears fell afresh. How were there more? I squeezed my eyes shut, trying to keep them in, and buried my face in my pillow. I breathed shallowly to keep the sound of my crying from carrying, in case Mr. Doswell was listening.

My body wanted nothing more than to sleep, but my mind had taken up its whirling again. The nape of my neck tingled where he'd touched me, a welcome whisper through the ache inside. I wouldn't sleep at all tonight.

Curse Frank and all this sorrow. Curse Mr. Doswell and all his goodness. And curse these tears over them both.

ELIAS

I'd hoped throwing myself into God's work would rid my mind of the previous night's encounter with Miss Byam. Unfortunately, the words to my sermon came slowly. As I paced my cabin, attempting to find thoughts of comfort to share with the men on Sunday, I listened for any sound coming through the wall. I didn't want to force my presence on Miss Byam, but the more I thought on our moments together, the more I wanted to charge over to her cabin.

Bumbling fool.

She needed space to grieve her friend. Space that didn't involve me, given the nature of my acquaintance with Mr. Walcott. The man had been many things I didn't like, but he deserved a period of mourning as much as any human. He'd meant something to her despite her frustrations with him. As much as I meant to her? More?

I knelt and straightened the rug, which had skewed. Comparing aided no one, but I couldn't help it. I ran a hand through my hair, which felt a little more windswept than I typically liked it. Too much fussing with it today. I'd probably brushed it back a hundred times. Whenever I thought on Miss Byam.

The memories wouldn't leave me be. I pushed myself to standing with a sigh. My arms couldn't forget the feel of her, how she'd clung to me, shaking. Her soft hair splayed across my hands. Most poignant of all was the sense of her near me, a mesmerizing fire that could not be contained by the darkness. I sought it everywhere I went on this ship. I wandered toward the wall, a moth to candlelight, and nearly leaned my head against it but halted.

"Sermon. Focus, Elias," I muttered, turning my back to the partition separating me from Miss Byam. I retrieved my Bible from the lid of my sea chest and flipped to 1 Thessalonians. *Wherefore comfort yourselves together, and edify one another, even as also ye do.* I nodded. That would do nicely, reminding the men to comfort each other in their trials. I slipped a pencil out from behind my ear and crouched by my sea chest to make note in my journal, awkwardly holding the book open with one arm while still keeping my place in the Bible. "Now, to weave this into the introduction."

"You talk to yourself while writing your sermons."

I startled at her voice, dropping my pencil. It skittered across the deck and caught on the rug. "Miss Byam?" She sounded as though she were in the room with me, not speaking through a wall. No shadow darkened the door's window. Her voice hadn't seemed to come from the gun room anyway. What sort of mischief was this? The longings of a heartsick mind? I glanced toward my tea box. Had I added something stronger than usual to my evening tea by accident? It hadn't tasted any different.

A muffled giggle from her cabin trickled through the partition. I took my lantern off its hook and moved toward the back of the cabin in the direction of the sound.

"There's a crack in the wall," she said.

After a moment, I found a sapphire eye peeking through the wood a few feet off the deck. She flinched at the light, and her eye disappeared. So, that was why she'd sounded like she was in the room. I rubbed the back of my neck, face heating as I pulled the lantern back a little. "When did that happen?"

Her eye appeared again. "I found it at the start of the voyage."

My skin crawled at the idea that I'd been mistaken in having privacy all this time. "And it's never been changed out when they've put the partitions back up?"

"I've found it every day."

Gracious, what had she seen? Me making a fool of myself, pulling faces and conversing alone? I adjusted my grip on the lantern, not wanting to think of other possibilities.

"Not to worry," she said almost too quickly, "I've . . . I've never peeked."

Except for tonight? I forced a smile. "The carpenter's crew could have fixed it."

She leaned away, the crack darkening. The partition's boards creaked as though she leaned against them.

I internally kicked myself. Carpenter's crew. Walcott's comrades. I dropped to the deck beside the hole. "Forgive me. I misspoke."

"There's no need to apologize." She paused. "They brought me one of his neckcloths today while they were preparing his belongings to be auctioned. I don't know why they did that."

I swallowed. Sometimes a memento or two were saved for dear friends or sweethearts. The rest of a dead sailor's belongings were auctioned off to crew mates and the money collected for the deceased's family. Walcott's friends would have known what she'd meant to him. "That was very kind of them," was all I could think of to say.

"It wasn't as though Frank had feelings for me."

I very seriously doubted that. My chest tightened. I'd seen the way he'd looked at her when she'd walked by. It had started as the same distasteful gaze he'd bestowed on Miriam but had heightened as the weeks had passed. I chewed on my lower lip. No, I wouldn't think so ill of the dead. Walcott must have appreciated Miss Byam for more than her looks. I had no proof that he didn't.

"I was a terrible friend," she said, voice pinched.

"Of course you weren't." She'd had the patience of Job with that man.

"You heard how I scolded him. That was the last conversation we ever had." Her voice wobbled. "I can't apologize to him now."

Without thinking, I leaned against the partition, just like she was. "Death rarely lets us wrap up our lives in pretty bows. You mustn't hold it against yourself." Never mind Walcott had deserved every second of her scolding.

She sniffed. "I was so angry at him. I shouldn't have let myself get furious." Was she crying? How I wished this wall were gone.

I traced the grain of one of the boards with a finger. "Don't let your regret withhold you from appreciating the time he was in your life." I opened my mouth to expound, but images of the past overwhelmed me. My mind flipped through moments with Miss Somer and all the others I'd given my heart to. Happy moments, painful moments, moments of hard lessons learned and reluctant growth. I'd let them all sour, drowning myself in the bitterness of things I'd wanted but could never have. It didn't have to be that way. Perhaps each broken heart I'd suffered had progressed me toward a happiness I couldn't imagine. With someone I hadn't foreseen. I slid my finger closer to the break in the wood.

"I feel like they dropped an anchor on my chest," she said, voice unsteady, as though speaking through tears. "I'll never be able to lift it."

I nodded, even though she couldn't see me. It would feel like that for a time as we all rebuilt our lives around the vacancy our missing shipmate left. For those who truly loved Mr. Walcott, the sensation would never fully go away. They'd learn to carry it. But I didn't tell her that now. "You do not need to lift it by yourself. I'll help you." Somehow, my tender thoughts toward her had infused themselves into my words, raw and unmistakable. If only I could see her face to know how she took them.

After a short silence, she said, "I'm glad you're here."

I swallowed, heart leaping. Whether from terror at starting this journey again or excitement at the trust lacing her words, I did not know. The one thing I did know—I would be here. For as long as she needed me.

Chapter 14

MAY

I trudged up to the forecastle, my feet heavy as lead. Though my mind would not still to allow me more sleep, my body regretted the two-hour rest deficit. Malta's harbor, where we'd returned for repairs, lay blanketed with purple light that peeked through the masts and shrouds of dozens of ships bobbing drowsily on the waves.

A figure stood at the starboard rail near the bow, the breaking sunrise catching his brilliant hair. The corners of my lips turned upward despite the heavy fog in my brain. I hesitated. He valued his time alone. Perhaps he wouldn't wish me to intrude. I'd already intruded last night.

The memory of his voice, warm as a newly poured cup of ginger tea, washed over me. He wouldn't refuse my company.

"Mr. Doswell."

He turned, eyes soft and eager in a way that made my toes curl. I bobbed a curtsy.

"Miss Byam," he said with a deep bow. Performed by any other man, it would have seemed awkward or mocking, but his sincerity made the gesture infinitely pleasing. "How do you feel this morning?"

I sighed, stepping to the rail beside him. "Awful."

"I'm sorry to hear it."

I couldn't look at him. At his gaze, my insides threatened to melt. He cared for me. That much was clear. Quarrelsome, stubborn, unfashionable me. It made little sense.

"Have you been up for long?" he asked.

Long enough that I'd heard him dressing for the day and leaving his cabin. And long enough to think so long on Frank that my thoughts had launched into a downward spiral that had left me fighting off tears. My weary eyes stung again, and I rubbed them roughly. "A couple of hours."

"It's difficult, isn't it?"

I let out a sharp breath and dropped my hands. "It shouldn't be." My musings had taken a very different turn this morning from where they'd been last night, and the frustrating confusion had finally pulled me from my hammock.

Mr. Doswell put a hand on my elbow, that comforting gesture I'd come to enjoy too much. "He was a good friend."

I shook my head. "But he *wasn't* a good friend. He hardly respected me or anyone else." Not the officers, not Mr. Doswell, not even the captain. "I cannot understand why I'm mourning like this." I'd spent the dark hours before dawn recalling how often he'd teased me when I'd asked him to stop or how he'd made suggestive jokes despite my continued discouragement. He'd been a flirt and a flatterer, and I'd fallen for his charms. Our acquaintance hadn't gone any deeper than that.

"He accepted you when no one else did," Mr. Doswell said quietly, regret in his voice.

I tilted my head and gave him an exasperated frown. He was, of course, talking about our first meeting. "That was a misunderstanding."

He shrugged, blushing. Why did his discomfort make me want to throw my arms around him and squeeze him tightly? I'd never had the desire to do that to someone not my kin before.

I brushed at my front curls, now a wavy jumble from lack of styling. I'd thought him a pompous dandy intent on judging me when we'd first met. A laugh bubbled up as I remembered his panicked expression when he had realized I wasn't a trollop. "I was so angry with you."

He ducked his head.

I turned to face him, leaning one elbow on the rail. "Little did I know you'd prove the greater friend." I pulled a little packet from my apron pocket and held it up, a whiff of peaches tingling my nose. I'd found it late last night while preparing for bed. All this time, I'd thought Frank had sneaked the dried peaches into my cabin. Of course it had been thoughtful Mr. Doswell. "These are from you, are they not?"

He didn't meet my eyes. "I was trying to make some sort of small reparation. And then I found some more when I went ashore yesterday and thought perhaps they'd bring a little light to your day."

My throat tightened until I couldn't speak to explain how much these meant—at the start of our journey and now. So I opened the packet and slipped out a piece, then offered one to him. He hesitated before accepting it.

The fruit's sweetness filled my senses as I bit into it, hoping the distraction would keep me from crying again. I watched him eat. The light had intensified, growing rosy as the sun awoke, and now brightened his features. Joy sparkled in his eyes as he chewed. I couldn't help tracing the line of his jaw with my gaze. How did someone like me catch the notice of a gentleman like him? I was hardly worthy of it and not simply because he came from the gentry and I from trade. What did he see in me that made him want to dry every tear?

He swallowed, and I lost myself in the gentle folds of his cravat that moved with his throat, remembering its smoothness against my face as I'd wept.

"Most everyone deserves to be mourned," he said. "We are none of us perfect. He was your friend, even if he had his flaws."

I pursed my lips. Mr. Doswell was right. It was so easy to think of Frank as all good or all bad. He was neither. I pulled my attention from Mr. Doswell's cravat. "As I've considered it, I think he wanted there to be something more between us." I looked up, waiting for Mr. Doswell's reaction.

He inclined his head. "To be fair to Mr. Walcott, who wouldn't?"

My pulse quickened, spreading heat through my body. I tucked the peaches back into my apron, uncertain where to look or what to think. I wasn't one of the dainty assembly room beauties the wealthy gawked at. I scolded carpenters' mates and shouted at boatswains' wives in threadbare gowns.

His hands wrapped around mine and held them between us. "I only wish for you to not berate yourself for mourning him," he said, voice humming in my ears and wrapping me in its tenderness. "He was taken suddenly in rather traumatic fashion. He was young, he was lively, and he made a place for you among the crew. We can acknowledge his faults while still grieving him and the ways he contributed to our lives. You aren't the only one affected by his death. Many among the crew have been affected." He would be the first to notice. I did not doubt it.

I gave an uncertain laugh. "But I am the only one who seems to not be capable of performing her usual tasks because of it." And here I stood at the break of another day of quietly tending to Mrs. Peyton's needs, lost in my sorrow while mingling with the captain, officers, marines, and seamen. Most of whom had practically already forgotten Frank. Yesterday, that realization had only sunk me lower into the waters of grief. I wanted to shake it, especially after this morning's musings, yet I couldn't.

"It simply shows the depth of your loyalty." He tentatively reached up and smoothed a lock of hair from my face. The tickle of his touch sent a thrill coursing through my veins. "You love so fiercely, even when you have been wronged. That is to be commended."

Papa. Lewis. Mama. Frank. I couldn't help but care, even in my anger.

"I'm tired of the hurt," I said, closing my eyes as he continued to play with my hair.

"Then, I'll try to . . ."

I opened my eyes as his voice trailed off. He cleared his throat, looking away quickly and releasing my hand. "Would you like to come ashore with me this morning?" he asked.

Yes, but even more, I wished to know what he'd been about to say. "If Mrs. Peyton does not mind, I would appreciate a few hours on land." I didn't have money to spend or duties to attend to, but it would be nice to have the ground under my feet for a short time. Perhaps I could convince him to finish his sentence.

"You should ask. I hope to leave after breakfast."

I nodded. "I will see if Mrs. Peyton is awake." I doubted it. She never rose early, though I couldn't blame her in her condition. A whole morning with Mr. Doswell. I stifled a grin.

I bid him what I hoped was a brief farewell and scurried down the hatchway. The ship suddenly felt impossibly cramped and dank. Just the promise of freedom to truly stretch and walk about made me giddy.

I hustled to the great cabin, nodding to the marine on duty, who nodded back his approval to pass. The door was ajar, and faint morning light touched the room. I halted at the sight of a figure in a chair in one corner. Mrs. Peyton? This was early for her to be out of the cot. A blue-clad figure knelt at her feet, his head in her lap.

The Peytons being young lovers again. I reached to pull the door shut to give them more privacy, but I halted. The captain's shoulders rose in harsh breaths. His wife ran her hand over his hair in the same soothing motion Mr. Doswell had fingered mine a moment ago. Her face creased with heartache as she murmured something to him. I held my breath, leaning in to hear.

"It wasn't your fault, love," she said. "You couldn't have saved him."

I retreated a step, raising my fist to my mouth. Frank's was the first death under his command. Under his collected facade, Captain Peyton was struggling as much as I was. I backed up farther until the scene of the Peytons huddled together disappeared behind the door's planks.

I'd been terribly wrong. About them. About Frank. About Mr. Doswell. The prejudices and impressions I'd once held to so tightly unraveled before my eyes. The deck felt unsteady beneath my feet as I trudged back toward the hatchway. How many times would I have to retract my own convictions? I hadn't let myself see these people for who they were.

Rung after rung, I descended toward the mess deck, the sun's encompassing light giving way to scattered lantern light broken by trenches of deep shadow. My narrow view of the past was marred by so many shadows, where the light of my understanding could not reach. Darkened by prejudice and grief, I hadn't cared to hold a light up to examine what might lay beyond the edges of my perception when I'd first boarded.

Mr. Doswell had made me reconsider. In the light of his goodness, I'd been forced to examine my first impression of him and had found someone tender and lovely and accepting. The longer I stood in his light, the more I realized the world was different from my limited understanding.

I stood at the bottom of the ladder, observing the deck as I gave the Peytons a little time alone. Sailors sat on sea chests, mending clothing and writing or dictating letters while they waited for their next watch. No one knew our captain was above, suffering for something that wasn't his fault. How many people had I forced to suffer or had wanted to suffer for something that wasn't their fault either? The Peytons, Mama, Elias . . .

I drifted toward my cabin. Elias. I had always thought of him as Mr. Doswell, as was right and proper, but the moment his Christian name popped into my head, I loved the feel of it. There was something warm and familiar about his name that fit this man who made me want to be so much better than I was. Dared I hope that someday I could be a woman deserving of a man such as he? I wanted so very much to try.

MAY

I brushed the sand-colored stone wall with my fingers as I walked along a gently curving street. The residents and visitors to Valletta, Malta's bustling port city, passed by, speaking loudly in a variety of languages. My head buzzed with all the sounds.

I glanced behind me. A young lieutenant had stopped Mr. Doswell, and I'd begged leave to walk ahead. The chaplain might not care about my standing, but I did not wish to make him have to bear the scrutiny of a potentially less-forgiving member of the gentry. If things progressed between us, we could decide how to manage that later.

A little smile crept to my mouth. I wouldn't mind taking a moment to think on the possibility of our relationship progressing. I'd walk to the little alleyway up ahead and then turn back around. That should give him plenty of time to speak with his acquaintance, and I didn't fancy getting lost in this unfamiliar place, fascinating as it was. With my head in the clouds, getting lost was too real a threat.

The Mediterranean sun warmed me through my makeshift bonnet as I wandered. Mr. Doswell had offered to replace it with a proper one when we'd passed a milliner's shop, but I wouldn't hear of it. I fingered the ribbon that trimmed the brim. It wouldn't pass for an elegant lady's bonnet. It was good, then, that I cared little for that and more for the sacrifice he'd put into making it over for me.

I paused at the alley and looked back at him speaking to the lieutenant. He'd offered to buy several things for me on this outing. I couldn't help but feel flattered, even if I'd refused each one. Though he had gone against my wishes only once in procuring a little lantern for my cabin and candles to fill it. This was a different sort of flattered than I felt with Frank. Frank's flattery had always bordered on ridiculous. Or scandalous. I could never tell if he were making me into a joke or if he truly meant what he said. With Mr. Doswell, it was almost as though he didn't know how to express his feelings in any other way than to give whatever he could—time, attention, gifts, praise. I fought against a grin as a little beam of the afternoon sun swelled inside me.

I cocked my head, suddenly wishing I hadn't gone so far and I could see his face more clearly. He glanced toward me with increasing frequency, as if he wished he could pull himself away from the conversation. Perhaps I could come to *his* aid. For once.

As I started back, a hand clamped around my arm and whipped me into the shadows of the alleyway. I screamed, but the man muffled it under grimy fingers and pushed me against the wall. Elias. I had to get to Elias. I blinked, unable to see in the sudden dimness, and tried to wrench out of my captor's grasp. Ice shot through my limbs. Elias wasn't far away. If I could just get his attention, he'd come. I tried to fill my lungs to scream again, drawing in the attacker's foul stench. I gagged.

"Don't scream, you ninny," he growled.

At the familiar voice, I froze. That Pompey accent. For a moment, images of Frank filled my mind. But the voice was too nasally to be Frank's.

The chuckle gave him away. He loosened his grip. With a snarl, I shoved his hand from my mouth, a mix of fury and elation welling inside. "Lewis, you idiot!" I wiped at my mouth with a sleeve. "You scared me half to death." And yet, there was something about the sight of him, the finding of a face I knew so well, in a city I knew very little, that made me want to grin.

"That's the greeting you give the brother you haven't seen in years?" Lewis spread his arms as though to embrace me.

"Yes, when you try to snatch me off the streets like a murderous fiend." I shied away. "When was the last time you bathed?" As my eyes adjusted, I took in his rumpled and dirty shirt, his lopsided neck cloth, his sock fallen around his ankle, and the ribbon wrapping his short queue coming undone. The navy prided itself on cleanliness, and Lewis was far from tidy. What was he doing in Valletta seemingly without an assignment?

"I bathed aboard the *Caligula*. Before they left me." He shrugged as though getting left behind by his commanding officers was a common occurrence.

"Lewis," I hissed, leaning closer. My nose instantly regretted it. "You . . . deserted?" He was a carpenter's mate. They wouldn't have just abandoned a skilled member of the crew, not in these days of scarcity.

"No more than you clearly deserted our mother." He didn't sound as furious as his words suggested.

I didn't react to his jab. I rubbed my brow, not sorry for my original greeting at all. Did he have an ounce of sense left in his brain?

Desertion could lead to a court-martial and death sentence at the worst. Flogging at the best.

"It really was not my fault I was too sick to crawl back to the *Caligula*," he said. "Stop giving me that look, May."

Too sick? Most likely from an overabundance of drinking. I didn't lift my eyebrows or untwist my mouth. He'd never held true to his promises to help support Mama. Why should I have expected him to honor his word in the navy?

"In any case, I am supposed to be in the Mediterranean," he said. "You, on the other hand, should be back in Old Pompey helping Mother."

I bristled. "Mama was forced to take a job at a manor in Fareham. We couldn't afford to stay in Portsmouth."

He didn't have the decency to put on a contrite expression, even under my glare.

"What about that widow lady who made you her companion?" Lewis wiped his hands on his loose trousers. "Did you come with her?"

"Mrs. Richardson died before I departed. I'm now employed by a captain's wife as her lady's maid."

"Huh. Waiting on someone hand and foot never seemed your type of work." Lewis smirked as if the thought were amusing.

I nearly defended myself and the Peytons, but I remembered similar conversations with Frank. They were trying to make me fight back. Engaging them in their games only made the situation worse.

"Who is your captain, then?" Lewis asked.

I straightened my posture. "Captain Peyton of the *Marianne*."

"Captain Dominic Peyton?" Lewis let out a low whistle. "How did you get all the luck?"

I hadn't considered myself lucky at the start of our voyage, but he was right. I had been greatly blessed, as Elias would say.

Elias. I swallowed. Using his Christian name, even in my thoughts, felt so intimate. Yet it suited him much more than Mr. Doswell. It was easier to imagine Mr. Doswell as a stuffy, self-important clergyman than Elias.

Lewis's eyes shifted. "May, you don't think Captain Peyton would let me sign on with the *Marianne*, do you?"

"If you deserted, heavens no." The calculating look in his eye made my stomach twist, and I guessed his thoughts before he said them.

"We wouldn't have to tell him I deserted."

I rested my hands on my hips. "I will not lie for you, Lewis." How dare he even ask. I wouldn't lie for anyone, let alone a brother who had practically ignored my mother and me since Papa had been sent to New Holland and then gotten himself into a terrible mess by his own stupidity.

"You wouldn't have to lie," he said quickly. "I'll do all the talking. Just don't rat me out for anything."

My hands went clammy despite the balminess of the day. I couldn't let him lie to Captain Peyton. To the crew. That was as bad as lying myself.

"Come now, May," he drawled, giving me a shamelessly pleading look to rival the best of begging dogs. "You wouldn't leave your own brother out in the cold." Never mind he was on a sunny Mediterranean island. "I've no funds. Nowhere to go." He grabbed my hands with his filthy ones. "Surely there's a space for someone with my talents. I'd even take work beneath my rank on the carpenter's crew."

I swallowed. There *was* a place for him. One the *Marianne* needed filled. "We don't have a carpenter's mate," I hesitantly admitted.

He squeezed my hands so hard my knuckles cracked painfully. "Then, you need me. You know I'm skilled at what I do. Don't deny it."

I couldn't. Lazy as he was, he did his work well when he put his mind to it. He would make a good replacement if he applied himself. "Mr. Jackson might have promoted one of his crew," I said. "I haven't heard."

Lewis released me and wagged a finger in my face. "But there is a place. Luck has smiled upon me again." He rested his hands on his hips as though he'd been offered his own command. "What happened to the previous mate? The poor bloke up and die? He didn't desert, did he?" He guffawed at his terrible joke.

I ground my teeth. Just this morning, I'd acknowledged my limited understanding of the people around me and resolved to open my heart. Frustrated though I was, even Lewis deserved a chance, didn't he? "The captain's aboard just now, if you'd like to seek his approval. I suppose I will see you aboard tonight if all goes well."

He seized me from behind in a crushing embrace like he always used to do before he went to sea. It might have been endearing if I weren't choking on his stench. "You're the best sister a sailor could ever ask for," he said, lifting me from my feet. His arms dug into my stomach. "That's what we Byams do. We look after our family."

Sometimes. This time I would try. Perhaps what Lewis needed was someone to reach out with kindness. I could be that person. "Let me go, you big oaf." I pushed against him, and he finally released me.

"I swear I'll make it up—"

I held up my hands. "Thank you is good enough for me." I might be trying to understand, but I couldn't bear one more empty promise.

"Miss Byam?" The worried voice washed through the alleyway like cool water in a desert. I practically ran toward the street. Elias caught me by the shoulders. "Are you well?" He squinted into the shadows at Lewis ambling toward us and took a step forward, partly blocking me.

I'd never seen him act so protectively. My heart swelled. He was braver than he wanted to believe.

I took his arm. "Not to worry," I said. "This is my brother, Lewis."

Lewis stepped into the afternoon sun. I winced. He looked worse in the light. The greasy hair that had fallen from his queue hung stringy and matted around his face. He had something in his teeth, and his once-white shirt matched the stone around us. I couldn't tell the color of the fabric's checked pattern.

Elias's brow rose as he glanced at me for certainty. I nodded. "I didn't know he was on Malta. He is . . ." What did I say? Of all the people in the world, I least wanted to lie to Elias about Lewis's desertion.

"I was discharged from HMS *Caligula* for illness, sir. Been looking for a position as carpenter's mate ever since." Lewis extended his hand, and it was all I could do not to grab Elias's to prevent him having to touch it. "Lewis Byam Jr., at your service."

Elias hesitated, then shook my brother's hand briefly. "A pleasure to meet another of Miss Byam's kin."

"This is our chaplain, Mr. Elias Doswell," I said. Lewis took him in from top hat to buckled shoe, the hint of a sneer about his mouth. Clearly, he bought into the common seamen's disdain for clergymen. I bristled but reminded myself to stay calm. "He has been a dear friend to me on this journey," I blurted, instantly regretting the words. My cheeks warmed. *Dear friend.* What a simpleton. To say something so easy to misconstrue in front of my brother. Lewis snickered silently. This trying to be understanding would take discipline on my part.

I turned to Elias, whose face looked a little rosier than it had before. Or perhaps it was just the afternoon sun that twinkled in his eyes. "Lewis is hoping Captain Peyton will give him a position on the *Marianne*," I said. Even without looking at him, I could feel Lewis's laughing gaze. I hadn't missed his teasing. If Captain Peyton approved, how long would I have to endure the taunting? Much as I did want my brother taken care of—preferably in a position where he could take care of himself—the thought of spending the next months, perhaps years, on the same ship. . . . No, I needed to stay optimistic. What if fate was giving me a chance to start making things right in our family? I'd make the best of it.

"I see." Elias studied me, and I couldn't meet his eyes. Of course he sensed something was off. He knew my emotions better than I did.

"If you'd be so kind, May, as to show me to the *Marianne*." Lewis raised his arm—was he offering it to me, being gentlemanly for the first time in his life?—but I quickly looped my hand around Elias's and pretended not to see. The feel of the fine wool through my sleeve settled the anxious stirring in my belly. If he was there, I could face life with Lewis. I could be understanding and look for the best. Elias and I had weathered many things in the couple of months we'd been together, beginning with our humiliating introduction. That felt a lifetime ago.

Elias cleared his throat and shook his head slightly as though pulling himself out of his thoughts. "If you will follow us this way, Mr. Byam, she isn't far."

Us. The simple word chimed in my head like one of St. Thomas's bells as we made our way toward the docks. He'd said it so naturally, as if we had always been friends. Confidants. Or perhaps something more.

I shifted closer to him as we walked, never minding Lewis's questioning looks. Let him laugh. I'd endured it nineteen years and hadn't let it fluster me before. Perhaps a new start with the support of a family member was just what Lewis needed. With Elias by my side, I wouldn't let my brother's ridiculous foibles deter me.

Chapter 15

ELIAS

Night's blackness hugged the *Marianne*, cool and thick, as I wandered the upper deck with Captain Peyton. No moon shone to hold back the dark. Only a spattering of stars through wispy clouds graced the skies.

"It's been years since I sailed the Adriatic," the captain said. I could barely see his face in the soft glow of a couple lanterns at the waist of the frigate. "There are some beautiful islands in the region."

"Are there?" Though a late October chill permeated everything it touched, a warmth that had taken up residence in my chest some weeks ago refused to let me truly feel it. Perhaps it was simply my scattered mind that refused to be bothered by the cold. It didn't register much of anything, to be honest, including the captain's words. Whether Miss Byam stood beside me or not, I could hardly focus on conversations enough to give well-thought-out responses.

"Sure to inspire the romantics among us." Even through my muddled thoughts, I caught the teasing in his voice.

"I look forward to seeing it, then," I said. Talking to the captain was better than walking the deck alone with my deluge of thoughts, but keeping up in the conversation was nearly as difficult as trying to fall asleep had been an hour before. As long as we didn't stray to the subject of Miss Byam, however. Then I'd never sleep. "Remind me of our orders while there." I'd been told before, of course. There had been little room in my lovesick brain to keep the orders straight.

The light on Captain Peyton's face grew stronger as we ambled toward the center of the deck. "We are to join with Captain Brisbane's squadron at Lissa. Napoleon has been attempting to build up his strength on the western shores of the Adriatic. It's the squadron's responsibility to thwart his efforts as best we can."

Ah, yes. That sounded vaguely familiar. We'd only received our orders that day. Or was it yesterday now? As chaplain, I couldn't be faulted for forgetting so soon. I wasn't involved in planning, like the senior officers, who had no doubt learned the orders by heart.

We climbed up to the quarterdeck, and Peyton wandered to the port rail. The only other men nearby were Mr. Sanchez and another helmsman speaking quietly.

"What do you think of our new carpenter's mate?" the captain asked.

That was drifting closer to the subject of Miss Byam than I needed. "I think . . ." What could I say? Mr. Jackson seemed near ready to seal the man in a locker and forget about him on account of his laziness. The rest of the carpenter's crew avoided him for fear of being disciplined by association. I'd overheard one of them say he caught Mr. Byam trying to light a pipe on the orlop too close to the powder magazine. It might have been a tale sprung from growing disgust rather than a truth, but somehow, I could readily picture Lewis Byam being that reckless. "I think it is still too soon for me to discuss Mr. Byam's merits. I hardly know him."

Peyton grunted. "He's a far cry from what I imagined the brother of Miss Byam to be."

There she was. I steeled my jaw against the smile that tried to overtake my face. It was getting more difficult not to react each time I heard her name.

"I suppose it was too hopeful of me to expect someone equally dedicated to his duty." Captain Peyton sighed, staring out to sea. "Every crew has its weakness. Some more than others."

I mumbled my agreement. Yes, Miss Byam was dedicated to anything she set her mind to. Her word became her creed. And that determination glimmered in her deep-blue eyes, even when she wasn't being challenged. The set of her mouth, the way she threw back her shoulders and charged ahead at every moment. Life itself had been a challenge, and she would not cower, nor would she shirk her responsibility.

"You're rather distant tonight, Doswell."

I snapped out of my reverie and cleared my throat. "Am I?" So much for trying to hide it.

"You should get some rest. You've been walking these decks later into the night than usual."

He'd noticed that too. I shouldn't have been surprised. Very little that happened on a ship went unnoticed by a good captain. But how could I retire when my mind wouldn't still? "Yes, Captain."

"I should retire myself. Georgana will be wondering where I've gone. She's been rather restless at night lately."

Clearly, we all were kept awake by our various agitations. She with her secret, he with the responsibilities of his position, and I with this growing flame I didn't know how to contain.

The captain nodded his farewell and headed below, leaving me alone at the rail and vulnerable to the firestorm of thoughts of Miss Byam and her strength and the tender feelings I couldn't help that I'd been trying to dodge all night.

I ran a hand through my hair. How could I keep all this inside? Sharing my heart hadn't gone well the last four times. But try as I might, I was an open book. Miss Byam would discover the truth sooner or later. I leaned against the rail, peering into the muted waves barely visible in the darkness. When the truth did spill out, it would be the end of this friendship as we knew it, for better or worse. A small piece of me yearned to know what it would be.

Tiny pinpricks of light burst into existence in the sea below me. Hundreds, then thousands trailing in the *Marianne*'s wake. I stiffened, breath catching. The little lights faded quickly, replaced by more as the ship meandered through the water. I held on to my spectacles, leaning farther over the rail. I'd read about this phenomenon. Not many people had the opportunity to witness it. Tiny creatures with the power of light. Could I have asked for a more perfect distraction from . . .

I glanced behind me at the currently oblivious crew. I didn't want to share this moment of discovery with them, but dared I wake the one person I wanted to see it?

That growing flame wasted no time in making my mind up for me. With one last glance at the shimmering ocean, I dashed for the hatchway, praying the dinoflagellates and their ethereal glow would still be there when we returned.

MAY

At the top of the ladder, Elias seized my hand with a vigor I hadn't experienced from him before, and I let him pull me toward the stern. I rubbed sleep from my eyes as we passed shadows of seamen on watch. If I had to be awoken in the middle of the night, it had better be Elias doing the waking, but was this really necessary?

The helmsmen gave us curious glances as we passed them, their faces barely illuminated by the binnacle lanterns. Elias led me to the stern rail and pointed.

"Thank heavens. They're still here," he said.

I tugged my thin coat over the dress I'd hastily thrown on, the chill night air quickly seeping through all my layers. If this was anything short of a miracle, I would find it very difficult to warrant him barging into my cabin this late at night.

I followed his gesture toward the sea.

"Is it not absolutely stunning?" he whispered.

For a moment, my eyes could not comprehend what they saw. The waves glowed, a brilliant blue light ebbing and flowing across their surface. "What in the name of—" I clasped the rail, my fingers curling over Elias's, as I leaned out to get a closer look.

"They're called dinoflagellates," he said, covering my hand with his other one. His warmth seeped into my skin. "Tiny sea organisms disturbed by *Marianne*'s passing."

"That's a rather dull name for magic." The light thinned and expanded as the ship crept forward. The blue danced over the wake, a billion azure stars melding into one undulating specter.

"Look!" He pointed a little ways off starboard.

I squinted. "I don't see anything." Just the swirling light.

He took a few steps to starboard, pulling me with him until I was nestled against his side. It blocked out some of the chill, and for a moment, I considered asking to share his thick, wool greatcoat. Most likely, he'd have just removed it and let me take the whole of its warmth. Elias would give me anything I asked and more. Until he had nothing left to give.

"Keep your gaze a few yards out," he said, breath tickling my cheek. "Let's see if they come again."

"They?" I did as he instructed and held my breath.

Elias's arm tightened around me. "I saw them for the briefest second. I hope they swim back this way."

"What am I looking for?"

He squeezed me. "Patience."

I grinned. Looking for patience was true enough, though as long as his arm stayed around me, I could wait for anything.

A sleek form outlined in blue glided out from the dinoflagellates' glow. I gasped, not trusting my eyes. Another followed after it. And a third. Dolphins, but they glowed like they'd swallowed the moon. "How do they do that?"

Elias remained silent for a moment, then said in a secretive voice, "Do you believe in mermaids, Miss Byam?"

"If I didn't before, I certainly do now." It felt as though I'd entered some fantastical dream. How could this sight be real? It was the stuff of fairy stories. I nudged him in the ribs with my elbow. "As a clergyman, is it not beneath your station to speak of myths?"

"Not if in jest."

The dolphins swam back and forth across *Marianne*'s wake, sometimes diving low and disappearing into the deep for a few moments before popping back up where we least expected them. I could almost imagine they were water nymphs playing under the cover of a velvet sky, the stars abandoning their posts to join in the merriment. Elias was right; I wouldn't have wished to miss this.

I glanced up at him to find him looking at me rather than the phenomenon before us. "What is it?" I asked.

He shook his head, the faint light catching his sheepish look.

"Come, now. What are you thinking?" Surely we were friends enough that he could tell me his thoughts, silly as he seemed to believe they were.

"I . . ." His eyes trailed from mine down my face to my lips. "I was simply thinking that tonight . . ."

I raised my brows. A funny pattering overtook my chest. Somehow, I knew what he meant to say. My heart, picking up speed with each shallow breath he took, hungered to hear him say it. But in my head, I cried out for time to halt. Once he uttered those words, there would be no returning to the camaraderie we'd had before. This could be the start of our final chapter. I swallowed. Or the prologue to a story I never imagined writing when I set foot on *Marianne*'s deck.

I wasn't ready to face that possibility yet.

"That tonight," he said softly, his tone so gentle my whole soul ached, "I wish I could kiss you."

A burst of brightness erupted inside me, and I straightened. "Oh," I said. Gracious, what was the matter with me? I shuffled to the side, breaking our contact, and turned my attention back to the dinoflagellates, which seemed to have dimmed since a few moments ago. "I'm not certain we really want to do that." I laughed shakily. My legs shook. Good heavens. Was I taking ill?

Elias said nothing, and I didn't dare look at him. I could feel his dejection through the cold air between us. Now what would we do? I'd have to pass him in the gun room every day, see his downcast face, know I did that to him. All because I was too afraid of the possibilities.

I focused on the trio of dolphins, trying to think of something to say. How did one change the subject after a declaration such as that? The creatures wove through the glowing sea, swift and powerful, then one by one, they dove and disappeared under the ship's keel.

Blast.

I chanced a peek in Elias's direction. He'd taken off his spectacles and now twirled them between his fingers. Blue light glinted off the lenses. He stood with elbows planted against the rail, the set of his brows in the faint light more resigned than heartbroken. Had this happened before? I attempted to burrow deeper into my thin redingote. Removed from Elias's warmth, the chill was penetrating my inadequate layers.

"How big are these creatures?" I asked.

He straightened, pocketing his spectacles. I'd killed his excitement over the discovery. I hunched my shoulders. What a mess. I'd ruined the night.

"They're quite small. Hardly visible to the human eye without assistance," he said.

Then the little pricks of light were not individual organisms but many together. I trained my mind on the revelation but could not conjure more curiosity. It was a wonder, to be sure. And still, I wished to return to my cabin to drown in my guilt.

I set my chin on my fist. Why did I feel guilt? Because I'd hurt him far more than his mistake at the beginning of our acquaintance had hurt me. What was more, part of me wanted the same thing he did—that closeness, that love. I just couldn't bring myself to trust someone to such a degree. The people I'd trusted in the past had all forsaken me. I shivered, folding my arms across my middle. Was that it? Was it trust that held me back?

"Are you cold?" Elias asked. I didn't detect any offense in his voice. Only the sweet concern he always showed me. He stood with one hand partially extended toward me, as though he wasn't certain whether I would want his care. I dug my fingers onto the cuffs of my sleeves. It wasn't fair to judge him based on my family's actions. If there was a single soul on this earth who wouldn't abandon me, it had to be Elias Doswell.

"It is a bit frigid." I couldn't let this chance slip through my fingers. What if the greatest moments life had to offer me lay in the love of this soft-spoken clergyman?

Elias reached up to pull his greatcoat from his shoulders. Before my head could catch up with my heart, I darted over, slipped between him and his coat, and pulled the garment's edges around the both of us. My back pressed against his chest, which expanded rapidly until I thought it would burst. He froze, arms still raised to remove the greatcoat. Facing away from him, I couldn't see his expression, but I could only imagine the confusion on his features.

"This is better," I said timidly, my mind awhirl at the feel of him against me and the jasmine scent wafting off his warm, wool coat. He didn't move. Mercy, what had I done?

ELIAS

My throat didn't work when I tried to swallow. A moment before she'd pushed away, and now she pressed against me, soft and comfortable, as though she hadn't just dashed my hopes. I hardly trusted my senses.

I lowered my arms to my sides, letting them hang awkwardly.

"Or perhaps this isn't better?" She turned her head as though listening for my answer.

Could she hear my thundering pulse as loudly as I did?

She started to pull forward. "I'm sorry."

I wrapped my arms around her, keeping her safely in the confines of my greatcoat. "Yes, this is certainly better."

She relaxed into me, leaning her head back against my shoulder. I rested my head on hers, struggling to believe this reversal. Standing in the pleasant night, cradling her in my arms, I could let the pain of the past fade into the darkness. She wanted something more, just as I did. I didn't have to guess or play Society's games. Perhaps I had simply moved too hastily.

Far too common with you, Elias.

I silenced the voice in my head. If I had to move slowly for May's sake, I would. The sea's glow swayed before us as though painting a picture of the excitement mounting inside me.

"Elias?"

A thrill coursed up my spine at the sound of my name.

"I'm sorry I refused."

With a smile, I hugged her more tightly to me. "You needn't be."

"I was frightened," she said. "I think I still am."

I kissed the top of her head, my face lingering against her soft hair. We were both in the service of the navy, in a matter of speaking. Neither of us was going anywhere. We had as much time as she needed, and I intended to give it to her.

She turned toward me, her hair tickling my face as she moved. "But I don't want"—our cheeks brushed. Then our lips. She paused, eyes widening. The magical light shimmered in their depths—"to be frightened."

I felt the words' vibrations against my lips as much as I heard them. I'd been too close when she'd turned. She hadn't anticipated my mouth being in the perfectly wrong place. Or right place. I didn't move, much as I longed to finish what we'd unintentionally started.

Her breath played across my lips, toying with my resolve. She hadn't backed away, but neither had she drawn into the kiss. We stood suspended between our desires and her fears.

Slowly, Elias.

I closed my eyes, pulling back to distance my lips from her, but at the same moment, she rose up and kissed me. My heart skipped, and the corners of my mouth lifted as I eagerly returned it. Her hands found the sides of my face, her fingers splaying across my jaw and down my neck. Gooseflesh shot across my skin as heat grew in my chest. I tightened our embrace. Warning bells sounded in the back of my consciousness, but I paid them no heed. We both had fears to work through. I wanted to face them with her.

She quivered, and I pulled the edges of my greatcoat more securely around us. I'd dreamed of holding her in my arms again since the night I'd comforted her in her cabin. I'd dreamed of kissing her, too, in moments of utter weakness. Dreams paled in comparison to the reality of feeling her against me, wanting me like I wanted her.

The *Marianne* tilted in a swell, and I steadied us against the rail. She broke away with a breathy laugh. "I'm not very good at this." Her hands fluttered down to rest on my waistcoat.

On the contrary. What she thought she lacked in experience was concealed in pure desire. "You're thinking too much."

"You aren't supposed to think when you kiss someone?"

Not that hard. "You're supposed to feel it."

She cocked her head, tracing the front edges of my waistcoat with her fingers. "Sometimes I don't like to feel."

I watched her fingers travel down my chest, meeting where the waistcoat overlapped in line with my racing heart. "Did you like to feel now?" I asked.

She ducked her chin, and I imagined a little blush across her cheeks, though I couldn't see it in the night. "Very much," she said in a whisper so soft I could barely make it out.

"You need not be afraid, May." I'd protect her with everything I had. Loneliness, abandonment, betrayal—these were part of both our pasts. They wouldn't be any longer. With her burrowed into my coat and my arms still through its sleeves, I couldn't reach her chin to lift it. I dipped my head until our lips met again, coaxing her back into a kiss. She melted against me with a sigh and let me taste her lips with soft kisses. She kissed me back, following my lead as she gripped the front of my waistcoat.

I couldn't remember the last time I'd felt so alive. It was as if the light of the glowing sea had permeated my skin, whirling through my veins and clearing my mind of bitter memories. A fresh start, and with this confident, loyal woman who saw my weakness and did not turn away.

I pulled back to catch my breath, and May studied my face. Was that affection on her face or just my own heart reflected in her eyes? She nestled her head against my chest, wrapping her arms around my waist. "I never want this night to end," she whispered.

My galloping heart wouldn't let me speak, so I pressed my lips to her forehead. The kiss would have to answer for me.

Chapter 16

MAY

I stood near the bow, ducking out of the way of seamen at their work in an effort to get a good look at the town materializing before us. Red-tiled roofs covered the coastline, which was flanked by tree-dotted hills. Little fishing boats bobbed everywhere in the harbor and a few ships, their proud Union Jacks rippling in the balmy breeze, anchored among them. It was nothing like the enormity and overcrowding of Old Pompey, yet the cheerful scene of the working citizens of Vis gave the town a feeling of home.

Off starboard, the gray walls of a growing fort adorned one end of the bay, with people as small as ants churning around it. Flecks of red indicated British soldiers seeing to the task. A reminder that even this secluded island dedicated to its fishing and vineyards was not exempt from Napoleon's war. Elias had mentioned last night that the town had already seen battle earlier this year, when the Royal Navy had gained control of it from the French.

I glanced behind me with the hope that Elias might have finished helping Captain Peyton with clerical work and come above, but the upper deck was a wall of the checked shirts and bare torsos of seamen. A ridiculous amount of disappointment hit me, and I quickly turned back to the little port town drawing nearer. I spent hours with him every day. How did catching sight of him still make my insides flutter like a loose sail? It was as if my whole being hoped on each meeting that this might be the time he'd finally kiss me again.

A few days had passed since our stolen moment on the quarterdeck. I leaned into the rail like we'd done that night and bit my lips between my teeth to keep from grinning like a ninny. Ships, especially little frigates such as HMS *Marianne*, weren't known for their privacy. We'd had the cover of dark and a drowsy crew while watching the dinoflagellates, but somehow I didn't think Elias would risk my reputation by kissing me in a public place again. I couldn't help growing impatient.

"May, May, devil to pay."

I straightened as my brother drew up next to me, trying to cover any emotions that might have crept onto my face. Over the last week, I'd avoided him as best I could in hopes he would not bring up Elias. Most of the time, he hardly acknowledged my presence. He was probably angry that I'd refused to let him share my cabin in the gun room, but as I much as I was trying to be understanding and generous, I had my limits. "Shouldn't you be repairing something?" I asked.

Lewis shrugged. "Ship's right as rain. Not a splinter out of place."

I refrained from plucking out the splinter on the rail near my elbow and sticking him with it. "It will be nice to make land." Not that it had been very long since we'd sailed from Malta, but the whole crew seemed to enjoy a break from the long weeks at sea we'd had at the beginning of our journey.

"I've heard some rumors about you." Lewis picked at something between his teeth.

I sighed. From the mates? Mrs. Hallyburton? She'd been giving me strange looks the last month or so, especially when she'd seen me in company with the esteemed Mr. Doswell. I'd decided he was the only reason she hadn't confronted me about whatever was on her mind. "No one likes rumors."

"On that you are wrong," he said. "We sailors love them. Every glimmer of shiny information." He raised a brow. "And the information I've caught spreading about you is rather shiny."

Gracious. He'd heard. I inhaled slowly, attempting to calm a surge of indignation that countered the acceptance I had tried to embrace the last weeks.

"A clergyman, May? You must be joking."

Heaven help me. I ground my teeth to keep from reacting. "You mean your friends must be joking. I've told you nothing about a clergyman."

He smirked. "You weren't going to tell your own brother about beslobbering the chaplain?"

"Lewis!" I scanned the deck, face flaming. Why had I agreed to help him get a place on this ship? I'd been wrong when I'd thought Lewis and Frank were cut from the same cloth. Frank had at least been friendly and pretended to be charming once in a while. Lewis took his teasing extremely past the limits.

He inclined his head in my direction. "And here I thought all your fraternizing with Doswell was a renewed self-righteousness and piety. Helping the miserable ship's orphans learn their letters and such."

I leaned away from him, folding my arms. "The people with whom I interact are none of your concern." Who did he think he was, Mrs. Hallyburton?

"As your nearest male relation this side of the law, I think it very much concerns me." He grinned, showing off a wooden tooth I hadn't noticed before.

Which side of the law he was on was subject to debate.

"And now, as practically your guardian, I hear that your study of the Good Book has some rather carnal motives."

"How dare you." Molten rage bubbled inside me, though I tried to quell it. He hadn't spared me a charitable thought in years, and now he felt it his right to advise me. Control me. "Elias is a better man than you can ever hope to be. He has been a perfect gentleman in word and deed."

Lewis lazily swatted his hair, which was long enough to fall into his eyes. "A regular donkey in the royal mews you are, daughter of a New Holland convict."

It was fortunate Mr. Hallyburton kept his cat o' nine tails properly stowed. My fingers itched to give it a try. "Remind me to never risk my livelihood standing up for your sorry hide again."

"Byams stick together, May, May, the devil to pay," Lewis drawled, thickening his Portsmouth accent. Why could I not resist it? I tried to cling to my fury at him, but that familiar sound loosened my grip. "You can't resist duty to family."

I sincerely wished to just now. I turned my back to him, ready to flee. Sitting below with Elias would be much more enjoyable than watching the harbor with my brother.

"It's been a hard six years, hasn't it?" Lewis said softly.

I paused. His jeering tone had vanished. "How would you know if it's been difficult or not for me?" I asked. "You've been at sea."

"That doesn't mean I didn't feel the effects of his conviction." He blew out heavily. "I didn't even get to say goodbye to him."

Didn't get to say goodbye. I hadn't thought of that. I faced Lewis, keeping a little distance between us. Mama and I had dealt with the pain of having Papa ripped from our home. Of watching them drag him onto a ship, never to return. But Lewis had never had the chance for a final memory, good or bad. The next time he'd returned to port, Papa had been gone, the house had been gone, everything about our former life had been gone.

"I didn't want to face it," he said, resting his chin on his hand and partially covering his mouth, almost as though he were embarrassed by the words coming from it. "I didn't want to see Mother broken or you working."

"Then, why didn't you send money?" I asked. We might have all pulled ourselves to our feet if Lewis had helped us. Instead, we'd been forced to seek work in a world with few jobs for women and fewer for women tainted by having a criminal husband and father.

He didn't look at me. "The burden was too much. I tried to escape it in any way I could. Put it out of my head."

That usually meant drinking and smoking and women. I bit the inside of my cheek. Why did my heart hurt for him even as he was admitting to squandering money that could have supported our mother, now practically a widow?

"Soon, there wasn't anything to send back. And I had to keep burying myself in . . ." He waved a hand as though expecting me to understand. "If I didn't have a distraction, the guilt and frustration would return. It came to a point that I couldn't change my ways."

I pressed my lips together, trying to calm my thoughts before speaking. It felt very unnatural. Lewis had never acted this way, always hiding behind his teasing and gruff manner. I wanted to handle this as Elias would. Perhaps gentility rather than my usual brashness would help fix things I'd thought beyond repair. "You deeply hurt us, Lewis. Mama should not have been forced into service."

He bowed his head meekly. "I know it."

"She deserves comfort after all she's endured. Not further grief." My throat hitched. How much had I contributed to her further grief with my attitude toward her new employment? I'd turned up my nose at her pleading to stay together.

"And you," he said. "You deserved assemblies and dinners with our friends and suitors just like Agnes."

I ducked my chin. "Even if you'd sent us every last farthing, we couldn't have afforded an experience for me similar to Agnes's." But it was sweet of him to consider it. Was that the goodness I knew he had deep inside coming to the surface?

"You've all carried a weight I should have helped shoulder, but I was too afraid to face my responsibilities."

Something in his tone hit me hard. It was so much like Elias, berating his weakness. Supporting a mother and sister was quite a lot to ask of an eighteen-year-old boy. He couldn't really be all to blame.

He grinned. "If I promise I'll do better, will you forgive me, May?"

For a moment, he resembled the older brother I'd toddled adoringly after, blue eyes bright and mischievous. How could I hold the past against him? We'd all fought and floundered through this new life without Papa. Some of us had borne it better than others.

"I'll find you something sweet in the town."

I laughed reluctantly. That had always worked when I was younger. "I will forgive you," I said. "After all, we Byams stick together."

He chuckled and rested his arm across my shoulders like he used to. I stayed still, trying to decide whether I liked this closeness as I watched the harbor. Fishermen we passed hardly gave us a glance. They must have seen many British ships in the last few years. Only a little boy stopped and pointed at the *Marianne*, speaking excitedly in words I couldn't understand. Lewis, Charlie, and I had watched the ships coming into Portsmouth in much the same way when we'd been that age, pointing out which ships we wished to captain and which had the nicest colors. I wouldn't have imagined someday truly getting to sail with my brother.

I leaned my head against his shoulder. "You are much more pleasant to be around after you've bathed," I said.

He made a face. "Charming as ever, May." But he squeezed my shoulder.

Lewis and I stood in comfortable silence amid the rattle of tackles and whine of rope as the crew eased the ship into port. Was it good fortune rather than ill fate that had brought us together? Lewis and I could start anew. Fresh. Our family could heal together, one small step at a time.

Regardless of the struggle, this voyage was turning out to be the best thing that had ever happened to me.

ELIAS

Clear afternoon sun bathed the ancient stone around us as we picked our way over the uneven floor of what had once been a Roman bath house. Greenery sprouted from the cracks between bricks and between the mosaic tiles that decorated the floors. An impossibly blue sky stretched above us, the barest wisps of clouds dusting its expanse. A vision of paradise, yet the only thing I could think of was the woman walking in front of me as I lamented the presence of the third member of our party.

I smoothed back a strip of hair that had fallen forward as I followed May and Étienne. I didn't really begrudge his presence. I wanted to act properly, even if part of me wished we could have come on our own. After all, he'd been the one to suggest the three of us explore the ruins while the rest of the crew saw to affairs of the ship.

We'd be patrolling the Adriatic with the town of Vis as our base and, at the most, would be only a few days out of the little port, but Captain Peyton didn't want to take chances of the *Marianne* being unprepared for a meeting with or having to chase the French. There was little for the three of us to do to help. Having a few hours of privacy, even with the extra companion, had been too tempting.

"Is Lissa very much like your home?" May asked.

The surgeon sighed. "It does remind me of Marseille, yes. None of the frigid winters we enjoy in the north."

I'd nearly brought my greatcoat on our excursion after how chilly the wind had been the last few days at sea, but the balmy afternoon made me wish I'd worn my linen jacket rather than my black wool one. It felt like a late English spring despite it being November. This was practically summer weather in some parts of the United Kingdom.

"Do you miss it?" she asked.

"Sometimes. But mostly, I miss my Lina." He paused his walking and looked back at me. "What do you make of these ruins, Mr. Doswell? You are the scholar among us."

I hurried forward to catch up with them. I'd been too swept up in watching the way the light glinted off a lock of May's hair that had fallen out of the bonnet I'd given her. Why she refused to let me replace it with something more suitable, I couldn't tell, but the fact that she held on to it with such fierceness made my heart swell. "I can't say Roman history is my specialty, but they are magnificently well preserved."

Walls as tall as I was rose around the main chamber, where we stood. We wandered in the direction of what looked like a double entrance with grand masonry separating the two openings. The roof had long since been lost, but the size and shape of the openings made them seem like doorways.

"Can you imagine this place teeming with Romans?" I asked, looking back the way we'd come. It must have been like a gentleman's club, with all the elite of the town mingling and vying for attention.

May laughed. "Dressed in white sheets and sandals?"

"Most likely not dressed in much at all," the surgeon muttered wryly.

Her face instantly reddened. Mine most likely did as well. She met my eyes, then we both quickly glanced away. Étienne would not have made a proper chaperone by any Society mother's standards. I'd been in company with my fair share of the strictest of them.

Étienne advanced toward the doorways. "Did you see the mosaic in the little room off to the right?" He pointed back toward a section of the ruins we'd passed. "It seemed more intricate than the rest of the floors."

"Should we go back and observe it?" I asked as the surgeon continued on his way. He winked at me over his shoulder but did not turn back. He meant to leave us alone. Yes, he'd be the chaperone of any gentry parent's nightmares. And the companion of every young couple's dreams. My heart did a little flip. He was giving us that moment of privacy I'd been craving the last two weeks.

A hand slipped around my arm. "I'd love to see it," May said sweetly and more innocently than I'd ever heard her speak.

I sighed. This bordered on improper. But there wasn't a door to close in the entire complex, so we wouldn't be completely alone. And it wasn't as if we hadn't been in the same cabin with the door shut on multiple occasions already. But this felt different. We'd as good as admitted our feelings about each other. Now we simply had to decide what to do with them.

May and I walked back the way we'd come, and she glanced around me as if to see whether Étienne was out of earshot.

"This is much better than the quarterdeck during first watch," she said. "Though I wouldn't have minded that a time or two over the last couple weeks."

I covered her hand with mine. "If the whole crew found out about the one time, think of what they'd say if it became a habit." A habit. I wouldn't mind if kissing May became a habit.

She shrugged, leaning on me to steady herself over a broken-up patch of stone. "Lewis already knows. He was the one I worried about knowing, but I don't think it will be a problem."

"Do the Peytons know?" I asked.

She winced. "If Mrs. Peyton knows, she hasn't mentioned it. And the captain, while very diligent and perceptive in matters of the ship and crew, clearly has much to learn about recognizing more sensitive matters. We already know one thing he's missed."

"She still hasn't told him?" I asked. May had seemed to think Mrs. Peyton meant to tell him when we made land.

"I'm shocked the whole ship doesn't know already. Her round gown will only hide it for so much longer."

My stomach sank. I had a feeling we were both about to get stuck in a marital disaster.

We came to the threshold of the room Étienne had indicated. On the floor lay four animal shapes made up of dark-gray tiles.

May released my arm and crouched to examine them. Then she looked up at me, cocking her head and grinning. "Dolphins!"

"Or some other fish." They had long tails that ended in flat fins and oddly teardrop-shaped bodies. Animals weren't the Romans' strongest subject when it came to art. I'd seen copies of Roman wolf mosaics that looked more like cats than anything.

"I'm going to call them dolphins." She straightened, and I held her elbow to help her up. I took advantage of the close proximity to wrap her in a hug and plant a little kiss on her cheek. She smelled of sunshine and sea breezes and stolen glances across busy upper decks, and I found I couldn't breathe in enough of her scent to satisfy me.

She pulled back with a coy smile and turned her back to me as she drifted farther into the new chamber. The room wasn't as little as I'd thought. Geometric designs crossed the length of the floor as though the poor artist who'd muddled his way through the dolphins on the threshold hadn't had the desire to try any more creatures.

"There's something I've been wanting to ask you," she said.

I hurried to catch up. "What is it?"

"I was just wondering . . ." She fiddled with the black ribbon of her bonnet, not looking me in the eye. This flirtatiousness was something I'd never seen from her. I had to admit I liked it. "How many other women have you kissed in your life?" she asked.

"I . . ." I rubbed the back of my neck, ears heating. It was more than I wanted to admit. Not more than many young men my age, to be sure, but far more than a clergyman ought to have. "Perhaps four."

Her eyes widened, and her mouth fell open in a dramatic gasp. "Elias Doswell, you rake!" she said, swatting at my arm. Then she covered a laugh with her hand, breaking her illusion of being appalled. "*Perhaps* four? You don't remember?"

I most certainly did remember. Each of them had broken my heart not long after. I brought my shoulders to my ears. "I wasn't doing it for sport."

She took my hand. "I am only teasing. After hearing about all of the mates' escapades, that hardly seems like very many. And who knows what Lewis has done since he left home."

Palm trees rustled from just beyond the walls as the mention of her brother silenced us. Though I felt terrible for thinking it, I wished we'd never run into him that day in Malta. He was back on the ship, and we were safe from his jeering for a moment. No need to grant him another second of our precious time.

"I suppose that with each one, you wished to marry them," she said, sobering.

I didn't want to admit to that.

"Were you refused?"

I looked away, then nodded. What would she think of that? The faces of all four women swam before me. My first love, Miss Durant, who had fallen for the Oxford friend I'd introduced her to. Miss Starle, who had quickly lost interest in me after a Season in London's grandeur. Miss Page, who had simply wished to ignite the jealousy of a gentleman too slow in proposing by giving me intense attention. And, of course, Miss Somer, the vicar's daughter who had seemed my perfect match.

May gave my hand a squeeze, pulling me from the memories that had once tasted so bitter. Now they dissolved into the crisp air, shadows of the past driven away by the midday sun to hide practically harmless in the recesses of my mind.

"I'm sorry," she said. "I cannot imagine having to endure such rejection, especially of someone as good and kind as you."

"God had other plans for me." Plans I hoped involved the woman before me, though I didn't know if I was ready to venture too far down that path of thought just yet. I tugged on her hand. "What made you ask?"

She focused on a little lizard scurrying across the mosaics before she answered with a bashful voice. "You seemed far more experienced than I did that night."

"Did I?" I chuckled sheepishly. How different this conversation was from our first meeting. The May and Elias who had met in such awkward a misunderstanding would not have believed this conversation was in their future. "And you? Have you . . . ?" I inclined my head. At the thought of her kissing someone else, I suddenly wished I hadn't asked so I could live on in blissful ignorance.

"Only once. It was a plot hatched by Lewis and his friend. They wanted me to keep my mouth shut about why they weren't coming to my aunt and uncle's for dinner. They claimed duties to their captain, but they'd already been paid off and wanted to burn their money at the tavern. Lewis had the brilliant idea that his friend kissing me would keep me quiet." Her mouth twisted. "He was right. I only realized I'd been used later."

"What a scoundrel." Would I ever find a redeeming quality about her brother?

"It was fortunate for me that my next kiss was far more pleasant." She tilted her head back, an expectant look on her face.

"Was it?" I asked. Étienne was nowhere to be seen in the chamber beyond, so I slipped my arms around her waist and pulled her close.

She slipped her bonnet from her head so it dangled down her back. "And the man kissing me the second time was much more handsome." Her arms encircled my neck.

"Was he?" I placed a little kiss on her brow. I was going to enjoy our assignment to this remote location if it meant moments like this.

She rose up on her toes with an impish grin and closed her eyes, bringing her lips toward mine.

"Miss Byam! Mr. Doswell!"

She pushed away from me. I released her and turned toward the shout. It wasn't Étienne. The voice sounded younger and clearly English. The serious edge to it made my insides tighten. Had they sighted a French ship?

A lanky young man came into view around a break in the outer wall. Walter Fitz? I took May's hand and hurried toward him as quickly as the uneven ground would allow.

"We're here," I called.

He bolted for us. "Byam's done it now."

"What do you mean?" May's hand tightened in mine.

Fitz halted, resting his hands on his knees and panting. "Mr. Byam was belowdecks, drunk as a lord, and Mr. Hallyburton caught him lightin' his pipe near the powder room."

Rumor indicated it wasn't the first time. A chill ran down my spine. I'd seen the effects of fire too close to waiting powder on my last assignment, and that had only been extra cartridges. Not a whole powder room that could blow the *Marianne* into the heavens like the French ship at the start of our voyage.

"Hallyburton tried to take the pipe, but Byam drubbed him."

May's face went pale.

"Broke his nose, I'd wager," Fitz said, rubbing his own nose as if he'd been the one hit. "Now Byam's in irons, and Mrs. Hallyburton wants him strung up for what he done to her husband. Captain's barely holdin' her off, but he looks near ready to let her do her worst."

May dropped my hand and bolted toward the harbor, bonnet bumping against her back as she jumped over rock and tile.

"May, wait!" I started after her, but Fitz stopped me.

"Where's Étienne? Hallyburton needs a doctor."

I nodded toward the doors. "He went that way." I didn't stay to make sure he found the Frenchman. May had nearly cleared the ruins, running like Cerberus himself was at her heels. I did my best to catch up to her. With every step, my head throbbed. This was not going to end well for anyone.

Chapter 17

MAY

My heart thundered in my ears as I stood before Captain Peyton's desk. I'd left Lewis with the beginnings of hope for a new future for our family. He'd been humble and sorry, though he hadn't said it clearly. It had seemed he wanted to mend things.

He couldn't have squandered that moment.

The captain sat back in his chair, kneading his brow. "I didn't expect this sort of trouble from someone you recommended, Miss Byam."

I swallowed with difficulty. I'd supported his story when Captain Peyton and Mr. Jackson had asked. Perhaps had even sung a few praises of his talent. I hadn't known then how he'd suffered as much as the rest of us the last six years. He'd had good intentions when we had talked earlier. Had our conversation made him feel the burden of responsibility too heavily again, turning him to drink?

"You can hardly blame her," Mrs. Peyton said from the window. "She was only trying to help her brother."

I wanted to dissolve into the floor. None of it made sense. I glanced back at Elias, who stood a little behind me, face strained. I wished I could feel the reassurance that should have come from the knowledge that Elias was at my side. Instead, I felt only cold as I tried to make sense of the events of the day.

The captain shook his head after a moment. "I don't blame her. He chose to get drunk in the middle of the day. But what a fix we find ourselves in."

Drunk. He'd been completely lucid when he'd spoken to me. How could he have managed so quickly? There must have been a mistake.

A knock sounded on the door. "Enter," the captain said wearily, the usual easiness in his tone completely gone.

Catterick walked in, brows lowered in a stony scowl. He made the motion of grabbing the brim of his hat in salute, though he didn't wear one belowdecks. "Sir."

"How is Mr. Hallyburton?"

"Dr. Étienne says his nose is certainly broken, but everything else is simply bruising. He does not think it will impede Mr. Hallyburton's duties after a little rest."

Thank heavens. It lessened the sickness in my stomach a tiny bit. Could that mean mercy for Lewis?

Captain Peyton leaned forward, placing his elbows on the desk. "That is fortunate." He rubbed his hands together, looking everywhere but at the other four people in the room.

Catterick shifted. "Mrs. Hallyburton . . ."

"Is crying for blood, I know it," the captain said.

Blood. My mouth went dry. I'd held a slew of things against Lewis the last six years, but none that made me wish him physical injury or worse. Surely that was an overreaction to what he'd done.

The ghost of a dry smile flitted across the captain's lips and was gone in an instant. "I've no doubt she'd take your place with a little too much enjoyment."

I stood rigid, not daring to think about what the comment implied. Lewis had broken many rules. More than Captain Peyton knew. By the laws that governed the navy, he should be punished.

Captain Peyton rose slowly. "Rig up a grating, Catterick. We'll pipe all hands in the morning."

"Aye, sir. How many?"

A grating meant only one thing. Uncle Byam and Charlie had talked about it as being the thing they liked least in their position as boatswain and boatswain's mate—tying up a shipmate and delivering a lashing at the captain's word. My limbs shook. Charlie had told me all the gory details of the floggings he'd witnessed. Captain Peyton wouldn't do that. He *couldn't* do that to Lewis.

"Twenty-five."

Twenty-five lashings! I gaped. For a drunken mishap?

Catterick saluted again and retreated from the great cabin.

The captain turned away from the door, toward his wife, who waited solemnly with hands clasped in front of her belly. Captain Peyton fussed with the black stock around his neck. "It has to be done. If I don't make an example of him, we both know what could happen," he muttered. "There's no helping it."

"No helping what?" I cried, my voice frantic. Bile rose to the back of my throat. His word was the law aboard this ship. If he didn't want to flog my brother, he didn't have to. The twinkle-eyed smile Lewis had given me earlier was not the expression of someone intent on harming or endangering others.

"I'll excuse you from the proceedings, Miss Byam," the captain said. "You do not need to watch."

"How noble of you," I muttered, still caught up in my troubled musings.

He sighed and turned to face me. "We have an order that must be kept in the service. If that order is not upheld, the navy will fall into disarray one ship at a time."

I'd seen prints of drawings made of floggings. Men tied up with all their shipmates watching while they were whipped with the cat o' nine tails. Now the image in my head had Lewis in place of the nameless criminal.

"But why so severe a punishment?" I shot forward, slapping my hands onto his desk. "Twenty-five? It does not fit his crime. He wasn't successful lighting the pipe. Nothing happened. Why are you punishing him as though something did?"

Captain Peyton's gaze grew distant. "If something had happened, there would be nothing left of him to punish."

"I thought the magazines were—"

"What is more," the captain said, riding over my protest, "lighting his pipe was not his only crime. Many a captain would have had him flogged strictly for drunkenness."

Lewis with his back covered in bloody stripes filled my waking eye. I tried to breathe. He didn't deserve this. He might not have been the best brother, but he was the only one I had. He was a Byam. We Byams looked out for each other. I couldn't let them do this.

"Most serious is striking an officer."

I threw up my hands. "Étienne said Hallyburton will be right as rain after a little rest." The burning anger in my core spilled out in surges I couldn't hold back. Lewis and I were turning a page. Making things right. He'd promised, hadn't he?

Captain Peyton settled his hands on the desk, a warning glinting in his eyes. "Perhaps you should pay a visit to the sick bay and see my boatswain's battered face for yourself."

"Hallyburton will heal." I folded my arms. "Much faster than Lewis will under the lash." A little voice in the back of my head told me I should have more compassion on the boatswain, but where was everyone's compassion for Lewis? Nowhere to be found. Someone had to care. It wasn't his fault our father had turned out to be a criminal, leaving him with too immense a burden for an eighteen-year-old boy. It had pushed him to this. Before this morning, I'd rarely thought on the responsibility laid on his shoulders, so caught up was I in my own struggles to survive. Upper crust Captain Peyton wouldn't be sympathetic to a poor boy's plight.

"That does not change the fact that he struck a superior," Captain Peyton said louder.

"Hallyburton is a warrant officer, not a gentleman," I shot back. "If the navy sees the two as different, why is the punishment the same?"

The captain groaned, glancing at his wife as though for help. "Your loyalty is commendable, if ill placed."

Hope snapped, cord by cord, like ship's lines breaking in a gale. Life had done this to me time and again, pulling things away just when I thought I was on the verge of happiness. All I could do was stand firm against life's pounding. I clenched my fists, my whole body tight as an anchor cable. I was wrong about Peyton. I thought him an understanding and fair captain, but he was just like every other haughty man of the gentry brought up to be a tyrant on the seas. "This is unjust!" My eyes stung. "You only want to look the part of a strong captain. This is to maintain your reputation. And you're willing to let my brother suffer for your ego." I dug my nails into my palms.

"May." Elias's soothing voice in my ear did nothing to cool the torrent within me. He tried to take my arm, but I brushed him off.

Captain Peyton's chiseled jaw went taut. "If someone had done the same to your uncle, Captain Woodall would have acted in like manner."

"Would he?" I scoffed. "I've heard he was nothing but a coward."

"Byam," Mrs. Peyton hissed, "that is enough." I'd never seen such venom in her usually serene expression. She'd never commanded me so forcefully before, like scolding a disobedient puppy. So she agreed with this abuse. It shouldn't have surprised me. She was raised in the navy. People in this world were deadened to its brutality. They thought only of advancement and prizes.

The old, familiar fury toward the Woodalls that had once resided inside me burst into life again and blurred my senses until it was all I knew. "Cowardly enough that he wouldn't let a capable woman on board to work with her husband and son," I said. She was going to kick me off the *Marianne* to find my own way back to England. I didn't care. The year of anger and grief at Charlie's and my uncle's deaths billowed to the surface, mingling with the indignation at Lewis's punishment. This family was responsible. I'd made myself swallow it, thought it would be for the better, but clearly, I'd been a fool. They cared only for themselves.

"There is nothing further to discuss," Captain Peyton growled. "You will not insult my family because yours has decided to ignore the laws and will, therefore, suffer the consequences. I do not understand why you would stand up for someone who does so little to support you."

How dare he. He didn't know anything about my life. He'd done nothing to help my family. This captain saw only his advancement in danger if he didn't exert his dominance over his men. "The same reason you protect your wife and child," I spat. "Because he's my family."

The captain froze, brow creasing. "Child?"

I couldn't stop it. My mind, dizzy with the deluge of emotions, pushed me forward like a ship with too many sails set in a strong breeze. The pain in my heart wanted retribution. I willingly set my sights on disaster, jabbing a finger in Mrs. Peyton's direction. "Look at her. You think she grew that belly from ship's biscuits? She's been hiding it from you since we left Portsmouth."

Mrs. Peyton shrank back, face pale. Elias's hand wrapped firmly around my arm. His shock at my betrayal radiated from his touch. It jolted me, cracking the rage that had mounted within. Why had I said that? Fool. My quarrel was with her unfeeling husband, not with her. She wasn't having Lewis whipped.

Captain Peyton dropped his arms to his sides. "Georgana?"

She breathed heavily, chewing on her lip. She took a step back, then another, until the bulwark stopped her retreat.

"What does she mean?" Peyton asked. He didn't sound angry, but he also did not sound joyful, as a soon-to-be father should on discovering his wife was with child.

"We should go," Elias said quietly. I couldn't hear much of anything in his tone, and I dared not look at his face. I didn't want to see the disappointment. He thought Lewis deserved this. That made him just like them.

With a jerk, I pulled my arm from Elias's grasp and flew from the captain's quarters. I kept my head down, not wanting to see anyone on the ship. Emptiness opened up inside me, gaping and raw. I didn't know what or who could fill it. I darted into my cabin and slammed the door, sinking against the wood.

Only one person came to mind who I wanted just then. Not Lewis, not Mama, not Charlie. Not even Elias. I couldn't make sense of it. What I wanted more than anything else was to be safely wrapped in the strong arms and hear the soothing voice of my papa—the person whose actions had turned my life upside down in horrible, unalterable ways.

I hugged myself tightly in the darkness as the tears fell.

ELIAS

"May?" I knocked again, but heard no movement. How I wanted to push back the canvas covering the barred window to see if she was all right. Instead, I trudged to my own cabin door. The officers eating at the gun room table were silent, but they watched me from the corners of their eyes. No doubt they'd heard May's shouting in the captain's cabin. The whole ship would know of it in half an hour if they hadn't heard it with their own ears.

I let myself into my cabin and lit the lantern, then sat cross-legged beside the crack in the wall between our cabins. What a disaster. I raked a hand through my hair, hardly knowing what to make of what had just happened. May said things she didn't always mean when she got this angry—I'd seen it firsthand—but I never would have expected her to tell Captain Peyton the truth about his wife without Mrs. Peyton's permission.

"May, please," I said.

No response. Had she not come to her cabin? I could have sworn I'd heard the door slam. Perhaps she'd crept down to the orlop to try to speak with her brother.

"I do not wish to discuss it," she finally said. Her voice was thick and tight.

I nodded, then remembered she couldn't see. How did I respond to that? She wanted me to leave her be, but I couldn't. "I'm worried," I said. The Peytons weren't unreasonable people. In fact, they were some of the most tolerant and good-natured people I'd met in the service. But May had crossed many lines that should not have been crossed. Enough that most members of the *ton* would have let her go without a moment's hesitation. What would she do if that happened? What would *I* do?

"I'm not." That stubbornness that had kept a barrier between us in the early days of the voyage had sneaked into her tone.

"You cannot say things like that and keep your employment." Perhaps I could talk to the Peytons. Emotions were high throughout the ship. It didn't excuse her, but it could convince them to grant some leniency.

"Yes, that is what you members of the gentry are taught. You demand respect from your servants, or you find others who will not speak their minds."

I pulled back from the partition. What was she saying? She'd rarely brought up our difference in class. I likely had less wealth than her father had, even before he'd started stealing from the rope yard. I did not see us as so very different, especially here on the *Marianne*. Clearly, she still did.

"This was beyond a difference of opinion," I pointed out. If they did end her employment, she'd have to wait in Vis until a ship came to the island and could take her to Malta. Then she'd have to find passage back to Portsmouth. It would be a long and unprotected journey. My heart faltered at the thought. "You greatly hurt Mrs. Peyton."

"She should have told him weeks ago." A hint of regret tainted her excuse.

I opened my mouth but couldn't find the words. I tried to remind myself that May was speaking from a place of hurt. "How can you say that? Where is your loyalty?" She was one of the most loyal people I knew. Someone who would keep her word no matter the consequence. At least, I'd thought that was who she was.

"My loyalty?" Her words seemed closer to the partition. "My loyalty is to my family, not some officer who couldn't care if I lived or died. Just like his father-in-law."

She hadn't noticed the strain of sorrow on Captain Peyton's face. The turmoil inside him at the thought of having to flog one of his crew. The pain when he'd made clear her brother's fate. Captain Peyton was a man who cared about those in his command. He included her among that number.

"Mrs. Peyton brought you here because she trusted you." May wasn't listening. I should hold my tongue until morning. Or tomorrow evening when the flogging was over and tempers had cooled.

"She brought me here because she needed someone's help while she lied to her own husband."

I dropped my forehead to my palm. How did I get out of this? "That wasn't your information to tell."

"I didn't ask for her confidence."

I ground my teeth. I needed some jasmine tea and quiet. Every line she spoke pummeled me as hard as one of her brother's strikes on the boatswain. She was better than speaking so ill of her employers when she knew the truth, but she'd latched onto the pain and wouldn't let go. "Can you hear what you are saying?" I asked.

Silence. I waited and, after a moment, heard shuffling. She must have given up. I tore at my cravat, but my yanking tightened the knot. Bothersome cloth. I didn't want her to give up; I wanted her to see the argument from another side. To think of how Mrs. Peyton must have felt being called out in front of her husband. May was blinded to anything but her and her brother's suffering.

"I thought you were my friend," she muttered.

The words bit into me like a boatswain's lash. The accusation in her voice made my heart quake. She'd said it so low, with so much finality, it was as if I'd made her brother break the rules and made Captain Peyton punish him myself. I'd simply stood there with her, aching at every word spoken, knowing how much it would crush her. She loved Lewis, despite his faults. It couldn't have been easy to listen to his sentence. I'd wanted to embrace her and ensure she didn't feel alone. But that meant nothing to her.

She was throwing my efforts back in my face, finishing her strike with a stinging *friend*. Was that all we were in her eyes? She knew me better than that. Surely she had to know the strength of my feelings for her. I'd do anything to take this away, but she didn't want that. She simply wanted someone who agreed that Captain Peyton was the devil himself and Lewis did not deserve a flogging.

I slumped against the bulwark, my strength suddenly gone.

You've done it again, Elias. Chosen someone you care for far more than she could ever care for you. Are you ready to give up yet? Or are you set on this unending cycle of misery?

I closed my eyes but could not block out the deriding voices whirling in my brain. We'd all been terribly misled by those around us. The captain. His wife. May. Me. What was the use in trying if everyone we loved somehow failed us in the end?

Chapter 18

MAY

I stood near the quarterdeck at the front of all the crew, hands folded and shoulders square. I'd locked up the tears that had flowed freely the night before. They wouldn't see me cry. I'd stand and watch their brutality, and I wouldn't give them the pleasure of seeing me go to pieces. Life had already broken me. There was nothing left for them to break.

Elias tried to catch my eye across the deck. I shot him a warning look before quickly pulling my gaze away. Much as I had fooled myself into thinking our little fairy tale could work, our lives were too different. The world didn't look kindly on children of convicts. The only thing we children of criminals could do was respond in like manner. Elias could go back to his world of drinking tea in the garden and strolling to cozy chapels on Sunday mornings. That life was not my destiny.

When the company was assembled, all crew and officers formally dressed, a hush fell over the deck. They looked ready to welcome an admiral aboard rather than witness a flogging. One more oddity of this strange navy world.

Mrs. Peyton stood a little behind her husband, a more obvious gap between them than usual. She kept her eyes on the wood planks at her feet, worrying one corner of her mouth, while he stood stiffly, resignation on his face. When he looked at her, she turned her head quickly. At the start of our voyage, they'd been so happy, the captain unable to hide his adoration and Mrs. Peyton bashful but charmed by his attention. They seemed an entirely different couple now.

My stomach soured so fast I nearly vomited on the deck. The clouds of fury cleared from my head on a harsh breeze of realization. It had been easy to swallow down my guilt last night as worry for Lewis had overwhelmed every other thought. Elias had been right. Whether I had asked for this confidence or not, I'd had no right to tell the captain. My defenses faltered. I'd caused their rift. Though in my mind I wanted to be satisfied with the discord, a pang rattled my heart.

The captain called for Lewis to be brought up from his confinement below, but I barely heard. I'd failed her. My posture slackened. I'd been the only person she could confide in on this ship, and despite giving my word, I'd failed her. I covered my mouth with my hand. I was practically a traitor who deserved to be flogged as much as my brother.

Two seamen escorted Lewis to the grate set against the quarterdeck like a sinister garden trellis. Lewis kept his head lowered, with his face impassive. They made him remove his shirt, revealing crisscrossing scars along the length of his back. I breathed in sharply. This was not his first time being disciplined in this awful manner. If it had happened before, how had he not learned his lesson?

I groaned within, pulling my eyes away. Lewis never learned. And I'd stood up for him, screaming at Captain Peyton on his own ship about the injustice.

I closed my eyes as my stomach roiled worse than it had in the gale we'd hit last month. Lewis had almost killed an entire ship's crew with his stupidity. Then he'd attacked an officer trying to stop him. Lewis knew the punishment for something like that. He had lived this life for years.

"Are you well, Miss Byam?"

I startled at Fitz's voice beside me. "Oh. Yes. I am well." He raised a brow, and I looked quickly away. Captain Peyton called for Lewis to be secured. His hands were tied to the upper corners of the grate. My brother didn't fight them.

I found the Hallyburtons, expecting a look of glee on the wife's face. She only stared at Lewis with unveiled hatred. The boatswain looked like he'd taken an anchor to the face, his nose, eyelids, and cheekbones a mass of ugly, purple bruising. He handed a bag to Catterick, who pulled a nine-tailed whip out of it. Each length of rope had a hefty knot at the end. The deck started to spin.

"Lewis Byam Jr., former carpenter's mate, has been found guilty of drunkenness, endangering the ship, and striking a superior officer," Captain Peyton said quietly. The only movement in the gathering was the faint swell that gently rocked the *Marianne*'s deck. "Is there any who objects to the punishment of twenty-five lashes?"

Twenty-five. I fell back a step on shaking legs. The number still seemed too great. But would he learn if it were fifty? A hundred?

No one said anything. They'd seen this before. If a member of the crew could not be trusted, he was a threat not only to their success but also to their very lives. Lewis had shown he couldn't be trusted. Just like our father. And with a ragged breath, I realized I had shown the same.

The captain nodded gravely.

"No, I'm not well," I whispered, unsure if Fitz heard. I'd wanted to stand here, strong and unmoving as an oak tree, not letting them see me cry or beg. Showing them what I was made of. But the captain, his wife, and Elias had already seen what I was made of last night, and it wasn't strength. They'd seen me lash out in the greatest weakness, not as a young woman as unbending as iron but rather as a little girl still unhinged from the revelation that her beloved papa was a lying, thieving scoundrel. A child who'd let herself be fooled by someone she loved. Again.

"Be done with it, Mr. Catterick," the captain said.

The whip cut through the air with a menacing whir, and I turned on my heel. I darted between the unyielding shoulders of a forest of stocky seamen who hardly spared me a glance. Lewis's shout echoed across the deck. I launched myself down the ladders into the belly of the ship, his cries of pain mingled with those of my own heart.

ELIAS

The sound of wood scraping wood brought my head up from my Bible. Men's voices carried from the cabin beside me. I stood quickly, snapping the book closed. The noise came from May's cabin. Why were there men in her cabin?

I crossed to my door in one stride and threw it open. Captain Peyton hadn't seemed as upset with May after last night's outburst as I had expected. He'd seemed too absorbed with what she'd revealed about Mrs. Peyton. Perhaps he'd kept in a deeper anger toward May than I had thought. Or he'd wanted to deal with her after getting her brother's punishment out of the way.

Two seamen carried her trunk out of the cabin and toward the hatchway.

"What . . . ?" I glanced around the gun room, but the few officers gathered seemed to be paying attention to maps and charts rather than the movement of a trunk.

May stepped out of her cabin, arms wrapped tightly around her middle. She wore her thin coat and carried her bonnet. Behind her, the cabin lay emptier than I'd ever seen it.

"What are they doing?" I asked, taking her by the arms.

She would not meet my gaze. "Taking my trunk above."

I pulled her back into the relative privacy of her cabin. "Have they dismissed you?" How could Peyton do that? Leave a young woman to her own resources on a remote island in a war-disturbed sea, where she couldn't speak the language and knew no one? Had the pressures of responsibility to the navy and family muddled his senses? Peyton had been one of the fairest and most understanding officers I'd met in all my years connected with the Royal Navy.

May pursed her lips and shook her head. "They should have, but they haven't."

"Then, why are they clearing out your cabin?" No more whispered conversations through cracks in the wall. No more greeting her each morning outside our cabins, trying to hide my grin at the glow I felt on seeing her. I didn't think things would return to how they'd been very quickly, but I'd hoped every moment that they would eventually.

"The captain sent someone ashore to procure a house for his wife near the docks," she said, voice flat. "We are to take possession of it by evening."

He was sending them ashore. Permanently, by the sound of it. A headache suddenly sprang up, and I released her to rub my forehead.

"I think it will be a better situation for all, Mr. Doswell."

I dared to hope there was a lie behind her steady words and formal address. "I don't want you to go," I blurted. "I'll . . . I'll miss your company." The fire in her indigo eyes. The way she almost smiled every time she saw me. The way just having her near made me feel like I could face anything the world had in store.

She shook her head. "I was foolish. I let myself think that because we shared a cabin wall, we were equals. But we aren't. We come from two different worlds."

"Marriages between classes are more frequent than Society likes to admit," I said. Her eyes widened at the word *marriage*. We'd never brought up that idea before, but surely she knew where I stood. I wanted to see her face each morning, not just for the duration of our voyage but for as many days as God granted us on this earth. I wanted to be the arms that comforted her in the storms of life, and I wanted to hold to her grounding strength when I felt I couldn't go on.

"It isn't simply money." A heavy breath escaped her. "Our lives are too different. *We* are too different. You deserve a sweet-tempered, accomplished lady who can make your home a haven. Someone your parish will love and admire for her thoughtfulness and grace. Someone trustworthy." She squeezed herself tighter. "You cannot marry a convict's daughter."

Her family's actions had nothing to do with us.

"I'm very sorry, Elias," she said. "I've mistreated everyone and for the stupidest reasons. I don't know what came over me." She paused, throat bobbing. "No, I do know what came over me—pride and misplaced indignation. Hurt and anger I didn't want to rein in."

She sniffed and blinked. "I don't want to hurt you, but I fear I could cause greater harm if we continue down this path. You deserve much better."

"May, please."

"I'm needed above." Her eyes glistened in the light coming from the gun room lanterns. "I've been the worst sort of lady's maid, and I have a long way to go to make amends for the trust I've broken."

I could only nod as I struggled to draw in the dank air. She was leaving and not just physically. "Can we discuss this further before you make up your mind?" I asked.

Here it comes again. What a simpleton. You thought it would be different this time. How very wrong you were.

She shook her head. "I've already made up my mind." She loosened her stiff posture and took my hand, raising it to her cheek. She breathed in, closing her eyes, then removed it and kissed the back of my hand softly. "Thank you, Mr. Doswell. You truly are one of the best of men."

May slipped out of the cabin like a specter in the night, stealing with her every tiny ray of hope I'd cultivated that someone could finally love me enough to stay.

MAY

With shaking hand, I rapped lightly on Mrs. Peyton's bedroom door. She'd gone to bed an hour ago with a mumbled good night and no request to help her change. I hadn't heard anything from her room since, but a faint light flickered under the door.

I wrapped my arms around myself in the dark, narrow corridor as I waited for a sound to signal her coming. To my right, a rickety flight of stairs led up to my new room, one of the two rooms in the narrow house Captain Peyton had let for us. Shadows edged every lonely, unfamiliar step.

The door half opened, revealing Mrs. Peyton still in her day clothes. Her blank gaze suggested fatigue, but I knew it was a defense as much as anything.

"Yes?"

"Shall I help you dress for bed, ma'am?" It was not what I'd come for, but perhaps that would make it easier to speak.

She shook her head. "I can manage."

I picked at the sleeve of my gown. "Would you like me to stoke the fire?"

"No. Thank you." Her stiff words seemed a valiant attempt at civility. A part of me wished she would scream at me instead of this gut-wrenching quiet.

"Can I bring you tea?"

She gave a single shake of her head. She didn't want to see me. I wouldn't have wanted to see me either.

I simply had to forge ahead, difficult as it was. "I don't know how I can ever make amends for what I did, but I am sorry. I had no right to tell him." My shoulders had drawn in of their own accord. How I wanted to shrink until nothing remained of my loathsome being.

"No, you didn't."

Especially not in the horrific manner I had. My face burned. Now what did I say? How did one go about making amends when there was no way to take back words?

"I'm surprised he didn't guess it before," she continued unexpectedly. "His duties as captain have weighed him down heavily of late. And it isn't as though he has spent very much time with women in his life." The faintest whisper of a smile flitted across her lips and vanished. "But that is not what pained me the most about your outburst."

I waited in silence. Whatever she wished to say to me, I would listen.

She gripped the doorframe with one hand, arm protectively across her as though I might inflict more hurt. Her voice lowered, full of warning. "My father is not who you think he is."

Aunt Byam's curses thundered in my mind. None of us had ever met this man we hated so much. He'd always been some grand gentleman in my head, cold and calculating and far superior to anyone he met. Mrs. Peyton was right. I had little founding for my opinion of him.

"When my mother died, he lost one of the only things he cared about in this world." She wouldn't meet my eyes, focusing instead on something behind the door. "I know your family was upset that my father refused your uncle's request to bring your aunt. She told Dominic as much when he brought her the news about Mr. Byam. But my father was only trying to protect me. I was all he had left."

The image of the haughty captain shattered in my mind, replaced by a fearful, grief-stricken father shielding his little girl from the world. I dug my fingers into my sleeves as the understanding I'd tried to cultivate in the last weeks extended toward Captain Woodall, this man whose very name had incited the worst in my family.

"Sometimes our love pushes us to do unwise things," Mrs. Peyton said.

Though said softly, the remark slapped me across the face. Love did make it difficult to be wise. It blinded you to faults and danger and reality. Love for Lewis had turned me into an imbecile far worse than I'd imagined Elias to be on our first meeting. Papa's love and desire to provide for us had turned him into a criminal. Elias's love for me . . . I couldn't think on that.

"It does. I know that now. I had no right to judge him." How could I blame Captain Woodall for his refusal when it had simply been out of fear for his daughter's safety? I'd let our grief, our yearning for someone to blame, villainize a man I'd never met and his family. My already-broken spirit sank lower. "Is there anything I can do, ma'am?" I asked. I didn't just mean to help her tonight.

"No. Thank you, Byam."

I made my way slowly up the stairs. The weight of the last two days seemed as though I'd carry it for the rest of my life. There wasn't a way to recover from what I'd done.

I didn't light my lantern when I got to the unfamiliar attic room. I'd grown used to getting ready in the dark on this journey. Besides, the lantern just reminded me of Elias.

It was a good-sized room with a larger bed than I'd ever had to myself and two windows, but in the empty night, it felt cavernous. I was too accustomed to a narrow cabin with a cracked partition and the sweetest neighbor a girl could ask for.

My fingers bumped against my trunk, and I knelt on the creaky floor. I winced at the sound that shattered the stillness. Mrs. Peyton's room was right below, and I didn't want to disturb her any more than I already had.

Instead of opening my trunk, I rested my head atop it. The grains of the old wood pressed into my cheek. I'd ruined everything. The path ahead looked impossibly bleak. I'd pushed away all friends, all family. For once, I couldn't blame my misfortunes on Papa's crimes. I alone carried the fault.

Trees rustled just outside one of the windows. A dog barked somewhere in the distance, then went silent. I never thought I'd miss the quiet mutterings of seamen settling in for the night, the *Marianne's* beams groaning as she lulled them to sleep with her rocking. But I did—desperately. I even missed the sound of footsteps on the ladders as the watch changed in the middle of the night. Frank telling jokes over cards. Mrs. Hallyburton scolding her husband in their canvas-sided cabin, where she thought no one else could hear. The Carden boys humming little Scottish tunes as they went about their work. Étienne's contagious laugh. Elias talking to himself as he prepared his sermons. I pressed my fist to my chest, trying to lessen the sting at the last memory. Now my solitary breathing filled every corner of the nearly empty room.

I needed sleep. I wanted nothing more than to throw my blanket over my head and pretend I was back in my hammock replenishing my energy for another day of navy life. What awaited me tomorrow, next week, next month? It didn't seem as though they'd punish me. The Peytons were far from the sort of employers who would beat their servants, and they'd had plenty of time in the last twenty-four hours to terminate my employment but hadn't. Would I remain here, living a silent life without the man I loved, until the navy called us home?

I opened the lid and dug into my belongings, searching for my brush. Everything in this trunk would remind me of him and what I did to him. He'd just told me of the young ladies who had rejected him. I'd pridefully thought I was better than they were, that I truly appreciated him for who he was. Perhaps I did appreciate him, but I'd wounded him as deeply as any of them. If only I could have been the woman he needed.

My hand closed around a little book amid the gowns and shifts at the bottom of my trunk. Papa's book of Cowper. I pulled it out. I hadn't read it since the beginning of our journey, huddled by the sliver of light from Elias's lantern.

I smoothed my thumb over the worn cover. I'd hidden the book in my apron pocket when authorities had come to take everything after Papa's conviction. That was not long before they'd set him on a ship bound for Port Jackson in New Holland. He'd cried that day as they'd led him and the other convicts past us in chains. I'd never seen him cry before. It hadn't affected me then. I'd been too numb to do more than hold Mama's hand and watch.

I flipped the pages one by one, even though I couldn't see them. Papa got the punishment he deserved, according to the law, but I'd also punished him daily in my heart. I hadn't been able to forgive him. In fact, at one point, I'd vowed I never would. I'd carried the pain and anger with me every day since, and it had eaten me from the inside, coming out in bursts of emotion when I thought myself wronged by others. The only times I could remember letting the weight of it go were the moments with Elias. Forgiveness didn't seem so impossible with him.

I reached for my lantern, locating it to the side of my trunk. With shaking hands, I lit it and sat with my back against the wall, much like I had the night I'd taken advantage of Elias's lantern light. I opened the book to the poem I'd been reading that night.

For thee I panted, thee I priz'd,
For thee I gladly sacrific'd
Whate'er I lov'd before,
And shall I see thee start away,
And helpless, hopeless, hear thee say—
Farewell! we meet no more?

It was as if Elias were speaking to me from the page. A tear trick-led down my cheek. What I wouldn't give to see the smiling face of Mama or Elias just now or read a loving message from Papa. I had no one to help ease this despair, and I only had myself to blame.

Chapter 19

MAY

"Will you join me on my walk today, Byam?" Mrs. Peyton asked from her seat at the empty table.

I turned at the doorway that led from the dining room into the little kitchen. "Pardon, ma'am?" For the first week of our internment on land, we'd said very little to each other. Mrs. Peyton had kept mostly to her room, except for meals and a daily, solitary walk. Anytime I'd entered her bedroom, she had closed her book of drawings and tucked it away. The last two weeks, she'd spoken to me a little more and had taken to working in the sitting room—if it could be called that with how cramped it was—cutting cloth. I didn't try to push her. I'd broken her trust and had no right to ask for it back, but the silence was gnawing at me like rats at the food stores.

I glanced down at the half-finished bowl of porridge in my hand and nearly full cup of tea in the other. She hadn't eaten much to have energy to walk. Still, I dared not dissuade her. "I cannot say no to more fresh air." I'd been outside a few times in the three weeks since we'd been banished from the *Marianne*, mostly to secure food from the market not far away, but even those excursions hadn't prevented the house from feeling like a prison.

She stood and nodded. "I'll fetch my pelisse and bonnet."

"I can—"

With a wave of her hand, she dismissed me and made for the stairs. I hurried to dispose of the dishes and wipe off the table. Mrs. Peyton hardly left a crumb after eating, but I was trying to do everything to perfection—make simple meals the best I knew how, keep the dust from the furniture and floors, clean the clothes and linens regularly.

I paused, the rag still pressed to the table's knotted surface. If only there were a way I could make amends with everyone I'd hurt. Making things right with Elias felt nearly impossible. I couldn't heal the bigger pain I'd caused, that of pushing him away. The look on his face as I'd left—the despair in his green eyes—was emblazoned on my mind.

I slowly straightened, studying the cheaply made table that had come with the house. I saw him in every cup of tea or well-dressed gentleman passing by our windows. Each time a pair of seamen in blue jackets would arrive at the house with a letter from Captain Peyton or a basket of food, I always hoped they would have something from Elias too. All I received was well-deserved silence.

When we'd tied on our bonnets and buttoned our coats, we set off into the breezy sunshine. Yesterday, rain had pummeled our house and rattled the windows, but morning had dawned with few traces of the storm beyond palm leaves littering the road. I gulped in the fresh sea air, even though I did not spare the harbor a single glance. Try as I might, I would not be able to keep from seeking out the masts of the *Marianne*.

Mrs. Peyton walked with purpose away from the water, and I hurried to keep up with her despite her shorter stature. She must not have intended for this to be a leisurely walk.

"Are we going somewhere in particular?" I asked.

"I usually walk up Whitby Hill. They've a telegraph at the top, and sometimes there is news."

I glanced around at the many green hills that enveloped the bay but couldn't see a telegraph through the foliage. It could be any of them.

"The one with the tower." She pointed to one of the taller hills with a medieval-looking ruin peeking up over the trees. It lay near where the army was building its fort. We'd get a very good view of the *Marianne* from that hill. I increased my speed. It was a pity we hadn't brought a telescope. Perhaps I'd be able to pick out Elias's red hair as he walked the deck.

But no. I slowed again. I wasn't supposed to be looking for our ship. I wasn't supposed to be trying to see Elias at all. I'd broken his heart and my own, and I was still trying to convince myself that it was out of necessity.

"Have you heard from the captain since his note yesterday?" I asked, fumbling with the buttons of my redingote. Though late November, the combination of sun and exercise made extra layers too hot.

"He only said they were sheltering from the storm in Vis, but he did not say how long they'd stay."

"Oh," was all I could say. Her tight words brought on a fresh wave of guilt. She must still be furious with me. Captain Peyton had visited only once, very briefly, since he'd confined us to the island.

Mrs. Peyton glanced back, looking me in the eye for the first time in weeks. Her brows knit. "He did say that he transferred Mr. Byam to the *Unité.*"

I nodded. When I'd said my goodbyes to Lewis, he'd told me of his demotion and impending transfer. He hadn't seemed as contrite as I'd desperately hoped, joking about Captain Peyton taking pity and stopping the punishment before Catterick had given him the full twenty-five lashes. I'd been a fool to hope he'd ever learn. And I'd likely not hear from him again for a very long time.

It was just as well.

I pulled off my coat and draped it over my arms. "Is the captain still very angry with you?"

Mrs. Peyton went silent for several moments as we passed the last line of red-roofed houses and started into the trees. "I think he was hurt more than angry. We all do foolish things when we're hurt and afraid."

Like pushing Elias away. I blinked at the uninvited thought. Rocks and pebbles appeared on the dirt path, and I moved closer to her in case she tripped. By now, she was nearing halfway through her pregnancy, and that was always the time Agnes started to feel off-balanced.

Pushing Elias away hadn't come from hurt or fear. Well, perhaps a little from fear—fear of what a future together would mean for him. And a little for me. Even though I knew how to behave since my family had lived the tea-drinking life, Society cared as much about who your family was as they did about genteel manners. How could we face constant opposition from our neighbors? The hurt of the moment and what I'd done with it had made those fears more serious.

Mrs. Peyton started to puff but held her brisk pace as the incline increased. I stayed a step behind her within reach. If something happened to her on my watch, Captain Peyton surely would never forgive me. That was, if he'd been able to forgive me for my outburst over Lewis, despite Lewis being a despicable, abandoning brother.

Perhaps I was scared about that as well. I hugged my coat. Every person who had meant something to me had broken my trust. I'd convinced myself that perhaps Elias would be the first person to stay, but *I'd* pushed him away. I couldn't keep trusting in people. The emptiness compounded with each person who cut ties and walked out of my life. It was safer not to trust, even if it was lonelier.

I kicked at a pebble and sent it skittering off the path. Maybe she was right. That was quite a bit of fear. It would seem we all carried it—Elias's fear of war, Mrs. Peyton's fear of being left behind, Captain Peyton's fear for his wife and child. Was life simply finding ways to push through the fear over and over until the last?

The path before us grew steeper, forcing my employer to finally slow down. Mrs. Peyton hunched but kept advancing with dogged determination. We weren't so different, she and I. Neither of us wanted to be left, though she fought by clinging to those she loved, and I fought by pushing them away. Her way seemed more difficult, but surely it also carried more hope.

"I forgive you for what you did," she said. "I want you to know that."

I started, coming alongside her. "Why would you? I hardly deserve it." I wouldn't forgive myself for something like that. Clearly, as I'd been harboring grudges for many people.

"For one, you have shown your penitence over the last few weeks."

I had certainly tried, though my efforts felt lacking. There was only so much I could do to repair what I'd done.

"For another, I understand, to some degree, the panic one feels when someone they love is in danger, even if they've made mistakes that put them there." She sighed. "Most of all, I do not want to carry this burden of indignation any longer. It's far too lonely a place to be." She gave me a hesitant smile.

I could understand not wanting to hold on to those feelings, but I could not comprehend how easily she forgave me. "Thank you. You are a better woman than I am."

"I never knew how much pain your family was harboring because of my father's decision. I was sorry to hear of it."

I shook my head. "It was not your fault." Her father couldn't have known what would happen, but Mrs. Peyton was least to blame.

"Still, I wish I had known." She gave me a sad smile that made my guilt burn and my heart ease all at once.

"How are you feeling, ma'am?"

"Better than I have since the start of the voyage." While tired, she looked more energetic and full of life than I'd ever seen her. It seemed the walking really had done her some good. "I'd nearly despaired of ever feeling well again." She gave a soft laugh.

A laugh. Had I heard her laugh at all in our time together?

"Do you think we will still be in Vis when the baby comes?" I asked.

"With four or five months left, I couldn't say. We are at the mercy of the service." A little glow had crept onto her face.

I couldn't help a smile at the sweetness of her excitement. I only hoped the captain could share in this sweetness when this tension I'd incited had settled. Perhaps he'd let us return to the ship while she awaited the little arrival. As long as we stayed on the orlop during engagements, she would be safe. Storms sank ships more than battles did, and the squadron had a comfortable harbor in Vis to weather any gales.

"Do you hope it's a girl baby or a boy baby?" I asked. The conversation was water rushing over the barren wasteland that had been my human interaction of late. I couldn't let it dry up too quickly.

She shrugged. "I couldn't care one way or the other. I think as long as it has Dominic's eyes, I will be happy."

I couldn't fault her for wanting that. For a brief moment, I imagined holding an infant, head covered with soft, ginger fuzz. I hadn't thought about my own children much, but suddenly, I wanted that little one more than I could bear. To see the man you loved reflected in a tiny bundle in your arms must be one of the greatest treasures of life.

Up the hill, an odd-looking contraption appeared over the trees. It had a straight pole like a mast with a perpendicular yardarm sticking out from one side. Attached to the arm were several balls and flags. A few people added more balls. That must be the telegraph.

"It's nice to talk to someone about the baby," she said. "I've really only talked to Étienne, and it was only in medical terms."

Very little seemed to pass the Frenchman's notice. "Not even the captain?" I closed my eyes. My fault again. She hadn't had much opportunity for such a conversation.

Mrs. Peyton suddenly grabbed my arm.

I jerked to a halt, scanning her for any sign of injury. "What is it?" I asked, supporting her arm.

She pointed toward the poles. "The telegraph. They're sending a message." Now the figures were taking down balls and adding flags. They worked rapidly. She started moving again at a similar pace to what she'd employed before. "Let's find out what they're saying."

"Who do you think the message is for?" How they could tell what the message said was beyond me. The series of flag-and-ball combinations moved so quickly I could barely internalize one formation before they moved to the next.

"The ships in the harbor," Mrs. Peyton said.

Something that could affect her husband. And my Elias. We scrambled the last stretch of path until we broke through the trees into the clearing around the telegraph. The men manning the contraption wore the checked shirts and wrapped queues of sailors. One man, more stylishly dressed, stood at the base of the telegraph with a book in hand, barking orders.

Mrs. Peyton strode directly to him. "What news do you have, Mr. Stone?" she asked breathlessly.

"Four suspicious sails to the south," he said, not taking his eyes off his book, which showed drawings of a telegraph with different signals.

Mrs. Peyton locked eyes with me. My breath caught. *Suspicious* could mean anything, but in these waters, it usually meant only one—French ships.

Elias's face, pale and creased with pain as he'd told me his past, filled my vision. Another battle. Would he be asked to push himself past his limits again in support of the crew? I glanced down at the harbor below us, where five ships of various sizes rested. What I wouldn't give to be down there right now. Even if I couldn't do much, at least I could encourage him. He had no one.

I glanced back at Mrs. Peyton, my yearning to be with him suddenly choking me. She was gone. I whipped my gaze toward the path in time to see her disappear through the trees at a run.

"Ma'am!" I took off after her. "Should you be running in your condition?" She ignored me, and at that moment, I hardly minded. We had to get back to that ship.

ELIAS

The *Marianne*'s decks swarmed like a kicked anthill with seamen and marines readying for departure. The moment we could catch a southeasterly wind to get us out of the bay, we would be off. For once, I welcomed it. Sitting in the harbor yesterday, waiting out the storm, seeing the rooftop of the little house where May and Mrs. Peyton resided every time I looked toward the shore, had tortured me more than expected. The ship was filled with enough reminders, but knowing she was there, just beyond my reach, made this hollowness in my chest pang with aching pressure.

I skirted Mr. Hallyburton shouting orders, his face green and yellow from aging bruises, and made my way to the forecastle. Clearly, I enjoyed torturing myself, but I couldn't help it. I wanted a last look at the rooftop before we left.

Someone had beat me to it. Captain Peyton stood with his telescope raised, the glass trained on the shore.

"Do you see them?" I asked, my heart pounding. I shouldn't want a glimpse of her when she wanted nothing more to do with me, but my heart never listened to reason.

"They just returned to the house." He twisted the telescope to focus it. "They were trying to get on one of our boats to come out here."

"Were they?" Why did I want that more than anything?

"Just as I expected." The captain released a sharp breath and closed his telescope. I bit back my disappointment. A hint of a smile played across Peyton's face in spite of his scowl. "She thinks I don't know her well enough by now to guess what she'd be up to."

It wasn't as ridiculous as he made it sound. She *had* kept him ignorant of her coming child for months, but I didn't think he'd appreciate if I brought that up. If only he hadn't anticipated the women's attempt to come aboard.

Why? So you could beg May to have you back? Cowardly, lovesick, pathetic Elias Doswell?

Yes. Because when she was near me, I didn't feel so cowardly or pathetic. I almost believed I had worth beyond the random facts in my head and silly talents rarely useful to anyone. She saw past the worrying chaplain to something more. Someone I wished I could become.

"She's safer there," the captain said in a softer tone.

"But that doesn't help wishing she were at your side." I couldn't entertain these thoughts. How was I to move on if I let her take up so much space in my mind? I should be steeling myself for the battle to come if the ships proved to be French.

Captain Peyton nodded slowly. "Life was so much easier before I set foot on the *Deborah*."

"I'm sorry, sir?" What did he mean by that?

He continued as though I hadn't said anything, his thoughts seeming to tumble from a cluttered mind. "I saw signs since the beginning of the voyage, but I didn't let myself see what they meant. The sickness, the fatigue, the withdrawing." He shook his head. "I had so many other things weighing on me. I determined that if there was something important, she would come to me eventually." He tapped his hand against the telescope. "Clearly, Georgana still has her secrets."

I looked away at the pain in his voice. Miriam had told me how difficult the first year of marriage was as two people realigned their lives to fit the new relationship. I wasn't sure why he was telling me—a bachelor despite my greatest attempts—all of this, but if he needed a listening and understanding ear, I could be that for him. If only I could relate my own struggles.

Peyton clapped me on the shoulder. "Come, Doswell. We're going ashore."

I choked. "Ashore?"

He strode toward the waist, where a few seamen were coming over the side with supplies from a boat that had just arrived. I hurried to catch up.

"I won't rest easy until I know she's safe in the house. I figured you wouldn't mind ensuring they're safe either."

My mouth went suddenly dry. I was seeing May again with my heart still bruised and battered. This was a terrible idea. But as I followed Peyton over the side, my hands and feet carried me all too quickly down the ladder to the boat. What a fool. A blasted, lovesick fool.

MAY

I halted my retreat to the kitchen when Elias walked through the door behind Captain Peyton. Three weeks without seeing him had only intensified his attraction. His red hair was set so as to look perfectly windswept but not wild. Though he wore his black coat, which was my least favorite of his coats, I didn't see the proper clergyman he was attempting to portray. I simply saw the man I loved. The man whose clear, green eyes looked everywhere in the room except at me.

The long days since I'd seen him hit me like an ocean swell. I wanted to run to him, to throw my arms around his waist, pull his coat around the both of us, and bury my face in his jasmine-tea-scented cravat. When had that aroma come to feel like home?

He focused on the captain and Mrs. Peyton, and I forced myself to look away. I had no right to wish for things to return to what they were. I'd broken his heart. Again. How many times could one heart be broken and put back together?

Captain Peyton took his wife's hands and squeezed them. "We don't have long."

"When do you sail?" she asked.

"As soon as we get favorable winds." He sighed, lowering his voice as if to keep their conversation private despite the tiny sitting room. "I wish you were coming."

Mrs. Peyton stood stiff and straight as one of the columns we'd seen at the Roman baths. I could hardly hear any emotion in her tone. "I can come."

It wasn't as if we'd missed the last battle. I clasped my hands behind me, imagining grasping an anchor. It was not my place to enter this conversation. He'd never agree.

A flicker of doubt crossed his face, an almost childlike yearning for what she offered. He brought her hand to his lips and kissed it tenderly, then he squeezed his eyes shut. He was the captain. He could tell her yes or no.

"I want you to be safe," he said, pleading. I'd never heard such vulnerability from the captain. "You and the baby."

I tried to catch Elias's eye. Perhaps we should give them privacy. He'd turned away and was gazing out the window toward the harbor. His stiff posture, with his collar plumb and coat seams masterfully fitted to the straight lines of his back, gave him that air of pride I'd imagined seeing on our first meeting on *Marianne*'s upper deck. His silence had added to that standoffish persona. But I knew he wasn't being proud now. He was holed up behind his defenses, trying to regroup before facing the next battle life threw at him.

I glanced back in time to see the captain gather his wife in his arms and kiss her as though for the last time. My throat tightened. If I hadn't said anything about the baby, would we be aboard for this battle, helping Étienne with the wounded? The captain broke away from her, and I thought I saw his eyes glistening.

"I'm not leaving you behind, George. I'm protecting you."

She didn't respond, but her head tilted slightly as though she weren't in agreement. He turned from her and squared his shoulders.

"Captain?" I asked, lowering my gaze to the floor. I kept my arms stiffly at my sides, gripping the edges of my apron. I needed to do this, as feeble and insignificant as words were.

"Miss Byam." Hesitancy clouded his voice.

"I'm sorry, sir." Humiliation burned in my chest as all the words I'd shouted that day screamed through my head. "For everything I said. I had no right to speak in anger. I was very wrong about Lewis and what he deserved." Why were apologies so difficult? I didn't know how to portray all the sorrow that had gripped my heart in our days ashore. Not sorrow for myself but for those I'd hurt.

"Thank you for your apology." His voice was softer, ever so slightly. It caught me off guard. I didn't expect any sort of warmth. When I looked up, he'd already turned toward Elias.

"Doswell, you needn't return with me if you wish to stay," the captain said. "I hope we'll be back before Sunday."

My breath caught. Stay? Elias hadn't moved a muscle from where he stood near the window. *Please*. I nearly whispered it aloud. My knuckles ached, I was clutching my hands so tightly.

He shook his head. "No, I will come."

I opened my mouth to protest. This was his chance to avoid the fighting that affected him so terribly. He wasn't going to take it? I didn't want his spirit shattered after the conflict again. I closed my mouth. It wasn't my place, I had to keep reminding myself.

"Whatever you wish." The captain retrieved his cocked hat from the little side table near the door. "We'd best be off. I'll send word as soon as I can."

Mrs. Peyton nodded. I hadn't been able to see her face through the whole interaction. Would she finally dissolve into tears when they left? I hadn't seen her cry the entire three weeks we'd been stuck ashore, but surely this would be the breaking point.

Elias held open the door for Captain Peyton, who paused on the threshold.

"I love you, Georgana," Captain Peyton said softly. Then he hurried into the street. Elias's hand tightened on the handle, but he did not hesitate for long before he nodded in our direction and closed the door behind them.

Nothing. He'd given me nothing. I shouldn't have expected anything, just as I hadn't with the captain. I didn't deserve it. But deep down, I had wished for some glimmer of hope. What a simpleton. I'd expected the captain's wife to break down, but I had instead. A hot tear escaped my lashes and ran down my cheek.

I rushed to the window to watch them leave. The men didn't look back, but Captain Peyton said something to Elias, who shook his head. The scene of Charlie and Uncle Byam leaving the house to board the *Deborah* rose in my head. It was the last I'd seen of them. Would I ever see these two men again? Would the dejected nod be my last memory of the chaplain who had loved me without reserve?

"Come, Byam. There's not much time." Mrs. Peyton's firm footsteps clipped along the bare floor.

I scowled, swiping at my tear. "Pardon?"

She stood at the base of the stairs, one hand on the rail and the other lifting the hem of her skirt. "We haven't a moment to lose." Her eyes weren't red-rimmed and wet. Her face wasn't blotchy. She looked calm, as if she'd just told me we were off to finish the mending.

I obediently followed her above, wiping my still-watering eyes on my sleeve. "What is it? Why must we hurry?" I asked.

Without answering, she pushed open the door of her room and hurried to kneel in front of a trunk at the foot of the bed. I held the lid open as she rummaged to the bottom of it. After a moment, she threw a pair of men's checked shirts, trousers, and sailors' slops onto the bed.

I gaped. "What are these for?" She couldn't be serious.

She cocked her head. "Do you want to go with them or not?"

Chapter 20

MAY

"This is madness," I muttered as I scurried down the street to the harbor after Mrs. Peyton. The thick canvas trousers bunched between my legs as I ran. I had to pull up the hems like a gown to keep from tripping, which was much harder to do with two separate legs rather than one continuous skirt. "Won't he recognize you like this?" She and the captain had, after all, met when she'd been similarly dressed as a boy.

Mrs. Peyton didn't spare me a glance. "I'm not planning on running into him until it's too late for him to take me back." She didn't seem uncomfortable at all in her wide-legged petticoat breeches and bulky gansey sweater that mostly hid her belly. She hadn't had to do anything with her hair but pull a knit cap over it. Dark curls—the remnants of the style I'd fixed this morning—peeked out from underneath the cap's brim, making her look like Étienne.

My own hair thumped against my back with each step. I hadn't braided it as nicely as Elias could have, but it made a passable sailor's queue once I'd wrapped it in black silk ribbon. It felt so strange to be out in public with my hair like this, and I prayed each person we passed took us for ship's boys rather than seeing through our disguises. One thing I knew for certain—when Elias found me like this, I would die of humiliation. This was much worse than out-of-fashion gowns.

We plunged into the masses streaming through the dockyard, which seemed primitive compared to Portsmouth's dockyard. Most boats were tiny fishing vessels rather than the gargantuan first-rates and East Indiamen that rocked in Old Pompey's harbor. Large or small, docks always seemed to have a crowd. I grabbed Mrs. Peyton's arm; otherwise, I had no doubt I'd lose her among the fishermen. Only a few we passed looked to be Royal Navy seamen.

"Isn't your husband going to be furious that you put yourself in danger?" I asked. Would he blame me for not stopping her? No, of course he wouldn't. He respected his wife's intelligence more than that.

"If we stay below, I'll be safe enough. Plenty of women have gone to war at sea in my condition," she said, scanning the water. "And the French like to take their prizes as intact as possible so they can restock their supply of ships. They aim for the masts so as to disable without excessively damaging their prizes."

"And the British?" We stopped. Nearby, a lanky sailor waved from a little rowboat barely visible above the dock.

Mrs. Peyton shrugged. "We like to win." She pulled me toward the boat.

I hung back. "I've already put you in too much trouble as it is. If I help you do this . . ."

She fixed me with a steady gaze. "Do you want to be there for them or stay here waiting and worrying if we'll ever see them whole and alive again?"

There was really only one answer. And Mrs. Peyton didn't wait for a response. She climbed over the edge and into the boat.

"What took you so long, Taylor?" The seaman didn't offer her a hand but let her clamber into the vessel on her own. "I came as soon as I could sneak away, just like you told me to." It took me a second to recognize the light hair and slight whistle in his speech. Fitz. He should have known better than to let a woman in her condition . . . Well, I supposed a woman of her condition technically shouldn't run down hillsides and sneak onto ships either. I'd excuse his manners this once. "The handsome cabin boy in the flesh," he said, resting his arms against the handles of the oars. "Busy powderin' your nose?"

"Stow it, Fitz," Mrs. Peyton growled with more authority than I'd ever heard from her.

I climbed down after her, and the boat wobbled under my weight. I seized the sides with a yelp, earning me a smirk from Fitz.

"Don't move, Byam," he said as he set the oars in place. I glared back. It wasn't my fault the boat was tipsy and we'd been on land for almost a month.

Fitz rowed us out into the glistening waves, haphazardly steering the boat through the maze of fishing vessels. The colorful shore, with its waving palms and red-and-white buildings, receded. The farther we strayed from the dock, the more the uncertainty in my chest grew. We were heading for battle.

ELIAS

Night was closing in as we pulled near the Portuguese merchantman with its green-and-white-striped ensign. The island of Lissa had faded to a dark shadow on the northern horizon, and even though I had left May on the opposite coast from the one in my view, I could not help looking back. She'd seemed so reserved when the captain and I had gone to say our goodbyes. I suppose I shouldn't have expected anything different after what had transpired at our last meeting, but it was unlike her usual energetic temperament I missed.

"That's Lieutenant McDougall on the forecastle," the captain said, lowering his telescope. I dropped my gaze to my book and made note of the sunset time with my pencil. Captain Peyton had asked me to take notes of everything on this chase to enter into the log later. I had a mind that he didn't mean notes about how far away Lissa and Miss Byam were.

Lieutenant Roddam grunted in surprise. "He can't have made it to Malta yet. He left just before the storm. How is he back so soon?"

Peyton closed his telescope. "We'll find out shortly. Take her southeast while we wait for Captain Maxwell's signal."

"Yes, sir."

The captain and lieutenant left to change the *Marianne*'s course, but I remained at my position near the bow. Captain Maxwell pulled the *Alceste*, a larger frigate than ours, alongside the Portuguese merchantman. To starboard, the other two ships of our squadron—*Active* and *Unité*—slowed to wait for orders from Maxwell. We were all frigates, and I hoped the Frenchmen we searched for weren't ships of the line.

You'll make a navy man yet, Elias.

I shook my head at the memory of my brother's voice. It wasn't the facts and figures that had driven me from the navy. I managed those plenty well. It was the inevitable bloodshed I didn't have the courage for.

I told you before—I think you are very brave.

I took a slow breath, not allowing my heart to pick up speed the way it had when May had so earnestly said that to me. Was it brave to come so close to taking your captain's offer to shirk your responsibilities and stay safely on shore? The only reason I hadn't stayed was because I had feared the young woman across the room, whose eyes I had felt on my back. How ridiculous to fear her presence more than the impending battle. It was better for May to be ashore and for me to be at sea. She was fulfilling her duty, and I would fulfill mine, safely away from any chance of hurting myself again.

I made another note of our course, and Lieutenant McDougall's presence on the Portuguese ship before closing my book and pocketing my pencil. He must have seen the French ships and made the merchantman turn around to give us warning. That was the only valid explanation. Ships would never get to their destination if they turned around to every fancy that popped into the captain's heart. They had to stay their course. And so did I. With one more look back in the direction of Lissa and my heart's desire, I quit the forecastle and made my way down to the lonely darkness belowdecks.

MAY

I hadn't minded the darkness as a child, but I'd never been on the orlop deck of a ship at night back then. Now, as I huddled between Mrs. Peyton and a coil of rope, it was all I could do to keep from fidgeting. If I didn't have the deck beneath me, I wouldn't have been able to tell which direction was up and which was down.

"Are we to sit here all night?" I whispered. Would we even be able to tell when night was over?

She shifted. "I hope not. When the crew retires, we should be able to find a more suitable spot."

"Fitz didn't procure us hammocks?" Of course a fifteen- or sixteen-year-old boy wouldn't think of such a thing.

"There wasn't time."

I sighed. My heart might have thought this was a good idea, but my hips were beginning to agree with my head, that we shouldn't have come. Cold, dank air seeped through my linen shirt and waistcoat, making me shiver. Why had we done this? I should have tried harder to convince Mrs. Peyton not to.

Somewhere above us, Elias was preparing to retire. I pulled my knees up to my chin and wrapped my arms around my legs. He'd be mumbling in practice for his sermon as he folded his cravat neatly and packed it away. Perhaps he'd be brewing a cup of jasmine tea in his veilleuse-théière at the gun room table while the rest of the officers readied for bed or the next watch. A little sliver of that peaceful life he dreamed of in the turmoil of his current circumstances.

Was he thinking about me? I shouldn't wish it, but secretly, I hoped so. What I wouldn't give to have his greatcoat around me. Preferably with him inside too.

"Mr. Doswell seemed out of sorts today," Mrs. Peyton whispered.

"Yes, he certainly did." On my account. Perhaps the captain had requested his presence and he hadn't been able to refuse. He had not appeared keen on the visit. Then he'd chosen to witness the impending battle over staying with me, which had stung acutely. I must have hurt him severely for him to make that choice.

"If something has happened between you, I'm sorry to hear it."

Was it terribly obvious that we were in a position for that to matter? Even in the cold, my face heated. If the whole crew knew about our moment watching the glowing waves, it was silly to think she had not heard of it. I cleared my throat. "I did it to myself, so I have no one else to blame." Would I have come to the conclusion that we were incompatible if Lewis hadn't been an imbecile?

Something skittered in the blackness not far away, and I flinched, bumping shoulders with Mrs. Peyton. I prayed it wasn't a rat. How much longer would we have to sit down here?

"He always seems to light up when you're around," the captain's wife said. "I never saw him do that on our previous voyage."

I didn't know how to respond, but the warmth in my middle chased away any thought of our current discomfort. Elias had a heart of gold to see something worthwhile through my rocky faults. How could I let him slip away? I wasn't vicar's wife material, but what did that matter if he did not care? If nothing else, I knew how to learn, to adapt, to stand my ground when the world told me to give up. I hadn't broken until I'd lost myself in my own misconceptions.

"He was rather quiet that voyage," she went on. "I suppose he still is, but it has been a comfortable quiet."

"I fear I hurt him immensely," I said, squeezing my legs tighter against my chest.

The ship creaked. Voices filtered through the deck above us, but I couldn't make out what they said. We were just under the gun room, so it would be officers' conversations. Was it Elias?

"Few things are irreparable if you are willing to try," she said.

I wasn't so sure. Could I repair it, this damage I'd done to his heart? Not many people in my life had tried to make amends when they'd wronged me. Elias was one of the only people. Surely I could try for him.

Mrs. Peyton shivered. If only we'd been able to procure coats instead of just shirts and waistcoats.

A little whistle wound its way through the belly of the ship. I straightened. A boatswain's call? No, it sounded too light for that. In a moment, I could pick out a merry tune as the sound grew louder. Seamen didn't whistle often, as some believed it brought bad luck. Who would risk his shipmates' displeasure? It couldn't be Fitz. He was as superstitious as any of them.

Footsteps accompanied the whistle.

"He's coming this way," I hissed. We couldn't see to hide. I glanced at Mrs. Peyton and could make out the shape of her face. A moment ago, I wouldn't have been able to see that.

I dropped my forehead to my knees. The captain couldn't be too terribly angry when this seaman reported us, could he? Not more upset than he'd been with Lewis or me. I'd faced him once, and I could do it again. But heaven knew, the thought made my insides crawl.

A form came around the corner, and light tripped across the walls from a swinging lantern. Mrs. Peyton and I flinched at the sudden attack on our eyes. I blinked rapidly, and for a moment, I thought Elias had materialized. No, this man was far too short. My frame involuntarily sagged. He had a darker complexion too.

The footsteps stopped, and the lantern moved toward us with its spears of light that made our eyes water. A low chuckle erupted from the newcomer.

"Ah, Mr. Taylor. I didn't expect to meet you again." The French accent was unmistakable.

"Dr. Étienne," Mrs. Peyton said.

He extended his free hand. "Perhaps you and Miss Byam would join me in rolling bandages for tomorrow's battle. It would be far more comfortable for someone in your condition than hiding in the cables." He helped Mrs. Peyton stand, then offered to assist me as well. I rubbed my eyes, which were finally adjusting to the light, and took his hand. He looked us both up and down, then gave a mischievous grin. "I have no doubt there is an interesting explanation for all of this. It is good, then, that I have many bandages to roll."

Chapter 21

ELIAS

"Ships! Ships!"

I nearly dropped the teacup I'd been holding to my lips as the shout echoed down the length of the *Marianne*.

Captain Peyton handed his cup to the nearest midshipman, who fumbled with it. The captain leaped nimbly down the steps from the quarterdeck. "Kingdon, my telescope. McDaniel, fetch Lieutenant Roddam." He barked orders to the mids as he went. The young men, some just boys, scurried to their assignments.

At last. We'd only just breakfasted, but everyone aboard had been pacing. We all knew the battle was nigh, but not knowing when it would catch us had put the whole crew on edge. I handed my cup and saucer to the midshipman who was taking the captain's below and followed Peyton forward, fishing my notebook and pencil from my pocket. I slid out my watch. Just after nine o'clock. My fingers responded stiffly as I made note. Though I couldn't yet feel the fear through my hollowness, my body had already started to react.

I positioned myself to Captain Peyton's right as he observed the little white dots on the horizon.

"Four," he muttered. "And one is flying the *tricolore*. French, no doubt about it."

I rested my book on the rail and scribbled rapidly.

"Did we find them?" Lieutenant Roddam bounded up to us.

"Signal the *Alceste*." A flicker of excitement lit the captain's eye. "We've a chase on our hands."

The lieutenant nodded once. "Beat to quarters, sir?"

"Without delay." He kept his focus on the enemy ships, and the lieutenant hurried away. I noted the time he'd given the orders. The captain lowered his telescope slightly. "I need you with me, Doswell."

My throat tightened. "Yes, sir."

"We're taking a prize today, and I will not allow the men to be cheated out of their rightful earnings. I need your record."

"I serve at the pleasure of my captain." I'd try to be useful, something I rarely was on this ship.

"You're a good man, Doswell." He clapped me on the shoulder in his usual way. "Would you tell Étienne he'll have to do without you today?" He lowered his voice. "It might be a busy one."

Drums erupted, their furious beat ringing in my skull. The ship came alive with men moving unnecessary objects below. I crossed under the shadows of our sails, all of which had been set since Lieutenant McDougall had given us the news last evening that the Frenchmen were forty miles south. To have found them so early in the day was a blessing—if all went well, we wouldn't have to chase through the night.

I entered a wave of seamen descending through the hatchway. I couldn't think about what had been asked of me. Captain Peyton needed me, and as a member of his crew, I needed to follow orders. I should have had a queasy stomach at the thought of standing on the quarterdeck again during battle, but I didn't. An unfamiliar numbness overtook me when I usually met fear in these moments.

On the gun deck, men were opening ports and stowing the captain's cabin. Seamen tied up hammocks and moved chests on the mess deck. They dismantled the bulwark that made up the gun room wall by wall, starting with May's empty cabin. What I wouldn't give to find her encouraging face in the cockpit with Étienne like I had in the last battle.

More men clambered about the orlop than usual, dark shapes eerily lit by orange lantern light. How many would last the day? It would be an even fight. Ship for ship. The Lord only knew what sort of fight the French would put up.

I ducked into the cockpit, which had already been cleared of the midshipmen's hammocks and sea chests. "Doctor, the captain wishes . . ." My eyes fell on a trio of boys standing to one side. Harvey Carden's eyes had gone as wide as eighteen-pound shot. Beside him sat an all-too-familiar dark-haired person in men's clothing whom I hadn't seen since stepping off HMS *Deborah*. My jaw dropped. Gracious! What was Mrs. Peyton doing here? And dressed in her old disguise?

Then I turned to the third individual in canvas trousers and checked shirt, whose face had gone crimson and who stood with arms folded protectively in front of their ill-fitting waistcoat.

I glanced at Étienne, who wasn't making any effort to hide his laughter, then back. When I'd thought I'd give anything to see her face, I hadn't expected her to materialize in sailor's slops and ribbon-wrapped queue.

"May?" I finally choked out.

MAY

Étienne had warned me Elias might come down, but it didn't take away the humiliation. Vicars, at least the ones who truly cared about their position, didn't want wives who dressed inappropriately. But here I was, and here he was, and there was nothing I could do about it now.

"How . . . How did you get here?" Elias tangled his fingers in his hair, worry flooding his features. Beneath it all was a spark of joy in the lift of his mouth and eagerness in his eyes, or was I imagining what I wanted to see?

"You're supposed to be in Vis." He turned to Étienne. "Did you help them?"

The Frenchman lifted his shoulders and threw up his hands innocently. "I simply found them and gave them a place to stay for the night."

"The captain . . ." Elias trailed off, features going pale.

"No need to tell him now," Mrs. Peyton said quickly. "I don't want to disrupt his focus."

Elias nodded slowly, rubbing the back of his neck. "I was sent here to tell you the captain requested my presence above and I won't be able to assist you, Doctor. It would appear you have all the help you need."

He was staying on the upper decks again? I gripped my shirt-sleeves, fingers digging into the thick linen. He couldn't.

Elias nodded a farewell and rushed out of the cockpit.

I followed on his heels into the darkness of the passageway, grabbing for his arm. I hadn't the faintest idea what I'd say, but I had to say something. "Wait. Just give me one moment."

His arm went rigid in my hand, but he stopped and looked down at me with brows pulled together. He took a measured breath and waited.

I licked my lips. Barreling into things was a specialty of mine, but this wasn't something to be handled with a bludgeon. Elias had all the delicacy. "I know there's not much time. And this needs more time than we can give. But I was wrong to push you away when all you wished to do was love and support me. So very, very wrong. And I'm sorry."

He didn't move, and I couldn't read anything through his guarded expression.

"I was hurt and scared, and I let it all come spilling out." Much like I was letting this apology tumble from my mouth in awkward and unfiltered phrases. "Before you go, just know that I'm proud of you and that"—I shouldn't say it, but there was no stopping—"I love you."

I took him by the arms and rose up to kiss his cheek quickly, but I didn't make it before a voice cried, "What the devil?"

I flinched and broke away from Elias, whipping my head around. Shelby, the gunner's mate, stood in the passageway behind me with an oil lamp in one hand and a spare cannon sponge on its long handle in the other.

"Miss Byam?" The gunner's mate looked me up and down with a skeptical scowl.

I shuffled back, every last inch of my skin aflame. Would I ever learn to keep control of myself?

"If you'll make way for working folk," Shelby grumbled, shaking his head and stalking past us.

"Perhaps we should continue this"—Elias cleared his throat, eyes flicking to my lips—"conversation later."

While I liked the sound of later, the trouble brewing didn't allow the pleasure to last long.

I squeezed his hand. "Be careful." The thought of him going above made my stomach tie itself in knots. I'd be here waiting, praying with everything I had that we'd have time to right all my wrongs when the smoke cleared.

ELIAS

Wind whipped at our hair and clothing as we flew after the two smallest French ships, which had broken off from the others. A chorus of popping from the larger frigates' battle to the east echoed across the water, though HMS *Alceste* and HMS *Active* were as tiny as children's toys on the horizon. Our companion, HMS *Unité*—which was large enough for eight more guns than our *Marianne* had—sailed along beside us, every sail bent in a similar fashion to ours.

I made note that it seemed *Alceste* was disabled. Through the spyglass, it appeared two of her masts were down, but it was difficult to tell in the mix of masts and rigging shrouded by smoke.

"We'll get our turn, boys," Captain Peyton muttered near the helm. "Hold fast."

I wouldn't mind if we lost them, even if it would sorely disappoint the crew, but I kept my thoughts to myself. We'd exchanged shots with the enemy vessels a few hours ago, which had whetted the crew's appetite. Then the French ships had darted away. They didn't seem keen on the opportunity to make a prize of us. Odd for French captains, but it could mean they carried precious cargo they didn't want falling into English hands.

If only I could go below with May. I'd reassure her that I was well so she wouldn't have to worry. For all her blunt exterior, she'd do anything for those she loved. That included me. My heart warmed despite the nipping breeze. How things had changed in a matter of moments. From numbing loneliness to dizzying shock. Perhaps there was an urgent message Peyton needed me to carry to Étienne.

And what would you do if you went below? Find a dark corner and continue your "conversation"? What an upstanding clergyman you are.

I winced at the thought. No, it was better for me to stay right here. May was right; we did have much to discuss. Things wouldn't go neatly back to how they'd been before, no matter how much the romantic inside me wanted to pretend the last three weeks hadn't happened, but I still wanted to try.

I brought the glass up again, this time pointing it forward toward the enemy ships we chased. The two Frenchmen, which couldn't be much bigger than *Marianne*, raced northward. They were running for Italy, no doubt. Perhaps with supplies. One of them had dropped back and seemed to be adjusting her course away from the other.

"She's turning northwest!" a midshipman shouted from the lower platform of the foremast. The news was repeated across the upper deck. They were splitting up, perhaps in hopes we wouldn't head them off and chase them back toward the battle.

"She's on our side," Peyton said to Roddam. "Signal Captain Chamberlayne to keep his course. We'll follow her." *Unité* was the larger of us, but the two French ships seemed similar in size. I prayed we were tracking the weaker and easier of the two.

Something about this ship seemed familiar, though perhaps I was simply reliving my memories of our battles on the *Deborah*. I trained the telescope on her transom as seamen scrambled to reset the sails and Captain Peyton gave Mr. Sanchez orders to turn. Yellow leaves scrolled above the stern windows of the French ship in a way I could have sworn I'd seen before. Such decoration was rather common among all of Europe's navies, but each ship had a slightly different design. I focused the glass on the small nameplate below the windows. *Saint-Germain.*

It couldn't be. I pulled away from the telescope and squinted as though that would help me see it better. There might be several ships of that name. Heaven knew the Royal Navy had plenty of repeated names in its fleets. This couldn't be the ship HMS *Deborah* had met near Antigua last year, which had dug in its heels and held on like a bulldog refusing to release its bone. So many had been wounded in that fight. So many had been killed. I glanced toward the hatchway. Including May's uncle. Twice that voyage, I had watched the ship leave after giving its all against a greater foe, as the *Deborah* had certainly outgunned her. Now it was an even fight. My skin crawled.

"Captain, did you see this?" I asked. "The name."

He joined me at the starboard rail and brought his own glass to his eye. After a moment, he leaned into the rail much like I had done. "Surely that isn't . . ."

"Look at her paint," I said. "The yellow and blue on black. That's hardly a common stripe pattern." But one that haunted my nightmares in moments of weakness.

He examined her again. "Well, this has taken an interesting turn." He closed his glass and tapped it against his hand. "I'd wager good money that's the very same privateer. She won't get away this time," Captain Peyton muttered. He pivoted and raised his voice. "Load the bow chasers. We'll give them a volley."

Gun crews at the bow sprang into action, readying their guns and waiting for the order to fire. Captain Peyton clasped his hands behind his back, thinly veiled anticipation on his face. Would he be so eager if he knew his wife was below? I bit the inside of my mouth. How had I been roped into keeping another bit of information about his wife from him?

"I wonder if she has the same captain," Peyton said. I couldn't tell if it was to me or to himself. "She's sailing much more cautiously."

Last year, her captain had been greedy and impulsive, and the *Deborah*'s captain had been wary and not keen on risking his ship or crew. Peyton was far more assertive, with a natural gift for navigating the seas and anticipating his enemy. Which would rule the day?

"Roddam, fire at will."

"Yes, sir."

I braced myself against the rail as the deafening roar of the big guns shattered the howl of the wind.

Chapter 22

MAY

I helped Étienne strap down a young midshipman as Hardy brought tools to extract the long shard of wood in the boy's arm. Mrs. Peyton held a lantern above the table to give the surgeon adequate light.

"Will I lose the arm?" the boy asked, chin quivering slightly. Poor lad. I wanted to hug him. He was trying so hard to be brave.

The Frenchman smiled as he plucked up a tool. "Not today, Mr. Greaves. Miss Byam, I think you'll have to hold his arm for me. These bands won't hold as efficiently as I'd like."

I moved around the table to stand beside him and took hold of the young man's hand and wrist. He gripped my fingers tightly. The enormous splinter was lodged deep, but I hoped for his sake that Étienne wouldn't have to dig too much.

"The *Unité*'s opponent already struck her colors, did you hear?" the midshipman asked. "One broadside." His voice rose in pitch as Étienne grasped the splinter with pincers and pulled.

Unité was Lewis's new ship. So, his crew hadn't had to fight long. I sent a prayer of gratitude heavenward. For all the trouble he'd caused, the thought of his safety was a ray of calm breaking through the tension. If only we could have been so lucky with our opponent.

"We clearly chose the wrong ship to engage," I said, keeping my gaze away from the wound. It took a moment to get used to the blood, even though I wasn't usually squeamish. *Marianne* had been on *Saint-Germain*'s tail for at least thirty minutes, but the French frigate had only just managed a true hit.

"Our foremast took a solid smashing," Greaves said with a waver. Attempting to distract himself from the pain. Clever boy. He'd make a good captain one day. "They've a good crew on their stern chasers. The guns have been causing trouble to the masts and rigging. But we're—" He clenched his eyes shut as Étienne pulled the splinter free. "We're gaining on them. We should draw alongside shortly."

And then the real fight would begin.

"Were there any other wounded?" I asked. And were there any casualties? Elias would have been on the opposite end of the ship, on the quarterdeck, but if it had been a raking blow, the shot could have caused damage down the length of the ship.

"No, miss." He paused and gritted his teeth as Étienne washed out the wound to try to clear any slivers of wood. I didn't envy him the sting of the saltwater. "A few had minor wounds and could keep at their stations. But Lieutenant Roddam insisted I come below." The jagged scrap of wood now lying on the floor, where Étienne had tossed it, seemed like it would inhibit anyone unfortunate enough to get it lodged in his arm.

"How do the officers fare?" He'd said no others wounded, but I had to be sure.

"She means Mr. Doswell, specifically," Étienne muttered as he warmed a plaster by the lantern candle.

I pursed my lips. He needn't have been so blunt about it. Perhaps it was the French way, but I preferred more privacy than that.

The boy's brows knit. "Doswell? He seemed well enough, I suppose."

Praise the heavens for that. Or was he just saying it? Had he even noticed Elias in the chaos? I closed my eyes and offered a silent prayer, more fervent than I'd said in years. Let him be safe and return to me unscathed. I'd give anything to make it so.

ELIAS

As the *Saint-Germain* sponged and reloaded her guns, I pulled out my pocket watch. Forty-five minutes since we'd taken the first shot in our duel. Haze from the spent gunpowder twisted around the frigates, muting the orange glow already appearing on the horizon, and soon we'd have to light lanterns in order to see to fire. A large risk with so much powder waiting on the gun decks. We'd seen how dangerous a night battle could be on this voyage.

"How many have we lost?" Captain Peyton asked.

I held my spectacles on as the deck pitched from a sudden wave and brought my notebook closer to my face. "One forecastle man dead, seven crew and a midshipman wounded. But two have returned to their posts, sir."

Captain Peyton nodded solemnly. We'd left nearly seventy men, including most of our marines, in port to defend Lissa against a French attack, giving us a hundred and five without the wounded and dead. *Saint-Germain* had a smaller crew, but they'd nearly matched us volley for volley. We couldn't know whether the dark would help or hinder us. If they could slip out of our grasp and lose us, they had a chance of making it to Italy. Perhaps they'd even meet up with the larger frigate we'd seen escaping the battle with HMS *Alceste* and *Active*. If we tracked them alone, we wouldn't have the firepower to battle both ships at once.

"What will you do, Captain?" I asked.

He set his jaw, staring down the enemy across from us. The French ship was banking in our direction for another shot. "Sanchez, one point to port. Don't let her rake us."

"Yes, sir," the helmsman said, adjusting his grip on the wheel.

The captain scanned the *Marianne*'s upper deck, then nodded once as though in decision. "Lieutenant, arm the crew." He nodded to the nearest midshipman. "Mr. McDaniel, tell Mr. Pindall to prepare the grappling hooks." The young man nodded solemnly and hurried away.

Grappling hooks. Captain Peyton meant to board. I swallowed, a difficult feat with smoke and dust permeating the air.

Lieutenant Roddam leaned toward the captain, head bowed to keep his voice from carrying across the quarterdeck. "We're boarding? We don't have our marines."

"They don't have any to speak of. She's a privateer in league with the navy. Our men are more disciplined than a ragtag bunch of corsairs. We will win the day."

"Of course. You know your men."

Peyton took him by the shoulder. "We make a stand now, Roddam, or we risk losing them to the night. Whatever their mission, we must foil it. If they make for Lissa with the other frigate that escaped, they could wreak havoc on Vis."

And endanger, in his mind, the wife he thought he'd left in a house near the harbor. I glanced toward the hatchway. Dared I tell him now?

"And if they aren't aiming to wreak havoc on our strongholds, they're meant to strengthen Napoleon's forces on the Italian coast, which we must prevent at all costs." Captain Peyton pulled away from the lieutenant with one last clap on his shoulder.

Roddam saluted and strode away to prepare the boarding parties.

"Mr. Hallyburton, Mr. Sanchez, take us in range for the hooks." The captain motioned to starboard. "We'll grab her and reel her in. Then the true test begins. Collect your cutlass and pistol as soon as you are able." He turned to me. "Doswell, mark the time, then take over for Sanchez once he's brought us in range."

Me? I saluted. Playing the part of helmsman in a battle was one thing, but with no one else about, the safety of the *Marianne* would rest squarely on my shoulders. Mine. The chaplain's. The school teacher, makeshift clerk, and sermon giver. The boy who'd run from the navy after his first experience in combat.

What is the captain thinking, putting a milksop like you at the helm? You'll lead them to—

But a new voice interrupted the naysayer in my head. *You can do this, Elias.* It was May's voice.

Odd. She'd never said that to me before, but I heard her as clearly as if it were a memory. It was with the same fervent tenderness that she'd told me she loved me.

She loved me. I closed my eyes, allowing myself the briefest moment to savor those words. What greater strength did I need than that?

"Keep her running east-northeast," the captain said. "We'll need as many men on that Frenchie's upper deck as we can spare, and Sanchez has more boarding experience than most of the crew."

"Yes, sir." I stood taller. I could keep the ship sailing. For England. For Captain Peyton. For May.

I checked my watch, noted that we were preparing to board just before five in the evening, and pocketed my book. Peyton would need these details for his report.

"And, Doswell."

"Yes?"

He threw me a grin. "I'm glad you're with us."

MAY

Mrs. Hallyburton barged into the cockpit with all the subtlety of a blast from a 32-pounder carronade. The handle of a pistol stuck out from her apron pocket. "Well, they've boarded that Frenchie. Time to pray and curse Boney." She threw Étienne a withering glance, as though she expected him to suddenly start singing *La Marseillaise* in protest, but he continued wiping off his instruments and paid her no mind. I sat on the deck assisting him, the cloth in my hand already stained. No doubt, he faced such suspicion regularly, but during a battle with tensions heightened, it must come out more frequently.

The boatswain's wife then turned her disapproving gaze on me, looking me up and down with a sniff. She'd discovered us earlier and had already given me a tongue-lashing for the indecency of dressing as a man. Knowing it displeased her almost dispelled my frustration at the inconvenience of wearing trousers, with their small pockets, chafing, and inhibiting trouble they caused when it came to relieving oneself. I couldn't wait to return to my gown.

From the corner where she attended to a wounded seaman, Mrs. Peyton lifted her head. "Is there anyone left on deck?"

"Just Mr. Doswell at the helm. The wounded have all been brought below."

I paused my cleaning. Elias was steering the ship again, this time alone. And Captain Peyton was leading every man he could muster in a full-blown charge into the enemy's ranks. It wasn't an uncommon tactic to leave a ship unprotected in an attempt to overwhelm the enemy, but it was a bold one. We shouldn't expect any less from Captain Peyton.

His wife went back to her task, but she moved rigidly. I resumed mine as well. Knowing they were in danger made simple work more difficult.

"You won't be getting any more wounded for a time, Mr. Éti-enne," the boatswain's wife said, resting her hand on her pistol. She said his name "ay-ten" without any attempt at correct pronunciation. "But you'll have plenty when the lads return."

"You told us you thought they were boarding, Doctor," I said, handing him a scalpel. "You were correct." The ship had rocked as though bumping into something not long ago, and he'd predicted one of the frigates had had enough of broadsides.

"I've participated in my share of boarding action," he said quietly as he put his tools in their places.

"Against good British tars." Mrs. Hallyburton sniffed.

I closed my eyes, clamping my teeth together. Étienne was as trustworthy as he was French, but engaging the boatswain's wife would come to nothing. Sometimes, it was better to bite my tongue and let the argument die. She hadn't outright insulted him yet.

The boatswain's wife kept an eye on the entrance, as if ready for Frenchmen to spring through it. "*Saint-Germain* is in for a shock."

Saint-Germain? Étienne and Mrs. Peyton glanced at each other, then at me. Wasn't that the name of the privateer HMS *Deborah* had fought when Uncle Byam was killed?

"Our old friend," Étienne muttered.

A chill ran down my spine. It didn't change anything about Elias standing at the helm, but somehow, the thought of this ship being to blame for my kinsman's death made my insides seize. I'd always imagined them as ruthless and greedy pirates, but never had I imagined actually facing them.

"If she couldn't handle our broadside, that bunch of yellow-bellied frogs won't do well face-to-face with true Englishmen," Mrs. Hallyburton said. Was she trying to convince herself that there was nothing to fear? Never mind that half our crew wasn't actually English. "We'll strike her colors for her in no time. Send the filthy matelots into the deep."

"Mrs. Hallyburton, might you accompany me to the stores?" Mrs. Peyton asked, rising. "I'm feeling a little faint, and I think I need something to restore my strength."

The boatswain's wife reached an arm toward her. "Of course, ma'am. You shouldn't be here in your condition as it is." She glared at me as though it were my fault the captain's wife was here instead of the other way around.

"Take a lantern," Étienne said, handing one to me. "You've had hardly anything all day. You must be famished as well."

My stomach rumbled at the thought of food. Étienne had brought us a few things throughout the day but not nearly enough for two grown women. And chasing enemies for hours left little time for finding nourishment without detection.

I took the tin handle of the lantern, a horrid thought popping into my head. With us gone and little Harvey the only seaman not wounded, Étienne could sneak away and do something terrible to help his countrymen.

He must have sensed my hesitation. "I will not sabotage the ship," he said with a wink. "You can trust in me."

Trust. That had been so hard for me to give anyone for years. But as I took in this wild-haired Frenchman with his impish grin, I couldn't help but believe him. Trust left one vulnerable. Elias had shown me that. But without it, what did one have? Everything good and beautiful in this world stemmed from trust—trust in deity, trust in others, and trust in yourself.

"We'll be back as quickly as we can," I said, then slipped out into the passageway after Mrs. Peyton and Mrs. Hallyburton.

The boatswain's wife led us through the maze of spars, cables, and crates until we reached the storerooms. She produced a key and opened the narrow door. I stepped in first to light the room. Water poured over my half boots, drenching the hems of my trousers. A cold, salty spray rained down on me from the deck above.

I cried out and stumbled back, sputtering and nearly dropping the lantern. I wiped at my face with my sleeve, but my soaked hair and cap kept dripping the seawater into my stinging eyes. Mrs. Peyton grabbed my arm and pulled me out of the storeroom.

"What is happening?" she asked.

Mrs. Hallyburton snatched the lantern from me and held it up. "We might have bigger problems than empty bellies on our hands," she said gravely, then swore. "Come, ladies. The frogs must have blown a hole in our hull. And Mr. Jackson went across with the crew."

Water quickly pooled in the storeroom. I raised an eyebrow at Mrs. Peyton. "I thought you said the French aimed for the masts."

It would appear this French ship was aiming to win as much as we were.

Chapter 23

MAY

Though I couldn't see through the hole's chaos of splinters near the top of the mess deck, every time the ship rolled, a new gush of ocean raced through it. We slipped over the deck as we hurried over to the hole. I kept my grip on Mrs. Peyton's arm to steady her, though my own instability made it of little use.

"We need a plug," Mrs. Hallyburton said, clinging to the bulwark. "And no doubt a fothering sail." She cursed and slammed the side with her fist. "We need Jackson. I'm no carpenter."

Water had crept up my stockings and seeped into the canvas of my trousers until I was wet well past my knees. I helped Mrs. Peyton toward an iron ring secured to the bulwark that she could hang on to. For the first time since I'd set foot on the ship, Mrs. Hallyburton looked shaken.

"How difficult would it be to locate him?" I asked.

Mrs. Hallyburton smirked. "Smoke. Darkness. Battle." She ticked them off on her fingers.

"Simple, then," I said. I pushed on before she could call me stupid. "I'll go above. See if I can find anyone. The two of you look for a sail." As the boatswain's wife, surely Mrs. Hallyburton could find a sail, even if she couldn't find a proper plug.

I thought Mrs. Peyton would tell me not to go, but she nodded. "Take care, Byam," she said very seriously. "Don't take unnecessary risks. We want you back safely."

I wanted to throw my arms around my employer. My throat tightened. She cared about me, even though I'd hurt her, and she implied that the captain did as well. I was wanted here. Needed here. And I'd do anything to protect this ship.

"You as well," I choked out. "Take care of her, Hallyburton."

The boatswain's wife harrumphed as though insulted that I would feel the need to suggest it. She reached into her pocket and pulled out the pistol. She checked it, then extended it toward me. "Do you know how to use this?"

I stared at the gun, shaking my head sharply.

"Then, for heaven's sake, don't. But it might give you a moment extra if they think you do know how."

"Where do I put it?" I asked. It would fall out of my pocket.

Mrs. Hallyburton huffed and skated over to me on the wetness of the deck. She checked it again, then shoved the barrel into my waistband. The cold steel weighed heavy at my side.

"Good luck, Byam."

I touched my cap in salute, like I'd seen the men do, not pausing to consider that that was most likely the nicest thing the boatswain's wife had ever said to me. I made for the hatchway as quickly as the water would allow.

"We'll need to start the pumps before too long," Mrs. Hallyburton said behind me.

I flew up the ladder, the whole time praying my waterlogged trousers wouldn't fall down from the weight of the pistol. I heard Mrs. Hallyburton and Mrs. Peyton make for the hatchway down to the orlop, but then the sound of shouting and clinking metal covered it.

I came up near the galley toward the prow of the ship. The big guns sat silent in their carriages, a few long-handled tools scattered about the deck. The captain wouldn't be pleased at that disarray, minimal though it was.

My shoes squelched as I crept along the eerily vacant gun deck toward the next ladder. I shouldn't find anyone here, yet I couldn't convince my brain that there wasn't someone lurking between the hulking cannons. What if they'd left one of the bodies here? My step faltered, and I covered my mouth as gooseflesh surged over my skin. How many had died? One or two? The crew wouldn't have left them on the gun deck, would they?

Gray twilight filtered through the gun ports. I scanned this way and that, hoping I wouldn't stumble across the casualties in the darkness. I could handle the death, but not right now. Not here, alone in the middle of war. Elias was above. I only had to run up this ladder and across the deck and I'd be at his side. I hurried forward and grabbed the sides of the ladder.

A grunt stopped me in my tracks. It came from near the stern, but I couldn't see movement. Was someone injured and left behind? My heart thundered in my ears. Dared I see who it was? Perhaps my mind was simply playing tricks.

"C'est trop étroit. La plupart des marins ne passeront pas."

My blood ran cold. That was not English.

ELIAS

I kept my eyes trained straight ahead and my hands firmly on the handles of the helm, but that didn't prevent my ears from picking up the sound of the battle. Every scream, every crack of a pistol rattled me. I wanted to run from it, like I had all those years ago. One person kept me where I was—May.

If the French overpowered us, what would happen to her? They were the enemy. Many in the French navy acted honorably, but this was a privateer. Did the same customs apply? Images of an oily-haired, mustache-twirling French captain—the sort you saw in newspaper caricatures—filled my head, his greedy eyes resting on the women we had belowdecks. Though my role in preventing our being overpowered was very small, I would fulfill it to the best of my abilities if it kept us one more step away from that fate.

Each time I heard Captain Peyton shout orders, I whispered a prayer of gratitude. We could win the day so long as we had him to lead. With night pouring in, the battle had to resolve soon.

Something whistled past my head. A bullet? I winced but did not move. My eyes stayed on the horizon, where the tiniest sliver of orange sunset still peeked over the black ocean. In the darkness, I put her face at the forefront of my mind. With her faith in me, I could do anything. Even brave my greatest fears.

MAY

I launched myself into the light of the cockpit, heart in my throat. Mrs. Hallyburton and Mrs. Peyton were nowhere to be seen.

"What is it?" Étienne lurched to his feet.

"There are Frenchmen," I cried. "On the gun deck."

His eyes widened. "How many?"

I put a hand to my chest, trying to breathe. We had a dozen wounded sailors, a French surgeon, a chaplain, a boy, and three women aboard. If they were trying to cross over and seize the ship while the crew was battling the rest of their shipmates on the *Saint-Germain*, how could we stop them? "At least two. They were struggling to get through the gun port."

The surgeon considered this. "Harvey, get me the knife. I'll see what they're up to." The loblolly boy retrieved it and presented it to him.

"I have a pistol," I said, pulling the weapon from my waistband. Something in the back of my mind screamed what a stupid idea it was to hand the Frenchman a gun. But this was Étienne. I trusted him.

"That is better than a knife." He accepted it, checked the mechanism, and pointed it toward the deck. "Bring a lantern, mademoiselle. Let us see what we can discover of their plans. There might be time to warn the captain."

I followed him back to the ladder. Water had already soaked the deck beneath our feet.

"Do we have a leak?" the surgeon asked.

I held the lantern up so he could see the ladder rungs. "Yes. I went above to try to find Mr. Jackson."

"There are times when I miss my army days," Étienne said as though talking about a childhood in the country or something equally picturesque. "They were less wet." We made it to the mess deck, slick with water. "From which direction were they coming?"

I pointed toward the stern. Were those voices? How many had made it through the gun port?

Étienne spoke quietly. "You come behind me with the lantern so I have the light, but keep your head below the deck. Do you understand?"

I nodded.

"If things go poorly, run for the orlop. You, Mrs. Peyton, and Mrs. Boatswain hide."

"Hallyburton?"

He glowered and shook his head. "I do not try to say that name."

We inched up the ladder, Étienne stopping at every rung to listen. He paused at the top, cocking the pistol. He glanced down at me, nodded once, then vaulted onto the deck.

"Stop! Don't move." It almost didn't sound like Étienne's voice. No Englishman would have mistaken him for a compatriot, but he managed a London tone well for someone with usually so stark a French accent.

"*Un anglais.*"

"*Soyez calme. Il n'y en a qu'un.*"

I wished I remembered my childhood French lessons. Étienne stood before the hatchway, gun trained on someone near the stern. Light from my lantern cast a strange glow upward on the surgeon. Shadows swung across the empty gun deck. I held the lantern up as far as I could without going over the edge of the hatchway. Was it enough for him to see his foe?

"Return to your ship. You've lost."

"*Qu'est-ce qu'on fait, Julien? Nous ne devrions pas combattre ici. Ils vont nous remarquer.*" There seemed to be two voices, one stoic and this one more expressive. Had only two of them made it through, or were they simply the leaders?

Étienne took a step back, lowering the pistol slightly. *"Que fais-tu ici?"*

I leaned to one side, trying to see the enemy. What was Étienne doing? Had the English accent not fooled them? The surgeon glanced down at me, bewilderment etched into his orange-lit face. My breath faltered. Something had caught him off guard. There must be a host of them.

Étienne motioned with his hand, a slight movement, as if shooing me toward the bow. I scowled. What could he mean by that?

"Qui est-ce?" the stoic-voiced intruder said.

"Personne sauf un mousse." Étienne mouthed, "Go."

If he thought I would hide while he stood between us and the enemy, he was greatly mistaken. I shook my head, but he motioned again. I couldn't just leave him. At his final emphatic wave, I lowered myself down the ladder. Very well. I'd leave him, as he insisted, but I wasn't about to hide.

Water splashed at my feet as I got to the deck. I hung the lantern on a hook coming from one of the beams. At least Étienne would still have a little light. Then I ran for the opposite hatchway. I had to get help.

My feet shot out from under me with the slickness of the deck. I landed hard on hands and knees with a grunt but didn't stop to acknowledge the pain pulsing through my limbs. It was a good thing my trousers were already soaked. I hardly felt the added wetness.

Water still poured through the hole in the hull. Where were Mrs. Peyton and Mrs. Hallyburton? Should I wait for them and warn them of the Frenchies? That would leave the whole ship and crew vulnerable to their plot. I pushed myself up. Sometimes risks had to be made for the good of the company.

I hauled myself up the forward ladder and crouched on the gun deck, letting my eyes adjust to the dimness. Several yards aft, Étienne still stood talking to the Frenchmen. Only two enemies, unless there were others hidden behind the gun carriages. One of them, the taller one, held a pistol pointed at Étienne's feet in much the same way our surgeon was pointing his weapon—in their direction but not aimed to kill. The other French sailor held a cutlass that gleamed dully in the faint light.

"*Que fais-tu? Tu combats tes compatriotes?*"

Why did they speak with such familiarity? I crept toward the ladder to the upper deck and grabbed hold of the rungs. Was Étienne in league with them? My stomach lurched. If he was, I was throwing Mrs. Peyton and Mrs. Hallyburton to the wolves along with little Harvey and all the wounded seamen. They hadn't a clue of our danger.

I gripped the wood. No, I had to trust Étienne. He hadn't betrayed us yet. I placed my feet carefully on the ladder and moved as stealthily as I could manage into the smoky evening air. Then I ran toward the helm, grabbing onto lines to steady myself as I went. I couldn't see well, but I didn't need to. As long as I kept moving forward, I knew I would find my refuge from the storm—the chaplain who held my heart.

Chapter 24

ELIAS

The thump of a body hitting the upper deck made my stomach turn. Another followed it. Then another. Wounded? Dead? I couldn't tell. Night had set in, and very few lanterns were lit on either ship. The battle had to be drawing to a close. No one could make out who was friend or foe in this lighting. I could hardly make out the masts before me.

Moaning from near the port rail signaled life. Praise the heavens. I wished I could go to them, help them get to the surgeon below, but I couldn't leave the helm unmanned. I could only pray the enemy wouldn't jump over the rail with them.

A figure dodged through the ship's lines, hurrying toward me in the mist. I tensed as my brain brought up each possibility of French or Englishman. The person was too short to be a seaman. They sprinted to the steps up to the quarterdeck.

"Elias!" a voice I hadn't expected to hear until the battle was won shouted.

I allowed myself a glance. "May? What are—"

"They've crossed over through the gun ports right below us." She moved in close, the binnacle lantern in its case in front of me revealing her taut face.

I clutched the handles of the wheel. "They've infiltrated the ship?" What could we do? We had little defense. "Where are they now?"

"Étienne stopped them on the gun deck. But he's alone." She grabbed my sleeve. "We need to help him."

"How many?" If they'd pulled a significant number over, they'd trap the fighting crew between the two ships.

"No more than a few, but they can easily overpower Étienne."

A few? They must be trying to sabotage the ship. Perhaps disable our guns or . . . Would they really go for the powder room? My blood ran cold. Very few ships actually sank in battle, leaving the orlop relatively safe for noncombatants such as May and Mrs. Peyton, but images of the burning ship after our last engagement still flooded my mind, brilliant fire against the blackness of night. We'd share their fate if those intruders weren't stopped.

"We have to find the captain," I said.

"I'll go." She released my sleeve.

My heart leaped into my throat. "No! They'll attack you. Look what you are wearing." They wouldn't stop to notice the way her waistcoat and trousers clung to her curves in a rather unmasculine way or the feminine line of her exposed arms beneath her rolled-up shirtsleeves. I was only too aware of them.

"Someone has to find him," she said.

"Give me the wheel," a voice grunted. A form limped up the steps to the quarterdeck. Mr. Midshipman Kingdon, the oldest of the young gentlemen.

May stepped around me to assist him. "You're wounded, Mr. Kingdon."

He gave her a confused stare, as though surprised at the woman's voice coming from someone he thought was a ship's boy. "I injured myself tripping on the deck," he said more gruffly than usual. Embarrassment over the injury, perhaps? "The captain insisted I return to the *Marianne* to not endanger myself or anyone else further." He reached for the wheel. "Let me be of some help."

I reluctantly let him take my place. Captain Peyton gave me instructions to do this and nothing else. But he hadn't anticipated the French counterboarding.

May pulled me toward the starboard rail. "Where was the captain, Mr. Kingdon?"

"At the waist. They haven't struck their colors. No one knows why."

"Elias, you don't have to do this," she whispered to me.

The last thing I wanted to do was plunge into that battle. Though I couldn't see the action, I could hear the clink of blades and shouts. "And let you go alone unprotected? Not on my life."

"Look." She dropped to the deck and rose with a long length of wood in her hands. "A spear. I'll be armed."

I sighed. "That's a boarding pike. Do you know how to use it?"

"No, but it can't be that difficult."

I took it from her, pointing the long, metal blade into the sky. It was more difficult than it looked. I hadn't held one of these in years, but the captain of the *Lumière* had made us train with them constantly when I'd been a member of his crew. The length and weight felt more manageable as a man of twenty-six than it had as a boy of twelve. "We'll go together."

She nodded. "Together."

MAY

I glanced over the rail. Grappling hooks held the two frigates together, but there was still a gap one could fall through into the ocean below. I gulped at the thought of being crushed between the two hulls when the waves knocked them together. It looked far too likely a scenario.

Elias held my arm. I could feel his fear in the stiffness of his fingers, but his care for me wouldn't let him stay behind. It was a great blessing but would also be a great responsibility. I had to make sure I never took advantage of it. Too many had already done so with him.

One of the gun ports below the quarterdeck had a rope connecting to the *Saint-Germain*.

"Elias, can you see that?" I motioned to the gun port.

"The rope? Barely. Perhaps we should . . ."

A form leaned out of *Saint-Germain*'s gun port. I seized the rail. Another Frenchman joining the others. "We have to stop them." Étienne would be overpowered in moments, if he hadn't already been.

We raced back to the quarterdeck. What could we do? Throw something at the mariner?

Elias held up the boarding pike. "We need to cut the line. You aim. I'll ram it."

I grasped the handle a little below his hands and positioned the weapon above the line. "Now."

He thrust the pike downward but missed the line. A cry of anger rumbled from the opposite gunport.

"Hurry," I said. "Again." Heaven knew what other weapons they had at their disposal. The next try also went wide.

The noise of battle almost drowned out a metallic click.

"May, get down!" Elias grabbed me and threw me to the deck. Something hit the rail, showering us with splinters. I tried to get up, but his torso pinned me in place.

"Are you hurt?" I clung to his coat.

"No, but he's reloading." The words vibrated in his chest, filling me with a comfort I shouldn't be feeling in the middle of battle.

Focus. "Let's cut the line before he finishes," I said. For a second, Elias didn't move. Then he jumped to his feet and hauled me up with him. This time, we both grasped the pike and wound up.

"Three, two, one," I said. And we slammed it downward together. The blade caught something, then slipped through. I hit the rail from the force of our blow, scraping my brow just under the brim of my cap, and released the handle. I dropped to the deck, holding my head. Something clattered against the *Marianne*, then hit the other ship. Angry French voices followed it.

"May! Are you injured?" Elias pulled me away from the rail. Another shot went off, sending more chunks of wood into the air.

I got to my knees. "Not badly. We need to hurry." My forehead pounded, and I wouldn't be surprised if the scrape bled. I hoped Elias wouldn't notice it.

We scrambled back toward the waist on hands and knees to a point where a grappling hook and line held the ships closer together. I took hold of one of the shrouds and pulled myself onto the rail.

Elias stopped me with a hand on my arm. "We're weaponless," he said. "The boarding pike fell." That must have been what hit the side of the *Marianne*.

"We don't have time." Was that glimmer in the night the gold braids of Captain Peyton's coat?

Elias released me and scooped something off the deck. Another long-handled boarding pike. But it looked to be missing its blade. I squinted. No, it had something blunt on the end. Elias joined me on the rail.

"What is that?" I asked.

"A sponge," he grumbled.

"We're fighting the French with a cannon sponge?"

He winced at the absurdity. "As you said, we don't have time."

The ship tilted on a wave, and I gasped, clawing at the shrouds.

"Hurry, the ships are closing in," Elias hissed.

I gulped, balking. The jump to the *Saint-Germain* was longer than I'd thought even with them moving closer. Elias would make it easily with his long legs.

The *Marianne* continued to slide toward *Saint-Germain*. "Before they hit—jump!" He leaped away, catching one of the French ship's lines and clearing the rail.

I jumped a second too late. My foot hit the *Saint-Germain*'s rail, sending a jolt through my leg that buckled my knee. I flailed, the black waters below us filling my mind as I fell forward. The ships crashed together with protesting beams. The force knocked me headfirst onto the deck, and I might have broken my neck if Elias hadn't caught me by the torso with his free arm. I grabbed hold of his leg, one of my feet still hooked around the rail. I wriggled in an attempt to get out of the humiliating position. Finally, I kicked free and tumbled the rest of the way to the deck, landing none too gently on my rump.

Not far from us, I spied a pair of shoes and the white-and-blue tails of an officer's coat. The captain. I pushed myself up, grit from the deck sticking to my palms. Captain Peyton had a Frenchman by the throat and had shoved him up against the mainmast.

"There he is." I darted toward him, earning an unintelligible shout from Elias. Debris littered the upper deck. I skirted a cannon lying on its side, wooden gun carriage smattered. A dark form in a heap beside it didn't move. I slowed, stomach wrenching. For a moment, I'd forgotten the cost of war.

A reassuring hand on my back kept me moving forward. I looked up at Elias. The faint light of lanterns pulsed in his sorrowful eyes. What person with a heart such as his could bear it?

"Captain!" I called.

As we approached, he loosened his grip on the Frenchman and stepped back. "Hallyburton, clap him in irons. He'll be delivering us the sword if we can't find the others." The boatswain took the enemy sailor and hauled him toward the hatchway. The captain pivoted to meet us. "Doswell! What the devil are you doing here?"

"Captain," I said.

His gaze fell on me. He blinked, studying me for a long time before realization dawned. He slowly closed his eyes, jaw working. He held his forehead for a moment, then dragged a hand down his face. "Miss Byam, what a pleasant surprise." Only he did not sound the least bit pleased. "I suppose this should not come as a shock to me. What has my wife dragged you into?"

I shook my head. No time for an explanation. "There are Frenchmen on the *Marianne*. Étienne is holding them off."

"Roddam, get them all below," Captain Peyton barked, sprinting for the rail. Elias and I ran to catch up. "Townsend! Bring your men back to *Marianne*."

"They came through the aft gun ports," I called.

The captain swept onto the rail and sprang across the gap, not even bothering with ropes to balance himself as he hopped deftly to the deck. Any Society miss would have swooned over a display such as that. Except for Mrs. Peyton, which I supposed was why he'd married her. A midshipman and group of sailors raced over the side, cutlasses at the ready.

"The fighting is mostly finished," Elias observed, helping me back up onto the rail. "Look."

I glanced back. The deck was eerily still. English seamen dragged tied French sailors below. Our officers and midshipmen shouted orders. A few straggling pockets of Frenchmen were detained. Why hadn't they struck their colors? They couldn't be carrying anything so precious as to warrant fighting to the death.

Somehow, the two French intruders must have had something to do with our enemy not surrendering. "Hurry," I said. "Let's get back."

ELIAS

May and I practically slid through the hatchway in our hurry to find Étienne. Captain Peyton stood not far from the ladder, hands behind his back, flanked by the party of seamen. The much shorter French surgeon stood beside him. Praise the heavens. Étienne looked unharmed.

"Well done, Étienne," the captain said. He glanced over his shoulder at May, who hugged herself as though remembering for the first time in several hours that she was wearing men's clothing. "I think you and Miss Byam helped us solve two predicaments tonight."

A lantern had been hung on a hook near the hatchway, casting a wavering light on the gathering. Toward the stern, two Frenchmen sat with wrists and ankles tied. The taller of the two, his brown hair tied back in a loose queue, glared at us. The shorter one, who had darker skin and curly hair cropped short, stared at the ground.

"Two?" Étienne asked.

"You stopped a counterattack that might have destroyed the *Marianne*," Captain Peyton said, crouching in front of the prisoners. He gave them a wry smile. "And you've found our missing captain."

Captain? What was a captain doing sneaking onto the enemy ship through the gun ports on a nefarious mission? He should have sent one of his officers.

Something flashed across the taller mariner's face. He couldn't have been much older than I, but shadows of conflict, of memory, flitted behind his eyes. Daring us all to cross him. *"Je suis le second, pas le capitaine,"* he muttered.

I glanced at our captain. Did he understand French well enough to know the man claimed to be the first mate?

"You are Bernard?" Peyton asked.

The taller man gave no answer, and his companion continued his silence. Étienne cleared his throat. "He is, sir." The first mate glared at our surgeon. He must know English to some extent. Perhaps as well as I knew his language.

"I regret to inform you that your Captain Demaret is dead," Captain Peyton said, a solemnity tinting his voice. *Saint-Germain's* captain had fallen? Then, the first mate sitting before us had become the captain without realizing it. "You will return with me, Captain, and strike your colors. Order your men to stand down and surrender their weapons."

The Frenchman shrugged helplessly. *"Je ne parle pas anglais."*

I don't speak English? He certainly seemed to understand. Étienne's face twisted. He didn't believe Bernard's lie either, but he quickly repeated what Peyton said in French. The other French mariner finally moved, turning his head to catch his new captain's gaze.

"Tell him his men have already been rounded up and taken below," Peyton said. "The boatswain put up an honorable fight, but we were too much for them. He told us you were now in command."

Bernard's scowl darkened the longer Captain Peyton spoke. Yes, he certainly understood. After Étienne relayed the message, Bernard barked a string of French curses on Peyton and all our crew. I removed my spectacles and wiped the lenses on the cuff of my shirtsleeve. I didn't want it to look obvious to the French captain that I was understanding almost every word. The captain might need my translation services later to eavesdrop on conversations.

"He says he will do it," Étienne finally interpreted. I glanced at our captain. That was certainly not what I'd heard.

Captain Peyton called for seamen to drag Bernard and his companion above, then turned to Étienne. "Thank you again for your service."

"I couldn't have done anything without the help of Miss Byam here." The surgeon nodded toward May, whose face reddened. "And you remember Mr. Taylor."

Mrs. Peyton stepped out from between the guns, arms folded. I hadn't seen her there before. She fixed her husband with an emotionless gaze. No embarrassment. No sheepishness. They stared each other down as though daring the other to break the silence.

A hand slipped into mine. May watched them with brows knit. I squeezed her fingers. If I knew anything about the Peytons, there was nothing to fear. Captain Peyton had become more serious under the weight of his responsibilities, but I knew for certain he adored and respected this woman.

The captain rubbed his forehead with an exasperated laugh. "What would I do without you, George?"

"You'd have a gushing hole in your hull."

Captain Peyton straightened. "She's hit below the water line?"

"Mrs. Hallyburton and I plugged it well enough," she said with a shrug, "but we should find Mr. Jackson as soon as we can and get men on the pumps."

"Yes, sir." Peyton saluted her, earning him a perplexed look from his wife. He crossed the distance and took her in his arms, and I glanced down at May. Sweat had curled the strands of hair around her face. The rest of it was starting to fall out of the ribbon-bound queue that hung down her back. A thin red line ran across her cheek where a shard of wood must have grazed it. Her lips turned upward in a small smile as she watched the captain kiss his wife. How I wanted to do the same to her.

Étienne appeared at my elbow, clearing his throat. "Will you direct the movement of wounded seamen down to the orlop, Mr. Doswell? Miss Byam, if you'd assist me below. I have a feeling we will be swarmed momentarily."

"Yes, of course," I said quickly.

"We'll speak after," May murmured to me.

I nodded. The next few hours as we cared for the wounded and righted the ship would be an eternity, knowing that May stood at the end of it, open and eager to have me once more.

Chapter 25

ELIAS

Waves crashed against the hull, sending bubbles and droplets trailing behind as the *Marianne* headed north with the *Saint-Germain* in tow. The French privateer's masts were in no state to make the journey to Malta and would need repairs at Lissa before Lieutenant Roddam took the prize ship and the prisoners to collect our earnings. *Saint-Germain* and her comrades had been carrying cannons from Corfu to Italy for the French navy. A fortunate victory for England and its allies. We'd celebrate with the crews of the other ships when we met them back in port.

I leaned against the rail on the forecastle, trying to sort through my emotions. We'd all had a very late night cleaning up the battle as best we could in the dark. There had been no time to talk to May, and she'd slept in the great cabin because Captain Peyton had decided to quarter Captain Bernard in the cabin May used to occupy. I'd heard Captain Bernard muttering late into the night.

Then this morning, I'd overseen the burial of eight of our brave seamen. There had been no time for discussions with May of the future, much less enthusiasm to talk about life when so many of our crewmates' lives had been cut short.

The upper deck had quieted after the funeral services. The crew dispersed to various duties about the ship. Étienne and the French captain walked the quarterdeck in low conversation. May, dressed in one of Mrs. Peyton's gowns from a trunk the captain's wife had hidden in one of the storage lockers, had gone below as soon as I had ended the services. I swallowed. Had she reconsidered what she seemed to have been hinting at last night, a reconciliation and future for us? Or perhaps I'd misinterpreted. Was she avoiding the conversation? I didn't know whether to seek her out or let her come to me. Could she be thinking the same?

Soft footsteps on the deck behind me made my heart leap. I dared not turn around, lest my enthusiasm startle some poor seaman I'd potentially mistaken for May. Relief shooed my worries away when she appeared out of the corner of my eye and rested her hands on the rail.

"That was quite a long 'later,'" she said.

"We have duty to thank for that."

She nodded. "You performed yours well."

Well, I didn't know if I could agree, though knowing she was near had bolstered my courage. I traced the horizon with my gaze until I picked out the dark smudge of land that indicated we'd reach Lissa in a few hours. "We all try."

"That is one thing I admire about you, Elias. You try, even when it's difficult. You put duty and compassion before your own needs or wants." Her shoulder touched mine briefly.

I wrung my hands. "Yes, but it isn't—"

She held up a hand. "Take the praise, Elias. It was sincere."

I nodded, unconvinced, though her words warmed me.

She gripped the rail, examining the too-short sleeves of her borrowed round gown. The hem was too short as well, at least for a day dress. She looked lovely, even if she wouldn't believe me if I told her. The way the wind played with her hair, tugging strands from its simple knot, mesmerized me more than it should.

"I believe we left off at 'I'm sorry for being a monster,'" she said. "Or something similar."

"I thought we left at . . ." I didn't dare speak it aloud.

She said she loved you. Why so little faith? Rarely did the voice in my head say something so positive. I'd had faith with all the other women who'd broken me. I'd gone so far as to propose to them. Why would this work for me now?

She licked her lips, drawing my gaze. I hadn't kissed her since that night watching the glowing waves. If things did not go well in this conversation, the memory of her warm lips on mine in the chill darkness would haunt me more than any kiss ever had.

"You are right. We left at . . ." She swallowed. "I love you."

A shiver ran over my spine to hear those words spoken so plainly and truthfully from the woman I adored. The walls she'd thrown up to keep me out on the day she'd quit the ship were gone.

"And I mean it with all that I am," she said quickly, searching my face. "Which I realize is not very much, especially after the fool I've been. My stupidity and irrationality have been painfully clear the last few weeks, and if I am to be perfectly honest, I do not know why you would forgive me." Her voice rose in pitch and speed the longer she spoke. "But I hope you will forgive me. I *desperately* hope you will forgive me." She hesitated and took a deep breath. "Now I am all lost and making a greater fool of myself."

I so rarely saw her flustered like this. If we weren't on the forecastle with a working crew constantly walking past us, it would be very difficult not to kiss her now. "We are reversing positions," I teased. "I am the one who makes a fool of himself when he speaks."

"Ha!" She shook her head. "I make a fool of myself far too often. I just don't usually realize it in the moment, as you do. I realize it weeks later when my heart is still sore from missing you and the regret for the things I said still chokes me."

A very small part of me wanted to take care. How did I know she wouldn't hurt me again? I couldn't recover from being turned away from her twice. At least not well.

She will *hurt you again, you dunce.*

Ah, the disparaging voice was back.

That's what happens when you love someone. The important thing is being willing to make amends. To learn from mistakes, make things right, and grow together.

Yes. That was it. Finding the right woman to love did not mean we'd never have trials between us. A person did not stay the same throughout his life. Love simply meant we'd see it through.

"I know it isn't an easy thing to ask," she said in the silence of my contemplation. "Heaven knows I am terrible at forgiveness and have no business asking for what, until now, I've struggled to give. I will do what it takes to make things right for you."

She looked up at me with wide, blue eyes. She awaited her fate—our fate—with no pleading. Her calm sincerity made it easy to believe she would accept whatever I said.

I took her hand. Little scratches covered it from the previous night's battle. She was proud of me. She loved me. And she was willing to do what she needed to for the ones she loved. Even if that meant stepping away forever. I'd never had the courage to willingly part with someone I loved as much as I loved her. I did have courage in one thing, however. Today I had the courage to put aside my fears.

I brought her fingers to my lips. I'd done it a few times on our voyage, but somehow, her skin against mine felt different this time. Rather than the jolt of lightning it had once given me, a deep-burning fire undulated through my veins. "Of course I forgive you, May."

She blinked as though not expecting that answer. "You do?"

I nodded.

"After how badly I hurt you by pushing you away, you would forgive me as easy as that?"

I caught a lock of her hair the wind had pulled out and smoothed it behind her ear. Together again. No strain between us. "What is love if not forgiveness?" Hadn't the greatest love known on earth come coupled with forgiveness all those centuries ago?

She gave a little smile, then leaned against me and laid her head on my shoulder. "I certainly don't deserve you, you know."

I snorted, wrapping an arm around her and holding her tightly. "We might have to disagree on that."

She mumbled something unintelligible as I rested my head on hers. I'd joined Captain Peyton to get away from love and courtship, with all their disappointments. How could I have guessed it would fall into my arms, awkward and imperfect, but somehow everything I needed?

MAY

The stocky Frenchman strolled up the path ahead of us, whistling a merry little tune and taking in the surrounding trees as though completely alone. I'd never experienced the bothers of having a chaperone before this voyage. I liked Étienne very much, but I wished we'd come on this walk just Elias and me.

I tugged at Elias's arm. "It's a treat to have Great-Aunt Étienne with us again," I said softly, hoping the surgeon wouldn't overhear.

Elias sighed. "I know several people who'd give anything to have him as their chaperone." He adjusted his cravat for the tenth time since we'd left the house.

He had a point. When we'd gone to the Roman ruins, Étienne had practically pushed us together. We'd almost had time to take advantage. "Do we really need a chaperone?" I was hardly a young lady of Society in need of a protected reputation, and it would take quite a lot for a gentleman's good name to be tarnished. Especially when he kept company with men of the navy, who were notorious for too much pleasure-seeking and rarely received any censure. And it wasn't as though the whole ship didn't know about our kiss.

Elias blushed. "I only wish to do things the right way." He straightened the front of his coat.

"You needn't be so proper all the time, Elias." It had been a week since we'd arrived back in Lissa, and we'd scarcely had a moment alone. I wondered if he'd planned it that way. It was driving me to madness.

"I promised Mrs. Peyton I would be a perfect gentleman."

I shook my head. As though he needed to make that promise. "When have you not been a perfect gentleman?"

"Perhaps when I tried to turn you away when you first boarded?" The uncertainty in his tone hinted that he still chided himself for that.

I hugged his arm. "You were simply trying to keep me from trouble. Mrs. Hallyburton is a formidable foe." And I couldn't be more grateful that she'd come to accept my presence, if not appreciate it. She seemed to have a new respect for me after I'd run into the fray to find the captain, and she had even given me one reluctant "Well done" after the battle.

He nodded absently. His arm was tense, and he walked stiffly, eyes forward. They kept shifting back and forth, almost as if he were reading something visible to him alone. He usually only did that before a sermon, and I always assumed it was his silent rehearsing. What was he rehearsing for now?

The answer hit me like a squall—the spontaneous dinner with the Peytons and Étienne at the house, the suggestion that we hike up by the fort to watch the sunset, his clear agitation.

He planned to propose.

My mind fuzzed. *Propose. To me.* The convict's daughter from Portsmouth, who might have been a scullery maid if she'd listened to her family. I breathed in so sharply I nearly choked. How could this be happening to me?

Did it matter? I glanced up at him out of the corner of my eye. We would never be rich by Society's standards, perhaps not even comfortable by its standards, but we would have enough. I would have a husband I could trust, who would love me with all he had, and he would have a wife who . . . I winced. A wife who couldn't control her tongue or her temper. But who adored him in return. In accepting him, I would certainly be receiving the better end of this bargain in more ways than one.

He fussed with his hair, which was touched with the warm light of the Mediterranean sunset just beginning to break. Oh, Elias. He already looked perfect.

Something came alive inside of me—a pulsing, radiating, worrisome, lovely thing I couldn't quite name, and I counted the seconds, hoping it would not be long until I found out if my wonderful imagining was coming true.

ELIAS

We stood at the top of the hill, not far from where the army had halted its work on the new fort for the day. To our left, the sun had sunk toward the horizon, spilling ocher light over the sea and island hills. Étienne had melted into the foliage, while May and I surveyed the scene. Would he spy on us from the tree line, or would he let us have our moment?

Our moment. I tried to swallow. What if she pushed me away again? She'd promised not to, but I was asking for more than friendship. More than flirtation and stolen kisses in quiet corners of the *Marianne.* I was asking for her world, for her heart, and—hardest of all—for her trust.

You're taking this too quickly. It has only been a week since you mended things.

So much had changed in that week. There had been tentative times, but there had also been so many moments of joy like I'd never felt before. Safety, relief, companionship, understanding. Things I'd felt with few people before, even those of my own family.

Might as well get it over with, then.

I would if the voice could ever be quiet.

May stood beside me, eyes closed as the breeze played over her face. She'd removed her makeshift bonnet, letting it hang down her back. The skirts of the Saxon blue gown she wore peeked out from under her coat and fluttered against my leg, and my heart fluttered along with them. A small smile graced her lips. If I could only get my mouth working, perhaps I could see scenes just like this every evening for the rest of my life.

Show life that it cannot beat you, Miriam had told me before the journey had begun. I would show it. I would quiet the voice of doubt in my brain. And I wouldn't only quiet it; I would conquer it.

"May?" What a way to start. I cleared my throat. I could do this. "I . . . I was wondering . . ."

She turned eagerly toward me, brows raised expectantly. "Yes?"

I gathered her hands in mine, hoping she wouldn't feel their trembling. "I wanted to ask you something. Something important."

She nodded. "What is it?"

I blew out a deep breath. I'd prepared this for a week, but what I wished to say still felt awkward and unrefined. I prayed it would come out with more finesse than the jumbled mess in my head. "I'm so very grateful for the time we've had together the last few months. You've made this voyage a wonder I never expected." I kept my gaze glued to her face, searching for any sign of what she was thinking, but she only watched me with silence and serenity. I gulped, stumbling over what came next in my speech. My head had gone blank as sand washed smooth by a departing tide. "I haven't much to give." Wait. That wasn't supposed to come next. Heaven help me.

She cocked her head. "You certainly have a great deal more than I do, whether we are speaking of desirable qualities or financial assets." She ran a finger down along the buttons of my coat and back up, sending a thrill up my spine.

"May." I was losing my head. And it was half her fault. My face heated as I looked down at the green waistcoat barely showing under my blue coat. Should I have worn something more muted?

She laughed, a light and giddy sound that quieted some of my anxieties. "I'm sorry. I've flustered you. Go on." She rested her hands on my chest and rose up to kiss my cheek. Her breath tickled my ear, and even though her lips barely grazed my skin, gooseflesh ran across my arms.

"Don't start that," I said as she pulled back. But I didn't want her to stop. I caught her hands, keeping them against my chest. "Then I'll never say what I need to."

She gave me a coy look. "Start what?"

"You know perfectly well." This was not going as planned.

She pulled her hands out from under mine and clasped them in front of her in an innocent gesture. "I'll be good. I promise. Ask me what you wish."

I couldn't withstand the teasing. Not from her. My shoulders slumped. "Now you are laughing at me." I should've expected I couldn't propose properly to this woman. Nothing about our courtship had been proper. I supposed I'd have to get used to that. Somehow, I didn't mind the idea.

She gasped, hands flying to her hips. "I am not laughing at you!" A smile threatened to break her mock indignation.

"You are giving me that look you have when you're laughing at me."

"You and your wild imagination." She shook her head, folding her arms.

I couldn't hold out anymore. I caught her in my arms and pulled her in tightly. She giggled, something I had heard so rarely from her. "Perhaps you should have just continued what you were trying to start since I won't be able to say what I wish to anyway."

"You mean start this?" Her lips eagerly found mine, and I didn't respond to her question. I couldn't respond to it. She stole my breath as she pressed fiercely against me. No shame, no timidity, just desire for me to be hers. And I *was* already hers. I had been for so long. Perhaps longer than I realized.

I trailed my hand up to her neck, holding her there as I returned her kiss. Somehow, I was always following her into these kisses. I hardly minded. I'd follow her love wherever it led us, to sunlit mountaintops or across star-kissed seas.

"I've missed that," she whispered, not breaking our connection.

"So have I," I whispered back.

She pulled away slightly, and I opened my eyes.

"You were going to ask?" she said.

"Ask what?"

She huffed. "Ask me to be your wife. Weren't you?"

Oh. That. "Yes, of course. I mean to say, I hope with every last breath that you will be." *Stop bumbling, and ask the question.* "Will you?"

She circled her arms about my neck. "Yes. What took you so long to ask?"

I opened my mouth with an exasperated exhale but was cut off from any protest with another laughing kiss. Life would never be dull with May, and at the moment, I could not think of anything that sounded more wonderful.

Epilogue

19 August 1812
Nine months later

MAY

Elias sighed that slow, resigned sound that signaled he knew he needed to rise for the day. Without opening my eyes, I rolled toward him and buried my toes under his calf. Never mind that it was August and the humid island air foretold a hot day ahead. My toes had never recovered from the cold damp of living on a ship. I hugged his arm under the thin blanket and nuzzled my head against his shoulder. He'd never be able to resist, and I'd get a few more moments with him before he left to perform his duties on the *Marianne*.

"You remember we're leaving this morning," he said softly.

I groaned, hugging his arm tighter. Those stupid patrols. I should be grateful. Most women married to men of the navy rarely got to see their husbands in times of war. I had to let mine go frequently, but I always knew he'd be back in days or weeks rather than years. That didn't make me enjoy the many goodbyes, however.

I loosened my grip on his arm and pulled my toes back. He chuckled softly. His weight shifted on the bed, and I finally opened my eyes to watch him stand and stretch. The summer sun had already risen enough to shoot a few bright rays into the attic room we shared on the topmost floor of the Peytons' rented house. The open windows let in the sound of birds trilling their morning tunes and carts rolling along the streets below on their way to pick up the morning catch from the harbor.

Elias pulled the curtains closed, and they danced lightly in the breeze. Even in the dimmer light, I could make out the lean lines of his chest through the open neckline of his nightshirt. I didn't know if I'd ever grow tired of seeing him in the morning, his hair mussed and eyes blinking sleepily as they adjusted to the light.

He opened his trunk and pursed his lips as he silently debated which pair of breeches and waistcoat he'd wear that day. I pushed myself up on one elbow to watch. He chose so carefully each morning. I'd laughed at this ritual the first few weeks of our marriage, as he'd even done it the first day when we'd stayed at the inn on Malta, but eight months later, I appreciated the moment to watch him without his notice. Sometimes I hardly thought myself a good match for him in both looks and fashion, but he always protested without hesitation whenever I mentioned it.

He was a good man. I hoped to deserve him one day. The congratulatory letter we'd received last week from my father in Port Jackson had said the opposite, that he hoped my chosen was worthy of me. Little did he know how it really stood.

An irritated cry from below announced that I shouldn't linger in bed. I sat up with a yawn.

"You don't have to get up," Elias said, pulling on his breeches.

"I should help Georgana with Alfie. He always knows when his papa is leaving." I swung my legs out from under the blanket and pulled my shift down over them. Eight months and I still sometimes felt self-conscious. Being married took getting used to, even when you shared a room. Many, perhaps most, couples in Elias's ring of Society didn't. While it would be nice to have the space, I secretly hoped that whatever little vicarage was in our future after the wars ended would not have enough space to warrant separate rooms. I'd grown to appreciate his calming presence through the night long before we'd married.

Instead of going to my trunk for clothes, I scurried toward him and slipped my arms around his waist, interrupting his task. The soft linen of his shirt was cool from the slight morning breeze. "Must you go?"

He laughed, embracing me and kissing the top of my head. "I wish I didn't have to."

"I hope you don't run into any Frenchmen, besides Étienne." I always prayed fervently while he was away that they'd return empty-handed. Almost as hard as I prayed for Sanchez's safety so he could continue to steer the ship as helmsman and allow Elias to stay below.

"We'll never make our fortune if we don't take prizes," Elias said.

I leaned my head against his chest, listening to the reassuring beat of his heart and relishing the warmth of his skin. "I don't care about prizes. Just your safety."

"I have a feeling you'll care a little more when we get back to England."

I let him get back to readying for his departure and reluctantly pulled out my stays. Someday, I'd wish for the return of these early months, when so few things bogged down our thoughts. I tried to remember to relish them, even if Elias had to leave so frequently.

Before I could finish lacing, Elias caught my hand and pulled me back into his arms. He'd put his ensemble together quickly and only needed a particularly fine straw hat to complete his dandy look. We'd have to wait to return to Malta, or even England, before he could get another. "I love you, May Doswell."

How I loved the sound of that name. "Aren't you glad I ended up not being who you imagined I was a year ago?"

I thought he'd laugh, but instead, he kissed me long and slow. "I'm simply glad the girl who walked up the gangway was you."

And as he kissed me again, I had to admit I was very glad of that too.

Acknowledgments

I've found that each book I've written comes with unique challenges, and this one presented more than its fair share when added to the out-of-state move, new baby, health issues, and a host of other adventures that presented themselves during the writing and editing of *Across the Star-Kissed Sea*. Because of that, I could not have finished this without the help of friends, family, and readers who encouraged me every step of the way.

My biggest thanks goes to Jeffrey, who, in addition to playing Super Dad, helped me remember my reason to write. Thanks for championing my work. And thanks to all my kids for being my biggest fans.

I could not do this without the support of my amazing critique group—Heidi Kimball, who won't let me settle for anything less than the deep and meaningful; Joanna Barker, who cheers for every little victory and inspires me to reach for the stars; and Megan Walker, who has been there for me through every peak and valley in this crazy writing life. Also thanks to my critique partner Deborah Hathaway, who has talked me through so many dark moments.

Thank you to my dear friend Jennie Goutet for always being willing to check my French. I am also extremely grateful to Christopher Sorensen, Michael Lamonica, and the Chatham crew for answering questions about naval history and sailing, as well as for being fantastic shipmates.

I'm very grateful to the Shadow Mountain team for all their help getting this book ready for the world, especially to my editor, Samantha Millburn, for being so understanding when real-life got in the way of edits.

Lastly, thanks to Sam Haysom, Sharleen Roberts, and Genesis Aleman for their help with beta reading, and to Nashelie Sanchez, Hannah McDaniel, Bree Kingdon, Meghan Merkley, and Alayna Townsend. An author couldn't ask for more wonderful readers.

ARLEM HAWKS began making up stories before she could write. Living all over the western United States and traveling around the world gave her a love of cultures and people and the stories they have to tell. She has a bachelor's degree in communications, with an emphasis in print journalism, and she lives in Utah with her husband and four children.